MONSTER SQUAD

BOOK 6

WAYWARD SON

HEATH STALLCUP

WAYWARD SON: A Monster Squad Novel
Book VI

©2015 Heath Stallcup
Edited by T.W. Brown
Cover by Jeffrey Kosh Graphics

Printed in the U.S.A.

ISBN-13:978-1506017334
ISBN-10: 1506017339

DEDICATION

To all the little monsters that invade my house, bite my ankles, hang on the drapes and swing from the rafters. Whether direct progeny or spawn of my progeny, you're all precious wee beasties and I wouldn't trade any of you. Even for bacon…well. Maybe for bacon. So check yourselves.

ACKNOWLEDGMENTS

Yes, I always thank my beautiful wife, Jessie. She's the one who challenged me to start this and she's the one who has given up so much so that I can.

I always have to give a shout out to the Tufo's. Sometimes those who offer so much ask the least.

Linda Coffman and my sister Sheila who proofreads these before Todd edits them.

Vix, who volunteered to beta read for me…not only to keep me true to the originals, but to keep me on course.

Last, but certainly not least, the fans who read these stories and keep the characters alive.

Thank you.
-Heath

1

Mitchell ground his teeth so hard he knew the men in the stairwell could hear it. He grabbed the closest security specialist and pulled him close. "You! Cover his six. *Nothing* happens to the XO, you read me, soldier?"

"Roger that, sir." Matt nodded then pushed the man into the elevator with Tufo.

Mark looked down from the top of the elevator and shook his head. "There's room for me in here, but if you expect me to pull your heavy ass up here, you better shed some of that gear." He shot the man a wink.

"Greene, Kowalski!" The security specialist waved over two more men and began hoisting them up into the overhead of the car. "Keep the XO safe."

"Ready on the east side," security reported through the radios.

Kowalski pulled his own radio. "Ready on the west side. Let's do this."

Personnel pressed the button for topside then stepped out of the elevators. Watching the doors shut, Mitchell whispered a silent prayer for all of the men.

*****

Jack slowly peered out from the base of the tower and stared at the large man wiping sand from his face. He watched as Apollo pulled a pistol from his thigh holster and began marching across the sandy beach toward the castle proper.

Jack stepped out and made his presence known. "Apollo?"

Apollo quickly turned and glared at the man who was once his best friend. "You." The venom in his voice was unmistakable.

"Apollo, what the hell is going on?" Jack asked, the wind knocked from his sails. "Why would you do this?"

"You traitorous son of a bitch." Apollo tried to run in the soft sand, his intention plain.

"Why?" Jack slowly began backing away.

"You never told me about Maria, you bastard. You should have told me about her and Hank!" Apollo jumped in the air and swung at his head. Jack ducked and rolled away from the larger man.

"What the hell are you talking about?" He was honestly confused and still trying to come to terms with why his friend would attack and try to kill them after all they had been through.

"You *knew!*" Apollo swung and connected a glancing blow with Jack's shoulder, spinning him. "You knew she was fucking the Padre, and you didn't tell me!" He attempted a flying kick that Jack avoided by leaping face first into the sand.

"Apollo, I have no idea what you're talking about!" Jack rolled to the side just as Apollo brought a heavy booted foot down.

"Don't try to lie to me, you little skinny bastard!" Another stomp would have crushed Jack's chest had he not caught his foot. Jack strained to hold the larger man's weight then pushed for all he was worth, throwing Apollo off balance and backwards.

"I swear to God I don't know what you're talking about!" Jack flipped back to avoid Apollo's flying foot,following with a kick up to land on his feet. "This is stupid, Apollo! If I had known anything about Maria and the Padre, I would have told you."

Apollo froze and literally growled at him. "You wanted me to stay focused on the mission. You couldn't risk me being distracted."

"Bullshit!" Jack dropped his hands and pointed at the man. "You were my friend. Brothers *first*! Always!" The glare that Jack shot at Apollo shook the larger man. For the first time since Sheridan came to him with the revelation of Maria and Hank, his faith in what he thought he knew was rattled.

Apollo shook his head slowly. "No. No, this isn't right. You had to know."

"I didn't dammit. If I did, I would have said something—"

"You KNEW!" Apollo screamed, catching Jack off guard. "You had to." His jaw trembled and his eyes threatened tears as he considered his actions. He felt his knees weaken and the fight left him as he realized what he had done.

He was the traitor. He had turned against his own people. He gave Sheridan's men intel that would help them take down the teams. He had drawn out detailed plans. He told them everything. *Everything.*

Jack stepped closer and shook his head, "Apollo, I have no idea who planted this shit in your head, but…"

"Sheridan." Apollo's voice was hoarse, his throat dry as he considered the consequences. Traitors deserve a traitor's death.

"Sheridan?" Jack couldn't be sure he heard correctly. "From Team One? That Sheridan?"

Apollo nodded as his legs trembled and his knees went out from under him, his large bodysinkingto the sand. "He showed me video of them." His eyes rose and met Jack's. "Marshall knew…he caught them."

Jack stepped closer, his shoulders slumped. "Oh God, buddy. Sheridan is a snake. You can't believe anything he says. He's supposed to be in witness protection. It was part of the deal for turning in those who hired him to kill Thorn."

Apollo lowered his face and sobbed. "I killed them, Chief. It's all my fault."

Mueller ran up from behind Apollo and slid to a stop. "The attackers are coming back for another hit! They've taken out most of the Lycans!"

Jack growled deep in his throat and fought the desire to shift. He stared down at Apollo then up to Mueller. "Get him out of here. I'll deal with them."

*****

Mick lifted Laura upright as she reached out and caught herself on the side of the airplane. "I'm sorry." Her voice was barely a whisper as she tried to catch her breath. "Did you say that they're under attack?"

"We pulled stills from a satellite, Ms. Youngblood. They are indeed." Pablo lifted his arm and allowed her to scroll through images on his ruggedized PDA. "We haven't been able to identify any of the attackers. They aren't wearing uniforms."

"Wait..." Jennifer pushed her way forward and reached for Pablo's arm. "You said that—"

Pablo pulled his arm away rudely, interrupting her. "This is classified material."

Laura reached out gently and took his arm. "She's with me, Pablo. Besides, she sounded like she may know what's going on." Her expectant eyes met Jennifer's.

"It was something my father said before we left." She shrugged and glanced away. "He said that they were preparing to attack the people responsible for taking me."

Laura felt her chest tighten. "Oh, no."

"Who is this man?" Pablo questioned. "Does he have such resources?"

Mick stepped forward, "Walter Simmons. Based out of Belize."

Pablo nodded. "There are rumors that he harbors werewolves."

Jennifer quickly turned to stare at Laura who gave her a subtle shake of her head. "He has a lot of financial resources." Laura stepped forward and wrapped her arm through Pablo's. "Can you escort us to our quarters? We're all exhausted and I'd like a chance to try to reach my people."

"Their communications are down, Ms. Youngblood."

"But maybe a cell phone is working. Or a hard line to someone else at the base and they can send support?"

Pablo nodded and motioned them to a waiting truck. "We'll get you settled and then I'll see to getting you to a phone."

"Thank you."

*****

"We got you covered here," Gus stated as he fired down the hallway. "They're concentrated on the other end. I wish I knew where these sons of bitches were coming from."

"I saw some boats approaching. But seriously, how many people can fit in those things?" Jimmy asked.

"If they are smuggling boats, more than you'd think," Rufus replied.

He rounded the corner at the base of the stairs and chanced a glance down the hallway. Men in civilian clothing and automatic weapons fired randomly down the hallway. He looked to Paul and shook his head.

He pulled Paul close, "I won't risk using the weapon on them in human form."

"The ones outside shifted. I saw them before the chopper tried to turn us to Swiss cheese."

Rufus motioned toward the door, and the two men darted across the short opening and for the front doors. "If you see a wolf, point him out to me." Rufus shifted the weapon on his shoulder and moved to the front again.

"Oh, you can count on that." Paul slid back in behind his brother and allowed him to be a shield. "You can bet those bastards are using silver bullets."

"*Oui.* You can feel it in the air." Rufus stifled a cough as he moved closer to what used to be the front doors.

He kicked at the shattered timbers and moved them out of his way. Stepping over the remains of door frames, he stepped out to the stone steps and swept the area with the weapon. Nothing.

The pair worked their way down the length of the house, following the sound of battle,rounding the corner to see wolves and other supernatural creatures slashing and dashing, swooping and clashing. The battle raged furiously as he leveled the weapon and took aim.

Paul rested a hand on his brother's shoulder. "Aren't you afraid you might hit some of our own wolves?"

Rufus shook his head. "Acceptable losses."

"Hey!" Pedro yelled as he turned toward the pair of vampires. "Is that the doo-hickey that Doc..." Rufus spun and aimed the device at Pedro. Gonzales saw the movement and dove to the side just as Rufus squeezed the trigger.

The ensuing blast lit the night sky and paused the fighting for only a moment as all eyes turned to the corner of the house. The second story veranda creaked as it teetered and fell, collapsing at the corner. Pedro got to his feet and ran to where the pair of vampires had been standing. There was a large blackened crater filled with pieces of the second story deck and bits of stone debris.

"Son of a—" A bullet whizzed by grabbing his attention once more. "Time to end this..."

*****

Sheridan slipped in behind the wheel of the van and drove it closer to the hangar. He sat in the front seat and watched as his men would slowly approach the stairwell entrance and set up on either side of the steel doors. One would snap the door open and another would toss a grenade inside just before the door was slammed shut. The men waited for the flashbang to report before throwing open the door and mowing down any unlucky soul close enough to take a bullet. Sheridan laughed with the giddy glee of a schoolgirl, beating on the dash and steering wheel as he watched his people slice the squads to ribbons.

Something caught his men's attention as they turned to the side, their weapons brought to bear. He soon realized that the lift doors had opened. Surely nobody was foolhardy enough to try to storm the upper level by elevator? He watched as his men slowly advanced on the lift car.

The men closest turned to the others and shrugged. Apparently the lift was empty. Sheridan shook his head, unable to comprehend what the purpose of...then he watched in horror as the men closest to the lift doors erupted in bloody gunfire. Shreds of meat and blood flew outward and downward, their bodies falling to the floor. The other men hit the floor or dove for cover.

The moment the firing began, the steel doors flew open; security forces flowed out, running and diving for cover of their own. Then the ceilings of the lifts fell out and men poured from the lift cars. Sheridan screamed into his coms. He barked orders to the wolves in the hangar, but most fired recklessly from cover, their rounds hitting far above their targets.

"No!" he screamed as he slammed against the steering wheel. "They've got people in the hangar now!" He clenched his jaw so tightly that he could feel his molars crack. "Use the flash bangs! Disorient them!"

Before his men could react, the building began to vibrate and the middle of the hangar floor actually split in half and lifted up and away. A large black pickup with a machine gun in the back rose from the floor like a phoenix from the ashes. From his vantage point, Sheridan could see two very large men inside the vehicle as it rose higher into the hangar. "Take them out! Don't let them get away!"

The weapon in the back of the truck came to life and began moving, targeting individuals. Short bursts from the .30 caliber machine gun shredded flesh and bone, sending sprays of blood against the metal barricades that they used to protect themselves from the small arms of the men on the other side of the hangar. Sheridan felt his guts tighten into a knot as he watched his troops being cut down before his eyes.

"Get out of there! Get out now! Shift if you have to, but get out!" His voice screamed so loudly into the coms that he was hoarse before he was done.

He watched as the squad members, emboldened by the reinforcement of the assault vehicle, began pouring from their own hiding places and advancing on his men. Man after man shifted and made for an exit. One jumped onto the hood of the large black truck and tried to tackle the motorized machine gun. He wrapped his large, hair-covered arms over the hot barrel and lifted, unable to render it from the mount in the back. The operator inside the vehicle moved the weapon again, trying to shake the new attacker off. The wolf braced one arm against the weapon's base, another against the barrel, and pushed with all of his might, actually bending the barrel. The wolf then leapt from the back of the truck and made for the large double doors and the parking lot Sheridan was now backing away from.

When Little John aimed the crosshairs of the targeting screen on a fleeing wolf and pulled the trigger on the joystick, the machine gun in the back of the truck destroyed itself. Bullets jammed in the barrel and the back-pressure destroyed the receiver. He slumped his shoulders and turned to Spalding. "I think I broke it."

"I think the wolf broke it," Spalding corrected.

"Maybe we could run them down? Put a wolf-shaped splatter on the front bumper?" John offered.

Spanky shook his head. "Unless Doc put a silver bumper on this thing, it wouldn't do much good."

The two men watched as their ground forces advanced, trying to take out as many of the fleeing wolves as they could. Those who were wounded or dying fought to the bitter end. Some dragged useless rear legs as they tried to bite or tear into the humans they had been sent to destroy.

Tufo pushed his way to the front of the crowd, putting silver bullets into the heads of anything he ran across. "Spread out. Make sure they're all truly dead."

He came across a pair of bloody wolves, their mangled bodies still smoking.He placed the barrel of his pistol to the head of one and squeezed the trigger. As he lifted the pistol to put down the other wolf for good, he noticed the slide locked back. He ejected his magazine and slid another home, racking a round as he did so. He straightened his arm, taking aim on the second wolf when a large hairy arm grasped his wrist and lifted the weapon up and away the bullet ricocheting off the girders.

"Live one!" Mark yelled as he struggled to pull his second pistol. The wolf pulled him down to face level, the smell of blood and bodily fluids strong as it growled directly into his face. Spittle mixed with blood splattered his face as he tried to wrestle his second pistol from its holster.

The wolf rolled to the side, taking him with it and pinning him underneath its massive body. Mark struggled with his pinned arm, but it was like trying to pull an appendage from a vice. He could feel the bones of his wrist being crushed as the wolf stretched his arm further away. He distinctly heard the clatter of his FiveseveN hitting the concrete floor of the hangar as the beast loomed over him. Rounds exploded over and around him and he heard someone scream to "Hold fire!" and "Don't hit the XO!"

Tufo tried to get a knee up and between the beast and himself, but it sunk into the ruined remains of the beast's abdomen. He felt the hot blood of the monster soaking into his uniform pants and down his thigh as he pushed harder to lift the creature from his body. "Get off me, you son of a bitch!"

The beast roared one long loud scream in his face, blood and spittle flying into his eyes and nose before it dragged a clawed hand across his torso from neck to navel.

Mark's eyes shot wide as the most intense pain he had ever felt exploded through his body. He swore he felt the bastard's fingers shred through his intestines as it dragged across his body, and his throat tightened to the point he couldn't suck in air. He lost all strength in his upper body and couldn't push back against the beast as it pressed against him.

He didn't hear the pointblank gunshot that splattered the wolf's brains across the floor next to him.

He didn't even notice as his troops pushed the beast to the side then circled him.

He heard somebody scream for a medic.

He suddenly felt very tired.

So sleepy.

God, it was cold on that floor…

*****

A loud wailing sound echoed across the ruined courtyard of Rufus' island home. The attacking wolves suddenly broke away and began rushing toward the eastern edge of the island.

Azrael landed next to Jack, his arm outstretched and pointing at the retreating attackers. "They're escaping."

"Let them," Jack heaved as he sucked in air. The battle had been draining and he saw no benefit in chasing after the attackers in the darkness. "I doubt they'll be back."

"We have decimated their forces. We should finish them while the advantage is ours," Grimlock added, his large body settling next to his brothers.

Jack patted the large gargoyle's shoulder. "Leave them. We need to assess the damage and treat our wounded."

"Something tells me we shall face these opponents again." Azrael watched as the dark figures quickly faded into the night.

"Not if they know what's good for them." Jack tugged at the reluctant warrior. "Come on. It will be daylight soon, and we need to see what we're dealing with."

Mueller stumbled up to the trio covered in blood. He nearly collapsed at Jack's feet. "I need to find Barbara and Bobby," he panted, his voice hoarse.

"Bob!" Jack collected the man and helped him to the side of the building. "Where are you hurt?"

Bob shook his head. "It's not my blood." He pointed to a body near the collapsed veranda. "He got the jump on me. I shifted and ripped his throat out." Pointing to his body he added, "Tends to get messy."

Jack sighed and settled in next to the man. "I'll find somebody to help you search for them." Jack glanced at this watch then turned to the gargoyles. "Fellas, you won't have much time before sunup. If you want to call it a night, I understand."

"We'll assist where we can." Azrael turned to Mueller. "Your female? She would have your scent?"

Bob gave the gargoyle a quizzical nod. "She would, I think. She's not a wolf, though."

"I shall begin the search." He stepped aside and lifted into the air.

Bob pulled himself to a standing position. "I thought this whole werewolf superpower thing gave us more endurance."

"It does. But we were fighting werewolves." Jack got to his feet, and the two worked their way to the front of the castle entrance.

Pedro trotted up from out of the smoke. "Jack! We need to talk."

"Hey, buddy." Jack waved him over. "Sorry about all this. I know you didn't sign up for any of—"

"Jack," Popo interrupted, "this is important."

Jack paused then motioned for Bob to go on. "Okay, bud, you have my attention."

Pedro sighed then pointed to the collapsed veranda. "We had a secondary mission. We weren't supposed to mention it to you unless we came up empty."

Jack gave his friend a confused stare. "Secondary mission?"

"Some of Doc's notebooks came up missing. There was some scary, nasty shit in there that had Mitchell and Tufo's panties in a twist." Pedro glanced to the side out of habit to ensure nobody else was listening. "The only person besides Doc who had access to it was Thorn. Before Groom Lake. We were supposed to look for the notebook—"

"Wait a second!" Jack interrupted, waving his hand in Pedro's face. "They think Thorn *stole* some of Doc's notebooks? Notebooks?"

"There were plans for a Doomsday weapon in there, Chief. Like, kill off anything that isn't 'human'. They were afraid that..."

"And of course, they just assume that the vampire had to steal it."

Pedro shook his head. "Jack, I saw Thorn with some kind of chromed out rocket launcher. That's what blew up and took out the corner of the castle." Pedro pointed to the rubble again. "He was aiming it at *me*."

Jack paused for just a moment and stared at Popo. "Over there?" Pedro nodded, and Jack took off in the direction of the smoking debris. "You're sure it was Rufus?"

"Jack, come on, of course I'm sure. There was somebody else with him, but it was definitely Thorn."

"Where did he go?" Jack stood over the fallen debris and stared into the scorched hole in the ground.

"He just...disappeared. There was a huge explosion, a flash of light and then there was nothing. Stuff collapsing, and fire and..."

Jack jumped into the hole and began tossing out chunks of debris. Pedro whistled for Gus and the two stepped into the blast crater with him, tossing out smoking chunks. "Do you really think he may have survived?"

"He's a fucking vampire," Jack stated as though that explained everything.

Pedro paused and sighed. "Jack,Mitchell wants the notebook back regardless."

Jack stood up and stared at Pedro. "Buddy, if it turns out that Thorn actually stole the plans for a Doomsday weapon from my teammates? He's going to have more to worry about than just the vampire council." The set of his jaw sent a cold chill up Pedro's neck.

*****

"Medic!" Kowalski screamed as he dropped beside his XO. His hands shook as he peeled back the sides of Tufo's shredded BDU blouse. "Holy…"

Greene slipped in next to him with a first aid box. "They're getting somebody now." He pulled open the white can and began ripping gauze bandages out and handing them to the staff sergeant. "He's going to be okay, ain't he?"

"Shut up and hand me more." Kowalski tried to press them against the shredded remains of Tufo's abdomen but the bandages disappeared and slipped inside his body cavity. Kowalski shuddered and pulled the soaked bandages back out. "This shit ain'tgonna cut it." His eyes met Greene's and he shook his head. "He needs a real doctor."

"Make a hole!" Mitchell shouted as Evan Peters slipped in beside Kowalski. "Let the Doc at him."

"We need to move him." Evan whispered. "His pulse is weak and thready. His breathing is shallow. I need an operatorium."

"Will your lab work?" Mitchell moved to the side as two men brought a stretcher in and placed it next to Mark's prone body.

Evan shook his head. "I need a real operating room." He pulled the stethoscope from the man's chest and pulled him gently to the stretcher. "Something fully sterile. With the right equipment. We need a ventilator, monitors…hell, I need an anesthetist."

"Where's the closest hospital that can handle this kind of trauma?" Mitchell yelled.

Evan looked up at the man and shook his head. "There are no hospitals set up to handle a werewolf attack, Colonel. You know this."

Mitchell clenched his jaw and his body trembled with anger. "I refuse to accept this. You have to save him!"

Evan pulled Matt aside and lowered his voice. "At this point, I don't even know if trying to turn him will save him." He glanced back at Major Tufo, a pallid blue settling in around his face. "He wasn't bitten by the wolf, he was *shredded*. He isn't infected. He was tortured. He's—"

"Don't say it, Doc." Matt had a finger in his face. "He's my oldest friend. You have to save him."

Evan turned back and studied the man on the stretcher. "Take him to my lab. Get me five units of whole blood. Match it to his dog tags. Go!" Turning back to Matt, he lowered his voice again, "You better call his wife."

*****

Apollo sat in the copilot's seat of the retreating boat as it sliced through the waves. His mind raced as he replayed the events of the last few days. How could he allow Sheridan to pollute his mind? How could he blame Jack for something that Maria and Hank did?

He lowered his head into his hands and fought the urge to sob in the presence of the remaining wolves. Lifting his head again, he did a quick count. Their forces had been reduced to a fraction of what he'd started with. Eight wolves literally licked their wounds in the craft as it bounced along the waves.

Apollo watched as the first fingers of sunlight crested the horizon, and he suddenly felt dirty. Very dirty. His righteous rage had turned to a dishonor that he couldn't rectify. Part of him wanted to shoot all of the remaining wolves and throw them overboard, but he realized they were just soldiers. Meat thrown into the grinder. They were taking orders. And he was the one who led them in the attack against an ally.

Apollo felt his rage rise again, and he knew it was Sheridan that should be made to pay. If he'd kept his damned videos to himself, if he'd stayed in witness protection, if he'd kept his plans of retribution to himself…

Apollo replayed events in his mind so many times that he made himself sick. There had to be a way to redeem the little piece of his soul that hadn't been tainted.

Leaning back in his seat, he watched the wolves during the ride as his mind wandered. *Who did they work for?* He remembered Sheridan saying something along the lines of being hired to do this job. As much as he hated to admit it, Apollo didn't pay any attention to him once he decided to join forces to get his revenge. Sheridan was a blowhard. A self-absorbed asshole that was only interested in his own agenda.

There wasn't much he could do at the moment, but as soon as they returned, he intended to find out as much as he could about who had hired Sheridan. Surely they had an agenda of their own. Maybe if he could determine who the money man behind this venture was, Apollo could do something about stopping the real monster.

2

Paul dragged the burnt body of his brother to the Monterey cabin cruiser from the thick underbrush they had been blown into. He knew that the house was under attack and that the docks were the only place not seeing battle. He pulled his smoking body across the wooden pier and onto the boat, tucking him below decks and onto the bed.

"I'm sorry, brother. I don't know where else to go." Paul collapsed onto the bed next to Rufus and sighed. "All hell is breaking loose out there."

Shortly, a wailing horn sounded, and the sounds of battle died down. Paul waited a little longer before opening the door to the cabin cruiser and sticking his head out. He could see the gargoyles circling the woods and people milling about the compound.

"It may be over." Paul turned to Rufus, still unconscious on the bed. "What should I do with you?"

Sounds of somebody moving topside froze Paul in his place. He slowly tried to close the door to the cabin cruiser when Marco jumped down onto the deck. "Mr. Foster." He looked over the vampire's shoulder at the charred body on the bed. "Is that Monsieur Thorn?"

Paul swallowed hard. "It is."

Marco nodded and cast a furtive glance over his shoulder. "They are searching for the two of you."

"Well, it would appear that we have been found." Paul squared his shoulders and prepared to open the door.

"No." Marco pushed him inside the cabin. "They are not pleased."

"What is the meaning of—"

"The soldiers are accusing Monsieur Thorn of stealing something from the human hunters." Marco stared past Paul and shook his head. "He will need blood. A lot of it if he is to recover."

"We have some here." Paul indicated the blood bar.

"He will need human blood if he is to recover." Marco glanced again back to the remains of the compound. "You and I both know that. Stay below and I will take you to the mainland. You can use the satellite phone to make arrangements. Have a car waiting for us below the dock. If we can get him someplace safe before the hunters can pick up our scent…" He gave Paul a knowing look.

Paul nodded. "Hurry then. Get us out of here."

Marco pulled the door shut and made his way to the controls. He quickly cast the lines from the dock and pushed the craft away from the dock. He prayed that nobody noticed the small craft start and leave.

*****

Matt paced just outside of Evan's lab while the vampire worked at a feverish pace. He attempted to stitch Major Tufo's intestines with the smallest of stitches, trying to secure all bleeders and make his insides leak-proof at the same time. He worked with magnifying lenses and had three assistants handing him fine sutures while his hands deftly sewed the man back together.

More and more bags of blood were pumped through Mark's body as Evan worked. With the lack of proper equipment, Evan literally held a silicone rubber hose in his mouth and would suction the surgical incisions with his mouth.

To their credit, not one of his 'assistants' complainedor even commented. The entire team worked non-stop, trying to save their executive officer, swapping duties as needed, running supplies, or kicking the rapidly piling mess from the location.

Matt had volunteered his two hidden bottles of scotch to help sterilize instruments and didn't even cringe when they pulled the top off the second bottle and began splashing it over Mark's wounds.

Jericho Jones quietly approached the colonel as the surgical team continued. "Sir? We have the casualty list."

Matt sighed and turned to face the young officer. "Do I want to know?"

Jericho shook head and handed him a list. "Fourteen dead. Eleven wounded. Eight critical."

"Where does Mark fall on that list?" he asked rhetorically.

"Critical, sir." Jericho turned and stared at the team working so diligently. "I'm not counting him out."

"I was supposed to call his wife." Matt's voice was barely a whisper. "I don't have the nerve."

"Not sure what to say, sir?"

Matt shook his head. "You've never met her, have you?" Matt shuddered. "The woman has nerves of steel. And a temper like…well, imagine *any* woman that could stand to stay married to him for as long as they have."

"Point." Jericho honestly did not envy the man.

"I don't suppose I could convince you to…"

"Not on your life, sir." Jericho chuckled. "Besides, you'd never forgive yourself if you didn't do it yourself."

Matt groaned. "You're right. I owe her that much."

He glanced at the makeshift surgical suite then turned and headed for the door. Jericho fell into step behind him. "Sir? You're leaving?"

"I'm going to go to their house and escort her here. Then I'm going to try to start putting the pieces back together. We *will* snap back from this, Captain."

*****

Jack watched as the gargoyles circled the woods, their search pattern slowly tightening until Azrael dove into the woods. He kept glancing at the horizon and the soft orange glow that threatened to rise in the east as the other gargoyles continued to glide over the area. Within moments, Azrael could be seen lifting into the air again, two humans clinging to him.

"Looks like he found them." Jack pointed to the sky.

"Just in the nick of time. The sun is almost up." Bob was suddenly nervous of the damage that a stone gargoyle statue could do to his family when dropped from eighty feet in the air with them clinging to it.

Azrael landed deftly next to the pair and set the wide-eyed Barbara and the extremely excited Bobby on the ground. "Excuse me, please. It is time for the stone sleep."

"Hurry." Jack waved him off and watched as he settled next to his brothers along the parapet of the castle. Within moments, all three were still, their eyes cast out over the ocean. "Amazing…"

"I'll say!" Bobby was nearly bouncing up and down. "Dad, when they wake up, can I go again? That was *so* cool!"

Barbara pulled her son close and squeezed him, "It's rude to ask a…" she glanced upward and then shook her head. "A…gargoyle…for rides, son."

Bob nodded. "Mom's right."

Bobby sulked and kicked a rock near his shoe. "Mom's always right."

Jack smiled and scuffed the kid's hair. "You're learning, kid."

The sound of a helicopter approaching set them all on edge. Jack turned to Bob and motioned toward the house. "Put them inside until we know what's going on." He glanced to Kalen, "Can you see who or what it is?"

"Another of those infernal flying machines." He pointed over the ocean toward the mainland.

"Is it the attackers?" Pedro asked, racking a fresh round into his receiver.

Kalen shook his head. "I do not believe so. They left by boat and…no. There is a woman in the front." He suddenly smiled and turned to Jack. "Your woman."

"My woman?" Jack pointed to himself. "My woman is with her parents."

"No longer." Kalen hopped from the tower and landed deftly in the sand. "My eyes tell me that she comes now."

Jack sighed. "Great." He looked around at the damage. "Rufus has disappeared, the place is blown up, and half the Lycans are dead or wounded…I don't need this kind of grief right now."

Gus stepped out of the house and held up a blue notebook. "Chief."

Jack glanced over his shoulder and saw the large man approaching. "What's this?"

"I found this in Thorn's study. It was in his desk." Gus handed it to Jack.

He thumbed through the pages and found a set that were more worn than the others. "Is this theDoomsday thing you told me about?" He held it out to Popo.

Pedro glanced at the diagram and shrugged. "That doesn't look like what he was holding. The thing that blew up? I mean…not unless you could shrink it down. Way down."

Jack closed the notebook and handed it to Popo. "I know who can tell us." His eyes met Pedro's. "Doc. He designed it. He'd know if it could be miniaturized."

"You're coming back with us?" Jimmy asked.

Jack glanced around the destroyed island compound. "With Rufus gone and unable to explain this, there's nothing holding me here." He glanced up and watched as the helicopter began its approach. "And I need some answers."

"Somebody may have something to say about you just up and leaving." Pedro pointed to Nadia gingerly stepping from the front of the helicopter.

Jack smiled when he saw her honey blonde hair and big blue eyes in the early morning light. "She can complain all she wants,but I have a job to do." He started to walk across the destroyed courtyard then turned back to his old teammates. "And I can't walk away from this until I know for sure where Thorn stood in all of this mess."

*****

Laura sat quietly as the Brazilian team drove them to their mountainside compound. As they approached the underground enclosure, she was reminded of the NORAD base at Cheyenne Mountain, only slightly smaller. The concrete archway built into the side of the mountain looked nearly impenetrable. Armed guards saluted as the trucks approached the compound, and tall chain-link gates closed behind them. She suddenly felt more like a prisoner than a guest.

"Do not worry. You will be safe here." Pablo smiled at her, and she didn't feel any better.

Laura did her best to return the smile but she was nearly certain it didn't come across as friendly. "Sorry, Pablo, I'm just exhausted from the trip. Please don't think we're not grateful."

"I understand. You've been struck with quite a bit since your arrival."

The truck stopped, and Laura looked out the dirty window. They were deep within the compound and men were disembarking the other trucks. Mick opened his door and held it for the two women. "Home sweet cave," he muttered as they passed him.

"At least it's cool in here," Jennifer stated as she took it all in.

"You must mean the temperature, because it feels like a tomb to me." Mick shuddered as they fell into step behind Pablo.

"Your quarters are down this hallway. They are not large, but there are beds and a place for your belongings if you have any. We will see to getting you a change of clothing. The lavatories are at the end of the hall." He paused and sighed at the two women. "I apologize, but we are not set up for women. If you will let us know when you plan to shower, we will make accommodations for you."

"Thank you, Pablo." Laura gave him a gentle squeeze on his arm as she walked past him. She took the first door on the right and watched as Mick took the room opposite hers. Jennifer took the next room on the right. Laura opened the door and found a small room with a single bed and a small nightstand and a two drawer cabinet. "This will do nicely. Thank you."

Pablo pointed behind them near where they entered the hallway. "The room there with the large glass windows. I will be in there. When you are settled, find me and we will get you to a phone."

"I won't be but a moment," Laura said. She turned and went to Jennifer's room, knocking as she opened the door. "I'm going to call and see if I can get through. I have to find out what's going on there."

Jennifer sat on her bed, her eyes staring off into nothingness. "Do you think he is dead?"

"Who? Matt?" Laura shook her head, giving the young woman a pat on the arm. "No, he's far too sly to have fallen for anything sneaky like that. If I know Matt, he's just fine. He's probably kicking back right now, sipping a scotch and puffing on a victory cigar."

"Please, Laura,let me know." The concern in her eyes seemed genuine.

"Trust me, I will." She stepped down the hall and tapped on the Plexiglas of the office. Pablo waved her in and Laura took a seat near the phone. She got the proper dialing sequence from Pablo for dialing the United States, then started going through the list of numbers that she had memorized.

*****

Sheridan pulled into the warehouse that they had been using as a staging area and shut off the headlights of the van. He heard the side door of the van open and felt the truck shift as the few wolves he encountered fleeing the hangar exited the vehicle. He sat quietly behind the wheel a moment longer. How was he going to explain their failure to his benefactor? With a silent curse, he opened his door and slid out from the seat.

He pulled his cane from behind the seat and hobbled into the abandoned office. He pulled the satellite phone from the charging station and punched the preset speed dial. He waited for the line to connect and then ring.

"Ah, Mr. Simmons. Yes, this is Sheridan." He paused while listening to the other line. "No, sir, not entirely. We dealt them a pretty tragic blow, but I'm afraid that—" He was interrupted as the other end blew up. "Yes, sir. But you need to keep in mind we attacked with untrained soldiers against some of the world's best. Considering the circumstances, we did some serious damage."

Sheridan slowly sat in the chair next to the work bench and listened to the tirade on the phone. "No, sir, I haven't heard yet how the attack on the island went. I can say that they wouldn't have had the same degree of opposition that we encountered so I'm sure that they did much better." Sheridan watched the wolves in the shop as they began tearing down their stations and prepared to leave the area. "Yes, sir. Once I know for sure, I will certainly be calling you again."

Sheridan sighed to himself and rubbed at his eyes as the man on the other end continued to yell. "Yes, sir. At once, sir." He clicked the end call button and placed the phone back in its charging cradle. "Please, Apollo, tell me that you had much better luck than we did."

*****

Little John and Spalding carried the body of Vince Carbone to a gurney where he was placed into a body bag. Spalding zipped the bag and placed an orange tag on it. This indicated the body had to be incinerated. He never really understood why their dead had to be cremated. They were infected with the wolf virus. It wasn't like their bodies would reanimate. Still, procedure was procedure.

Technicians and soldiers alike worked side by side cleaning up the topside, spraying down blood with antiseptic and preparing it for decontamination. Bodies of wolves that were shifted were placed into special body bags made for larger beings. Those who were killed prior were bagged and tagged, both given incineration tags. Only those who were support personnel and killed in the battle would be allowed a true funeral.

Little John almost envied them as their families would have an opportunity for some form of closure. He stood and stretched his wide shoulders, the realization of why operators for the squads were chosen from those who didn't have ties to the 'normal' world.

The sound of approaching helicopter blades caught the attention of everybody topside. Fearing another attack, techs began looking for cover and security personnel and operators grabbed their weapons and formed up at the open doors.

The Chinook hovered just outside the parking lot and Spalding watched through the ACOG scope as the side door opened and third squad fast roped out the door and into the parking lot. He breathed a heavy sigh of relief and called the men down. He stepped out and held an arm up to Dom.

"What the hell, man? How come nobody is answering coms?" Dom slowed and looked at the hangar. "Holy hell…what happened here?"

"We were hit," Spalding answered as the rest of third squad caught up with their team leader. "Hard."

"Oh, my God. Anybody hurt?" Dom walked past Spalding and entered the hangar. Rivers of blood running to the drains in the floor caught his attention. "Please tell me that's tango blood."

"Some. Not enough of it, though," Little John answered. "They hit the XO. He's bad."

"Tufo?" Dom paled as the words hit home. His mind instantly returned to the bond he formed with the man when he first returned to the squads. Tufo was the only one that treated him like he wasn't a China doll, ready to break if he wasn't handled with kid gloves. "Where is he?"

Spalding pointed down below. "Doc's working on him."

"Why the hell is Doc working on him? Why didn't they medevac him to a hospital or a trauma center?" Spalding and Little John lowered their heads and refused to meet his eyes. "What aren't you telling me?"

"Dom, a wolf shredded his guts. The damned thing sliced him from bellybutton to throat." Spalding choked up.

Dom felt his knees weaken as the words hit home. Hammer was at his side and propped him without being asked. "Let me get you to a chair, boss."

"No. I'm okay. I just need…" Dom turned slow circles and stared to the ceiling. "Why the hell couldn't we have been here for this? We could have made a difference."

Darren pulled his buddy aside, away from the support personnel still cleaning up the mess. "Believe me when I tell you, had you been here, you would have either ended up pinned down like we were or worse."

"What's worse than not being able to do anything?" Hammer asked.

Little John pointed to the body bag containing Carbone's body. "Being carried out in one of those."

"Who is that?" Hammer asked, not sure he wanted to know.

"Carbone," Sullivan replied. "He went down fighting."

"All of them did," Darren corrected. "Just because they weren't squad members didn't make their sacrifice any less noble."

Dominic repeated a silent prayer over Carbone's body then crossed himself. He turned to Spalding, his eyes angry, "Who was behind the attack?"

"We can't be sure. All we know for sure is that they were wolves."

Ben watched as they continued to scrub the coagulating blood and bits of flesh from the structures. "Should we turn in our weapons and lend a hand or…"

Dom shook his head. "Negative. We have a cleanup crew still in the field." He turned to Hammer, "Stay here and help them get the coms back up. That's priority one. As soon as they are, reach out and touch me, brother."

"Roger that." He turned and headed for the stairwell to turn in his weapon and grab a tech crew.

Dom grabbed Ben. "Give him a hand with it. We can cover for you in the field but those coms are essential. I'm going to check in on the XO. The rest of you replenish our ammo. We're lifting off in twenty."

*****

Apollo continued to replay the events of the last few days through his mind as the helicopter sliced through the early morning sky. One of the wolves had opened the side door, and the air whipping through the cabin carried a chill. The smell of the salty sea threatened to carry his mind elsewhere, but he forced himself to evaluate exactly where he allowed himself to be swayed.

He couldn't put his finger on the exact moment that he stepped into that dark chasm, but he knew what had caused it. It was the video of Maria. He only thought that he had her out of his system. To find out that she didn't really care for him…that she, in fact, loved someone else, was more than his fragile psyche could handle.

He closed his eyes and leaned his head back. The emotional turmoil of the last few days was more than he could handle, and the constant adrenaline rushes were causing a crash.

What have I done? he asked himself. *Why did it take seeing the Chief in person to drag me back to reality?* He knew Jack wasn't lying when he said he held nothing back from him. He knew that the man wouldn't lie to him about something as important as Maria. How could he have let Sheridan get inside his head? He wasn't that weak-minded. He wasn't some hormone driven teenager. He fought the urge to punch something as he sat upright in his seat and stared out the window.

The land zipped by and he watched as the patchwork quilt of the land below passed beneath them. He quietly continued his mental assessment until the thought of Sheridan came back around. What had he said about their benefactor? He had an axe to grind with the squads? He was the one who provided the wolves? Apollo shifted in his seat and studied the wolves trying to unwind and come off their own battle highs.

He scooted closer to the wolf closest to him. "You and your boys did well out there. We couldn't have known that they'd have gargoyles and shit."

The wolf gave him a broad smile. "If they hadn't had those flying rock monkeys, we would have handed them their heads."

"You got that right." Apollo gave him a light elbow. "Hey, where'd you boys learn to fight like that, anyway?"

The wolf shrugged. "We're all pretty good in a scrap." He pointed to the wolf in the front of the helicopter. "Davidson is from the states, and he used to fight mixed martial arts."

"No shit?" Apollo feigned interest. "Where the rest of you from?"

"Most of us are from different packs down south." The wolf shifted closer so he wouldn't have to yell as loud. "The three of us are from Columbia. There are some from Brazil, some from Peru. All over South America."

"Seriously? I wouldn't think that many different packs would come together for something like this." Apollo rubbed at his chin thoughtfully.

The wolf laughed at him. "We didn't come together for nothing. Mr. Simmons hired us. We're all enforcers for him."

Apollo raised a brow at that one. "Paid enforcers? Mercs?"

"You could say that." The wolf nodded, liking the sound of being called a mercenary. "Yeah, a private army for a very wealthy wolf."

"That's cool." Apollo eyed each man as the chopper continued along its flight path. "How long y'all been with this…Simmons?"

"Yeah. Simmons." The wolf shrugged. "Different times really. I have been with him for nearly five years. Most of these guys over ten years." He scooted closer and lowered his voice somewhat. "Once his daughter come up missing, the old man went bat shit crazy and started spending his money on all kinds of security. He has a compound in Belize that would blow your mind. All of his cars are armored. He has dozens of wolves patrolling all the timejust to keep his daughter safe."

"Wait, I thought you said she went missing?"

"Well, she did. But then she came back. She was gone for nearly ten years…wait. So…you don't know who I'm talking about?"

"Brother, I have no fuckin' clue." Apollo shrugged.

"Your people were the ones that had her."

Apollo gave him a disbelieving look. "My people?"

The wolf laughed again. "Yeah, man. That's why the old man wants them all dead. They held her for nearly ten years."

"We didn't hold nobody." Apollo's face was twisted in confusion.

"Yeah they did. Had her on ice. Literally." The wolf leaned in and spoke into his ear. "Little blonde gal. Spoiled rotten? This shit seriously isn't ringing any bells?"

Apollo shook his head. "No, man. We didn't have nobody like that. We weren't set up for holding prisoners."

The wolf leaned back in his seat and smiled. "Maybe you should talk to your people?"

"Yeah." Apollo leaned back and watched as the landscape slid by underneath them again. "Maybe I should."

*****

"It's not good."

"Define 'not good', Matt." Tracy's eyes hardened as she stared at him, her heart sinking in her chest.

"Like maybe you should come with me." He held the door open for her and watched the color drain from her face.

She backed away a half step, her head shaking. "I-I can't just…I mean. I have to…the dogs. And…"

"Tracy." Matt placed a hand on her shoulder. "Now."

She felt a lump form in her throat as her body responded, moving her forward even though her brain was screaming at her to run.

She nearly jumped as he shut the door and circled the car to get in behind the wheel. She felt her hands begin to shake as her mind raced, playing a thousand possible scenarios. "What happened?"

Matt started the car and pulled out onto the pavement, turning toward the hangar with purpose. "We had a mission and had just released from it. The next thing we know, all hell broke loose." He slowed slightly then drove through the stop sign. "We were under attack."

"Who in the name of..." Her mind couldn't conceive of anybody stupid enough to attack a squad of monster hunters. "Who was it?"

"We don't know yet. All we do know is that they were mostly wolves." Matt pushed the car past the legal limit, ready to hit the red and blue emergency lights if they happened to run afoul of any base police. "Anyway, they were in retreat. Mark and a couple of others were putting down the wounded and—"

"Putting *down* the wounded?" She stared at him open mouthed. "Did nobody think about interrogating them?"

He ignored her. "One of the wounded tore into him. Literally shredded him from throat to waistband."

Her breath caught in her throat as she thought of her husband being torn open by something as vicious as a werewolf. "Did he..."

"He's still alive, Tracy. They're working on him as we..." He turned and gave her a sympathetic look. "He *was* still alive when I came to get you. It's bad, though."

"I understand what you're telling me." Her lip quivered, but she refused to allow herself to cry. "Just hurry."

"As fast as I can." He pointed to the hangar. "We're almost there." Matt slid the car to a stop outside the double doors and was halfway out of the car before the engine had stopped running. "This way." He helped Tracy out of the passenger side and guided her past the mess and toward the elevators.

"Why is he here and not at a trauma center, Matt?" The shock was beginning to wear off as the elevator car carried them deeper below the hangar.

"How do we explain a werewolf attack at a trauma center?" When the doors opened, he directed her out and to the left. "Doc has him over there. We need to stay out of their way."

"I want to hold his hand." Her voice was soft but steady. "If something happens to him...he needs to know that..." She choked and turned away.

"Tracy, he doesn't know what's going on," Matt tried to explain. "But let me see if we can get you in there."

"Oh, my God…is he…"

Matt pulled her aside so that she wasn't looking directly at the surgery. "Doc may be one of…them, but he's one of the best."

"He's got a straw sticking into his guts, Matt!" Her voice carried and one of the assistants glanced over quickly then turned back to the job at hand.

"He has to keep the surgery site suctioned clean." Matt pointed to the bag of blood hanging overhead. "They're putting it in faster than he's losing it."

"Barely," Doc stated through clenched teeth.

"Is there a chance he'll turn?" She turned and faced Matt. "He wouldn't want that."

Matt shook his head. "No. He can't turn from what Doc's doing. And Evan said that he wasn't bit, this was all done by claws. He's not infected."

She trembled as she stared at the scene, unable to see her husband behind the flurry of work. "I need to be by his side."

"Of course. Let me…"

"He's flat-lined!" a tech stated, pulling a stethoscope from his chest before pulling the rubber sheeting away. "Prep a heart needle!"

Tracy froze and her grip on Matt's hand tightened. "No."

"Let them work," Matt's whispered voice soothed. "He's a tough old bastard. He isn't going out like this."

"I couldn't take it if anything…" She turned and buried her face in his shoulder. Matt clumsily stroked her shoulder.

From the lab he watched the tech look up to Doctor Peters and shook his head. "He's gone."

3

As Marco pulled away from the docks in the black SUV, Paul cradled his brother's burnt body in the back of the vehicle. "We need to get blood in him fast." He kept his voice steady, but the urgency was apparent.

"We have emergency blood stored off-site. I'm heading there now."

Paul glanced out the window and watched as rows of commercial buildings whizzed past. "Emergency blood? Do you mean animal blood?"

"No, sir. Emergency as in human blood." Marco took the left turn a little too quickly and caused Paul to lose his balance, slamming into the side of the SUV. "It's bagged blood, but it's human. It will have to hold him until we can get a donor."

"Donor?" Paul glared at the driver. "Take me someplace where there are people, and I'll convince them to donate."

Marco's eyes hardened as he stared at the vampire in the rear view mirror. "Monsieur Thorn wouldn't want it that way."

"Rufus may have no choice!" Paul leaned across the rear seat back and pointed at Marco, "Get me a live person. He needs fresh, human blood, and lots of it. I don't care if it's a prostitute, a homeless person, or the president of the United fucking States."

Marco ground his teeth as he accelerated the large SUV through the commercial areas. He knew a place where professionals worked. Ladies of the night...but at this early morning hour, he doubted any would still be lingering. The dock workers would be too obvious and there would be too many prying eyes if he approached any. That only left the homeless or the illegals. Shaking his head, he turned toward the heart of the city. "This is on your head."

"Of course it's on my head," Paul repeated. "Not that he'll actually remember it once he's come back."

Marco drove near the closest home improvement store. He spotted a few day laborers hovering near the entrance and slowed the truck. "Stay low while I lure them inside."

Paul sunk low in the rear of the SUV. "Nothing like ethnic food."

Marco rolled down his window and whistled to the small handful of men. In Spanish he announced that he needed two men for a day's work. A pair of young men jogged toward the truck.

"What are you working on?" the taller one asked.

"Just cleaning up a rent house. Mostly hauling off trash maybe a little painting. If things work out, it might turn into a couple days' worth of work."

The two men nodded and slipped into the truck. One crawled into the rear seat while the other sat up front. "How far is it?"

"Not far. In fact, just a few blocks from here." Marco pulled out and turned back toward the warehouse district. "First we need to pick up some equipment though."

As they drove, the man in the backseat leaned forward. "Hey, do you smell something burning?"

Marco studied him in the rear view mirror and shook his head. "Nope. Damned allergies, I can't smell a thing."

He pulled into one of Thorn's abandoned warehouses and hit the button to shut the door of the building. As Paul leaned across the back seat and grabbed the man closest to him, Marco punched the other man in the front seat, effectively knocking him out cold.

"Try not to make a mess, will ya?"

*****

"Move!" Evan yelled as he spat the rubber tube from his mouth and slid in next to Major Tufo. Raising his fist into the air, he brought it down hard onto his chest, effectively shocking his heart into beating again. "I need a heart needle and adrenaline."

The technician near Mark's head held a stethoscope to his chest and listened. He pulled it away and shook his head. Evan pelted his chest again, careful not to hit too hard lest he shatter the ribcage and send splinters into his heart. An assistant slipped in next to Doctor Peters and handed him the long needle. "Adrenaline."

Evan slipped it between the ribs near the sternum and plunged the liquid directly into the muscle. "Come on, dammit. Beat!" He began doing chest compressions while another assistant bagged him, effectively breathing for the man. After the third round of compressions, he stopped and they checked for a pulse again.

"I got it!" The tech moved the stethoscope up near his neck and listened for the heartbeat at the jugular. "It's weak, but it's there. Let's push more blood."

Evan stepped aside while they hung another bag of blood then donned clean gloves. He waited for the go ahead to begin stitching the man up again. None in the surgical area heard the sobbing from feet away as Mitchell kept the major's wife from collapsing.

Evan continued to work at a feverish pace, praying to any god that would listen to a vampire's prayer that he could save the man. He barely noticed when a masked woman appeared near the major's face and took his hand in hers. She whispered sweet words of encouragement in his ear as he continued to work.

Mitchell paced, his eyes casting furtive glances toward the surgery. Finally he approached the group and asked, "How much longer?"

Without looking up, Evan reached for another suture and replied, "I'm about to close his lower abdomen. I've stitched together his insides as best I can."

"Will he make it, Doc?" Mitchell's voice cracked, dry from worry.

Evan shrugged slightly. "To be honest, Colonel, I'm shocked he's made it this far."

Matt stood by and watched as Evan inserted drain tubes, then wrapped Mark with layer upon layer of sterile gauze. The entire team then wrapped him tightly with thick tape then placed him ever so gently on a clean gurney with fresh sheets and prepared to wheel him to a room. Evan pulled the mask from his face and Mitchell cringed at the coagulated blood crusted around his mouth and stuck between the lines of his teeth. He felt a sickening twist of his guts as he realized *where* that blood had come from, but he shook it off. Mark wouldn't be breathing if it hadn't been for Evan's efforts.

"What are his chances, Doc?" Mitchell watched as they wheeled him off to a junior officer's quarters and prepared to convert it to a recovery room.

"Don't ask me that, Colonel." Evan stripped his gloves and pulled the smock from his chest. He worked his mouth and spat a coagulated glob into the floor drain. "By all rights, he shouldn't have even made it down here, much less survived the surgery."

Matt lowered his face and felt his eyes threaten to betray him. "But you're sure he won't…"

"No. None of the damage was from a bite. And from the amount of blood we pushed into him, I would hazard a guess that we thoroughly transfused him." Evan nearly collapsed into a chair and ran a hand through his hair. "Not that a transfusion would save him had he been infected. I was just saying that…well…no. He's not infected."

"You're exhausted, Doc. The sun's up. You should get some rest." Matt patted the man's shoulder as he stepped past him. "Whether he makes it or not, I need you to know that I…" Matt's voice trailed off as the words caught in his throat.

"I understand, sir." Evan stood and met his gaze. "Perhaps you should check on the rest of the operation. Make an appearance anyway. Let them know about Major Tufo."

"Yeah. You're right." Matt turned and headed for the doorway to the stairwell.

"I'll check in on him and I'll have my field medics rotate in and out as well."

"Thank you, Doc. If there's any change in his status, let me know."

"Of course." Evan watched as Mitchell disappeared through the doorway and sighed. He stared at the pile of bloody gauze and sponges that lay at the floor of his lab and the coagulated puddles that jellied as they streamed toward the floor drain.

He knew that he should clean his lab now while it would still be somewhat easy, but he debated with the demon inside. Major Tufo was loved by all. He would be missed as much or more than anyone with the squads. He knew in his heart of hearts that the man couldn't survive his wounds. He had been so tempted to 'accidentally' cut his finger or stab himself while suturing and squeeze enough blood into a major artery that perhaps…

He shook his head to clear his thoughts. No. He wouldn't wish his existence on anybody.

Still…

What would Mrs. Tufo do?

*****

"Jack!" Nadia tried to waddle-run to him in the soft sand, and Jack rushed to meet her. He smiled at the sight and prayed that she would think that he was simply happy to see her. Picking her up, he swung her around then kissed her gently before setting her back on her feet.

"Nadia, why are you here?" He walked her toward the castle and further from the slowing blades of the helicopter. "If you had shown up earlier, it could have been very dangerous."

She stopped and jerked his arm. "It was dangerous whether I was here or not, Mr. Thompson."

Uh-oh. He knew that tone. "Sweetheart, that's what I do. Remember? I'm the head of…"

"Do not pretend with me, Jack!" Her voice caught him off guard with her genuine concern. "You enjoy battle. Even with my warning, you stayed here in hopes…" Nadia's eyes fell on Pedro, Jimmy and Gus.

Jack followed her gaze then tried to set her mind at ease. "No, Nadia…no." He spun her back around and faced her. "No, they're the good guys. They arrived here to help and they did. They helped to fight off the attackers and…"

"And who were the attackers?"

"They were, uh, wolves." Jack pointed to the bodies of some of the fallen that were slowly shifting back to their human form. "Yes, we did lose a few Lycans in the battle, but we came out victorious in the end."

Nadia huffed and pushed past him. "The castle is in ruins. The outbuildings are destroyed. The stables have been demolished. The beaches are mutilated. Were you not able to save anything?"

Jack looked around at the destruction and shrugged. "There were a lot of them." She glared at him, as if he had just proven her point for her. "They had a helicopter gunship. It's sort of hard to beat one of those."

"If you had listened to me in the first place—"

Jack interrupted her, his tone suddenly a mixture of anger and bitterness. "Then I'd probably be dead. I invited my squad mates here and they had the experience and skill needed to turn the tide of this battle. If they hadn't been here, we'd have lost a lot more Lycans, and more than likely Robert and I both would be dead."

She nearly staggered back from the tone of his voice, her eyes wide. "I never…I mean…I saw the attack and you were…"

"Yes, we were under attack, Nadia, but my people weren't the ones behind it. As you can see, they're still standing and the only reason I am is because they were here."

"Ahem." Kalen cleared his throat and leaned heavily on his bow.

Jack blushed then stepped toward his warrior Elf friend. "And Kalen and Horith as well." He paused and turned quietly to Kalen. "If you need to check on him, I totally understand. With Rufus AWOL, I'm betting the mission to Geneva is off."

Kalen shook his head. "They will send word one way or the other."

Jack nodded solemnly. "Words can't express how bad I feel for what happened."

"What did happen?" Nadia asked from behind him.

"Horith fell in battle." Kalen stated plainly. "I sent him back to the Wyldwood."

"We counted nine leaving by boat," Bartholomew stated as he approached the trio. "Considering the bodies scattered about, they had a force of over fifty. Heavily armed, too." He tossed an assault rifle on the ground at Jack's feet.

"And you have no idea who sent them?" Nadia raised a brow at Jack, her hands planted firmly on her hips.

Jack knelt and retrieved the assault rifle. "This is a Sig 552 Commando." He wiped the sand from the receiver and pulled the spent magazine from the weapon. "Practically new, too."

Kalen reached for the weapon and examined it. Sniffing it he wrinkled his brow and handed it back. "All I smell is wolf. And gun powder."

Jack looked around the remains of the battlefield. Motioning to Robert, he held up the rifle. "Have you collected their weapons?"

"All that we've found are being stacked near the entrance to the castle." Robert hooked a thumb over his shoulder in the general direction of the pile.

"Are they all Sigs?"

"Yup, commandos and a few P226 Tacticals." Robert turned to Jack and closed the distance to the small group. "Why? What's up with the weaponry?"

"It's just that...these aren't exactly common weapons for the U.S. These are SOG weapons for most European teams."

Robert nodded in agreement. "And some South American nations use them as well."

"As soon as the bodies finish shifting, get a collection of prints. We need to get them to Colonel Mitchell and see if he can run them for us." Jack turned to Pedro. "Break out your coms, Popo. You need to fill the colonel in on what's happened here."

"What exactly do you want me to tell him? Are we headed back to Tinker?"

Jack rubbed at his chin and tried to avoid Nadia's eyes boring a hole into his head. "Tell him the mission to Geneva is cancelled. I'm sending the Lycans back to the pack with Nadia for now. Meanwhile, I'll come back with you and we can regroup."

"And what of us, Chief Jack?" Kalen shifted his weight on the bow. "We were promised a chance at vampires and yet...we've only taken a few wolf pelts." He glanced at the gnome near his leg and smiled.

"I'm hoping you'll come with me. We may need to regroup, but for now, the threat from the council isn't over. I'd rather have a ready force than none at all."

Kalen nodded in agreement. He turned and glanced to the parapet of the castle. "Perhaps we should wait until nightfall then. I fear that attempting to move them might be hazardous."

"Where is Rufus?" Nadia asked, her eyes betraying the fear growing within.

Jack turned and wrapped an arm around her shoulders. "About that." He gently directed her toward the castle and to a place where she could sit and rest. "We need to talk."

*****

Laura placed the phone carefully back into the cradle and rested her head on the desk. "Still can't get through?" She lifted her head and noted the concern on Jennifer's face as she leaned against the doorjamb.

"It's like they just disappeared." She sighed and rubbed at her eyes. Pablo stepped briskly back toward the duty office and Laura raised a hand to catch his attention. "Can I ask another favor?"

He smiled an easy, carefree smile and nodded. "If it is within my power, Ms. Youngblood, it is yours."

"Is there any chance that you have satellite access?" She quietly prayed that there was still a way that she could at least ensure that the hangar building was still standing and not a fiery inferno.

Pablo hung his head. "I'm afraid that is not within my power. We do not have such luxuries."

Laura exhaled a long, slow breath and leaned back in her chair. "If only there was some way I could access our own satellite."

"What would you need?" Pablo stepped inside and sat down at the computer console across from her.

Laura shook her head. "Honestly, I'm not sure. We were given an old satellite to use, but…" she stretched her neck as she tried to find the right words, fatigue eating away at her ability to think. "But I just didn't take the time to learn anything about it. I was supposed to have been gone by now."

Jennifer placed a reassuring hand on her shoulder. "I'm sure they're fine. Remember what you told me?"

"We still don't know who…or *what* may have attacked them."

Pablo rolled closer and lowered his voice, "There is still the possibility that it was simply an attack on their communications. Just because they lost the ability to communicate does not mean that somebody was foolish enough to attack them head on."

Laura had an uneasy feeling in the pit of her stomach and shook her head. "I don't think it's that simple, Pablo. Would you simply take out somebody's coms and not attack them directly?"

Pablo lowered his eyes and shook his head. "No."

"Yeah, I didn't think so." Laura picked up the phone again and began dialing again.

"Did you think of another number?" Jennifer asked hopefully.

"No, I'm just going to keep trying the ones I know until somebody picks up. Surely if..." she paused and stared off at nothing. "I mean, *when* the survivors of the attack realize their communications are down, they'll want to get them back up ASAP."

*****

Apollo weighed his options and debated on how best to deal with Sheridan when he finally stepped off the helicopter and confronted the man. Did he pull him aside, put him in a choke hold and squeeze every last drop of information that he could from him or did he continue to play along, milking him for every drop of intel that he could? As much as it might please him to feel the man's trachea turn to mush under his probing fingers, Apollo knew that nobody could speak if they couldn't breathe.

He jumped from the hovering chopper and strode purposely toward the warehouse, his mind still bouncing between his two options. As soon as he entered the gloom of the warehouse, he saw the drastically reduced forces packing their meager gear. He had to force himself not to smile as he realized that the crew at the hangar did more than just hold their own against the attack.

Bigby lay back on a cot, his shoulder bandaged and soaked with blood. Apollo grabbed the nearest wolf and pulled him aside, "What happened?"

"We thought we had them. Bastards opened a hole in the floor and brought up this big black truck with a chain gun in the back. They sliced through our offensive line in no time. We had no choice but to retreat."

Apollo shook his head, feigning concern. "That must be something new."

"Or some secret machine they hadn't told you about." The wolf turned back to the gear and continued packing.

"Why are you packing? Planning to bug out?"

He cast a furtive glance over his shoulder toward the office then looked back to Apollo. "Our boss ain't too happy with Sheridan. We've been called back home."

Apollo nodded. "And where's that?"

The wolf stiffened slightly and gave him a cautious stare. "You weren't told when you were recruited?"

"I didn't care to know then." Apollo motioned around him, "But it's not exactly like I'm qualified for much else. I'm gonna need some kind of job."

The wolf considered his logic then rubbed at his chin. "Belize for the most part, but Mr. Simmons has properties all over. We might get assigned to any of them. He likes his security like he likes his women."

"What? Burly and covered in hair?" Apollo laughed at his own joke.

The wolf shook his head. "No, *thick*."

"Ah." Apollo glanced toward the office and dreaded the next part. "I guess I better go pack what little I have."

"Make it quick. We leave tomorrow."

He entered the office area to find Sheridan slumped in a chair, rubbing at his temples. He lifted his rummy eyes and looked to the large ebony man hopefully. "Please tell me you had better luck than we did."

Apollo straddled a stool and spun around to meet his gaze. "It was almost as if they were waiting on us. I was hoping we'd get there before my team did, but they were already there." Apollo ground his teeth as he recounted the battle and the bitch-slapping wakeup call that Jack gave him. "Plus, the man had a bunch of *others* there. They sliced through my team like a hot knife through butter."

"Fuck!" Sheridan slapped a pile of papers from the table and hobbled to his feet, his anger forcing him to try to walk off the nervous tension. "What are 'others'?"

"You know...supernatural beings? Elves and shit. He even had a bunch of flying fucking gargoyles. Tore shit out of our chopper."

"How did you get back so quickly?" Sheridan glanced over his shoulder and out the dirty window to the warehouse.

"We stole another one." Apollo glanced over his shoulder to see what the man was trying to look at. "What?"

"How many men did you lose?"

Apollo grunted and pushed off the stool. "Nearly all of them. I think we came back with eight plus me."

Sheridan's eyes bulged and he had to lean against the counter. "Bloody hell."

"Oh, it was bloody all right." Apollo allowed a slight grin. "I ain't for sure, but I think we took out the vamp that owned the place, though."

"Thorn?" Sheridan shook his head and slowly sat back down. "It was his forces we needed to take out. Anybody that had to do with the squads. Your Team Leader and my 'best friend' Mr. Thompson was number one on the hit list. Any chance he was fragged in the attack?"

"Nope. Lucky fucker is still breathing."

"So he knows that you've switched sides?" Sheridan's voice was cautious as his mind tried to devise three different ways to use the information as an advantage.

"Oh yeah. And he knows that you're involved as well." Apollo pulled a toothpick from behind his ear and stuck it in his mouth.

"He…he *what*?" Sheridan paused and stared at the man as if he had grown a second head. "How could he have found that out?"

"Because I fucking told him." Apollo turned a defensive stare to the man. "They got the drop on me, had me dead to rights, and instead of killing me, he took me prisoner."

"And you had to spill your guts!" Sheridan shook with rage as he took to his feet again. "You realize that you've just signed my death warrant? Not just mine, but every man that used to work with me. They'll all be hunted down and…"

"You wanted a war!" Apollo was on his feet and closing the distance between the two. "Well now you got it, sweetheart. Jack knows everything. Well…not *everything*. He don't know who's financing this little army of yours."

"Why in the hell did you tell him that—"

Apollo interrupted him again, "And I hope the son of a bitch goes running to the squads and rats me out. Rats YOU out. That way, instead of gunning for them, they'll come hunting for us. We can set traps, we can prepare. Rather than trying to attack them in their fucking *strongholds*, they can come after us on our terms."

"You're an imbecile." Sheridan shook his head as he stared at the man. "Our anonymity is the only thing that was keeping us alive."

Apollo waved him off. "Fuck anonymous. I want them to know." He stared out the window at the handful of wolves packing their gear for their trips home. "You need to call your boss and order us some new soldiers." He turned on Sheridan and glared. "This time have him send some REAL soldiers. Not just knuckle-dragging grunts that can shift. We need people who are trained how to fight. Between the two of us, we sacrificed over a hundred men, and for what? To ring their fucking doorbell and announce that we wanted to punch them in the nose?" He threw the stool across the room and let it clatter to the floor. "Fuck that. We need men who can fight. If he can't do that, then he ain't serious about his revenge."

Sheridan watched the mountain of a man stomp out of the office and grinned wickedly as he picked up the satellite phone. He knew that Mr. Simmons wouldn't be happy, but with a force like Apollo on their side and angry? He'd be a fool not to take advantage of that weapon.

*****

John helped where he could, but the technicians were thorough and needed little help in repairing or replacing the equipment damaged or destroyed in the attack. He felt like a third wheel as people all around him scurried about, performing their duties as he simply stood and watched.

Finally he found a group of men bagging up the dead wolves that were slowly shifting back to their human form. "Can I give you a hand with that?"

The men in the HAZMAT suits shrugged and offered him a pair of rubber gloves. "You may already have the virus, but a lot of them are still messy as hell."

John pulled the gloves on and went to work bagging and tagging the bodies. They were quickly stacked on a push cart so that they could be fingerprinted before cremation. As John was tossing the last of the bodies onto the cart Dave Marshall trotted back into the hangar. "Little John! Give me a hand out here." He waved the large man over toward the door.

"What's up, Dave?" John stripped the gloves and dropped them in the garbage on his way.

"We're trying to get the dishes back up and operational. We have the smaller ones back up, but we need someone big to help push the larger one up and help hold it in place while Hammer anchors it."

The duo trotted to the rear of the hangar and lifted and pushed the large dish up while Hammer ran stabilizing cables out to anchor the larger mesh dish. Marshall lifted along one side while John lifted the other and kept the dish upright. Dave finally caught John's attention. "Hey,I heard you were in the back of the truck and sliced through their front line. That's heavy fuckin' duty, man."

John chuckled to himself. "You heard wrong. I was safe and sound in the armored cab with Spanky. Doc installed a remote trigger in the console. There's a real nice crosshair TV screen mounted in the dash."

Dave rolled his eyes. "I should have known. The way stories get stretched around here…give it a week and you'll have *thrown* the truck up to the main deck, then climbed in the back and breathed fire from your nostrils while you were shooting them down."

John broke into laughter which brought a stern stare from Hammer. "Please hold it steady."

"Sorry." John kept snickering as he thought about Marshall's warning. "Any advice for when that happens?"

Dave gave him a toothy grin. "Just ride the wave, baby. Nod your head, tell them 'hell yeah, that's exactly how it happened' and ride the wave of fame while you can."

"Really?" John couldn't see himself being a glory hound.

"Hell yeah. Because next week it will be somebody else, and you know they'll do it." Dave hiked a brow at him. "Especially if it's me. I'll blow that shit up 'til they think I'm Superman."

"Well, if it's all the same, I think I'll stick with the truth." He saw Dave's face fall. "No offense, I'm just not the embellishing kind."

"Hey, whatever floats your boat, baby. I'm just saying we all do it. More to blow off steam than anything." Dave felt the dish shift and he quickly adjusted his grip and realigned it. "So no offense taken."

Hammer stepped back and eyeballed the work. "I think that's it. Let it go so we can see if the cables hold." Both men gently released their grip and the dish remained solid. Hammer nodded as he turned back toward the hangar. "We should have coms again and I'll order up some concrete so we can get these posts reset."

"We got eyes and ears again?" Dave asked. "You sure?"

"I'm not positive, but the dishes were the only components actually damaged. We should."

"Excellent. I don't want to miss my soaps." Dave trotted past the two and made for the door.

Hammer turned to John and gave him a questioning look. "Was he for real?"

"God, I hope not."

4

Doctor Peters collapsed onto his bed and ran his hands through his hair. In the extremely dim light of his bare room, he sighed heavily and cast a quick glance at the framed photograph of Laura that sat beside his tiny bed. How he missed her in times of stress. She was truly his anchor.

After they had said their good byes, he truly feared he wouldn't see her again. To come back to Oklahoma and find her waiting at the hangar nearly made his heart start beating on its own again.

The nights they had spent together afterward, carefully pushing the limits and boundaries of their physical relationship, to him it almost felt as if the two had been bound together. He metered out his bites to her, keeping them limited to places where the punctures wouldn't be seen. The blood bond that formed between them grew and continued to grow each time they did it.

He watched her carefully. He wanted to be sure that she wouldn't accidentally become addicted to the rush she got from his bites. He smiled to himself as he recalled the one time he nearly lost control and bit her neck right at the moment of orgasm. It had sent her so far over the edge that he wasn't sure he would stop. Luckily for them both, he had bitten far enough back on her neck that her hair or uniform or both covered the bite marks that quickly faded.

Completely sated and feeling much like he had as a human at Thanksgiving feasts, he lay back on his cot and felt the massive amount of blood in his stomach literally slosh as he moved.

Without a proper suction machine, he'd been stuck keeping the wounds clean, and he knew he couldn't just spit it onto the floor. He had drunk enough to keep him full for weeks.

Rolling to his side to try to get more comfortable, he felt a headache spike between his eyes and a wave of nausea strike like he had never felt. Groaning, he wrapped his arms around his swelling stomach and tried to relieve the pressure that was building.

He honestly felt sick and slowly sat up on his cot. He pulled the waste basket from his small desk beside his cot and held it between his feet as his head spun and his stomach threatened to revolt on him.

Evan Peters felt himself break into a cold sweat and knew that something was wrong. Although he had never attempted to drink so much at one time before, he knew that something wasn't right. This wasn't from overeating. This was...something else.

With a violence that he'd not known possible, his stomach emptied itself across the room, painting the wall with such force that it sprayed the ceiling and the back wall of his domicile. Brownish black globules of coppery blood dripped from every surface as his head spun and the room began to tilt. He glanced down at the trash can and for a fleeting moment found it somewhat amusing that the only place free of vomit was the very receptacle he intended to barf into.

Evan found himself panting for breath and his extremities shook as he reached for the can. "This is wrong," he mumbled. He tried to stand and found his legs had turned to rubber. As he went down, he reached out and grabbed for his desk to break his fall.

He lay on the floor, the can upended between his legs and watched as the ceiling above him slowly twisted and turned. "I need to tell Colonel Mitchell..." he moaned as the darkness over took him.

*****

Rachel remained in the rafters of the warehouse while Damien worked. Her eyes watched him much like a hawk would watch a mouse scamper in the grass. She could feel the last vestiges of humanity seep away as he drew ever closer to seeing her brought back to her full potential.

She couldn't remember why she had resisted seeing the plan through to completion. On the few occasions that she allowed herself to remember her 'other' self, she quickly dismissed the pity she felt for the humans that she would soon rule. They were of no more importance to her than ants on a sidewalk were to the humans who trampled them during their daily grind.

As Damien finished the preparations, he looked to the rafters and called to her, "Mistress, it is prepared. We are ready."

She stepped out and floated to a gentle landing behind him. "Are you certain?" She walked slowly around the stainless steel container, staring at the dark red blood within. It's surface reminding her of a polished mirror.

"Yes, my queen. I am certain." Damien held his head high as he watched her.

"You're certain the blood is pure?"

"I tasted each source. It is pure." He bowed slightly as she continued to pace around the perimeter.

"Prepare the final sacrifice." Her eyes never lifted from the blood as she spoke, but Damien knew exactly what was expected. He walked to where the elder was held captive and dragged him from his cage.

The man was bound and gagged, his eyes screaming for help as he struggled against Damien's grip. Rachel refused to watch as Damien pulled the elder to the foot of the vat and forced him to his knees. "For your glory, my beloved."

"All things for my glory."

He jerked the elder's head aside and sunk his teeth deep into his neck, ripping huge chunks of flesh from his quaking form.

Damien barely chewed before swallowing the gooey chunks and biting another chunk loose. As the elder began to convulse, Damien punched through his chest and pulled his dead, withered heart from his chest. He quickly shoved it into his mouth and sucked the black blood from his fingers as the elder's power began to surge through him.

He felt the centuries add to his own power and it knocked him to his knees. Rachel felt the corners of her mouth draw into a smile when Damien fell to the ground. It was time.

She raised her hands to the moon and began an ancient chant in a language not spoken since the dawn of man. The blood in the vat rippled as the ground shook, and Damien watched as the lights inside the warehouse dimmed. He smelled something akin to ozone forming inside the warehouse and saw a hazy fog forming, moving quickly around Rachel as she continued to chant.

Damien slowly pulled himself to his feet and watched as she continued to chant, her head back, eyes closed, mouth forming words that he couldn't hear. A buzzing sound seemed to have come from nowhere and washed out everything…or…or was it just him. He could feel himself growing weaker. But…how could that be? He just ate the heart of an elder. He knew he had gained centuries from it and yet…he could barely stand. He felt so weak. His head was spinning and he could *feel* the power being sucked from him. Whatever was causing it, it felt like it was draining him.

His legs collapsed from under him, but his hands refused to let go of the sides of the steel vat. He could feel it warming under his grip. The cold of the steel giving way to heat from…something. It wasn't totally uncomfortable, yet, but it continued to grow in intensity.

He mustered all of his strength and raised his head, his eyes settling on Rachel. Rather, on what was left of Rachel. Her withered corpse still stood at the end of the vat, her jaw barely moving as the last mutterings of the chant fell from her lips. He watched as her body fell to the ground and he could have sworn he saw dust rise up into the air. For the briefest of moments, he hoped that she actually survived the transition. He had grown accustomed to her.

He felt the blood in the vat bubbling, sloshing, something within it thrashing about. He tried in vain to stand so that he could see his beloved rise from the ashes, but he didn't have the energy to speak, much less to stand. He felt his head wobble, and he couldn't hold it up any longer.

He collapsed, his body drained, but his hands refused to give up its grip on the side of the vat. He gasped for a breath and prayed that he'd have the strength to call out for her help when his grip finally released and he fell to the ground. He lay on his back and stared up at the ceiling of the warehouse, unable to turn his head or even blink his eyes.

Damien watched as his beloved Lilith rose from the blood and stepped from the steel tub. Nude and covered in blood, her long dark hair appeared even darker when slathered to her body by the blood of the virgins. She didn't look at him as she stepped over his prone body.

Damien sucked in enough air to croak out a single word. "Help."

Lilith paused and turned back. She looked to him and cocked her head to the side, studying him as he lay on the ground. "You weren't as strong as I'd hoped." She shook her head at him in disgust. "You would have survived this if you had been strong enough."

Damien's poor starved brain raced as he considered her words. *Would have survived? I still live!* Lilith stood erect and turned away from him. She came back a moment later wearing the robe that Rachel had been wearing and considered his predicament.

"I suppose I could toss you into the blood. If you have the strength to save yourself, then maybe I can find a use for you."

Damien's mind was begging for her to do something. Anything. He watched in horror as she bent and grabbed him nonchalantly. As she lifted him, he caught a glimpse of his withered self. His hair was white and his wrinkled, leathery skin hung off of his bones. She tossed him into the vat of blood and he could feel himself floating for a moment before the thickening blood saturated his clothing and allowed him to sink.

Damien didn't have the strength to swallow as the blood entered his mouth. The best he could hope for was that enough could work its way down his throat to nourish him before it was too late.

*****

Colonel Mitchell paced outside of Mark's room and prayed for a miracle when Jericho Jones approached. "Colonel?"

Matt groaned as he turned. "Yeah?"

"Sir, we have coms back up. And the hotline was active while it was down. We actually have another report, sir."

"Son of a—" Matt bit off the curse. "What is it this time, Captain?"

"Vamps, sir. Looks like a small den wreaking havoc in California." Jericho handed him the report.

"Verified?"

"Working on a secondary, sir. Could have it at any moment."

Matt chanced a glance through the window into Mark's room before turning away and marching down the hall. "Who's up?"

"Sir, at this point, I don't think we can go by that. We have parts of First Squad scattered. Third Squad is still in the field. Second isn't slated for this, but they're the only complete team we have available."

"Of course." Matt stopped and rubbed at the back of his neck. "Okay, Captain. Notify Spanky to get his team prepped. And tell them to be on their toes. The full moon is right around the corner. Things are liable to get stupid out there."

"Roger that, sir."

"Gather what qualified members we have and get them ready for the mission. If we can get this underway in time, I'll take OPCOM again."

"Sir, I've got this rotation." Jericho knew that the colonel would rather be at the XO's side. He also knew that it was his shift to be OPCOM actual but there was something in the man's voice.

"No. I need something to…" he glanced back down the hall. "I need the distraction."

"Copy that, sir." Jericho pulled his copy of the report and headed topside to find Spanky.

Mitchell stood in the hallway a moment and tried to gather his thoughts. Without Mark there, this wasn't going to be 'right'. Maybe he could have Jericho take his spot in the OPCOM. Maybe he could have Doc on standby in case the shit hit the fan again. Maybe…he rubbed at his eyes and blew out a breath. Maybe he needed to stop second guessing everything.

*****

Apollo stood in the warehouse and sucked in deep breaths, trying to calm himself. He had fought the urge to rip Sheridan's throat out, and while he congratulated himself on accomplishing that minor goal, he was left questioning himself. He had returned intent on discovering as much as he could about the man behind the attacks. Now he was putting himself as the point of the spear for a war.

He could hear Sheridan in the office speaking to somebody, obviously over a radio or telephone. It must be the Simmons guy that he'd learned of. Still, he didn't think he had enough information to take to the teams just yet. One name and the location of their warehouse would get him thanks before they sunk a silver bullet into his head for turning traitor.

Apollo wandered the warehouse watching the handful of surviving wolves as they packed their gear and debated simply killing the rest of them off and calling in Mitchells cleanup crews to look for whatever evidence they could find.

A hand on his shoulder startled him and he turned to find Sheridan hobbling up beside him. "The man behind the curtain is sending his best enforcers. All that he has with any kind of military background."

"How many?"

"He didn't say. But he did say that it should be enough to more than hold our own when the squads come knocking." He sounded pleased with himself. "I have to admit. The last time I called him, he wasn't pleased with the outcome. Once I hit him with your idea he changed his tune."

"Like we gave him much choice."

"True." Sheridan rubbed at the back of his neck as he thought about Walter Simmons. "Still, he seemed almost excited now. I think the idea of them knowing that you and I were involved and having them go on the attack intrigued him. I don't think he was expecting such a move."

"You didn't."

"No. I'll admit you had me on that one." Sheridan looked past the man and watched as the wolves packing each stopped and checked their phones at nearly the exact same time. To the man, they each put away their phone and began unpacking the gear they had been preparing to take back. "Looks like he's put the wheels into motion."

"When will they be here?"

"They're loading now. Should be here tonight." Sheridan turned back for the office then paused. "By the way. You're now in charge of this canine army."

Apollo raised a brow at that announcement. "You ain't the boss no more?"

"Oh, I'm still the boss. Just not over the tactical movements. That's all you. So if this goes to shite, it's on your head."

*****

"So he's just gone?" Nadia's eyes were wide with disbelief as she probed Jack's face for some tell-tell sign that he was pulling her leg.

"We've searched everywhere and Pedro saw him go up in a huge explosion. My best guess is that he vaporized himself."

She shook her head as she tried to wrap her mind around the possibility. "I can't believe it. I've known Rufus since I was...well, my entire life."

"I know." Jack patted her hand and avoided her eyes.

"There's more, isn't there?"

"I don't..." his voice trailed off.

"I'm a big girl, Jack. Tell me. Please. I need to know." He looked up and saw the tears forming in her eyes.

Jack swallowed hard and tried to think of a way to put what he needed to tell her next that wouldn't make Rufus out to be the bad guy. There was no easy way to say it. He opted for the Band-Aid approach. Rip it off quickly and let the sting fade. "There's evidence that he stole secret plans from the squads and attempted to build a Doomsday weapon. It was that weapon that exploded on him and—"

"No!" Nadia exclaimed, pulling her hand from his. "Rufus is an honorable man. He would never do such a thing."

Jack held her by the shoulders and stared deeply into her eyes. "As I said, there is evidence. That doesn't necessarily mean that he did. Until I can find out more..."

"I refuse to believe that Rufus is capable of such a thing."

Pedro stepped into the room and held the notebook out to her. "It was a Doomsday weapon that targeted natural born supernatural beings. Not just vampires, not just wolves, not just elves...all of them." He held the notebook at arm's length, but she refused to accept it from him.

"Why would he do such a thing?" Her tone was defiant as she glared at the man.

"Who knows? The last time this notebook was seen, it was in Doctor Peters' lab."

"Why would your vampire create a weapon to destroy vampires? That makes no sense." She was slowly shaking her head, refusing to accept what her heart already knew.

"He didn't set out to design it. As I understand it, he was trying to figure out a way to differentiate. So that it wouldn't be a 'kill-everything' weapon, and instead could be used more like…well…like a sniper rifle."

"I refuse to accept this based on your say. I've known Rufus my entire life. He is simply not capable of such subterfuge."

Jack turned her attention back to him. "And I'm going to try to figure out if it's true."

She turned wide eyes up at him and shook her head. "You're not returning with us to the pack? If Rufus is truly…gone, then our pact with him is nulled."

Jack closed his eyes and sighed. "I'm still officially his Second until my duties are discharged. You know this."

"No, Jack. If he is truly gone then you cannot be Second to him." She tried to stand and pushed his hands away from her. "Why do you do this? Answer me truly."

Jack stood and faced her. "If he's not dead and he's still out there? He could have copies of this. Which means there's nothing to stop him from building another weapon."

"But you found nothing when the weapon blew up and—"

"And Foster is missing. As well as some of the wolves. And a watercraft." Jack exhaled hard and turned to Pedro. "Give me a minute, will ya?"

Pedro stepped out of the room and his footsteps could be heard clicking down the stone hallway. Jack turned back to her and his eyes unsettled her. She had seen this look before…in her visions.

Before he ever uttered the words, she knew what he was going to say.

"As long as a threat like this is out there, I can't just sit around and do nothing. I need to be out there trying my best to stop it."

Nadia felt the tears running down her cheeks without realizing she was crying. "Jack, this is Rufus we are speaking of. He is not a threat."

"If he's trying to build a Doomsday weapon, then he *is* a threat. And pact or not, Second or not…friend or not. I will stop him."

"No, Jack. Please, come back with me. Be a husband and a father."

"I will be, sweetheart. But not until this threat is neutralized. How could I ever rest knowing that at any moment he could set off a device that could take out *all* natural-borns? You, me, our child?"

"Jack…" she sobbed. "Please?"

"Your father. Your mother. Everybody you've ever known or cared for is at risk as long as he has the ability to recreate that weapon, Nadia. Can you really ask me to sit aside and do nothing?"

She collapsed into her chair and sobbed into her hands. When Jack reached out for her she pushed him away and turned her face from him. "Go!"

Jack stood and stared at her sobbing, his heart breaking. It took everything he had not to reach out and pull her to him, but she didn't want him. She was too upset. He turned for the door but paused at the doorway. "I love you, Nadia. I will come back to you."

She turned away from his voice and continued to cry.

*****

"Seems like we just got back from a mission." Lamb smirked as he double checked his gear.

Ing chuckled. "Ah, the life of a military operator. Travel to strange, exotic lands, meet new and exciting people…"

"And kill them." Little John finished the joke for him as he finished checking his gear. "Anybody hear what this one is?"

Spalding hung his pack back on the pegboard and stretched his neck. "Supposed to be a small vamp pack."

"Easy-peasy," Donnie chimed in as he finished checking his own gear.

"Never assume, Donovan." Spalding looked up from his team and saw Jericho approaching them from the leader boards. "Heads up."

"Secondary just came in. Time to lock and load, boys." He handed Spanky the operations sheet then turned back for the hallway leading to the OPCOM. "For the love of God, be careful out there."

"Roger that, Cap." Spanky browsed the operations sheet then handed it to Donovan. "Be on your toes, boys. We got some mixed signals on this one. California border town. People disappearing. It doesn't look pretty."

Little John reached for the sheet and checked it. "Cali, huh?"

"El Cajon. Mean anything to you?" Spanky asked.

"I had family out there. On the outskirts of town, anyway."

"Maybe if we get done soon enough you can stop by and say hi." Lamb patted the large man's shoulder. "I'm sure they'd appreciate seeing you."

John shook his head. "She's long gone." He hung his pack up and turned back to them. "My grandmother."

Spalding held a hand up to get their attention again. "Gear up, check out your weapons, grab plenty of ammo and be on the tarmac in twenty."

"We Chinookin' it again, boss man?" Donnie asked.

"Negative. We're trying to get set up before sundown this time. We'll be taking a fast mover. The faster we're wheels up, the less chance of having to jump out of a perfectly good airplane." He shot the crew a wink. "Move it, ladies."

*****

Laura rested her head on her shoulder as she slowly pressed the buttons, dialing the hangar again. She'd grown so sick of the tone announcing that the number was out of service and suggesting that she try her call later…she wanted to scream. Now she was just bored as she alternated between fingers to keep them from blistering. When she heard a ringing tone, she feared she had accidentally dialed a wrong number. She sat upright and cradled the phone closer against her ear.

"Duty officer," the voice announced.

"Holy…who is this?" she asked.

"Please announce yourself."

"This is Laura Youngblood. I'm trying to reach Colonel Mitchell."

"Oh, Ms. Youngblood. This is Lieutenant Daniels. I apologize, ma'am. The colonel is in the OPCOM preparing for a mission." She could hear the phone rustle as the duty officer shifted it. "Can I take a message?"

"Negative, Lieutenant. It's imperative that I speak with him. Is the XO available?"

She noted a longer than normal pause and dread swept through her. "Ma'am, I'm sorry, but…Major Tufo was attacked. He's in really bad shape. I'm not even sure if I'm supposed to be telling you this or not."

"Oh, my God…what happened?" She shifted in her seat and listened carefully, hoping to pick up any hints the man might give her.

"We were…uh…there were multiple assailants. They pinned most of the personnel below decks. Communications were down for quite some time. They were eventually repelled but…we did lose some. Quite a few were wounded as well."

"How bad is the XO?" She couldn't hide the anxiety in her voice as she asked.

"Ma'am, I honestly don't know. Doc's got field medics and a couple of the nurses watching him around the clock."

"Doc?" Laura's mind raced as she considered the numerous possibilities of why Evan would be in charge of Mark's recovery. She could only come to one conclusion. "Lieutenant, were the assailants…" she tried to think of a way to ask her question over what she knew was an unsecure line at best. "Were they what we normally send the squads out against?"

She noted the long pause on the other end of the line then heard him clear his throat. "Ma'am, you know I can't say. But I can say that sometimes you should 'trust your gut'." Laura's hand went to her mouth as she realized that the squads had been attacked by *something* and not someone.

"Understood. Can you patch me through to Doctor Evans?"

"Ma'am, as I understand, he's down for the day. He was in surgery for a long time, but I know he'd be happy to hear from you. If you want to leave your number, I can send somebody to try to wake him and have him return your call."

Laura smiled at that and nodded, "Yes, please. I'm at the Brazilian base with Pablo and his team. Do you have a pen?"

*****

Paul Foster sat beside his brother in the quiet of the empty warehouse. Waning sunlight seeped through cracks in the walls or through old exterior doorways, but the pair were deep in the shadows of the building, stuffed back into the abandoned offices in the rear. Desks had been pushed together and an old mattress placed on top for Rufus to lie on while Marco was out hunting down more 'donors'.

Rufus hadgreedily drained the first two and was beginning to look closer to normal, but still he slept, his body attempting to heal itself from the massive burns and multiple crushed and broken bones. Paul could only guess at the internal injuries he had suffered absorbing the brunt of the blast.

Paul had only suffered minor burns from the explosion. Finishing Rufus' scraps had easily healed him and given him the strength to break through the concrete floor to rid them of the bodies. He barely lifted his eyes as the overhead doors opened once more and Marco drove the SUV inside again. The sunlight pouring into the warehouse told him that it was still unsafe to be outside.

The truck slowed to a stop near the office and Marco opened the door then walked around and opened the door for a petite blonde who stepped out and looked around the warehouse with wide eyes.

She chewed her gum loudly, popping it between her jaws as she spun in slow circles. "So this is where you film your movies?"

"It sure is," Marco replied as he shut her door. "It doesn't look like much, but trust me, hang a few drapes, set up some false walls, some furniture, you can't tell it from a real house. One soundstage is as good as any other."

"Fuckin' sweet." She pranced around the front of the truck, swaying her hips in an exaggerated manner as she walked. Her high heels clicked on the concrete floor, and Paul noted the large hoop earrings dangling from the sides of her face. She glanced back to Marco and smiled, "So it's a grand to do the porno then what's my cut of the sales?"

"One percent," Marco answered as he walked her closer to the office. "That may not sound like much, but when you consider that most of our movies gross over a million a month, that's ten grand for each actor. You don't see a lot up front, but it really pays off in the end." He stopped and wrapped an arm over her shoulder. "And that's counting our internet sales, our over-the-counter DVD sales, pay-per-view, satellite, cable...it all adds up."

She snapped her gum again and smiled up at him. "There must be a ton of perverts out there."

"Sugar, you have *no* idea." He continued walking her toward the office. "We have to wait for the guys to show up with the lights and cameras. Our interior decorators are on their way and some of the other actors should be here any minute."

She stepped into the office and saw Rufus lying on the desk. "He looks like somebody already rode him silly." Paul raised a brow at her then shot a questioning look to Marco.

"Mr. Foster here is our producer. Mr. Foster, meet Judy. She's going to be our next star."

"Is that so?" Paul sat upright and looked at the skinny blonde haired girl with too much makeup. "What makes her so special?"

"I got no gag reflex," she bragged, still popping her gum. "Want me to demonstrate?" She walked up to Paul and dropped to her knees, reaching for his crotch as she did so.

He grabbed her wrists and held them. "Thank you, no."

She glared at him and spat her gum to the floor. "What's your problem? I ain't got no diseases."

"No worries," Marco interrupted, reaching over her shoulder and taking her hands from Paul. "Mr. Foster prefers...older women."

"Yeah, right." She smirked at Foster. "I bet he *prefers* boys. What are you?"

Paul smiled sweetly and stood, his hand slowly reaching for the young woman. "My dear, sweet, young lady." His hand stroked the side of her face, and her eyes showed fear for just a moment. "I'm your worst nightmare." He flashed his fangs at her just before he launched himself at her throat.

5

Mark groaned in the narrow bed, his IV swinging slightly as he moved with the pain. Images flashed through his mind that he couldn't begin to explain as he fought to wake. He could feel hands on him, holding him down. He struggled to push the blankets off…the heat…the cold…he could feel himself dying.

His eyes fluttered open and it took a moment for him to realize where he was. He saw Tracy sitting beside him, squeezing a rag out into a bowl of water then reaching to wipe at his brow again. "Am I dead?" he croaked.

Her face tightened and she tried to smile, but it looked more like a sob. Her eyes were red and swollen, obviously from crying. "No, you're not." She sniffled and reached for his face with the rag again. "But you are feverish."

"So I wasn't attacked by a werewolf? I'm just delusional. Good."

"No, sweetheart, you were…" she choked on the words for a moment and had to take a deep breath before continuing. "You were attacked. And now you're fighting a fever. I think you have some kind of infection."

"Fuck me," Mark groaned and turned toward the wall. "I'm infected, aren't I?"

"No." She was emphatic and for a slight moment, he believed her. "Doctor Peters assured me that there were no bites. Just tears and cuts from claws. You aren't infected."

Mark's hand shot up and caught Tracy by the wrist. "I don't want to be one of them." His eyes were wild, and he shook with the chills from his fever. "Don't let me become one of them."

"Mark, you're going to be fine. They're giving you antibiotics and you're going to be just fine." She grimaced slightly at the grip he held her with. "Please, honey, let go…"

He shook with rage for just a moment before releasing her. As he collapsed back onto his sweat-soaked pillow he stared at the ceiling. "When I first came back I thought…I thought I wanted to be like them." He slowly turned his head and faced her. He saw what he expected. Shock. Denial. "I feared getting older. Weaker. Feeling my body break down and betray me with age." He shook his head slightly and turned his eyes back to the ceiling. "But after seeing the true cost…being cut off from family…I knew. I couldn't do that. Ever."

"You're not infected." She wiped at his forehead again then soaked the rag once more. "You need to quit dwelling on the thought. You're not helping yourself by thinking negative thoughts."

"Trace…I can *feel* it. It's in me."

She stiffened and held the soaked towel in her hand. "You can't be."

He finally turned and stared at her. "Are you wearing the crucifix I gave you?"

Her hand went instinctively to her neck. "Why?"

"It's silver. If I'm not infected, then it won't do anything." He held his hand out to her and she saw his fingers shaking. She didn't know if they shook from weakness or from fear of the possibility that…

She placed the towel into the bowl and unclasped the chain. "Okay, but once you've proven that you aren't infected, will you try to rest and get better?"

His eyes relaxed as she slipped the cross into his hand. "Yes." He closed his hand on the silver crucifix and waited. Nothing happened. Slowly she smiled at him when she realized that he wasn't going to burst into flame. He opened his hand, and she reached for the chain but he pulled it away. With a grunt he pushed the tape and bandages down from his chest. When he saw the first line of the stitches that crisscrossed his chest, he took one end of the crucifix and inserted it into his broken skin.

His eyes widened and he bit back a scream as a small wisp of smoke rose from the wound.

*****

Lieutenant Daniels stuck his head into the OPCOM and motioned to Colonel Mitchell. "Sir,can I have a word?"

"We're about to start another mission, Lieutenant. Can it wait?" Mitchell signed off on the logbook and was just sitting in his chair when Daniels interrupted.

"Negative, sir. This is priority." Mitchell turned and saw the look on the man's face. "Jones, you have the OPCOM. Get me if any intel changes."

"Roger that, sir."

Mitchell stepped outside the OPCOM and shut the door, turning on the young junior officer. "This had better be good, Daniels, or so help me…"

"Sir, Ms. Youngblood called in. She asked for you or the XO. I gave her as much of an update as I could. She asked for Doctor Peters and—"

"Spill it, Daniels." Mitchell's patience had worn too thin to listen to much more rambling.

"Sir, we found the Doc in his quarters. It looked like a slaughterhouse in there. Blood…*everywhere*. He was unconscious on the floor. It took quite a bit to revive him."

Mitchell's concern instantly shifted. "Where is he now?"

"We have him in his lab and we're pumping him full of blood."

"Full of...are you kidding me? He must have sucked down five units from the XO during surgery." Mitchell's mind spun as he tried to piece together the different puzzle pieces.

"Sir, he claims that the XO is..." Daniels checked over both shoulders to ensure nobody was within hearing range. "That the XO is infected. That's the only thing that could have caused the reaction he had. It took longer to affect him because it had just happened. But he's certain that the major has the wolf virus."

Mitchell felt his legs go weak under him. He considered the possibilities then stood upright. He squared his shoulders and placed a hand on Daniels' arm. "Does Major Tufo or his wife know yet?"

"Negative, sir. I came here first thing."

"Good. Let's keep it that way." Mitchell glanced back through the OPCOM door and checked the red dot on the screen indicating how far out Team Two was from the mission. "Go inform Doc to keep this under his hat. I'll inform the XO and his wife."

"Sir? Is there any way to counter the virus?" Daniels asked.

Mitchell shook his head. "No, Lieutenant, there isn't. Nothing short of a silver bullet. The upside is the virus will help him heal faster. And he'll heal completely."

"So it's a good thing?"

"Depends on who you ask, son. If you were to ask Major Tufo, the answer would be a definite 'negative' on that one."

"Understood, sir."

"Double time it soldier. Make sure nobody approaches the Tufos. They are not to hear about this until I can talk to them."

"Consider it done, sir."

*****

"So Matt is okay?" Jennifer asked again.

"Yes. He's fine. They're in the middle of a..." Laura sighed and rubbed her hands across her eyes. "Dammit."

"What's wrong? You said that he was okay."

"It's not that. It's…" she paused and shook her head. How do you tell someone that you were scared for someone else's life? Not because you seriously cared if he lived or died, but because you wanted out of a job so badly that you were scared to death that if he didn't make it, you would be stuck with his job from then on? She knew how petty it sounded and it made her angry with herself. She should be feeling sad for Mark, but she really didn't know him that well. He was a prankster pain in her ass.

"What's wrong, Laura? You look like you're about to cry." Jennifer suddenly gasped. "Was your lover harmed in the attack?"

Laura snapped out of her pity party and gawked at the younger woman. "What? No. I just…one of the other officers in charge was hurt badly and might not make it. He was…a good man."

"Was? Do you not expect him to live?"

Laura sat back in her chair and exhaled. "I honestly don't know." When Evan had called her back, he sounded sick and she could tell that he was exhausted, but just hearing his voice made her feel better. Until he told her just how badly Major Tufo was hurt. She could tell that there was something else he wanted to tell her but he held back.

"Where there is life, there is hope." Jennifer's eyes seemed to twinkle as she spoke and Laura couldn't help but wonder if she actually believed such naïve things.

"Sure. If you say so." She stood and stretched her shoulders. "I need to get some rest."

"Very well." Jennifer stood and looked out the window of the office. "Do they have designated areas for us to shift?"

Laura stiffened and shook her head. "Look,there's something you need to know about the squads here. They may be infected with the wolf virus, but they aren't aware of that. They take a mixture of wolf's bane and some other things to prevent them from shifting. They…" she sighed and sat back down. "Look, if you need a place to shift, you're going to have to find it on your own.

They *can't* know that you're a wolf. Or that Mick is a cat. Otherwise…they're liable to try something stupid."

Jennifer's face fell. "Seriously? You brought us to the den of hunters under the auspice that we would be safe."

"And you are. As long as they don't find out that you're shifters."

"Just before a full moon?" Jennifer's eyes narrowed.

Laura threw her hands up, "I'm sorry, okay? I thought Matt would be here right away and…" She dropped her head into her hands and fought the urge to sob. "I didn't know what else to do."

Jennifer closed her eyes and inhaled deeply. "What would you suggest?"

"I don't know. Go for a stroll, find a place to shift. Shift in your room. Something. Nothing. I don't know."

"Was this a ploy to keep us moving until we were back at your base?" Jennifer's tone was more than just accusatory.

Laura raised her head and stared at her. "No. Never."

"Good. Because I'm never going back there." She lifted her chin and thrust her jaw out slightly in defiance.

Laura snorted and leaned back in her chair. "Then you may as well go home to daddy now." She watched as Jennifer's face changed to near shock. "Because I can tell you this. Colonel Mitchell may be pulled by his wolf, but he is still in charge. He'll never leave his men, so that means he won't ever leave that base unless he's dragged away kicking and screaming." Laura stood and pointed a finger at the shorter woman. "So if you ever had a serious thought of hooking up with your 'Fated Mate' you're going to *have* to go back to that base. Otherwise, all of this is for nothing. If you just wanted to meet the guy so you can tell him to piss off? I can relay that message for you."

Laura pushed past the woman and pulled the door open. "If you decide that all of this was for nothing, you need to let me know so I can start planning my return trip home. Otherwise, I think you need to open your mind a little to other possibilities."

*****

Rufus sat on the edge of the makeshift bed and assessed his wounds. He could still feel pains in his chest when he took a deep breath and knew that most of his ribs were either fractured or cracked. One leg ached with such ferocity that he feared it would never be right again. "I don't remember what happened."

"That shiny Doomsday gun of yours blew up in your face," Paul said as he leaned back in the office chair, his feet propped up on the desk in the corner. "I don't know who built it for you, but I think I'd demand my money back."

Rufus looked up at him and Paul fought the urge to cringe. One of his eyes was still singed white and the side of his face bore the scars of the intense heat or radiation or whatever it was that caused the blast. "Your humor is less than amusing, *mon ami*."

Paul watched as Rufus continued to take inventory of his aches, pains, and breakage. "I wasn't joking. I think if I were you, I'd hunt down the bastards responsible for selling me that piece of junk and eat them."

"*Non*! We do not eat…" Rufus paused and shook his head slightly. "How have I healed so quickly?"

Paul stopped rocking and purposely avoided his stare. "Yeah,about that."

"Tell me you did not do what I think you have done."

Paul sat upright and turned to face his brother. "It was the only way to save you."

"Fool!" Rufus yelled as he tried to hop off the bed and to his feet. He collapsed in a heap, yelping in pain. Paul was there in an instant, scooping his brother up and placing him gently back on the mattress.

"Don't try to move yet. You aren't completely healed."

"Obviously," Rufus shot back through gritted teeth, his fangs extended from the pain.

"Look. You may not like it, but animal blood wasn't going to save you. You were too far gone."

Rufus lay back on the mattress and groaned. "I would rather have died than take the life of a human."

"Who says you took their lives?" Paul lied. "You do realize that you can feed from a human without killing them?" Rufus turned his head and stared at his brother with his one good eye. "Yeah, just like you do with your precious animals. If it's good enough for sheep and cattle, can't it be good enough for people, too?"

"*Non.*" Rufus sighed and closed his eyes. "People become addicted to the bite. They want more and more until they are dead."

"Some, maybe. Others donate their blood, and it's stored in bags. Not the tastiest way to get human blood, but still better than goat blood, wouldn't you say?"

As if on cue, the roll away door opened and Marco drove into the warehouse again. Pulling up to the office he parked the SUV and stepped out, cooler in hand. He pushed open the door of the office and opened the cooler. "We have O positive and some AB negative for your dining pleasure."

"Monsieur will have all of the above." Paul waved him toward Rufus who lay still on the mattress.

Marco grabbed an IV stand and pulled it close to the bed. "Which arm should I put it in this time?" he asked Paul.

"Oh, he's awake now. He can drink it straight from the juice box." Paul stood up abruptly and walked toward the door. "Don't forget the straw."

Marco placed two bags of O positive on the mattress next to Rufus then helped him to a sitting position. "Hungry, boss?"

"Famished." Rufus took the bag and sunk his fangs into the plastic bag. As he quickly drained the first one and handed the empty bag back to Marco he glanced out the office window to Paul who stood in the middle of the warehouse and stared at the ceiling. "Tell me, Marco, have I been feeding only from bagged blood?"

Marco tossed the empty bag into a trash can and handed him another full bag. "No, we gave you some of the mixed blood from the bar on the boat. It didn't do anything for you. Mr. Foster knew then that you'd need human blood." Marco didn't exactly lie, but he omitted a lot of the truth. "As I drove the boat, Paul forced as much of the beast blood into you as he could to keep you alive."

Rufus glanced at Paul again and noticed that his blind eye slowly began to focus once more. "So he truly does care?"

Marco gave him a puzzled look. "I would think so. He could have left you to die and inherited everything. As soon as he found out that the human hunters were searching for you…"

Rufus turned and gave him his full attention. "Why were they looking for me?"

"They weren't happy. Something about stealing something from them. A notebook and something to do with a weapon."

Rufus inhaled deeply and felt the pain in his chest lessen as his ribs healed. "They know."

"Yes, sir, they know. And as I told you, they aren't happy."

"And Jack?"

Marco avoided his eyes. "He was *most* unhappy."

*****

Jack watched the helicopter take off, his wife and future child literally fading into the sunset. He tried twice more to get Nadia to understand and twice more she rebuked him. When she finally left, he pulled her aside and forced her to listen. He told her that he loved her and he had to do this to keep her and the baby safe. She refused to accept it.

It broke his heart to watch her leave, but he knew he had to see this through. "You gonna be okay?"

Jack turned and saw Gus approaching him from behind. "I dunno, Gus. She's my everything."

"Does she know that?"

"I tried to tell her, but she doesn't want to hear it right now." Jack leaned against the pillar still standing in the front of the castle. "I couldn't make her understand that I need to see this through for her and the baby."

"She'll come around." Gus placed a hand on Jack's shoulder and gave it a slight squeeze.

"What if she doesn't?"

"She will. You're fated, right?"

Jack rolled his eyes. "For whatever that's worth."

"It will work out." Gus stepped past him and out into the courtyard. "You just need to hurry up and do whatever it is you have to do."

"Right now, I'm planning to head back to base with you boys."

"And us," Kalen added. Neither Jack nor Gus had heard him approach.

"Right…and them." Jack paused then turned back to Kalen. "If the mission to Geneva is off, why are you guys still hanging with me?"

Kalen motioned for Jack to step aside. The two walked out into the sandy area between the castle proper and the beachhead. "The Wyldwood has requested it. When the Wyldwood requests something, you do it."

"Oh, I get that. I just don't understand why."

Kalen shook his head. "Our elders have been having visions of something dark, Chief Jack. Something ominous. It has them fearful."

Jack stopped walking and pulled Kalen to a halt. "Wait, do you mean visions like they had back when the Sicarii first rose up?"

Kalen shrugged. "I do not know. I just know what the Wyldwood has told me. Stay with Chief Jack. He shall lead you."

Jack sighed and stared at the setting sun. "I think I need some answers my friend." He turned and headed back toward the castle.

"Where do you go?" Kalen called out.

"To make a phone call." Jack entered the castle and took the stairs two at a time.

He trotted down the hall and pushed the remains of his door out of the way. The attack from the gunship had splintered the heavy English oak to shards and most of his heavy antique furniture was ruined. He pushed his way past the trash and detritus in the room and bent low to retrieve the ornately carved box from under the bed. Pulling it out, he cleared a spot in the floor and set the box down. Sliding it in front of him, he carefully opened the lid and stared at the bundle inside wrapped in simple cloth. With both hands he carefully lifted the bundle out and placed it onto the floor, then slid the box out of the way.

Very carefully, Jack unwrapped the cloth and lifted the large polished stone from its wrappings. He placed the stone gently on the stone floor and smoothed the fabric beside it. Jack closed his eyes and recited the short chant that he had been taught then blew lightly on the cloth. Slowly, letters began to appear on the cloth.

Jack held the cloth up to the window and tried to look through the letters. Taking a corner, he gently folded one side across to the other. Then he folded it the other way. He lifted the cloth again and looked at the setting sun through the gossamer material. The letters that had previously made no sense to him, now created words that he could read. Jack quickly read the lines in the form of a chant.

He picked up the polished stone and rubbed it while repeating the chant. Slowly the stone became opaque and a murky light emitted from it. He held the stone in his lap and stared into it. "Loren? I'd really like to speak with you again."

He waited a moment longer and was about to give up when her radiant face appeared in the stone. "Chief Jack, it is good to see you."

"And you." Jack waited a moment hoping she would volunteer the information he was seeking but her image simply smiled at him. "I need information."

"Of course. What I have is yours."

"Kalen tells me that the elders are seeing things again," Jack blurted out. "Visions. Something dark and scary?"

Loren's smile almost appeared sad for a moment, but she quickly recovered. "He is very young. He should have kept that to himself."

Jack gave her a puzzled stare. "Why is that? Should I not be made aware of possible threats?"

"Oh no, Chief Jack, it is simply that we aren't sure what the threat may be. It is true that the elders are having visions of another dark threat. An ancient darkness that threatens to rise up once more, but..." She paused, as if searching for the right words. "There isn't a clear consensus on what that 'threat' may be." She actually appeared to blush.

"Any kind of heads up would be appreciated here, Loren. I mean, if it points us in the general direction."

"I understand what you ask, Chief Jack, but alas, I cannot give what I do not have. Some foresee a period of great darkness, some foresee a darkness rising and then quickly extinguished. Others see a threat that rises and then...like waves on the water, it ripples out."

"So nothing specific?"

"I fear not." The look in her eyes told him that she believed the threat to be real, but she could no more pinpoint it than he could. "And Kalen should have kept such knowledge to himself until we knew more. Forgive him, Chief Jack, he is but a child and has been thrust into a position of—"

"Whoa! Wait a second. A child? How can you say that?" Jack had to stop and think for a moment. Kalen? He was more than a child. The guy was huge as far as Elves were concerned.

"Yes, a child. He is only seventeen years. He is a most capable warrior. He was trained by his own father from the age of three. His brother Horith was set to become Captain of our Guard. The Gatekeeper. But now..." She lowered her eyes a moment and shook her head.

"He didn't make it?"

"Horith? He is healing. But he will be unable to defend us again. Kalen must become the Gatekeeper."

"You said he's only seventeen?" Jack had trouble accepting that. "He looks older."

"He is Elf, Chief Jack. A warrior Elf at that. His years were not easy."

"Understood." Jack sighed as he considered what she had told him. "Okay Loren. I know you're busy so I'll leave you to your work. But if any of your elders get a clearer picture of what this threat is, please let me know as soon as you can."

"As you will, Chief Jack."

"Peace be with you." Jack saluted her.

"Peace be with you."

*****

Damien awoke and thrashed in the coagulated blood. It felt like cold pudding around his body as he fought to pull himself to the surface. For the briefest of moments, he couldn't remember where he was and as his head broke the surface of the vat he had to hang an arm over the edge to keep from slipping back under. He gagged and sucked air into his throat, coughing and spitting as he hacked the blood up and out of his lungs. Damien clung to the side of the vat until he cleared his lungs and could calm himself.

Slowly he remembered the events as they played out. Rachel had recited the chant, the blood of the virgins had restored her original body and the elder…he had eaten the elder. And his energy had been sucked from him.

Damien tried to stand and felt weak as his body fought the weight of the coagulated blood clinging to his clothing. He hooked a leg over the edge and slid over the side and into the floor. He lay gasping on the cold concrete floor, trying to come to terms with what had happened. From the corner of his eye he saw movement and he quickly turned his head to see Lilith sitting on a stack of crates watching him.

"You survived," she said drolly. She slipped from the top of the crates and stepped closer. He took in her bloody nude form as she bent down and grasped his face by the jaw. "You're nearly restored. I'll be."

"What happened?" he croaked.

"You nearly died." She stood, and he couldn't take his eyes off her shape. The same shape he adored in the lower levels of the bunker in Nevada, except now, in the flesh, she was more perfect than he remembered. "I'm surprised you were able to pull through."

"You saved me?"

She laughed deep in her throat and it unsettled him. "You didn't save yourself."

"Thank you, my beloved." He rolled over and coughed up another chunk of coagulated blood from deep in his lungs. "I don't know what I would have done without you."

She continued walking until she reached the emergency shower. Dropping her robe, she pulled the chain and let the water flow over her body. Damien watched her shower and couldn't fight the arousal he felt. He smiled as he pulled himself to his feet and stumbled to the shower beside her. As he wrapped his arms around her, she spun and slammed an open palm into his chest knocking him across the open space and sliding across the floor. "You'll not touch me."

He rolled to his knees, gasping for air and coughing up more blood from his lungs. "W-w-what the hell was that for?"

"You are not worthy." She continued to shower, her back to him. "You shall not touch me."

Damien rocked back and sat up on his knees, his eyes searching her for some kind of answer. "What do you mean?"

"Exactly as I said." She turned and glared at him. "You would do well to heed my words."

"Fuck that." Damien struggled to his feet. "I *made* you, bitch."

Lilith paused and slowly turned her eyes ablaze with anger. She lowered her gaze to him and cocked her head to the side. "What did you just say?"

"You fucking heard me. I *made* you." He staggered toward her, his finger pointing toward her. "You were mine before I put your jerkied ass back together, you're mine now."

Lilith snorted and turned back to her shower. "Watch your tongue, little man."

"Watch my..." Damien stopped and stared at her. "Who the hell do you think you are?"

She held a hand in the air. "I am your queen. And you shall bow in my presence."

"The hell I will—" Damien didn't finish his sentence before he felt his legs go out from under him, his kneecaps smashing into the cold hard concrete. He heard the crack before the pain registered with his rattled brain. He opened his mouth to scream, but Lilith pinched her fingers shut. When she did, his mouth sealed and he screamed through a closed mouth, his desperate gasps for air blew globs of drying blood out of his nostrils.

"I *am* your queen." She turned and stared with evil behind her eyes. "And you *will* bow in my presence."

6

"This place doesn't look too vampy to me," Jacobs whispered as he observed through binoculars. Cars zipped past on the nearby freeway and trash blew past his location as he studied a small mission style church.

"It's supposed to be empty but the spotter reported comings and goings and he verified fresh prints." Lamb pulled the binoculars from Ing's hand and stared at the Spanish style stucco building. "Add the recent increase in missing people and Bob's your uncle."

From another vantage point Spalding and Sullivan watched the west side of the church building. Spalding stared at the building through his scope while Sullivan counted the minutes to sundown, watching the orange orb steadily glow to a darker red as it sank deeper on the horizon. Spalding tapped Little John's shoulder. "Is that movement at your 3 o'clock?"

Sullivan pulled his rifle up slowly and peered through the scope. "Negative. Civilian outside the fence." He continued to observe the dogwalker and added, "Unless the vamps have started using poodles as a ploy to throw us off the scent."

Spalding keyed his radio, "Bravo Four. Sitrep."

"All clear from the eagle's eye, Bravo One." Donovan shifted his position to get a better angle. Atop the nearby tower, he would be shooting nearly straight down into the courtyard of the church if anything came out. "You have clear access to both entrances."

"Roger that." Spanky hit the button on his shoulder making his throat mic hot and linking it to the OPCOM. "Bravo units, converge on target. Maintain radio silence until bingo."

A series of clicks verified that all of Second Squad copied the order. From his peripheral vision, Spanky could just make out Jacobs and Lamb working their way through the knee high grass toward the front entrance while he and Sullivan worked their way to the rear of the church.

It was slow going closing on the church through so much open terrain, but they wanted to maintain their element of surprise. Both teams had closed the gap by half when Sullivan raised a closed fist, halting Spalding. Spanky whispered into his radio, "All units hold."

Sullivan slowly brought his rifle up and peered through the scope. "What the—"

Spalding didn't wait for Sullivan to explain. He came to one knee and brought his own weapon to bear. Looking through the scope, he saw what appeared to be a person dressed from head to toe in black moving swiftly and silently across the rooftop, a sword strapped to their back. Whoever it was moved quickly, their face covered by a black hood.

"Who the fuck is that?" Lamb whispered through the coms.

"Bravo One, report." OPCOM demanded.

"Wait one, sir," Darren whispered as he watched the black-clad figure do a silent front flip and land deftly on the rear porch. Placing their hands on the edge of the porch, the acrobat did a hand stand, kicked out and swung out then in toward the rear door, kicking it in and rolling into the church in one deft move.

"All units converge, now!" Darren ordered.

Lamb and Jacobs ran for the front door and knocked it out of its frame as both men hit it with their shoulders, tucking and rolling into the darkened interior. Rolling to their feet again, they flipped the lights on their rifles as soon as they were up and in the ready position.

Spalding and Sullivan heard muffled screams and banging as they ran past the side of the church near the rear door. Darren stacked on the left and John entered in a low crouch. Sweeping left and right, they found black blood splattered on interior walls and ashed vampire remains still smoking on the floor as they slowly made their way through the smaller rooms of the rear.

A loud scream broke the near silence and a burning body shattered through a wall near John who turned and put two silver rounds into what was left of the dying vampire. He stepped to the side and looked through the jagged hole the body had been thrown through. He saw the black clad person expertly swinging a sword while simultaneously fighting off four vampires. As the swordsman sliced and diced, flames and ash sparked from the bodies of his opponents.

"We have a bogie," John announced into his coms.

"Who is it?" Jacob's voice came through his earpiece.

"Can't tell. They're dressed like a ninja, but they can damned sure use a sword." John jumped back into the hallway and pushed his way forward. As he was about to step into the open room where the four vampires were fighting the 'ninja', a body hit the wall of the hallway and exploded in a sparking pile of ash.

Spalding grabbed him by the neck of his uniform and pulled him back just as the vampire erupted into a fireball and John stared at the embers slowly rising into the darkened room. Growling low in his throat, Little John took a long step and jumped the still burning remains and rolled into the room, his carbine coming to bear on the lone occupant standing in the middle, sheathing his sword. "Halt!"

The black-clad swordsman froze in place then slowly turned. John couldn't see the man's face and barely had time to react before the spinning roundhouse connected a foot with John's jaw. As he fell, the smaller and quicker figure jumped to the side, kicked off the wall and landed deftly on John's shoulders, essentially riding him to the ground.

Little John hit the hardwood floor and rolled, taking his attacker with him. His hand shot up and grabbed the swordsman by the tunic and pulled him off balance as he continued his roll and ended with John on top of him, his pistol shoved into the man's face. "Who the fuck are you?" he growled as he jerked the hood away.

John saw long dark hair fall to the side but the face was still covered with a black wrap. He grabbed it and pulled it away just as a fist came up and caught him in the solar plexus. With the wind knocked out of him by surprise, the swordsman brought a hand up to knock the pistol from his grip then caught his arm in an armbar hold. Rolling over the top of him and pulling him off balance, John was essentially pinned by his own weight.

He looked up through narrowed eyes and gritted teeth to see… "Brooke?"

The swordsman froze then glanced down at him. "Dad?"

Her grip lessened just enough for John to pull her over him and to the side, freeing his arm. As she rolled back to her feet, she came up and stared at him, her eyes wide. "This isn't possible…"

"No, Brooke, it's okay." John stammered.

"No!" she screamed, her foot jutting out and catching him across the chin before she launched herself out the window and into the cool night air of El Cajon.

"Was that who I think it was?" Spalding asked as he held a hand out to John.

John took his hand and pulled himself to his feet. "Yeah, it was."

Lamb and Jacobs stepped into the room. "We only found three." Lamb stated as he looked around at the ashed vampires. "Looks like you hit the mother lode."

Spanky watched Sullivan as he stared out the window, searching for the black form in the night. "It wasn't us."

Jacobs rested his arms on his carbine and gave him a cautious look. "The ninja looking dude that was hauling ass across the roof?"

Spanky nodded. "Except it wasn't a dude. It was Little John's sister."

"No way. Dude…" Lamb shook his head. "Of all the places." He paused and nodded toward John. "Wait. If she's *killing* vamps, do you still want to hunt her down and…well. You know?"

Spalding shrugged. "We have no idea what her purpose was here. She could be removing competition from her territory. She could be doing the dirty deeds of her master. She could be…anything."

Jacobs nodded. "The way she was dressed, I'd think assassin."

"It doesn't matter." John pulled his head back in from the window. "She's gone. I guess I'll never know."

"Dude, you don't even know if she was turned. She could still be human."

John shook his head. "She still looks eighteen. I have no doubts what she is." The disappointment painted across his features was impossible to miss. "Still, I wish I could have just asked herwhy?"

Donovan's voice crackled across their earpieces. "Do you want me to keep tracking her?"

*****

"Sun's setting, Chief." Jimmy plopped down in the sand next to him and handed him a beer. "You got your stuff ready to go?"

Jack nodded solemnly. "This isn't going to be easy." He glanced back over his shoulder. "I know it's only been a few months, but this place had become home."

Robert finished coordinating with the wolves that were staying behind and then approached the pair. "Those who are staying are going to try to rebuild this mess."

Jack took a long pull from the long neck and planted it into the sand. "What about Barbara and Bobby? Are you going to leave them here or bring them with you?"

Robert rubbed at the back of his neck and stared off across the ocean. "Honestly, Jack, she wants me to stay." He noticed that Jack didn't seem surprised. "I'm thinking...well...maybe I should stay here. You know, just in case Thorn returns."

Jack chuckled to himself and nodded. "That sounds like a hell of a plan to me, Bob." He pulled himself to his feet and stuck his hand out, grasping Robert's. "I understand completely. Trust me."

Robert turned sad eyes to his boss. "Do you really? Because I'll be honest, Jack. I'm feeling like I'm leaving you hanging out to dry."

"No, buddy, you brought your family out here so you could be a wolf and if Barbara got infected...well, the two of you could do your own thing. I get it." Jack motioned to the island with a sweep of his hand. "This place is perfect. You're surrounded by other wolves, nobody to try to hunt you. A safe place for Bobby when folks shift. You need to stay here."

Robert glanced over his shoulder and saw Barbara pull Bobby closer to her, her eyes glued to the three men on the beach. "You sure? I mean...if you really need me, I can always..."

"Bob, stay here. You're family comes first." Jack pulled the man into an embrace and slapped his back. "You made a great second. Now go be a great husband."

"If you end up needing me, call," Robert made him promise.

"If I need you, trust me, I have your cell." He pushed him toward Barbara. "Now go. And tell Barbara not to worry."

"Thanks, buddy." Bob gave him a wink as he turned.

Jimmy took a long pull from his beer. "You two should rent a room."

"You're going to look real funny walking around with my foot shoved up your ass." Jack sat back down next to him. "When's our ride supposed to be here?"

Jimmy shrugged. "After dark. Apparently there's a mission so the duty officer was vague." Jimmy stretched out in the sand and happened to see a gargoyle spread his wings in the darkness. "Fuck me."

Jack spun his head around and saw the giant creature step from the roof and glide to the ground. "Impressive, aren't they?"

"Hell yeah." Jimmy sat up and turned to better see the three mythical monsters. "I wouldn't mind having one on my team."

Jack snorted. "They're coming back with us, so that may not be out of the question."

"Be still my beating heart," Jimmy laughed. "I wonder what a gargoyle acts like after a few beers?"

"Let's not find out." Jack leaned over and poured his into the sand. "I watched Grim pick up a crashed helicopter and throw it into the ocean. With that kind of strength, a drunken gargoyle is not something I'd want to have to deal with."

Jimmy looked at his own beer and quickly poured it out as well. "Have you decided where to start searching for Thorn?"

Jack nodded. "I was his Second. I have access to all of his papers. That includes all of his properties." He hooked his chin back over his shoulder. "I packed them all. He owns a lot of different places but it shouldn't take too long to search them."

Jimmy sat and stared at the waves crashing on the shore. "What about the teams, Jack? You plan to come back for good or what?"

Jack shrugged. "I don't know, TD. I figure I'll talk with Mitchell and see what he thinks. I figure, at worst, I can give him the intel I have and he'll say 'thanks, now beat it'. If that happens, I guess I can search for Thorn on my own."

"You know he won't do that. You were his number one operator." TD stood and offered Jack a hand up. "You just might want to tell him if your return is temporary."

Jack exhaled hard and stared toward the water. "I honestly don't know if he'll have me back, Jim."

"Why? You're a Tier One operator, Jack."

Jack nodded. "Once upon a time. But you have to know something." Jack turned and faced him, his eyes solemn. "I stopped taking the bane months ago. I'm a shifter now."

*****

"Here's a change of clothes." Paul tossed the clothing to Rufus and fell into the chair again. He did his best to appear bored as he picked at his nails.

"Do you have a plan for once I'm finished healing?" Rufus asked as he pulled his burnt and blood covered clothing from his body.

Paul shot him a glance and laughed. "Me? I thought you were the brains of this outfit."

Rufus paused as he was pulling his shirt on. "You were the one with the foresight to drag me to safety. You knew to trust Marco. You knew that human blood would get me back on my feet. Why would I not trust your judgment now?"

Paul sat up and stared at his brother. "Now? After all of these centuries? Now I'm responsible enough to trust?"

Rufus sighed and sat back on the makeshift bed. "*Mon ami*, you were always loved. Trusted? *Non*, but loved, *oui*."

"Just not enough to trust. I see," Paul snorted and reclined in the old squeaky office chair again.

"It wasn't from a lack of affection. It was because you acted untrustworthy." Rufus pulled the charred remains of his pants from his body, old chunks of burnt flesh still clinging to them. "At this point, I'm not even sure where is safe to go."

"Ah, see? There ya go. You put all your eggs in one basket and you handed it to that Boy Scout, Thompson. Now that he's turned on you, you have nothing that he doesn't know about." Paul waved him off. "Your first mistake was in trusting him."

Rufus hung his head and nodded. "*Oui*. You are right. I should not have trusted him so completely." He lifted his head and turned to Paul. "So now I am at your mercies."

Paul rolled his eyes. "Don't sound so melodramatic. It isn't that bad." He rolled the chair closer to Rufus' bed and leaned back again, propping his feet up on the mattress. "You have holdings all across the Americas, yes?" Rufus nodded. "Then we pick one and use it for a short while, then move to another. As long as we keep moving, the odds of him stumbling upon us are slim."

Rufus nodded. "What about the underground facility in Nevada? The one where we staged the battle against the Sicarii?"

Paul shook his head. "No place where the authorities might stumble upon us. Too risky. No, we should use properties you own and simply bounce from place to place." Paul's mind kept racing as he thought. "We can call in reinforcements to act as security if we need to. We just need to figure out where a reliable source is."

"The wolves, of course."

"The wolves, of course," Paul mocked. "Thompson *is* a wolf. Do not think for one moment that he wouldn't go to them first and report his concerns. You know how the wolves are about pride and honor and all of that spew. If they think for a moment that you did anything to break their pact?"

"*Oui*." Rufus knew exactly what the end result would be.

"So we have to avoid the wolves and the human hunters. And we need security that we can trust."

"Vampires."

"Correct. Vampires." Paul kicked away from the mattress. "And since you still have control of my people, we have plenty of them to call."

Rufus leveled dead eyes at his brother. "Make the call."

*****

95

"So what's the cure, Mark? What do I need to get? Garlic? Holy water? A flea collar?" Tracy sounded desperate as she gripped his hand.

Mark closed his eyes and clenched his teeth, his jaw bulging from the pain. "There is no 'cure'. Trust me on that." He opened his eyes and met her worried gaze. "Except a silver bullet."

"No,I don't accept that," she whispered, her hand squeezing his harder. "There has to be something."

He turned slightly away from her and stared at the ceiling tiles of the room. "You know, when I first came back and Jack told me that they were infected with the wolf virus, I really thought I wanted their strength and speed too." His voice cracked and he sucked in a sharp breath. "But then I saw what Matt when through. I saw what Mueller went through. The risk to your family is too great. You can't control the shift or what the beast does when you transition." He shook his head slightly. "When it was just you and me, I thought, 'what the heck'. We could be wolves. Never grow old. Never be weak. Shift once a month, that's a hell of a tradeoff."

Tracy lowered her face and pressed her forehead to his hand. "I can't believe you ever considered something like that."

"I thought about it. But now with grandkids and…who wants to live forever, right?" He gave her a tired smile.

"Not if your entire family dies around you."

"And I wouldn't wish this curse on any of them." He coughed slightly then winced in pain. "Remind me not to do that again."

"What about a transfusion?" Her face was suddenly hopeful, but his eyes quashed that hope.

"I'm already eaten up with it." He lifted her hand to his face and she could feel the heat radiating from him. "It's the reason my body is burning up."

"What do we do?" She feared the answer he was going to give her.

"I already told you. I have a mineral deficiency. I need a high velocity dose of silver."

"That's not funny." She punched him lightly in the shoulder.

"I wasn't joking." He reached for her hand and pulled it closer to his mouth. Kissing her knuckles her closed his eyes and inhaled deeply, trying to memorize the scent of her. "I want you to do it."

"You can't ask me to do something like that."

"You threatened to smother me in my sleep when we first married. Surely you can press a barrel to my head and squeeze a trigger."

"Please don't joke, dammit." The tears poured freely and she tried to pull away from him. He gripped her hand tighter and refused to let her go.

"I have to. If I let it sink in…I'll lose it." He reached up to her face and stroked her cheek. "But this has to be done."

"Surely somebody else can do it." She stood in the small room and stared at the IV bag. "Maybe they could put something in your IV. You could just fall asleep and never wake up."

"I'm not a dog." He smirked. "Well, yet. But even then, it has to be silver. A bullet is quickest and painless. Anything else would hurt like hell."

Tracy hung her head and shrugged. "How am I supposed to find a silver bullet? I'm not the Lone Ranger."

"In our closet. Top shelf." He coughed lightly and gripped his chest again. "There's a .38 revolver. Jay Wolf made me some special rounds for it. Just in case."

"Jay *Wolf*? Are you kidding me?"

He shook his head. "Swear to God. That's the man's name. He makes our ammo for us."

She shook her head defiantly. "Matt drove me here…"

"So have him drive you back. Tell him…anything. Just get it."

She inhaled deeply and squared her shoulders. "Fine,I'll get it. But I'm not using it." She turned and reached for the door. She paused in the doorway and turned back to stare at him. "Whatever happened to, 'for better or for worse'?"

"It was for better or for worse, not for better or for cursed."

*****

As the large overhead door closed behind the stolen buses, Apollo stood to the side and watched as the men inside disembarked. Each man stepped off the transport and looked around the previously abandoned warehouse with a scowl of disapproval on their collective faces.

The driver stepped to the side of the bus and opened the covers to the storage bins holding their gear. "Grab your shit and get it stowed."

Each man dug through the piles and retrieved his personal belongings then worked his way to the bunk areas. "I don't think they approve of the accommodations," Apollo commented to Sheridan. "Maybe next time we can put them up at the Ritz."

"They'll get over it. They've stayed in worse places." Sheridan watched the men and tried to assess them as Apollo did. "What's your take?"

"Hard to tell just by looking at them. Some look mean enough to have potential. The real proof will be in whether they can fight."

"According to Mr. Simmons, these are the best of the best." Sheridan hobbled back to the office and left the door open for Apollo.

After he walked into the office, he shut the door and watched Sheridan ease into a chair. "The last group he sent was supposed to be able to fight, too. They didn't do too good."

"True enough. But look at who they're going after." He flipped through the drawings that Apollo had given them. "Maybe we should have used gas?"

"Where would you have gotten it?" Apollo hopped up onto the counter and continued to watch the men through the dirty window. "First thing in the morning, I'll put them through their paces. We can figure out where they stand as warriors." He turned and addressed Sheridan directly. "You need to get us weapons. And a lot more ammo ASAP."

"Yeah. About that." Sheridan ran a hand across his face. "We cleaned out your man's supply of silver when we absconded with his ammunition. I doubt they've had a chance to resupply him."

"All of it?"

"Yes, and unfortunately, the wolf that was loading the ammunition for us was killed in the assault on Tinker."

"Fucking great." Apollo hated loading cartridges. It was make work and boring as hell. "We'll find out if any of the new guys know how to cast bullets and get them started then."

"We have a pretty good supply still, but if you are expecting the squads to track us and hit us here, we'll definitely need more."

"Oh, we'll need more than just bullets. I want RPGs, claymores, frags, smoke grenades, you name it."

Sheridan's eyes lit up. "Well then. Make me a shopping list."

Apollo reached into his shirt pocket and pulled out a folded piece of paper. "Already done." He tossed it to Sheridan and leaned back, staring out the window again.

"You don't want much, do you?" Sheridan's voice dripped with sarcasm. "I'm not an armory, you know."

"No, but you know the money man. Somebody needs to make it happen. You know who we're about to go up against."

Sheridan read through the list again and nodded in agreement. "Very well. First thing in the morning, I'll start contacting my people on the black market."

*****

Mick sat quietly in his room, his ears straining to listen to anything going on outside his door. Convinced that he was alone, he pulled his travel bag out from under his bunk and unzipped it. He rifled through the leather bag and pulled out his shave kit. He set the contents next to the sink in his room then stepped beside the door once more. He listened intently for another moment then went back to the sink. He reached for the canned shave cream and unscrewed the bottom of the can. He pulled a small black electronic device from the bottom of the can and pressed a button along the bottom. Two LED lights lit up and he waited to see if the device could broadcast through the thick concrete walls of the underground facility. The red light remained lit and the green light flickered, and then went out.

Cursing to himself, Mick held the device in the air and walked around the edges of his room, holding the device both high and low, praying for a signal. Nothing.

He debated on risking getting caught with it and knew he had no other options. He pressed a series of buttons and then began tapping out his message in Morse code. As he finished, he pressed another series of buttons which stored the message for burst transmissions as soon as signal could be had.

Mick shoved the device into his shirt pocket and headed for the door. He paused then quickly turned back and screwed the bottom back onto the shave cream can. *Just in case somebody comes looking for me.*

Mick stepped out into the hallway and found it empty. He turned and headed toward the exit. He was certain that there would be a flurry of people in the massive central part of the facility. The same central area that he would have to walk through to get outside. He prayed that if he walked with purpose, nobody would challenge him.

As he reached the end of the hallway, he saw the office with the large windows in it. One man sat inside, his head down, writing in a logbook. Mick walked past him and continued out into the central part of the facility and past the line of vehicles that had carried them here. He could see the doors of the facility open to the darkening sky and prayed that he could get outside and the transmitter could do its thing. It would only take a moment…

"You there!" The voice sounded agitated and Mick froze in mid-step. He slowly turned, trying his best to seem surprised.

"Me?" He pointed to his chest.

"Where are you going?" He saw the man from the office staring at him, his hand slowly creeping down to his thigh holster.

"I was just stepping out for some fresh air, mate. Thought I might catch a smoke and a short walk." He hooked his thumb over his shoulder toward the door.

"You are not authorized to travel without an escort." The man's heavily accented English was easily understood.

Mick nodded and sighed heavily. "Okay, mate. I don't want to break any rules here. I didn't know. Nobody said anything to us about having an escort." He started toward the man then stopped. "Tell me, though,do I need an escort to just stand in the doorway and get a breath of fresh air? I mean, if I don't go walking off?"

The man from the office stared at him suspiciously for a moment. "Why would you ask this?"

Mick gave him his best smile. "I don't want to put anybody out, mate. I know you boys have your hands full. Everybody has a job to do, and I don't want to take anybody away from theirs just so I can stretch me legs." He pointed toward the doorway. "If it ain't breaking any rules, I can just stand there and get a bit of fresh air and nobody will be any wiser. I'll not wander off, nobody has to be my babysitter and we're all happy. It was just feeling a bit stuffy in my room is all."

The guard studied him for a moment then nodded. "Do not leave the shadow of the overhead. Stay in eyesight at all times."

"Of course, mate. I'll not be a moment. I just needed some fresh air before I call it a night."

The guard watched him as he strolled toward the doorway. Mick stood in the doorway and took several deep breaths of the cooling night air and stretched his tall frame in the large open space. He had to admit, despite the ruse, it felt good to be atop the mountain and catching a glimpse of the moon and stars before he crawled into that tiny little bed for the evening.

He shoved his hand into his pocket and pulled the transmitter out. Green light. Mick smiled to himself and slipped it back into place. "Of course I'd forget my lighter. Bring my smokes and no light." He threw his hands into the air for show. Turning back he saw the guard still watching him. "I guess it's the fates' way of telling me I should quit, eh?" He began walking back and shot the guard another quick smile. "Thanks, mate,I appreciate it."

Mick walked easily back down the hallway and to his room. He slipped back inside then quickly pulled the transmitter from his pocket and tucked it back into the bottom of the shave cream can, screwing the bottom on tightly. He actually breathed a sigh of relief as he shoved the contents of the shave kit back into his bag.

"Mr. Simmons, you are going to owe me so big when this is over."

7

"Bravo Team, report!" Matt sat on the edge of his seat, his eyes scanning the screens above. He turned to the electronics technician on watch and ordered they bring up the helmet cams from Bravo Four. Donnie's cam came to life and the whole of OPCOM shifted to see the screen. A lone person, dressed in dark clothing, was being observed running from the area. "Who the hell is that?"

"OPCOM, Bravo actual." Spalding sounded like he was running as he spoke. The overwatch cam shifted and the four operators were seen chasing the fleeing subject, their body heat registering much higher than their target. "We are in pursuit of a person of interest."

"Person of interest?" Matt turned to Tufo's chair, expecting a smart assed remark, and felt his guts tighten into a knot as he was reminded once more that his XO didn't have his back. He shifted back to the screen then nodded to the flight officer. "Get me visuals from the bird."

"On it, sir." The flight officer keyed commands into his keyboard that were instantly relayed to the drone operators. Moments later, visuals were fed to the OPCOM screens from the drone circling the area.

"Go low and get me a tight shot of whoever it is they're chasing." Matt keyed the coms again, "Bravo actual, Predator is dropping low. We can drop the subject in a matter of—"

"Negative, sir!" Bravo Five yelled through the coms. "The suspect is my sister!"

"Sister?" Matt turned to the communications tech. "Tell me the coms are fried. It sounded like he said, 'sister'."

"Affirmative, Colonel. And coms are five-by-five." The tech adjusted the coms for a brighter gain and to adjust for the higher volume of the operator's voices.

"Say again, Bravo Five. Did you say sister?" Matt stood and walked to an empty station, keying up Sullivan's record.

"That is affirmative, sir," Donovan huffed as he jumped a low fence and spread further to the right in hopes of cutting her off.

Matt scanned his record and saw no mention of a sister. "You have no sister Bravo Five. Has your team been exposed to any gases or foreign substances?"

"Negative, Colonel," Jacobs reported as he and Lamb spread further to Brooke's left hoping to flank her. "No exposure."

"Then would somebody please tell me how the hell this person of interest suddenly became Bravo Five's sister? And if she is related, why is she running from him?"

Donovan's cam showed him jumping to the rooftop of a nearby building and running as fast as he could in parallel to the chase. "Long story, OPCOM," he huffed loudly as he landed and rolled on a flat roof then took off at a dead run, doing his best to keep the team in sight. "She went missing when Five was a kid."

"Are you kidding me?" Matt grumbled to himself. "So we just go off mission because somebody thinks…" He clenched his jaw so tight he surprised himself that he didn't snap a tooth off. "Bravo Team, you are *off mission!*"

"Negative, sir," Spalding responded. "Mission is complete. All tangos accounted for and ashed."

"Then why the hell are you chasing…" He forced himself to stop and squeezed the bridge of his nose. "Get me the visuals off that Predator. If we can't stop them, we might as well assist."

"Suspect is wearing a hood of some type, Colonel. We can't get a clear shot of her face," the flight officer stated.

"Fine. Put the drone in a head-on and have it light up the ground in front of her. See if you can stop her long enough for the squad to catch her."

The flight officer typed the commands into his keyboard and moments later the camera from the drone indicated the flight corrections. Matt watched as the craft banked, tilting the skyline at a sharp angle then realigning in front of the running woman. When the drone went weapons hot, tracers ran a line across her path causing her to slide to a stop. It distinctly reminded him of someone sliding into second base.

"She's all yours, Bravo Team," Matt whispered into the coms. "This had better be worth it."

*****

"None of us are surprised, Jack." Pedro rested his arms on his carbine. "We knew as soon as you left that you'd quit with the bane."

Jack half expected his old teammates to reject him once they knew that he was now a slave to the moon. "So, you aren't pissed?"

Jimmy shrugged. "Why should we be?" He looked to the other squad members. "You married a wolf, Jack. You're expecting a...pup? Cub?"

"A baby, you jackass." Jack elbowed him. "It's a baby."

"Jimmy can't help it," Gus said. "The Good Lord didn't bless him with an abundance of brains."

"Well, I didn't know if..." Jimmy stammered. "Nevermind."

"I just wanted you guys to know up front. I had told Mitchell and Tufo, but I didn't know if they spread the word or kept it under their hat."

"It's not like they announced it, but hell, I think we all sort of expected it." Pedro slapped the man's shoulder. "No skin off our teeth, brother. It's just like anybody else. As long as you don't go hunting humans, we ain't got a problem with it." He shot the man a quick wink.

Jack started to reply with a smart remark when he saw Grimlock wave him over. "Um, excuse me a moment, fellas. The big guy needs something."

Jack worked his way across the courtyard, wondering how they were going to fit all of the operators into a helicopter with the three gargoyles. As he approached,Grimlock, the large gargoyle, appeared troubled. "Is there a problem, Grim?"

"Not a problem, but something troubling," his voice rumbled low and deep. "The Wyldwood has ordered the elder warriors back."

Jack's face fell as he stared at the oversized ebony gargoyle. "She what? I just spoke with her a little while ago and she said nothing."

"We just got word." He pointed to Kalen who was speaking with the other supernatural warriors.

"So, who are the 'elder warriors'?"

Grimlock inhaled deeply and let it out slowly. "You will be allowed the youngest from each clan. The rest must return."

Jack shook his head in disbelief. "The youngest? What the…" He gave Grimlock a questioning stare. "Why?"

"It has been seen. She must obey." Grimlock turned and started toward the crowd.

"Please tell me that you're the youngest of your clan," Jack pleaded.

Grimlock snorted and Jack could only assume it was a laugh of some sort. "From the gargoyles you shall be left with Azrael."

Jack shrugged. "Okay,that's not so bad. I thought maybe you were sending somebody for me to babysit like a punishment of some kind. I can't imagine changing a gargoyle diaper."

Grimlock paused in mid-step and glared at him. "No warrior gargoyle wears diapers."

"It was a joke, big guy." Jack patted his shoulder as he walked past him. "Calm down."

As Jack approached Kalen he heard him trying to explain to the others. "Once you are prepared, I'll take you back to the Anywhere. You should say your farewells now. The others will be going with Chief Jack and me."

Gnat picked up his bow staff and handed it to Kissum. "I'd rather use the hammer if you don't mind."

Kissum nodded solemnly and pressed the hammer to his forehead, his eyes closed as he chanted something under his breath. When he handed it to Gnat, the procedure was repeated. "I bestow unto you the hammer of our fathers. Use it to defend the three realms and protect the lives of innocents."

"Would you like to explain to me what the hell is going on?" Jack asked.

Kalen turned and lowered his eyes. "The Wyldwood contacted me and—"

"How?" Jack interrupted. "How did she contact you?"

Kalen's face wrinkled in puzzlement. "The speaking stone." He pointed to the bracelet on his wrist. "She alerts me when I am needed."

"Why didn't she tell me when I spoke with her?"

Kalen shrugged and lowered his eyes again. "She came to me urgently. All of the elders, the seers, those who have visions…they all saw the same thing."

"And that was?"

"The darkness comes," Kalen stated bluntly.

"And so they pull the grand majority of our team?" Jack threw his hands up in the air. "Look, if I'm supposed to lead the group that defeats this darkness, then why is she leaving me with the youngest of the groups?"

"I cannot say, Chief Jack. I can only do what she tells me to do."

Jack growled low in his throat. "Fine. Great. Superb. So who's left from this assault team?"

"Me, Gnat, Azrael and you." Kalen held his head high as he announced the names.

Jack groaned. "A four-man team."

Grimlock squeezed his shoulder gently, "That is better than a no-man team."

As Jack stared at the group he shook his head. "Not much."

*****

Laura paced along the outer edge of the hangar. She didn't know why Evan hadn't called back and could only assume that something else had happened. She chewed nervously at her thumbnail and would pause only long enough to glance at the office then return to her nervous pacing.

"Miss Youngblood,you have a call." She spun so fast that she didn't even look at the young man waving to her from the office. She trotted past him and pushed through the door.

Laura snatched the receiver from the desk so quickly that she must have seemed frantic. "Evan? Tell me everything is okay."

"I'm sorry, Miss Youngblood. Dr. Peters can't come to the phone right now." She felt her throat tighten at the message. "We sent someone to get him and…" the pause was enough to choke her.

"Is he okay?" She tried to steady her voice but found it cracking slightly as she spoke.

"He will be, ma'am. If you hadn't called and requested a callback, we might not have found him." The duty officer tried his best to fill her in, but without knowing the full details of what exactly ailed the doctor, all he could truly tell her was that Evan was on the mend. "We have him on a transfusion of sorts. He says that he should be fine, but he still feels pretty sick."

"Does he know what caused it?"

"If he does, ma'am, he isn't saying. He just wanted me to call you and tell you that he's going to be right as rain before you return. He promises."

Laura suddenly felt very tired. "Thank you. Please tell him that my thoughts are with him." She reached across the desk to hang up the phone when Pablo took the receiver from her.

"I take it that Colonel Mitchell will not be coming?"

"I…" she began, then stared at Pablo. "I honestly have no idea."

"Perhaps you should ask him?"

"They're on mission at the moment. He isn't taking calls." Her voice was barely a whisper.

Pablo nodded and rose from his chair. "My men are preparing for a mission as well. While they are out, I will have to ask that your people remain within the mountain. It isn't safe outside these walls at night."

"I understand." Laura rose and slowly turned for the door. "If anybody calls for me, please, have somebody wake me." She felt as though somebody had drained her batteries with that call. All of her nervous energy was now gone and her body begged for rest.

"Of course." Pablo walked her to her room before heading back and going deeper into the facility to prepare for the mission at hand.

Laura tried to second guess what Matt would do now. Considering the circumstances, would he still try to come here to meet with Jennifer? Could he *not* still meet with her? Would his wolf allow it? She rolled to her side and stared out across the tiny room that she now called home.

Just as he eyes grew heavier and she felt sleep creeping up on her, she heard a light knocking at her door. Fearing that she was receiving another call, she rolled from the narrow bed and quickly answered the door. Jennifer stood outside her room, her eyes cast downward. "Are you lost?"

"Most of the time." Jennifer gave her a weak smile. "I thought about what you said."

"And should I book a single, one-way ticket home?" She didn't mean for her voice to have such a hard edge, but the fatigue had removed the filter from her mouth.

Jennifer shook her head slightly. "As much as I hate that place, no. I'll go with you."

Laura cocked a disbelieving eyebrow at her. "Why?"

Jennifer leaned against the doorjamb and stared up at the much taller woman. "Let's just say, I gave it some serious thought, okay? I mean, I'm not really keen on the idea, but I'm willing to do it to meet my Fated Mate."

"Don't misunderstand me, as I'm thrilled that you're coming around, but you have to understand, I'm not seeing a 'why' in what you said."

Jennifer sighed and shrugged. "I just put myself in his shoes. Or, rather…I tried to. I mean, he's in charge of all these people and they just got attacked. The full moon is days away. You said that he'd never leave. Add all that together and put it on one big plate and…"

"And?"

"And I realized that it was time to pull on my big girl panties and do what needed to be done." Jennifer pushed off the doorjamb and squared her shoulders. "I may hate that place. I may hate the people working there. Hell, I may even hate him and not realize it. But if I want to find out, I need to do what has to be done. Whether I want to or not."

"And you're not worried that somebody will try to snatch you up again?" Again, Laura didn't mean to add as much sarcasm to her voice, but it crept in.

"No. I'm not." Jennifer crossed her arms and gave her a stern stare.

"What if they're attacked again?" Laura's voice softened. "Aren't you afraid that something might happen to you?"

Jennifer shook her head. "If he's truly my Fated Mate, he won't let anything happen to me. He'd take a bullet for me if he thinks that I'm the one."

"You sound pretty sure of yourself."

"If you were a wolf, you would understand."

Laura snorted. "Ah, the old '*it's a wolf thing, you wouldn't understand*' argument."

Jennifer shrugged again. "Yeah,I guess so."

Laura peered past Jennifer and noted the empty hallway. "Fine. The Brazilians are preparing for a mission. I'm dead tired and have to get a couple hours sleep. As soon as somebody from the base calls me, I'll get word to Matt that we're headed his way."

"Thanks." Jennifer turned to leave.

"Hey,do you think Mick will take us the rest of the way or will we need to fly commercial?"

She shook her head. "I honestly don't know. I can ask him when he wakes."

"Let me know as soon as you can so I can alert Matt."

Jennifer nodded her agreement then slipped back into her own room. Laura shut the door and practically collapsed onto her narrow bed once more.

Across the hallway, Mick paced rapidly in his room, clenching and unclenching his fists. *Mr. Simmons will not like this at all.*

*****

Tracy pushed aside the shoebox at the top of the closet and wrapped her fingers around the cold steel of the revolver. She felt a shudder travel through her body as her hand gripped the inanimate object and a queasy feeling rose from her stomach and threatened the back of her throat. She nearly gasped when she pulled the weapon from the top shelf of the closet, even though she knew exactly what it was. Even though it was the reason she had returned home. Even though it was the only thing that ran through her mind during the entire trip. Now that she was physically holding it in her hand, she wanted nothing more than to be as far from it as she possibly could.

She placed the pistol carefully on the bed and stared at it with a curious fascination. A certain horror intermingled with the idea that this cold, unfeeling tool, this mindless utensil of destruction, this *thing* that her husband had brought into their home for their protection, would now be the harbinger of his undoing.

She sat down hard on the end of the bed and ignored the silent specter beside her. She knew that if she didn't take it to him, he'd only find another from somebody else at the base. She also knew the risks involved in letting nature take its course. An accidental infection of a loved one could mean the transfer of the curse. She wanted so desperately to curl into a ball and weep; to simply cry herself to sleep and wake to find out that it was all a bad dream.

She held her head in her hands and sobbed silently, praying that somehow they both were wrong. Praying that somehow, everything would be okay. She lifted her face to find Hank licking at her foot.

"What do you want?" Her voice cracked as she reached for his big square head. "Do you miss daddy?"

Hank yawned and smacked his jowls, then rested his head on the top of her foot. The added weight pulled on the mattress and caused the pistol to slide across the comforter. Tracy caught it with her hand and nearly jumped when she felt the coldness of the steel again.

"I don't know if I can do this." Hank closed his eyes and grunted, wiping drool on the top of her foot as he rested his heavy head. "Infected or not, I want daddy to come home again."

Hank's head slipped off her foot and he slid to the floor in a large sleepy pile. He had no idea why the human he allowed to feed him was so upset, but he had a tired-on that demanded a nap.

*****

Hammer entered the lounge and peered into the gloom. The televisions were all off and nobody was in sight. He stepped over to the entry to the gym and stuck his head in, but again, the room might as well have been a ghost town. "Where the hell are you, Dave?" he mumbled to himself.

Making his way down the aft stairwell, he entered the CQB training area. Rather than walking through all of the rooms that were set up, he strained his ears but couldn't hear anybody.

With a groan, Hammer backtracked and made his way topside. Finding Chad 'Mac' McKenzie assisting the tech crew run new cabling he caught the man's attention. "Have you seen Marshall?"

Mac thought for a moment then pointed him toward the other end of the hangar. "They're collecting the dead for cremation down there. I'm pretty sure I saw him helping them load body bags."

Hammer scratched at the side of his head and turned toward the deuce and half parked at the north end of the hangar. As he rounded the stack of crates between himself and truck he found Marshall loading bodies in the back of the truck, pausing after each one to mumble a short prayer and perform the sign of the cross over the body. "I didn't know you were the religious type."

Marshall gave him a sheepish grin and nodded. "Yeah, well,after all the things we've seen and heard, it just seemed the natural choice."

Hammer watched him reach for the next body bag and he grabbed the other end, helping him stack the body into the back of the truck. "I thought you were in a hurry to catch your soaps."

Marshall paused and blew out a long breath. "I didn't want to say anything because…"

"What? You were afraid we'd rib you?"

"Pfft. Like I'd care about that." He turned back to the body recently added to the stack and repeated the same short prayer and sign of the cross. Turning back to Hammer, he shrugged. "I guess I was afraid you'd try to stop me."

"Nobody ever tried to stop the Padre."

"But he was a man of God." Dave searched the larger man's face. "I mean, he was…ordained or something, right?"

Hammer shrugged. "Beats me." He crossed his arms and smirked at Marshall. "Would it matter if another *person* gave him permission to serve?" Neils could almost see the light bulb go off in Marshall's head. "The Padre did what he believed was right. Nobody would dare try to stop him from that. Even if they disagreed with him."

Marshall leaned against the truck and ran a hand through his hair. "I don't see how anybody who fought in the desert with us could possibly disagree with him. I mean, we had a vampire who was once one of Christ's disciples. We had a werewolf who was there when he died on the cross. Both were cursed to live forever. Fathers of their own cursed lines. Both of them had seen things that…" his voice trailed off.

"Don't strain your brain trying to figure it out, buddy." Hammer clapped his shoulder. "People have argued for and against the whole God-no God, religion versus nature thing for centuries. If you've found something that works for you, run with it. Just don't let it get between you and your job."

"No, never. I just," He paused and turned back to the bodies. "I felt like they needed somebody to say something over them." He turned back to Neils and his eyes began to redden. "That Carbone needed someone to…say…"

Hammer nodded and gave the man's shoulder a squeeze. "I understand,I truly do." He turned back to the remaining bodies. "Let's finish up here so the techs can do their jobs."

The two men finished loading the bags into the truck, each being treated to a personal prayer from Marshall while Hammer watched on.

I'm sure they all appreciate the thought if nothing else. Neils thought.

*****

"Our forces are gathering. We'll have a small army here before morning." Paul slipped back into his chair and eyed his brother. "How are you feeling?"

"I feel angry." Rufus stood and paced the small office. "I haven't fed on human blood in so long that..." He shuddered, and Paul felt the wave of energy ripple from him. A ripple that cause the hair on the back of his neck to stand on end. "I'm finding it difficult to fight the urge to hunt."

"How long were you on animal blood?" Paul's voice was barely a whisper, his question more rhetorical than anything.

"Too long." A growl came from deep in Rufus' chest. He turned and shot his brother a feral stare. "I crave more."

"Then you aren't through healing." Paul rose and waved Marco in. The large man all but trotted into the office with the cooler in hand. "You need to finish healing so we can get you back onto your special mixture." Paul stifled his smile as he reached into the cooler and withdrew another bag. "Here. Feed."

Rufus tore into the bag and sucked it flat in short order. Paul was standing by with another when the first was simply dropped to the ground. "Hmm. Perhaps we should get you a live donor in here. Let you feed from a source with more than one unit in it?"

Rufus sucked greedily from the plastic bag, his eyes darting side to side. "*Non.* I do not think I can control..." He sat on the makeshift bed and rolled his eyes back into his head. "I need more."

Paul looked to Marco and gave a slight nod. Marco nervously set the cooler down beside Paul and slipped from the room. He reentered a moment later with a woman in tow. Her hands were bound behind her, her mouth taped shut. "Oh, look at what Marco found. A 'donor'." Paul slipped from his chair and practically glided to the door. He wrapped an arm around the quivering young woman and escorted her into the room. "Look, brother, a donor."

Rufus' eyes shot open as soon as he smelled the human. He could sense her fear and it excited him even more. He dropped the nearly empty bag of blood and stared at her, his fangs still extended. "Where did you..."

"She volunteered, didn't you, sweetheart?" Paul's hand gripped the back of her neck and gently nodded her head for her even though her tears and sniveling told a different story. He bent her head to the side, exposing her neck. "And look, she *wants* you to get better brother. She wants you to feed from her."

Rufus' hands shook as he reached for the half naked young woman. "I do not think I can stop if I…"

"Do not worry, brother. I will help you." Paul's voice sounded like silk as it slid across the room and caressed Rufus' ears. "Just enough to help you heal."

"*Oui*. Just enough to help me heal."

He rose slowly from the mattress and reached for the woman. She tried to recoil from his cold touch but Paul held her tight. Rufus launched himself and was attached to her neck in a moment. The initial shock and fear gave way to a moan of ecstasy as he sunk his fangs into her and began to feed. She melted in Paul's grip and he had to increase his hold to keep her upright. Eventually, he let go and allowed Rufus to hold her while he fed.

Marco stood in the doorway and watched the macabre dance. His hands shook with both fear and anger as he watched Mr. Foster manipulate his master. Rufus was obviously out of his mind to do such a thing, but to have Paul coerce him so? Marco couldn't stop watching. He saw Paul slowly turn and give him a smile that made his blood run cold. He knew exactly what he was doing.

When Rufus let go of the girl and she tumbled to the floor, her ashen skin the color of death, Marco knew he had crossed that line that he swore he'd never cross again. Marco lowered his eyes and prayed to whatever god would listen that Rufus would get his rightful mind returned.

Rufus stood and stretched his arms outward. He could feel his bones knit back together, his internal organs heal and the last of his burns return to normal skin once again. "It is finished."

"Yes, it is." Paul kicked the body of the girl aside and leaned against the desk. "So…tell me, brother, how do you feel now?"

Rufus turned and glared at him with feral eyes. "I feel like a vampire once more."

*****

Lilith paced slowly while Damien remained prostrated on the floor. "I need you to fetch me things." She stopped and placed a heel on his shoulder. "You can do this, can you not?"

"What do you need, mistress? Tell me so that I might please you."

She watched him patiently, waiting for him to lift his eyes to bask in her radiance. When he didn't, she smiled to herself and removed her foot. "I am in need of ingredients for a spell. You can obtain these things, yes?"

"Or die trying, mistress."

She kicked him hard across the ribs and sent him sprawling. "There is a difference in blind obedience and proficiency. I need somebody capable of getting me what I need." She bent down and pulled him to her face by his shirt. "Can you do this or are you a liability?"

"I can do this, mistress." Damien choked as she tightened her grip on him. "I swear I can."

She threw him to the ground and stood over him. She watched him carefully and knew she had him when Damien's eyes finally broke from the ground and glanced up at her still naked form. He turned slowly and stared at the body he had fallen in love with and his breath came in choking gasps as he stared. "Eyes to the ground." She stepped over him and watched him scramble to press his forehead to the cold concrete once more.

Lilith stared off to the west and considered the physical things she would need. "A white dove. A raven. Two runestones. A silver chalice. A dagger. Four black candles. Salt. Lots of salt." She turned quickly to Damien's prone body. Can you remember that?"

"Yes, m'lady. I have it." He began crawling away from her and toward the door.

"Stand like a man or you'll be baked in the sun before you can finish."

Damien pulled himself to his feet and bowed deeply to her. "As you will, so mote it be."

"And hurry, Damien. My legions await."

8

Tracy slipped back into Mark's room and quietly shut the door behind her. She leaned against the cold metal and stared at his still form on the bed, her mind traveling back to the first time they met. The first time he screwed up the courage to ask her out. Their first kiss. When he asked her to marry him. Their first child…his travels with the Corps. She lowered her head and squeezed her eyes shut. Her hand slipped into her coat pocket and her fingertips brushed the cold metal of the revolver.

"I didn't hear you come back." He sounded as if he had been swallowing sand. She lifted her face and tried to hide her grief.

"Let me get you a drink." She stepped beside his bed and poured a cup of water. Placing a straw into the cup, she bent it so that he could sip from it. "Drink it slowly."

He stared at her a moment, refusing to take the straw. "Did you get it?"

"Drink the damned water, Tufo, before I shove my foot up your ass." She pushed the straw closer to his mouth and watched as he swallowed a mouthful. He choked slightly and coughed, then went back for more.

Once he had finished and she had retaken her seat he turned rummy eyes to her again. "Did you?"

"Maybe I'm not ready to let you go that far." Her voice was firm, her jaw set. "If Matt can live with this…whatever the hell it is, then you can, too."

Mark shook his head slowly, his eyes closing. "Matt doesn't have a family that he could infect."

"So don't bite anybody." She sat stiffly in the chair and stared down at him in his bed. "It's really not that difficult. It's not like you're home that much anyway, are you? You're always here with your nose up Matt's ass and..." her voice cracked and she choked up. Her hand went to her mouth to stop her from saying anything else she might regret.

"No, don't hold back. Tell me how you really feel."

"Fine. Maybe I will." She refused to look at him and stared at the bag of saline hanging from the hook above his head. "I've decided that even though you're a major pain in my ass, I'd rather keep you around."

Mark grunted and she wasn't sure if it was a laugh or a grunt of displeasure. "Pain in your ass?"

"Besides, Tufo, you're worth more dead than alive." She finally cracked a sarcastic smile at him. "Remember, we cashed in your life insurance years ago to pay for college tuition, and now that you're back with the squads, your military life insurance isn't squat."

"You can't be serious." He slowly rolled a bit on the bed to better see her. "This isn't a game, Trace. This is the real deal here."

"And what you're asking of me is a permanent solution to a temporary problem."

"Temporary?" Mark's voice rose to almost a shout. "There's no cure for this. This is anything *but* temporary."

"You know what I mean." She pointed a finger at him. "I'm not letting you take the coward's way out. There has to be ways to deal with this."

Mark sighed and slumped deeper into the uncomfortable mattress. "Like what? Lock myself in the silver cells downstairs every full moon?"

Tracy turned and stared at him. "There are silver cells downstairs?"

Mark's eyes widened as he realized he had just stepped in it. "No."

She started slapping at him, causing him to wince as he tried to defend himself from her blows. "You son of a bitch! You had me thinking you were going to be tear-assing through the house and hiking on the furniture, and biting people.And all this time there are silver cells in the basement?"

Mark groaned as he did his best to defend himself from her blows. "I'm hurt here. Please—"

"I'm gonna kill you, you goofy…" she stopped hitting him and pulled him closer, wrapping her arms around him. "You, stupid, selfless, goofy…" she cried as she started kissing him about the face.

"So you're not going to shoot me?"

"Pull something like that on me again and I will."

*****

"We're about ready to leave. Has anybody seen Kalen?" Jack asked as he turned a slow circle in the middle of the courtyard.

"Last I saw, he was walking the majority of the others back through a large boulder." Gus pointed to the boulder that the group had come through earlier.

"Have everybody gather their gear and muster out here. We're gonna travel back through the portal."

"What about the chopper? It's inbound now. Should be here any time." Gus glanced out over the ocean in the general direction of the shore. "There should be plenty of room for who's left."

Jack shook his head. "I'm going to direct them to strip the bodies here of weaponry and anything that might help point us to who sent them. By the time they bag what's left, that transport will be stuffed with gear."

Gus scratched at his chin. "Do you really think we can track them down just off what these guys might be carrying? Most mercs strip themselves of anything identifying."

"Do you really think these guys were mercs? I mean, did any of them fight like they were trained soldiers?" Jack pointed to the sheer number of dead that the wolves were now stacking behind the castle proper for burial and disposal. "They nearly overwhelmed just because there was so damned many of them. But I'd bet a month's pay, none of them were pros."

"Point taken," Gus agreed. "And you said something about their weapons?"

"Sigs are primary weapons all over Europe and some areas of South America. There's a slight chance we can trace them by the serial numbers." Jack nodded to where the weapons were stacked. "It may take a while to find a trend or commonality, but once we do, we'll track down who was behind this."

"Too bad Apollo bailed. He could have just told us." Gus spat on the ground as if the name had left a bad taste in his mouth.

Jack paused and lowered his head. "I don't want to think what could be going through the big guy's head right now. How he could turn against the squads and do something like this…it's just beyond me."

"Chief Jack." Azrael pointed out over the water. "Another of those flying machines approach."

Jack noted the apprehension in the young gargoyle's voice and placed a hand on his arm in an attempt to calm him. "Easy there. These are the good guys." The gargoyle turned questioning eyes to him and Jack gave him a reassuring smile. "They're with us. They're coming to help."

"If you say so." Azrael seemed to stand down, but kept his guard up.

All eyes suddenly turned toward the large boulder as a golden light shone from the edges and it slowly opened revealing the tall Elf standing within. Kalen stepped through and waved his hand over the stone again, sealing the doorway behind him. "They are safely home once more."

"The chopper is on its way," Jack stated as he approached him. "Once we get them briefed, you can escort us to the base." Kalen nodded his face somber. "Is something wrong? Did Horith take a turn for the worse?"

"No, he is improving. The Wyldwood is caring for him well." Kalen stared off into the night sky. "She simply passed on some disturbing news."

"Care to spill it?" Jack suddenly felt perturbed. He was starting to not like the idea of being the last to know things. "This whole 'getting information second hand' is getting really old, really quick."

Kalen turned to Jack and took him by the arm, leading him aside so that they could speak quietly. "What did she say when you last spoke?"

"Not much really. Care to enlighten me?" Jack crossed his arms, his jaw set.

Kalen exhaled slowly and leaned against his bow. "She has informed me of our fate."

"Our? More visions I take it?"

Kalen shook his head, his eyes downcast. "Mine and the others." He finally lifted his face and met Jack's hard gaze. "We are to follow you unwaveringly."

"I should expect so." Jack's voice took a tone that he hadn't intended, but the message was clear. Neither was happy about the situation. "She's pretty much left me standing here with my dick in my hand. I mean, I'm stuck with the graduating class and from what I understand, these guys may be warriors, but they're just kids."

Kalen nodded, not quite understanding everything he said, but understanding the gist. "There is a reason for her actions Chief Jack, but she did not offer an explanation. She simply said that our youth is necessary to complete the mission at hand."

"And what exactly is our mission? I don't guess she bothered to inform you, did she? Because the last I heard, I requested back up in dealing with the vampire council and those plans pretty much blew themselves up."

Kalen slumped his shoulders and shook his head. "She did not enlighten me. She stated only that the mission would soon become clear. The darkness would—"

"Hold on," Jack interrupted. "Your youth is necessary but she won't say why. Our mission would soon become clear, but she didn't say what. I hate to say this, but I'm getting a distinct feeling that we're being played."

"Played?" Kalen turned a quizzical look to him.

"She's messing with us. She has no clue what's going on so she tells you what she thinks you want to hear." Jack snapped his fingers and rolled his eyes. "Dammit. That's why she pulled the older, more experienced fighters home. She's expecting the shit to hit the fan in her realm, and she wants the biggest and strongest there to defend their homes, isn't it?"

Kalen shook his head. "She has assured me that the darkness cannot reach our realm. The elder warriors cannot assist in our battle. I do not know why, but it must be the youth…"

"Bullshit." Jack turned and started to stomp away. "Hey, you know what? It doesn't matter. If she doesn't want her people to help, we don't need you. The squads have dealt with bad asses before, we can keep on doing it."

"Chief Jack!" Kalen shouted to get his attention. He quickly shot a furtive glance to either side to ensure he hadn't caught any undue attention. "There is more."

Jack crossed his arms and stared down at the Elf. "So spill it, Spock."

Kalen didn't grasp his sarcasm but continued in a more quiet tone. "There will be others who will join us. But…they aren't from the Middle Realm."

"Oh, do say," Jack huffed. "And where the hell are we supposed to find these other 'others'?"

"She did not say. Only that we are to expect two more others to join us."

"Sure we are." Jack turned at the sound of helicopter blades slicing the night air. "If you'll excuse me, I have to deal with this. Then you can open us a doorway to the base. You can do that, can't you?"

Kalen sighed at the chief's exasperation. "Yes, I can do that."

"Good. Try not to screw it up and send us to Greenland."

*****

Little John jumped a short fence and rolled to a stop in front of Brooke, his hands out in front of him trying to stop her. "Brooke! Please, just wait."

She faked left, then right, then tried to leap over him. John jumped with her movement and caught her leg, dragging her back to the ground with him. "Dammit, stop!"

She kicked out at him and rolled away, coming to her feet and ready to bolt once more. She raised her eyes and stared down the barrel of a carbine. "I wouldn't," Lamb deadpanned. "You're not that fast."

She spun to the side and came up facing yet another barrel. "Nope, wrong again." Ing wiggled the barrel of his rifle under her nose. "I really wouldn't do that."

Brooke slowly turned her head and felt the blood drain from her face as she realized that she was surrounded. Her eyes darted back and forth as she looked for a weakness in their line. "Don't even think it, sweetheart." She looked up and saw Donovan standing on the rooftop, his rifle leveled on her as well. Her shoulders slumped as she raised her hands in surrender.

"Why did you run?" John asked as he tried to catch his breath.

She turned and gave him a 'duh' look. "Aren't you part of the famous 'Monster Squad'?" Her voice instantly took him back to his youth. It really was Brooke. "I may stay below the radar, but even I have heard of your exploits."

John felt the tension slip from his body as he tried to find the words to explain. "Brooke...I..."

"It's Raven." She shot him a dirty look. "I haven't gone by that name in nearly a lifetime."

John stared at her open mouthed, unsure what to say. "I'm sorry. I know you as Brooke. My big sister."

"She's dead." The woman stared at him with such anger in her eyes that he nearly cringed. "She died a long time ago."

"Look, missy," Spalding stepped between the two siblings,"I don't give a tinker's damn what you call yourself. Either you're John's sister and we give you a chance, or you're not and we ash your ass right now." One look at his face convinced her that this man was all business, regardless of what her brother may or may not want.

She took a half step back, her hand moving toward the blade strapped to her back. She paused as the carbines leveled on her registered once again. "At one time, I was." She looked away from the two men and cast her eyes to the ground. "That was a long time ago."

"So why were you in the mission killing those vamps?" Spalding's tone made it clear that she had better come clean the first time. He wouldn't tolerate being lied to.

"It's my job." Her voice was low and whisper quiet.

"You're an assassin?" Spalding's grip tightened on his weapon as he assessed her response.

She shook her head slowly. "No,I'm one of them." She suddenly lifted her face to meet his gaze. "I mean, I'm a vampire as well, but I don't kill like they do." She quickly turned and faced each of the squad members. "I mean, I drink blood,I have to...but I don't kill people."

"Do you feed from animals like the *Lamia Beastia?*" John asked as he pushed closer.

She shook her head again. "I steal from blood banks." She swallowed hard. "When I can't steal from blood banks, I'll feed off people, but I only take small amounts. I haven't had to kill to feed in…a *very* long time."

"What happened, Brooke?" John pushed past Spalding and towered over his older sister. "That night, I mean. I…I never gave up on you." His voice cracked as he spoke.

Raven turned away, unable to look at her little brother. "My life ended that night, Johnny."

"But you're back now. And you don't kill, so…" He turned and quickly looked to Spalding for guidance. "Surely we can figure out something, can't we?"

Spalding lowered his weapon and hiked a brow at his crew. "I think if Ms. Sullivan here will give her word to cooperate, we can cut some slack."

She turned untrusting eyes to Spalding. "You kill vampires. I'm supposed to just trust you?"

"You kill them too. Sounds to me like we may be on the same team." Spalding shot her a crooked grin. "And you wouldn't be the first vampire to work with us."

Her wide eyes turned to John who nodded. "We have a genius doctor who's been helping for…well…forever." He held a hand out to her. "Come on, Brooke. Come home."

She pulled back slightly and stared at his huge open palm. "I…"

"It's okay." John extended his hand further. "I promise,nobody will hurt you."

She lifted her gaze to meet his and suddenly saw that same ten year old boy that once idolized and terrorized her when she was human. For the briefest moment she wanted to cry. Instead she stiffened and squared her shoulders. "I'll go back with you. But I make no promises on staying." She turned and walked past the other members of the team leaving John standing with his hand still extended.

Spalding placed a hand on the larger man's arm and slowly lowered it. "Don't worry, buddy, she'll come around."

"I hope so."

*****

Matt ordered the cleanup crews to the El Cajon mission and a fast transport to retrieve a portion of the team. Apparently Little John, Donovan, and Ms. Sullivan were returning to ensure they arrived before sunup. The rest of the squad had set a perimeter guard while waiting.

With the fires put out, the hangar being repaired and the mission complete, Matt suddenly felt exhausted. He poured a cup of coffee and walked down the stairs to check on his XO. He really didn't want to be the one to do what he was about to do, but if anybody were going to break the news to Mark, he'd rather it be him.

He knocked lightly on the door and waited for Tracy to open it. "Can I have a word with the two of you?"

"We need to have a word with you, too." She pulled the door open for him and Matt stepped into the small room, suddenly feeling very crowded in the small space.

"I have some news that…" he paused and tried to think of a way to put it that might soften the blow.

"You mean that Mark is infected? We know." Tracy sat in the chair beside Mark's head and saw Matt do a convincing fish imitation.

"H-how did…w-who told you?" Matt's mind raced, trying to figure out if he could legally kill somebody under the UCMJ for spilling the beans.

"I could feel it inside me. And the fever, it wasn't natural."

"But that shouldn't have…" Matt shook his head as he tried to wrap his mind around the situation.

Tracy lifted her crucifix and shook it. "Silver. Burned his wounds."

Matt groaned as he leaned against the door. "I didn't think about…" he trailed off. After a moment, his eyes met Mark's. "I'm sorry, buddy."

"I tried to get her to shoot me," Mark stated plainly. "She wouldn't do it."

"If you don't knock off your crap, I still might. I just won't shoot you where it will kill you." She looked to Matt. "A silver bullet in the ass wouldn't kill him would it?"

Matt choked on his coffee. "Um, I honestly don't know. I wouldn't want to test it."

Mark nodded. "Highly allergic to silver now. You can't even drive a silver car. It could kill me."

Tracy stared at him questioningly. "Are you serious? Is there real silver in the paint?"

Mark shook his head. "No. You just drive like a crazy old bat."

She stood and started to swat at him again. Matt quickly grabbed her hands and pulled her back. "As much as he might deserve to have his ass kicked for calling you 'old', he needs to heal."

"Screw that. Nobody tells me I can't drive." Tracy kicked out toward him and barely brushed him with her boot. "Tufo, I'll plant a foot in your old, wrinkled ass."

Matt pulled her back and pushed her toward her chair. "It would seem that he is on the mend." He then turned to Tracy. "And you should be nominated for sainthood just for putting up with him all these years."

"Kissing up to her will do you no good. She sees right through all of that crap."

"A little kissing up would do you some good." She glared through narrowed eyes.

"Believe it or not, I actually have work to do." Matt reached for the door. "Is it safe to leave the two of you alone?"

Tracy reached into her coat pocket and withdrew the pistol. She handed it to Matt with a huff. "I told him I wouldn't do it, but damned if he isn't pushing me to reconsider."

Matt shoved the revolver into his belt. "I think I'll keep this in my desk." He pointed at Mark. "You be nice and get healed up." Turning to Tracy he gave her a wink. "If he keeps giving you grief, let me know and I'll dig this back out for you."

*****

Paul stood near the partially open overhead door and listened to the sounds of the city at night. He desperately wanted to hunt but he didn't dare leave his brother behind at such a crucial time. He was almost certain he had converted Rufus, but now was not the time to be weak. He had to ensure that the taste for human blood had stuck. The bodies scattered about the periphery of the building was testament to the toll his recovery had taken, but in order to prevent him from swinging back to his old way of thinking, Paul had to make sure that any future feedings seemed to be Rufus' idea.

He inhaled deeply of the night air and could almost taste the life floating on the breeze. A slight squeeze of his shoulder had him turn and gazing into his brother's face. "You can almost feel the vibrations, can't you?" Rufus inhaled deeply and sighed as he exhaled. "The golden strings of energy that ties all life together…you can almost see it if you look hard enough."

"Almost." Paul's voice was barely a whisper. His face appeared feral in the moonlight and he wanted nothing more than to sink his fangs into a soft warm body.

"Our army approaches. I can feel them." Rufus pulled Paul back into the warehouse and toward the office. "Once they are here, find them safe places to bed down for the day. But tonight, show them where to hunt. Feed them. Get them strong so they can better fight."

Paul fought the urge scream 'hallelujah' at those words. "And what of you, brother? Do you hunger?"

Rufus stretched his neck and flashed his fangs. "I always hunger." He continued toward the office. "While you're out, pick me up a snack. Another female, I think."

"As you will."

Paul lowered his face but watched as his brother disappeared into the darkness. *His transition is complete.*

*****

Little John sat across from Brooke and watched her closely. The noise from the helicopter prevented any meaningful conversation, but his eyes never left her. She had withdrawn inside her hood again as soon as she sat, her face hidden from him. Her hands fingered a silver looking amulet as they sliced across the night sky. John shifted in his seat to try to see it better, but she slipped it back into her cloak. It was almost as though she could see him through her cloak and didn't want him getting too curious.

Donnie watched the uncomfortable reunion and, to his credit, kept his comments to himself. He couldn't imagine what it must be like for the larger man. To have lost his sister at such a young age, spent years convinced there were monsters out there, finally getting a job where you could hunt them down, and even after you convince yourself that you would drop her for her own good the moment you see her…here she is. He was stymied as he watched John be transported back to his youth the moment he laid eyes on her. Rather than being a thirty-year-old operator facing an eighteen-year-old girl, he was ten again and seeing his big sister for the first time in two decades.

John reached into his pocket and pulled her photograph out. He ran a finger along the side of her face and for the first time in years, he noticed just how faded and crumpled the photo appeared. He looked up again and tried to see Brooke's face but the hood still had her blocked from his eyes. John sighed and started to put the photo away. He paused, the photo still in his hand. Without thinking, he stood and moved to the seat next to her. He handed the photo to her.

"I never stopped looking for you," he yelled above the drone of the engine.

He noticed her head shift slightly under the hood, and then she turned away. He continued to hold the photograph out where she could see it. "What happened to you, Brooke?"

She shifted herself in the seat, turning her back to him as much as she could. John's shoulders slumped as he withdrew the photo and slipped it back into his breast pocket. "I never gave up."

"You should have." Her voice was a whisper, but John's enhanced hearing picked up every word.

"I couldn't. You're my big sister." He placed a hand on her leg and patted it. Her hand shot out and swept his away.

"I'm not that person anymore." She shifted further, turning more of her back to him.

"You'll always be my sister, Brooke. Being a vamp doesn't change that." John sighed and stared across the other seats, his mind replaying the night she was taken. "I would have stopped them if I could have. I was just too little to do anything."

"You did more than you know." John shifted his head, trying to hear her better. He could almost swear that her voice cracked as she spoke.

"What do you mean? I couldn't do anything but…"

She turned in her seat so swiftly that she startled him. "Do you really want to know why I hunt vampires now, Johnny?" His blank expression must have read as a 'yes' to her because she continued. "I hunt them down because I have to. You see, they took me to use as bait. For the first few weeks, I was used to lure others in to be fed on. Then they turned me. Had to keep me 'young'. They *used* me as bait to catch people so they could eat."

"That's not your fault, Brooke. You were just a kid yourself."

"That's not all, Johnny." She turned more and he could see her face. Tears streaked her cheeks. "The highest crime a vampire can commit is to kill another vampire. Do you understand what I'm telling you? Do you know why? It's because we have no soul. When a vampire is killed, that's it. There is no afterlife. It's just darkness."

"I don't get why you're—"

"They said that the new girl is good, but they needed somebody that could lure more people in. They wanted a kid. They wanted to go back to the house and get *you* Johnny. They wanted to use you like they did me. Use you for bait so they could catch some unsuspecting soccer mom…or other kids your age. I couldn't let that happen."

"Brooke, what are saying?"

"I killed them, Johnny. I killed them all." She pointed to the sword that Donnie now held. "I used that blade and I sliced them all to ribbons. I watched as they turned to ash right before my eyes."

"Brooke…I had no idea…"

"I did it to protect you, Johnny." Her face tightened and her eyes hardened. "I turned against my own maker. I killed my entire coven to protect a single human. From that decision on, my life wasn't worth a bucket of warm spit. From that moment on, it was kill or be killed." She shifted her body again and stared straight ahead. "So I kept killing. Any time there was a sign of a vampire, I hunted it down. I hunted it and I destroyed it. I kept killing and I kept killing until there was nothing left of me anymore."

"I don't get what you're saying, Brooke."

"Brooke is dead, Johnny." She pulled her hood down further, blocking her face entirely. "There's only the Raven."

9

A soft knocking had Tracy pulling the door open. She wasn't prepared for who stood in the doorway, peering over her shoulder at the body on the bed. "May I come in?"

She cast a quick glance toward Mark who nodded. "I hear I owe my life to you." He tried to pull himself upright more in bed and failed. The pain shooting through his torso was simply too much to tolerate. "Thank you, I think."

Evan hung his head as he lingered against the far wall. "I suppose you know about the infection then." He paled even more as if that were possible. "I am so sorry, Major. I did everything in my power to…"

"Doc, don't. This wasn't your fault." Tracy helped pull Mark up to a sitting position and stuffed another pillow behind his shoulders. "You did everything you could."

"I honestly thought I'd have known sooner." Evan took the chair that Tracy offered and practically fell into it. His skin appeared so pale in the blue fluorescent lighting that it almost seemed transparent. Dark veins crossed his face and neck and Tracy tried not to stare. "I never thought that the virus would take so long to affect either of us."

"Hit ya pretty hard, did it?"

Dr. Peters nodded. "The expression, 'vomited everything I'd eaten since Kindergarten' came true tonight. Or…is it day? I've lost track of time."

Mark shrugged. "Who knows, Doc." He closed his eyes and leaned his head back. "I wish you hadn't saved me."

"Mark!" Tracy chastised as Evan's head popped up. "You shouldn't say such things."

"Major, we couldn't have known about the infection. The wolf never bit you. You were torn open by nails and—"

"And the damned thing spat blood and slobber all over me as it tore into me. Teeth or fingernails. If there's spit mixed in, I don't think it would matter if he stabbed me with a damned screwdriver."

Evan contemplated that little tidbit and had to give the major the benefit of doubt. He definitely made a good point. "At least you weren't infected by a vampire." Evan's voice chilled as he spoke. "That truly is a death sentence."

Mark slowly rolled his head to stare at the vampire. "And this isn't?"

"You couldn't possibly compare the two." Dr. Peters appeared honestly shocked. "To become a vampire you must truly *die* first. To be infected by the wolf virus, you still live. Hell, you live a lot longer and healthier. You just have one day a month where you have to be careful."

"So, it's like PMS to the nth degree, is that what you're saying?" Mark didn't try to disguise the venom in his voice.

Evan sat taller in his chair and tried to square his shoulders. His hands shook as he pointed at the executive officer. "I'm not saying that at all. I would not begin to belittle your condition, Major. But I also think the same respects could be paid to me." He pushed up from the chair and turned for the door. Turning to Tracy, Evan placed a shaking hand on her shoulder. "I'm sorry, my visit didn't go as planned."

She merely nodded as he stepped past her. As Evan reached for the door, he turned slightly and addressed Mark once again. "You say that you wish I hadn't saved you. I understand your thinking that the infection is a curse, and in some ways it might well be. But that very same virus is now fighting like hell to keep you alive. I wonder if you're even worth saving any longer."

*****

Rufus watched from the shadows of the office area as Paul addressed the vampires assembled to act as personal security. When he felt the time was right, Rufus stepped out and approached the group loosely scattered about within the warehouse.

"Gentlemen, so good of you to come on such short notice." He knew that they had no choice but to drop everything and rush to their aid, but he also felt it was in their best interest to be diplomatic while addressing them. "It would seem that your services as professionals are very much needed. My team of wolves," Rufus noticed Marco still hovering near the rear and corrected himself, "save one, seemed to have abandoned me in my time of need. And these are trying times, indeed. The vampire council has decreed a meeting this very full moon. My wolves have turned against me and may very well be attempting to turn the Monster Squad against us." He inhaled deeply for dramatic effect and shook his head. "I fear that we find ourselves between the proverbial rock and hard spot, *oui*?"

Paul nodded and stepped forward, speaking out on his brother's behalf. "Your primary mission is to guard our master. Rufus *will not* be harmed."

"*Non*. To protect us both." He draped an arm over Paul's shoulder and squeezed his brother affectionately. "I have you back now. I will not lose you again."

Paul nodded sheepishly then turned back to the vampires he was addressing. "Once the sun sets, you'll all go out and hunt. Build up your strength. We can't afford you to be dim witted if you are protecting either Rufus or myself. We will prepare a small team for Geneva. That mission must be completed. The rest of you will be sent on to another of Rufus' homes here on the mainland. You will secure the property and ensure that the grounds remain cleared."

A wolf near the front stepped forward and nodded to Paul. "Is the Honor-pact between Viktor's wolves and us now dissolved?"

Paul turned to Rufus who sighed, his head shaking. "I must speak to Viktor before I answer this truthfully. But my Second, Jack Thompson, is now *persona non grata*."

"Who then acts as your Second?" another vampire asked.

Rufus clenched his jaw and rolled his head on his neck. "I have yet to proclaim a formal Second." He glanced to Paul who simply shrugged. "For now, I name my brother. He saved my life and nursed me back to health. He has displayed more than ample loyalties. Consider him my Second." Paul's jaw hung open as he stared at Rufus. This went beyond any of his initial plans. Then again, he went astray of his initial plans a long time ago.

"Which of your properties would you prefer us to secure, sir?"

Rufus turned his attention back to the security detail and considered them for a moment. The only property that he thought Jack might not be aware of would be the Aspen estate. A risky move, to be sure, but he had little choice. He turned to Paul and pulled him aside. "If you were Jack and you were aware of my holdings, how would you go about checking them?"

"How do you mean? Which ones first?" Rufus nodded. "I'd go for the ones furthest away probably. The ones that I thought were abandoned. Then work my way in to wherever he calls home."

"As would I. But I would send multiple teams to inspect as many as possible. I somehow doubt that Mr. Thompson will have those kinds of resources." He turned back to the security detail. "Aspen. The estate there has plenty of rooms in the main house, the guest house holds more and the land surrounding it is not only clear enough that we can see if anybody approaches, there are no neighbors."

"Colorado is awfully close to Oklahoma. If Jack went back to the squads…"

"I kept no paperwork on the estate in Aspen." Rufus gave him a wicked grin. "The registered owner is a fictitious name."

*****

Laura hung up the phone and leaned back in the chair. She rubbed at her eyes and wished she hadn't. It felt like she had rubbed sand deep into the corners and now her eyes teared. "What's the verdict?" Laura looked up to see Jennifer leaning against the door frame.

"Colonel says that if we don't have our own ride, let him know, and he will gladly authorize two Business Class tickets to the U.S."

"Business Class?" Jennifer feigned shock. "He does realize that I'm supposed to be his Fated Mate, right?"

Laura chuckled lightly under her breath and waved her off. "When the government is paying for it, that's a marked improvement from coach." She stood and stretched, feeling her bones crack in protest. "At least it isn't a military hop. With those you're lucky to get a wooden bench to sit on."

"Business sounds good." She stared cautiously down the hallway. "Are you going to ask Mick, or do I have to?"

Laura shrugged. "He's your friend. Besides, we have tickets. We don't need to ask him."

"I know, but I feel like we owe him the opportunity to see this through." She turned away and stared out the open door. "He's running from my father every bit as much as we are now."

Laura placed a reassuring hand on her shoulder. "Then go ahead and ask him. The worst he can do is say no."

Jennifer shot her a sideways smirk. "No, that's *not* the worst he can do. Trust me on that one."

*****

Apollo finished stacking the crates next to the aluminum shipping containers. He made a mental checklist and marked off a few more boxes from his list. "Yo, Sheridan,where's the M203 grenade launchers?"

Sheridan's shoulders slumped and he hobbled toward Apollo. "Not everything is being delivered at once, old chap." He pulled Apollo aside and tried to lower his voice. "I had to use more than one supplier to keep expenses under control. This bloke wanted too bloody much for the launchers, so I went with another supplier."

Apollo planted his hands on his hips and stared at the much smaller man. "Let me guess. You got a budget and figured if you cut corners you could pocket the rest."

Sheridan sighed and ran a hand through his wavy hair. "My friend, you are every bit as observant as you are large. Just trust me when I say that they are on the way. Your launchers *and* the grenades for them. I give you my word."

Apollo groaned but turned back to the crates. "I'm bustin' open every one of these to make sure we get what's coming. If they be short by so much as a holster, somebody's head is gonna roll."

"Be my guest." Sheridan made a grand sweeping motion as Apollo marched past him.

Grabbing two other English speaking wolves, Apollo began to unstack the crates and going through the contents. Sheridan stepped back, but even on his way back to the office, he could hear the man arguing about where to stow the equipment. He paused and checked the time. The next wave of reinforcements were due in that afternoon, and he needed to be sure that everything was in place. Food stores were in place, the shipping containers with the silver webbing were stacked in place for the men to shift on the full moon if necessary and housing containers had been brought in and set up. Potable water trucks and port-a-potties were brought in. From what he could tell, they were ready to make a short term stay in the industrial park.

*****

Jay Wolf parked his Excursion in the parking lot behind the hangar and watched the flurry of activity as personnel continued to replace damaged equipment and run new cabling. As soon as he stepped away from the large truck, two security guards flanked him. "Identification, sir."

Jay paused and turned on them slowly. "Jay Wolf here to see Colonel Mitchell."

"ID, sir." The guard held his hand out in a no-nonsense manner.

Jay opened his mouth to say something and thought better of it. Whatever was going on here, the men were obviously on high alert. He slowly reached for his back pocket and retrieved his wallet. Pulling his driver's license out, he handed it to the large man.

The guard looked the ID over then handed it back. "Colonel Mitchell doesn't have you on his calendar, sir."

Jay nodded. "I couldn't get through by phone. It's pretty important, son. I need to talk to the man."

The guard shook his head. "Not without prior authorization."

"If you would just contact him and let him know that I'm here, I'm sure he'd—"

"NOT without prior authorization, sir." The guard squared his shoulders and stepped between him and the hangar.

Jay deflated and placed his license back into his wallet. Nodding, he reached for the door of his Excursion. "Fine. But do this, will ya? Tell the man if he wants any more *silver ammunition* then he'd damned sure better talk to me." Jay watched the guard as he spoke and noted the nervous tick form in his jaw. "I'm just going to sit in my truck while you make that call."

The guard looked to the other one and gave a slight nod. The smaller guard stepped away and pulled a radio from his belt while Jay sat effectively pinned in his truck. Moments later Colonel Mitchell came stepping out of the hangar, yelling something to the guards who seemed to melt back into the background. Jay stepped out of his truck cautiously and looked for the large men, but they had effectively disappeared.

"They're good. I'll give them that."

"What's up, Jay? Why are you here?" Mitchell looked like he had been through hell. Jay noticed the dark circles under his eyes and the haggard look of his uniform.

"Have you slept?"

"I don't have time, Jay. Why are you here?" Mitchell crossed his arms over his chest and stared at the man.

"I know silver isn't the easiest thing to get in bulk. Not the way you need it. I may have found a source, but..."

"But?" Mitchell raised a brow at him.

"But it's expensive Matt. I just don't carry that kind of pocket change."

"How expensive?" Matt asked as he turned and headed toward the hangar. Jay fell into step behind him. "My funds are limited as well, and after what happened, I can't just drop a chunk on bulk silver."

"I understand...wait. What happened?" Jay asked as they stepped into the hangar. His eyes took in the effects of the carnage and he stood still in shock, his eyes darting from scene to scene.

"This is after we've cleaned up and repaired most of the damage." Matt's voice was low and quiet. "We got hit."

Jay felt a hand on his shoulder pulling him toward the elevator doors. "Who in the hell would have the balls to attack you guys? Don't they realize what you do?"

"We're working on it." Mitchell pressed the button and pulled Jay back so the doors could close. "My team is tracking every scrap of information they can. As far as we can tell, they're using weapons stolen from South American military units. Most likely sold on the black market."

"Son of a..."

"You were talking about silver." Matt held the elevator door for Jay who stepped out and moved toward the offices.

"I've got an idea. I don't know how effective it would be, but it might stretch the silver out quite a bit." Jay entered Matt's office and took the first chair. "You know we manufacture the Trident round, right? It's a machined brass alloy that breaks into three distinct pieces once it hits its target, but it's still effectively armor piercing."

Matt shook his head. "Honestly, I hadn't kept up. Too many other irons in the fire." He took his seat behind his desk and poured a cup of coffee. He held the pot up for Jay who waved him off. "Are you wanting to machine some Tridents out of the silver?"

"Yes and no." Jay smiled mischievously. "I want to use the same cold dipping procedure we use on the .30 caliber rounds on our Tridents. They'd still have a brass core, but they'd have a silver jacket. If we make them as thick as the .30s, I really think they'd be just as effective."

Matt leaned back in his chair and considered Jay's idea. "How much further could you stretch the silver?"

"At least three times. Maybe slightly more, but effectively, let's say three times. As far as cost, it will be about the same, because each round has to be hand-machined. You can't cast these bullets. But once they're silver jacketed, you're talking a nasty silver round."

"I'm guessing you have the ballistic testing to back up your claims." Matt sipped from the bitter nectar and watched him carefully.

"You know I do or I wouldn't be suggesting it. You can go to our website and see a lot of the testing, and I'll give you the password to see the stuff that nobody else can see. The armor piercing tests, the gelatin tests, the Kevlar tests, etc. I keep all of that on a secure server."

"What about the .223 ammo? Would you be loading them with your Tridents as well?"

"I can if you want me to. I think once you see what this round does in gelatin; you'll probably want me to have some heavies machined up for the .308s as well."

Matt nodded as he thought about Jay's offer. "If your silver jacketing is as thick as what you did for the .30 caliber stuff, I think it will work." He sat up and placed his coffee cup on the desk. "But, Jay, this may be a stopgap. If the rounds don't measure up in the field…"

Jay stood and held his hands up. "I understand completely. If they don't perform, there's no sense in using them. Hell, send them back and I'll reload them with the solids for you. But I really think you'll like them once you field test them."

"Make it happen." Matt turned and walked to his safe. "Now. How much do you need to get this bulk silver?"

*****

The largest of the three boulders behind the hangar gave a soft yellow glow before a seam appeared along the edge and a brighter golden light burst forth. Wallace, Gonzales, and Gus Tracy all stepped through and took up defensive positions. Once they determined the area clear, they radioed the hangar guards and informed them that the rest of the island team was coming through the portal. When they received an 'all clear' signal they waved through the rest of the party.

Gnat stepped out into the darkness followed by Azrael and Jack. Kalen stepped out last and waving his hand over the portal sealed the boulder behind them. "Home sweet home, eh, Chief?" Pedro remarked.

Jack looked at the beat up old hangar and felt a sudden pang for Nadia. "Home is where the heart is, Popo."

"Copy that, Chief." The three operators slowly stood and with a final sweeping motion, fell into step and moved toward the hangar that had once been home.

"Someone approaches," Azrael stated softly, his hand holding Jack back by the shoulder.

"Good to see your ugly mug again, Phoenix." Dominic blocked out most of the security light as he stepped from the shadows. "As soon as they said you boys were coming in, I wanted to be first to welcome you back."

Jack patted Azrael's hand. "Friendly." He turned to Dom and was nearly crushed in a bear hug.

Azrael studied the large man squeezing his commander and shook his head. "He does not appear to be acting friendly."

Dom dropped Jack and stared behind him. "Whoa. Who are your friends?"

Jack sucked in air and placed a steadying hand on Dom's shoulder. "These are my…team." He pointed them out one by one. "Azrael, Gnat, and you've met Kalen."

Dom gave them a toothy grin. "*Your* team? I thought you had a team of spec op wolves?"

Jack sighed and shook his head. "Yeah,so did I." He turned back toward the hangar. "What say we get these kids settled into some kind of bunks and maybe get them fed."

"Hell yeah, we can do that." Dom slapped Azrael on the back and nearly jumped back as the gargoyle's wings fluffed under his hand. "What the?"

"He's a gargoyle. Grimlock's baby brother." Jack pulled Dom toward the hangar. "I'll fill everybody in as best I can once everybody is settled."

"Well, it's still a mess. We're trying to get shit picked up and fixed and cleaned up after we got hit and…"

"Wait. The hangar was hit, too?" Jack stopped and stared at Dominic. "The guys on the chopper didn't say anything about that."

"They probably didn't know. The first thing they hit was our coms." Dom pointed behind them to the large dishes that still had support cabling holding them in place while the concrete cured. "The chopper was dispatched just before the attack."

"How bad was it?" Jack asked. "Was anybody hurt?" Pedro, Jimmy, and Gus all moved in closer to hear Dom.

"Yeah, well…Major Tufo got tore up real bad. Doc patched him up though. We think he might make it." He sighed heavily and then turned to the three operators. "I'm sorry, guys, Bone bought it in the attack."

All three operators were struck hard. They didn't know the new SEAL that well, but he had seemed like a solid warrior and had more than pulled his own weight. Jack pulled Dom closer and stared at his eyes. "Who else? Was anybody else hurt?"

Dom nodded. "Yeah, we had quite a few hurt or killed. But those are the ones from the squads. The rest were support personnel."

"Where's Laura? Is she still…" Pedro asked, his voice nearly cracking as he asked.

"She's still out. To be honest, I don't know exactly where she is, but I think she's headed back since all this happened." Dom turned and headed toward the hangar. "Let's get you settled and we can get you caught up."

"Apollo was with the team that attacked us." Jack didn't know why he just blurted it out, but it froze Dom in his tracks. He spun on the smaller man.

"What did you just say?"

Jack nodded. "You heard me. Apollo led the wolves that attacked us on the island." Jack could see the gears turning in Dom's mind. The larger man glanced up and looked past Pedro, half way expecting Apollo to be standing behind his men and grinning at him as though it were a big joke.

"That can't be. Not Apollo…"

"He said something about Maria and me lying to him and…" Jack trailed off, shaking his head. "Sheridan put him up to it."

"Sheridan? Your old pal from Team One?"

Jack grimaced. "He's not my pal. But yeah, same asshole."

Dom stiffened and shot a glance back at the hangar. "The colonel needs to know this."

*****

Damien unloaded the meager supplies and began setting them up under Lilith's direction. He would make the smallest of adjustments according to her careful eye. He didn't know why everything needed to be just so, but he knew that if his goddess wanted it so, it would be.

Once he had everything exactly as she thought it should be, he stood to the side and watched her. She walked around the ceremonial site twice and inspected everything exactingly. Damien had painted the glyphs on the floor exactly as she stated they should be. He painstakingly placed each object where she stated they needed to be. He even located where true north was rather than trust a compass to tell him where magnetic north was. He didn't dare be off at all for her.

"Mistress, if I may ask…" His voice was dry and hoarse as he whispered his question. She continued to study the placement of each object, staring with an intensity that he couldn't comprehend. "What is the meaning of all of this?"

"You may ask." She stood and strode purposefully to the next item, studying it's placement for what seemed an inordinate amount of time.

Damien cleared his throat and stood slightly taller, "Mistress, what is the meaning of all of this?"

"I already told you. To call my Legion to me." She continued to study the placement and shook her head. "Something is *off*, but I can't tell what."

"What is your Legion, Mistress?"

Lilith stood and stepped away from the pentagram on the floor, the double layered circle around it drawn and painted with perfection. Slowly she turned to him and cocked her head slightly. "Poor little vampire. You truly have no idea, do you?"

Damien tried not to cower in her presence, but he could feel himself shaking as she stared at him. He watched with a fascinating horror as she raised her arms to him, inviting him closer. "Come to me, child."

Damien wanted nothing more than to run and hide. To put as much distance between himself and her as he possibly could, but...her call called him like a magnet pulled steel. His body moved toward her as though he no longer controlled it. He wanted to scream or cry or plea for forgiveness as her arms wrapped around him and he felt her fingers stroke his hair. "You want nothing more than to sink your fangs into me and taste true power, isn't that right, little vampire?"

Damien tried to recoil with horror. "N-no, Mistress. I would never..."

"Tsk-tsk, Damien. You and I both know that you prefer the ghoulish ways. You prefer meat in your stomach to blood." She held her arm out to him and taunted him. "Go ahead, child. Eat of my flesh."

Damien felt revulsion even as his mouth opened and he felt his lips wrap around the tender flesh of her arm. He could taste the copper of her blood as his fangs sliced into her flesh and although his mind screamed 'no' his body refused to listen as it bit deeper into her muscle and ripped a large chunk free from the bone. He could feel her warm blood running down his chin and neck as he chewed and savored the taste of his goddess.

With horrid fascination he watched as her flesh renewed itself before his very eyes, his mouth still full of her flesh and blood. He swallowed and felt...not a surge of energy from millennia of power built walking the earth, but memories. Memories of a simpler time. When mankind wore skins to cover himself and protect from the elements. When the first thoughts of civilization began to take root. When man first domesticated animals for food and beasts of burden. When plants were first cultivated...he was watching it all from her eyes. And he knew. She wasn't the first vampire...

Damien fell to the ground as his body fought the flesh now churning in his stomach. Images continued to flash across his mind and the harder he fought against them, the harder they pierced the veil of his own memories, forcing their way to the forefront and threatening to explode his eyes from their sockets.

He saw mankind as it manipulated fire. As it prayed to rocks and clouds in the sky. As it made gods of anything it didn't understand. He watched as the hairless apes slowly developed into things more akin to the food source he knew today.

Damien rolled over and got his knees under him, pushing up and trying to force the foreign flesh from his body. He gagged and hurled, lurched, and spat; but the offending flesh clung to his guts like a parasite, forcing the memories into him.

Damien saw the garden. The beauty of it astounded him. He saw the Adam through her eyes and, although it called to him, she pushed it away. She had been created from the earth itself just as the Adam had been. She was his equal and would not be subjugated. He watched as she left...hovering just outside the gates...watched as the Eve was created from the Adam's rib. He could feel her anger, her betrayal. He watched as she ran blindly into the wilderness.

Damien tried once more to expel the flesh but it refused to give up its grip on him. He gasped for air as he lay on the cold cement floor. Rolling to his side, he curled into the fetal position and surrendered to the visions.

She ran to the mountains. Her anger fueled by pain...pushing her to run further, faster. And then she saw *him*. So tall. So blindingly beautiful. His alabaster skin, soft blue eyes, yellow hair and...yes...wings. White and soft, like the wings of a dove. His skin glowed with a radiance she'd never seen. His beauty was like none other.

He was her first lover. She surrendered herself to him willingly, and he showed her things that she never knew possible. He promised her everything. She would live forever. She would rule this earth. He would give her a Legion to command. Six thousand bloodthirsty warriors…hers for the taking.

She gave herself willingly. Heart, mind, body and soul. He was her master now. Her creator was no more. She turned her back on Him entirely. She belonged entirely to Samael.

The images flashed through his mind so rapidly that Damien couldn't breathe. He tried to suck in air and he felt bloody foam forming in his throat…the images of her life, running from village to village, forced to live off the blood of people like a vampire. A *daywalking* vampire. She can walk in the light!

Rome! Rome was her undoing! She was caught! Oh, the terrible things they did to her. She prayed to him. Samael, save me! But he didn't come. The tortures they invented just for her. As she lay stretched out, naked, scarred, about to be drawn and quartered, he came. Finally. But he didn't save her. "The time is not right," he whispered. With a single kiss to her forehead, he gave her the knowledge. Now she knew how to call her Legion. Now, when it was too late. She stared up at his beautiful form, his dove like wings folded behind him as he stood over her. "Your day will come again, my love."

Darkness…

10

"You're absolutely certain it was Apollo? *Our* Apollo?" Mitchell found his chest tightening and a lump forming in his throat. He had been so preoccupied with the mission and the cleanup from the attack, then the next op immediately afterward, he had completely forgotten protocols. Namely, mustering his personnel. Then he remembered that he had granted the man leave along with the others from his team. His mind spun as he considered Jack's words and the second guessing was muddying his thoughts.

"Yes, sir,I'm absolutely certain it was him. We had a very tense…conversation." Jack studied his old commanding officer and could see the multiple emotions trying to cross his features. "He singled me out of the entire group. Blamed me for something to do with Maria?" Jack studied Mitchell who gave him a blank stare.

"You mean her death? Jack, you had nothing to do with that."

"I know that, sir." Jack sat up straighter in his chair and cleared his throat. "Sheridan got to him, sir. Got into his head. Convinced him that there was more going on with Maria and the Padre than what we thought."

"Sheridan?" Mitchell was on his feet, his eyes bulging. "That son of a bitch is supposed to be in WitSec!"

"Understood, sir, but Apollo was pretty adamant. Sheridan had a video of Maria and the Padre together and…"

Mitchell glanced down, his jaw ticking. "And?"

"And somehow Marshall knew. Apollo says he caught them or something. Anyway, Sheridan used it to get inside his head and twist him all up." Jack stood and paced to try to burn off the nervous energy. "Sherry got him so twisted up that he blamed the entire team. Convinced him to attack us at the island. A lot of good men died out there."

"Mueller?" Mitchell's eyes indicated he was asking about more than just Robert.

"Negative, sir. He and his family are safe. They stayed behind to let me know in case Rufus returns." Jack reached into his blouse and retrieved the blue notebook. "I believe this belongs to Dr. Peters."

Mitchell took the notebook and flipped through the pages absently. "So the bastard did steal it."

"And he tried to build something from there, I'm afraid." Matt's head jerked around and met Jack's gaze. "I can't say for sure that it's the Doomsday weapon that Doc told you about, but whatever it was blew up when he tried to use it. The only thing left was a smoking crater."

"Did you direct the crews from the chopper to pick through it and bring back whatever they could find?"

Jack smirked and fell back into his chair. "Of course, that was one of the first things I did. I wanted to know if there were any remains in that hole as well."

Mitchell sat back into his chair and ran a hand across his face. "So if I'm putting the pieces together correctly, Sheridan is behind the attacks. But why?"

"He may have recruited Apollo, and he may well have been behind the attacks here, but he's a merc, sir. A hired gun. He doesn't have the resources to hire a bunch of werewolves and have them put their lives on the line for money." Matt looked up and studied him at that. "Wolves fight for honor, for their pack, or because their Alpha tells them to. They don't fight for material wealth." Jack shook his head. "No, if Sheridan is behind this, he was hired to direct it, but he's not running it. Somebody more important is."

"Great. Valuable intel, but we're still no closer to knowing who's behind this." Matt stood and made his way to the door, notebook in hand. "Go check on your team. I'm going to return this to Doc. Maybe he'll finally relax a bit."

"Once he finds out that Thorn had prototypes built, he's going to need some industrial strength Xanax."

*****

After escorting Little John and his vampire sister back to base, Donovan quickly made his report then went in search of Major Tufo. He had no desire to watch any more of the drama that was the life and times of the family Sullivan. The entire command was abuzz with what happened with the XO and the rumor mill was running on overtime. He had a sneaky suspicion and needed to either put it to rest or try to help his friend in dealing with what he knew he was facing.

After discovering what room the Tufo's were tucked into, Donnie double-timed below decks and found a corpsman exiting as he approached. "How's he holding up?"

The corpsman turned and shook his head. "Cranky son of a bitch."

"I can hear you," Mark shouted from inside the room. Donnie shot the withering corpsman a smile and patted his shoulder as he passed him.

"Don't worry, he's always like that."

"And the white horse you rode in on, Donovan," Major Tufo called through the closed door.

Donnie looked to the corpsman and shrugged. "See?" he whispered. He knocked lightly on the door and stuck his head in. "Permission to enter, sir?"

"Denied! Get the hell out," Mark barked and tried to roll over. Tracy rolled her eyes and gave Donovan a look that he could only describe as 'exasperated'.

"Has he been this pleasant the whole time?" Donnie asked as he stepped into the room.

"Worse," Tracy answered as she stood and stretched her neck. "He has some periods where he's a total ass, but then his mood really sours."

Donnie gave her a reassuring smile and a gentle hug. "Why don't you go grab some coffee. Give me and Major Pain here a little bit to visit."

"My pleasure." Tracy stepped past the man and reached for the door. "You have my permission to beat him if he gets too hateful."

"Yes, ma'am." Donovan shot her a wink as she headed down the hall. He pulled the chair over and sat facing his XO. "So."

Mark turned his head slightly and opened one eye. "So? So what?"

"So, how was your day?" Donnie gave him a silly grin and Mark's face turned red.

"Are you kidding me? I had my guts ripped out by a fucking wolf and you ask me how my day was?" Donnie watched as the veins in his neck bulged.

"Feeling a bit aggravated? Depressed maybe? Ready to eat that silver bullet yet?" Donnie crossed his arms and continued to shoot him that same stupid silly grin.

"What the hell would you know about it?" Mark scooted slightly further away and turned his face toward the wall.

"Major..." Donnie sighed and ran a hand over his face. "Mark, look at me. Give me your attention for just a moment, will ya?"

"Why should I?"

"Maybe because you and I share something more than just a working relationship. Maybe because we're friends." Donnie leaned forward and lowered his voice. "Tink-tink-tink…"

Mark's eyes flew open and he snapped his head around to stare at the man. "What the hell is that supposed to mean?"

"It means I'm not ready to give you that Viking funeral just yet." Donnie stared at him intently and Mark noted the seriousness of his face.

With a sigh, the major pushed himself up, his face breaking out into a cold sweat from the pain. "Okay, Donovan, say what you have to say then get the hell out."

Donnie grunted and leaned back in his chair. "What you're going through isn't unusual, but it will pass." He spoke slowly and softly, his eyes focused on a spot far, far away. "Others…other survivors, they've all reported the same thing. As the infection spreads through them, their first and only thoughts are how to get rid of it. Even if it means killing themselves." He finally turned and looked at Mark who seemed to be hanging on his every word now. "Slowly, they come around and realize that it's not a death sentence. Some may still consider it a curse, but it's a manageable one."

"How the hell would you know? You were a test tube conversion." He didn't try to hide the bitterness in his voice.

"True. But there are a lot of others who weren't. And I took the time to talk with them." He leaned in again and stared at the man. "Just like I took the time to figure out how to deal with certain woodland Sprites."

"You keep that shit to yourself, you hear me?" Mark shot a furtive glance to the door then pointed a finger back at Donovan. "Not a word, you understand?"

"I have no idea what you're talking about, Major. What happens in the field stays in the field." Donovan sat back and stared at him again. "But you need to understand that this anger and bitterness and…well, all of it. It's part of the transition. Not to mention a bit of survivor's guilt tossed in, I'm sure."

"Pfft. Listen to Doctor Phil, here."

"Just experience talking." Donnie stood and pushed the chair back. "But I wanted to toss something out for you to think about before I left."

"What's that?" Mark spat.

"You *just* got infected. You *know* what infected you. It hasn't been a full moon yet." Donnie leaned against the door and watched him, waiting for the lightbulb to come on over his head.

"So? BFD, bub. I guess you're going to tell me that, since I know what it was, I can make proper arrangements and all will be right with the world, huh? I can keep my family safe if I lock myself up downstairs in the silver cells and howl at the moon every month?"

Donnie shook his head as he watched his XO bark at him. "Negative." He turned and opened the door. "But we both happen to know an organization that has these little black pills you can take that might very well keep the whole thing at bay." He saw that bulb light up and fought the smile curving the edges of his mouth. "Seeing as how you just got infected, it might be a good time to see about getting a big supply of those pills. Don'tcha think?"

*****

Little John escorted Brooke deep into the hangar and below decks, security personnel on either side as they walked. "Are they necessary? I came of my own volition."

"Sorry, sis. Rules," John mumbled. He pointed to a door at the end of the hall where another security guard stood. The man opened the door and John escorted her inside the bare room. A lone table with two chairs sat in the middle.

Brooke looked around the room before sitting in the chair opposite the two way mirror. "An interrogation room?" She crossed her arms over her chest and sat stiffly, her face straight ahead.

"I'm sorry," John whispered. "It's all just a precaution." Brooke sat stonily opposite him and stared at the mirror facing her. As John milled about she caught herself stealing a furtive glance at him and catching the similarities between him and their father. She almost felt a pang of regret as memories flooded her mind; memories of a simpler time when her biggest worry was maintaining her GPA.

The steel door flew open and Colonel Mitchell stepped inside with Jack in tow. Little John stiffened slightly and Brooke noticed immediately his change in body language. "Colonel?" John motioned toward Jack, his eyes narrowed.

"John Sullivan, Jack Thompson." Mitchell had a folder in his hands, his face buried in it.

Jack reached out a hand and accepted John's. He tried not to let it show how unnerved he was at meeting somebody even larger than Apollo in such tight quarters. "I'm here as a courtesy to the Colonel."

"And your purpose here?" John's curiosity piqued as Jack did a double take at the question.

"Evaluator." Jack held the door open for John who stared at him blankly. "We'll need a few minutes alone with her, thank you."

Mitchell didn't look up from his papers when he stated, "Sullivan, don't you have a weapon to check in and a preliminary report to file?"

Little John stiffened, the veins in his neck bulging as he stepped toward the open door. "Yes, sir."

"We'll inform you of our findings," Jack said, his face unreadable. He let the door pull shut behind John then turned and took a seat at the table. "I can see the resemblance."

Brooke turned cold eyes to him. "It's the facial hair, isn't it?"

Mitchell glanced up from the file and fought a smile. "I think she likes you, Jack."

"Don't they all, Colonel." Jack continued to study the young woman, his face stoic. "What's your story?"

"I'm a vampire." Brooke stared at him, her dark eyes unblinking. Jack waited for her to continue but she apparently thought those three words were enough.

"And I'm a werewolf. That isn't the whole story."

"It should be enough." She tilted her head slightly and studied him. "You weren't always a wolf, were you?"

Jack shook his head. "You weren't always a vampire. I guess we have something in common."

A light knock at the door raised Mitchell's head and he stood to answer it while Jack continued to play the game with the young woman. He opened the door to find a rather anxious Elf standing on the other side trying to peer over the man's shoulder. "I must speak to Chief Jack."

"He's a little busy at the moment." Mitchell tried to pull the door shut when Kalen shoved his foot into the way, blocking the door.

"I must speak with him. It is most important."

"Unless we're under attack again, it can wait." Mitchell lowered his voice and glared at the young Elf. "Trust me, now is not the time."

Kalen lowered his own voice and pointed over Mitchell's shoulder. "If that is the female vampire slayer that he is speaking to, there is something he must know!"

Jack's ears picked up the entire conversation and he assumed that their guest did as well. He stood from his chair and turned to the door. "I got this, sir." He pushed past the colonel and stepped into the hallway. "What is it, Kalen? I'm in the middle of something."

"The Wyldwood, she has sent word." Kalen's face appeared ashen. "The young woman inside?"

Jack felt a knot in his stomach at the mention of the Wyldwood and more than just a touch of anger that she didn't come directly to him with information that was supposedly so damned important. "What about her?"

"She is one of the two we are to expect. She is the missing warrior."

*****

"But when? The full moon is just tomorrow." Mick stared wide-eyed at the two women. "You will need some place to shift."

"What about you?" Laura gave him a sideways look.

"I'm a cat. We aren't controlled by the moon." Mick waved her off.

"So, what? Litterboxes?" Laura's attempt at humor was not well received.

"Werecats shift at will. Nothing controls them." Jennifer stood and paced. "Much like other cats, they are aloof and are not easily controlled. Werecats are the same."

"Thanks. I think." Mick studied her with curiosity. "Why the sudden rush to get there?"

Laura noted a change in Mick's voice but she couldn't place a finger on what exactly that change was. He seemed almost apprehensive about them returning to the states. "I need to return to work and Jennifer would like to get this meeting out of the way. See if…I dunno. If maybe the chemistry is right?" She shrugged.

"I don't know what will happen." Jennifer plopped onto the bed and avoided both of their gazes. "I just need to do this."

"But do you need to do it now?" Mick asked.

"Why?" Laura stepped closer, her arms crossing her chest. "Is there a reason why maybe she shouldn't?"

"What?" Mick suddenly turned and gave her a blank stare. "Why would you say that?"

"Why would you try to stop her from returning there?" Laura turned to Jennifer, who was staring at both of them, her face twisted in confusion. "It's almost like you know something that we don't know, Mick."

Mick shook his head, almost too much at first. "No, not at all. I don't know anything." His mouth suddenly went dry and he licked at his lips. "I just...that's an awfully long flight for a light craft and..."

"And Mitchell authorized commercial flights." Laura cocked her head to the side. "But you didn't bat an eye at flying us here."

"Well, heh-heh...that's really just a hop and a skip compared to..." He cleared his throat and reached for the water pitcher.

"Mick?" Jennifer reached for his hand and he quickly pulled away. "What is it? You're not acting yourself."

Mick's hand shook as he poured a quick glass of water and drank it. He looked down at the ground, shaking his head. "You don't understand. I was just trying to protect you, that's all."

"What did you do?" Jennifer asked as she moved closer to him.

"I was just trying to keep you safe."

"Spill it, Mick." Laura took a step closer, effectively cornering him in his own room. She knew that should he get aggressive, she couldn't stop him from hurting her, but she hedged her bets that he wouldn't try anything with Jennifer there.

Mick took an instinctive step backward, his eyes glued to the floor. "It was just to keep you safe, Jen. That's all."

"Tell me, Mick." She reached for his hand, and he jumped at her touch. "Mick?" Her eyes pleaded with him as her voice tried to sooth his rattled nerves.

"Your father..."

"Oh, great," Laura moaned.

"My father? What does he have to do with anything?" Jennifer edged closer, and Mick continued to shake his head. "Tell me, please."

"He just wanted to keep you far away from there. To keep you safe, that's all. I promised him I'd fight tooth and nail to keep you safe, too. He knew I would. He knew…"

"What happened? Mick, you're starting to frighten me." Jennifer edged closer until she was right beside him. "You have to tell me."

"He sent his people to attack the hunters. They're not done. They won't stop. They'll never stop until they're all gone." Mick finally raised his eyes to meet hers. "He said to keep you away from there at all costs. To keep you safe. He said that he'd hunt me down to the ends of the earth if I let you anywhere near there…"

"Ohm my God." Jennifer's face paled and she turned to Laura.

"Your father was behind the attack on the squads." Laura turned and opened the door to Mick's door.

"Where are you going?" Jennifer's hands shook as she saw the determination set in Laura's eyes.

"I have to call Matt. He needs to know."

*****

Apollo finished his inventory of the supplies and noted the discrepancies. They were short too much material for it to be considered acceptable losses. Either somebody was skimming and cooking the books or somebody wasn't supplying what was being ordered.

He tucked the inventory under his arm and marched into the office he shared with Sheridan. "You're short."

"No, you're simply very tall," Sheridan joked, spinning in his chair to face the large ebony skinned man. "Oh. I see you weren't making a joke about my height."

Apollo threw the inventory down on the workbench in front of Sheridan. "Tell me you ain't skimming."

Sheridan sighed and pushed the inventory away. "I already told you, due to the overwhelming amount that we needed, I had to go through numerous suppliers. Not everything has been delivered yet."

"This is what we're supposed to have. That's what we *don't* have. Somebody has been skimming to the tune of about thirty percent." Apollo straddled the chair across from Sheridan. "That's a pretty good amount. It could mean the difference in winning and losing."

Sheridan shook his head. "There's more coming, trust me. When the time comes, we'll have more than enough supplies."

"What you doin' with all the extra?" He narrowed his gaze at him. "You pocketing the money, or you storing up your own little armory?"

Sheridan fought back the urge to scream. "I already explained to you—"

"No. You already tried to lie to me." Apollo stood and raised a brow at him. "Now, you about to tell me the truth. Or me and you are gonna have some serious issues."

Sheridan lowered his eyes and stared at a spot under the workbench. He contemplated maintaining the lie and hoping that Apollo would believe it. He contemplated making up a new lie. He even thought about letting him on the truth.

He opted for the latter.

"I'm building my own little cache of weaponry."

"Now why the hell you wanna go and do that?" Apollo moved forward and took his seat again.

Sheridan shook his head. "You wouldn't understand."

"Try me." He glared at the man. "I ain't going nowhere, and I ain't got nothing but time."

Sheridan inhaled deeply and let it out slowly. "Call it an insurance policy."

"For what?"

"In case this mission goes south." Sheridan looked up and met his gaze. "I'll need a way to defend myself while I beat a hasty retreat, and I'll probably need a way to defend my position once I get there. I'll need start up weaponry to start my own little…"

"What? What you gonna start?"

"A mercenary-for-hire contractor can't very well expect all of his clients to provide the weaponry, now can he?" Sheridan crossed his arms and gave him a stony stare. "One can't be expected to be taken seriously if you don't have the arsenal behind you."

"So, you going freelance once this is done?" Apollo found his story only a smidge above total bullshit.

"That's the plan. And I was hoping you'd come along as well." Sheridan raised a brow at him. "You and I both know that, as much as I adore Big, the man doesn't have the skillset you do. I'm in no shape to fight like I used to."

"So you thought you'd hijack a ton of weapons then sweet talk me into being the hired muscle." Apollo shook his head at him.

"Nothing quite that simple, but if you must boil it down to bangers and mash…yes."

Apollo stood and headed for the door. "If that's a job offer, I'll consider it." He paused then turned back to Sheridan. "But you better get a helluva lot better at cooking books if you hope to get shit like this past the folks financing this cluster fuck."

*****

Rufus waited while Paul went through the enforcers man by man and hand chose the group to accompany them to Geneva. Once the group was chosen, he walked through them and gave them the once over. Even though their power was strong, their abilities unrivaled, he knew that they were walking into the belly of the beast. Literally. Their powers would be minimal compared to the central guards of the council. They would be centuries older, their strength unparalleled, and their abilities untold.

Rufus dismissed them to their meals and retreated to the office, all the while knowing that their only hope still was with an attempt at diplomacy. He contemplated the many ways that the trip could go wrong and feared that should such a thing happen, all of the good he had tried to do in his life would be for naught.

A light knock at the office door caught his attention and an enforcer dragged a young woman through to him. "You need your strength, master." He offered her to Rufus and felt his fangs descend before she came within his grasp.

He pulled her close to him and saw the terror in her eyes, yet she made no sound. He opened his mouth and drew her neck closer to him when he felt the unmistakable ebb of power emanate from her. He knew at that moment why she did not scream. She had been manipulated. Entranced. Hypnotized.

He pulled back and stared at her. Her shivering body, her wide eyes, the snot running from her nose as she quivered in place. She could not run. She could not resist. She could not scream. She knew what was about to happen to her, but she couldn't do anything about it. He placed her gently in his lap and stared at her as she tried not to cry.

"You know why you are here, *oui*?" She shook her head. "You did not volunteer yourself to nourish us?" Her eyes widened even more and she shook her head again. "You were about to be eaten alive. You knew this, *oui*?" Her eyes rolled back in her head as she tried to pass out, but he patted her face awake again.

"Speak to me, child," Rufus commanded. "What is your name?"

She mumbled something, but the words were unintelligible. It was as if her mouth had been numbed. Rufus stood and dumped her to the floor, his anger rising.

He threw open the door and found Paul leaning against the doorjamb, licking blood from his fingers. "That last one was a bit too lean." He pushed his way into the office and saw the young girl cowering in the corner. "That one should just about top me off. You done with her?"

"She did not volunteer herself." His voice shook with anger as he pointed at the girl on the floor.

Paul paused and stared at him wide eyed. "Huh? She…didn't? You sure about that? Because I'm pretty sure that they all knew what they were getting themselves into."

"Did they?" Rufus' voice was barely a whisper, but the anger screamed loud and clear. "Truly?"

Paul withered slightly and gave his brother a weak smile. "Well, I'm almost positive they did." He shrugged. "What difference does it make? I mean, hey…look at you. You're back, right? You're vampire again. You're strong, healthy, and robust."

"And about to face the council as the head of the *Lamia Beastia* and beg them to overturn the edict. They will know that I am no longer Beastia." He closed his eyes and shook with rage. "It would have been better had you let me die."

"No!" Paul grabbed him by his shoulders and spun him around, away from the cowering figure on the floor. "You have a destiny, remember? You are going to face the council and you are going to convince them that you are the man to take down Lilith. Because we have an in with her maker."

Rufus' eyes settled on Paul and he shook his head. "*Non*. Not her maker. Her reanimator, perhaps, but not her maker."

"Semantics. You know what I mean." Paul led his brother to the door of the office and pointed out toward all of the enforcer vampires scattered about the warehouse. "You have an army at your disposal. Not a huge one, true, but an effective one. A very strong one. More than capable of taking out Damien and some big-tittied bitch that he's dragging around with him."

"You over-simplify things once again."

"And you're over complicating things." Paul dragged him out of the office and into the warehouse. "If you want to load up on sheep blood and ox bile and whatever your heart wants, just let these guys know and they'll make it happen. Hell, they'll hit the closest butcher shop and drain every last drop from whatever there is. But don't you dare start second guessing your mission. You have a destiny."

Rufus nodded and stepped into the crowd of gathering vampires. "My friends, we have one more errand this night. I require the blood of…" Paul stepped back toward the office while his brother went into 'leader' mode. He gently shut the door behind him and turned on the young girl still cowering in the corner.

"As for you…" He flicked his fangs down into attack position.

11

Tracy pushed open the door to Mark's room and froze. He sat on the edge of the bed staring at the IV stuck in his arm, his finger absently picking at the tape holding it in place. "What the hell are you doing Tufo?" Her voice betrayed the anger she felt but didn't waver as she pushed her way into the room.

"I was sick of lying down." Mark continued to pick at the tape and refused to make eye contact.

"I don't care if you—"

"Trace." Mark stood up and held his arms out to the side. "I'm nearly healed."

The color drained from her face and she nearly fell into her chair, the coffees she held threatening to spill. "That can't be." Her voice was little more than a whisper as she stared at him.

He reached a tentative hand up and peeled the tape from the multiple layers of gauze and folded back an edge. Although the dressing was soaked with brown stains of dried blood, his skin held bright pink scars, the stitches having been pushed from his body. "I know it can't be, but look." He pulled back more of the thick padded gauze and showed her more of the wounds. "They're all like that."

Tracy stood and stepped closer, inspecting his wounds. "Well, everywhere except where we touched you with silver." She reached out and gently pressed a finger to that area of the wound.

Mark grimaced and pulled away from her. "Damn, I had no idea that…" He turned from her and faced the mirror, leaning to his left so that he could see the wound more clearly.

"Mark, what's going on? Even infected, you shouldn't have healed this quickly." Tracy's voice wavered behind him, her eyes straining to see what he was staring at.

His fingers probed at the pink scars and traced the long crisscrossing slashes that ran from his chest to his navel. "I honestly have no idea, honey." He glanced up in the mirror and she noted the fear in his eyes and could only imagine it matched the fear that reflected in her own. "Shortly after Donovan left…I just felt…" He shrugged and shot her a crooked smile. "Better."

"What did he say?" She was on her feet now, standing behind him, her hands gently squeezing his shoulders.

"He reminded me that nobody knows wolves more than we do. And that we have medication that can prevent the virus from manifesting." He met her gaze again and noted the happy tears running down her cheeks. "And he informed me that all of the stuff I've been feeling is normal."

Her eyes widened as she realized what he meant. "So…no more talk of shooting yourself?"

He shook his head slowly. "I guess it isn't the end of the world." He turned his attention back to the mirror. "But this still isn't right."

"So what do you do now?"

Mark blew out a nervous breath and shook his head. "First things first. I need to get on the bane before the full moon." He turned and faced her, pulling her into a tight embrace. "The full moon is right around the corner. I honestly don't know if I'd change that fast or not, but I'd rather not chance it."

She nodded and guided him back to the bed. "I'll talk to the doctor and get the pills for you. For now, do me a favor and lay back down. I know you may be feeling better, but I'd be happier if you'd shut up and listen this time."

Mark nodded and kissed the top of her head. "Yes, boss."

*****

"What do you mean you *need* her?" Mitchell shot Jack a withering stare but Jack stood his ground.

"Exactly that, Colonel. She's supposed to be part of a new group that I'm supposed to lead. At least, according to the Wyldwood and her soothsayers." Jack glanced back through the narrow glass in the door and watched the young woman scrape at her thumbnail with another finger nail. "I still don't have all the facts or even the 'why', but according to Loren, this group that I brought in will be key in stopping something big."

Mitchell leaned against the wall and ran a hand across the back of his neck. "I swear, between you and your favors and all of these mystic visions people keep having of the end of the world, I just don't know how much more of this I can take."

"I didn't have the vision, sir. Maybe if I did, I'd have a better understanding of what the heck was going on." Jack shot a glance over Mitchell's shoulder to where Kalen stood, his shoulders slumped. "Seems like she doesn't tell anybody the whole story these days."

"But we're supposed to throw protocol out the window and do what she wants because…" Mitchell shrugged. "Help me out here, Jack. I've got nothing."

"Because she's the Wyldwood?" He had no other answer.

"Because, without the Wyldwood, you wouldn't have had the assistance of the *others* in your battle against the vampires in the desert." Kalen suddenly seemed more sure of himself. "Without her, the other clans and tribes would have turned their collective backs on you. It was she who convinced them that the anywhere would be threatened if they didn't assist."

Jack turned to Mitchell and nodded. "There ya go. Sounds like as good an answer as I'd ever come up with."

Mitchell groaned and opened the door to the interrogation room. "She's all yours, Chief."

Brooke looked up expectantly as Jack walked back into the room. He sat down across from her and reached for her cuffed hands. Withdrawing a key from his breast pocket, he unlocked the handcuffs and slid them across the table.

Brooke raised a brow at him. "A bit trusting aren't we?"

Jack leaned back in his chair and studied the young woman. "Looks like me and you may have a future."

"You're not my type." She smirked at him.

Jack smirked back. "And I'm married." He pulled the folder over and opened it again. "That's not exactly what I meant."

Brooke tried to see what was in the folder but Jack held it up too high. "What is that?"

Jack glanced at her then dropped the folder on the table. "Everything we could dig up on you prior to your abduction."

"It's pretty thin."

Jack nodded. "Apparently you were a very boring person."

Brooke bristled and leaned back in her chair. "You aren't winning me over."

Jack slid the folder across to her and let her go through it. "I'm not trying to win you over." Jack stood and gripped the back of his chair. "But I am recruiting you."

Brooke's eyes shot upward at him. "Come again?"

"You heard me. You're about to join my merry band of misfits."

"You didn't say please."

"Because it wasn't a request." Jack turned toward the mirror and waved at somebody. "Kalen. In here."

Brooke sat stoically as the door slowly opened and Kalen slipped inside. He shut the door behind him and turned to Jack. Brooke continued to stare away from the pair but after just a moment, she sniffed at the air and turned her attention fully to the light haired warrior standing just feet away.

"You called me, Chief Jack?" Kalen tried to ignore the young woman sitting behind the table and focused his attention on Jack.

"I want you to contact Loren again and get me some freakin' details on…" Jack turned and stared at Brooke who had silently slipped from her chair and now stood behind Kalen, inhaling deeply. "Are you okay?"

"You smell like fresh baked sugar cookies." Her voice was whispered and heady, her eyes closed as she inhaled Kalen's scent.

Kalen shuddered and turned to face her. "Because I am Elf. My blood calls to you."

Brooke shook her head as if clearing it from a dream. "What's that? An Elf?"

"Yes, a Northern Greater Elf." Kalen squared his shoulders and glared at her.

Brooke stepped back and bounced her gaze from Jack to Kalen and back to Jack. "I suppose that's supposed to mean something to me, isn't it?" She stepped back further and leaned against the table. "Sorry. I don't know any Elves. You'd be the first one I ever met." She allowed herself to take in this tall, tan, light haired young man with the pointed ears and deep blue eyes. She fought to not react physically to him as she allowed her eyes to drink in all that was him. She cleared her throat and moved back to the far side of the table. "Sorry about the whole sugar cookie thing."

Kalen nodded to her slightly then turned back to Jack. "I do not know if Loren will speak with me. You know how she can be when it comes to receiving an audience."

"Then keep trying. Leave voicemails. Text her. Whatever you have to do. I need answers." Kalen nodded, still unsure what exactly Jack had told him. He turned for the door when Jack added, "And find out all that you can on this last member we're supposed to be getting. I hate surprises."

*****

Laura waited patiently for Mitchell to answer the phone then with a surge of nervous anxiety hung up and called the central number to have him paged. When he finally picked up she let out a breath and closed her eyes. "Mitchell." His voice sounded so familiar yet it felt like it had been ages since she had actually seen him.

"Colonel! Thank goodness." Laura inhaled to hit him with all that she had learned, but was interrupted.

"Laura! I was becoming worried about you. With everything going on here, I was really—"

"Sir! I have some intel that I think you need." She paused a moment to allow him to shift gears and realize that this wasn't a social call or a simple check in.

"Go ahead, Laura,I'm all ears."

"Sir, I have a lead on who it was that attacked the base. It was Jennifer's father, a Walter Simmons. I don't have a lot of information on the man himself other than he's not the soft and cuddly type."

"Simmons?" Mitchell leaned back in his chair and shook his head, trying to take it all in. "How in the…why would he…are you sure about this?"

"Positively, sir. The pilot who flew us here informed us that he was directed by her father to keep her away from Tinker. That this wasn't over."

Mitchell felt the color drain from his face and suddenly felt that the increased guards weren't enough. "How are you doing Laura? Is this pilot a threat?"

"Negative, sir. In fact…" She paused and glanced down the hallway to ensure that neither Mick nor Jennifer were within earshot. "I'd bet good money that he's in love with your Fated one."

"You don't say?" Mitchell leaned forward, his wolf screaming to be released.

"Yes, sir. He's not a wolf...he's a cat. But he's got what I would call real feelings for her." Laura leaned against the duty desk and listened to him breathe through the phone.

"What would you suggest, XO?" Laura bristled at the title and prayed that Tufo would make a speedy recovery. Then she felt guilty for having thought it.

"Part of me thinks that ditching him here would be best, but another part of me thinks that he may have more Intel on Simmons." She shrugged as she gripped the phone tighter. "Honestly, sir, it's your call."

Mitchell exhaled hard into the phone and rubbed at the bridge of his nose. "Drag him here. Kicking and screaming if you have to. If nothing else, we can hang his carcass outside and send a message to Simmons' men."

Laura nodded even though she wasn't entirely good with the decision. "Very well, sir. The full moon should be tonight. After that, we'll be headed toward you."

"Have you figured out a place for Jennifer to shift?"

Laura stared out the window of the duty office and shook her head. "Negative, sir, but we will figure something out."

"Call me if you need me. Mitchell out."

Laura hung up the phone and for the first time since discovering who was behind the attacks, felt like she had betrayed a friend. She glanced down the hallway again toward Jennifer's room and wondered why she felt such a thing.

*****

Matt hung up the phone and stared at the receiver. He could feel the nagging pull of the full moon, but unlike the past, it was more like a tickle in the back of his mind...a reminder that he needed to be cautious. And soon.

A soft knock at the door pulled his attention from his wandering thoughts and he barked a quick, "Come."

Captain Jones stuck his head in and looked about the colonel's office. "Busy, sir?"

"No more than any other time, Jericho. Come on in."

Jericho Jones entered and quietly shut the door. He handed Mitchell a list of names. "Our dead, sir." He stood at attention while Mitchell scanned the names. "Some of the men would like to have some kind of memorial service."

Mitchell glanced up at him, surprise painting his features. "After what we've been through? You do realize we could be attacked again at any time. This isn't the time to drop our guard, Captain."

"Understood, sir. But a lot of the men…" He averted his eyes, unsure how to broach the subject.

"Spill it, Captain. I don't have all day."

Jericho cleared his throat and decided to toss it out. Perhaps he could pick through the pieces and make it all make sense once it was laid out on the floor. "Sir, they never got the chance to mourn First Squad when they were lost. Now a lot of their coworkers were killed. Security forces worked side by side with a lot of the techs. Even the new guy, Carbone, was pretty well liked. The men just want a chance to do something to give them closure."

Mitchell inhaled deeply and stared at the list again. "I guess it wouldn't hurt to do a little something. Maybe throw something together to honor those who fell." He handed Jericho the list back and gave him a solemn nod. "Make it happen. Keep me informed."

"Thank you, Colonel." Jericho turned to leave when Mitchell cleared his throat, grabbing the man's attention again.

"Captain, keep something in mind as you put this together." Mitchell's eyes indicated the seriousness of what he was about to say. "I was serious when I said that we could be attacked at any moment. However you set this up, keep that first and foremost in your mind. Don't do this any place that could put our people at any further risk. Don't let them get isolated or sealed in. Don't—"

"Understood, sir," Jericho interrupted. "We'll keep it brief."

"I don't mean to take away from what you're trying to do, Captain. Hell, I understand and appreciate it." Mitchell stood slowly and approached the man. "I'm just not ready to lose anybody else."

Jericho nodded as he reached for the door. "Understood, sir."

Colonel Mitchell watched the young officer leave and contemplated everything that had occurred over the past few days. Losing Apollo to a twisted psycho. Having the squads attacked on their home turf. The loss of a squad member and numerous support personnel. Jack returning with a handful of 'others'. Sullivan's sister showing up out of the blue and being a friggin' vampire for shit sake.

Mitchell turned and instinctively reached for the bottle of scotch he had kept hidden before realizing he had volunteered it for Mark's surgery. He fell into his chair as the realization of how close he had come to losing his best friend hit home. He watched his hands shake as he reached for the coffee pot. *Just what I need. More caffeine.*

*****

Paul Foster sat back in the overstuffed leather seat of Rufus' jet. He swirled the mixed animal blood in the large snifter and inhaled deeply. It still surprised him that it could smell and taste so similar to human blood. He just had to remind himself to *sip it* and not gulp.

Foster lifted his eyes and watched as Rufus sat back, eyes closed in the chair opposite him. "Tired?"

"*Non.*" Rufus barely moved as the plane shot through the air and crossed the Atlantic.

"Afraid of flying then?"

Rufus actually snorted a quick laugh and shook his head. "Thinking." He opened his eyes and seemed to study his brother a moment. "If the meeting with the Council were not already set, I believe I would not attempt this now."

"Bad timing?" Foster sat forward, his voice low and conspiratorial. "Afraid that this ordeal with the human hunters has cast a shadow of bad luck on your endeavors?"

Rufus exhaled hard and shrugged. "*Oui un non.* The timing is right, your Damien has seen to that. This is our best chance to convince the Council that they need us alive more than dead." He turned and stared out the window at the dark waters crossing below. "But I also think that perhaps having my Second turn against me at such a critical time…"

"*I* am your Second now, brother." Paul sat upright and squared his shoulders. "Or did you intend for my position to only be temporary until you could get your dog back under your control?" The venom in his voice did not go unnoticed.

Rufus shook his head, a pained smile crossing his features. "Your standing as my Second is not in question, brother. I fear that my judgment may be questioned though since I appointed Jack to that position only to have him turn on me."

Paul nodded as he sat back. "Your point is conceded. But I don't think you have anything to worry about. At least, not with your own people."

"It is the Council I worry about."

"They needn't know." Paul set the snifter of blood aside and crossed his legs. "All they need to know is that you appointed me as your new Second. If they are so rude as to inquire why, simply remind them that blood is thicker than…well…Milkbones." He chuckled at his own joke.

Rufus gave him a wan smile and turned back to the window. "What are the odds, dear brother?"

"Odds of what?" Paul picked up his snifter again and took a small sip.

"That Monsieur Thompson will be waiting for us in Geneva?" He turned slowly and watched Foster pale as the realization sunk in. "He does know my plans. He knows how important this meeting is. He knows that regardless of anything else that may or may not be happening, I would need to attend this meeting. If I were a betting man, I would assume that he would be there waiting for us."

Paul swallowed hard and shook his head. "We brought security. We should be…I mean…" He turned a worried look to Rufus.

Rufus nodded. "*Exactement*."

*****

Apollo slept fitfully in the small bed. Images of Maria and the Padre continuously replayed through his mind and he ground his teeth as he tossed his blanket to the floor. Sweat formed on his brow and he gripped the metal edges of the cot as he fought the urge to scream. He could see her wrapping her arms around the other man then lean in to kiss him and Apollo wanted to shoot them both for the betrayal. He saw Marshall in his dream, sneaking about, watching the two as they stripped down and danced the dance of lovers.

Apollo sat up in the small bed with a start, his mind racing as he stared into the darkness, his mind attempting to gather its bearings. He forced himself to slow his breathing and swung his legs off the edge of the bed. His throat was dry and he needed to walk off some of this nervous energy.

He went to the water cooler and swallowed three large cups of the chilled liquid, feeling some of the nervousness slip as he rehydrated. He leaned against the wall and shook his head. "Get a grip, man. Get a grip."

He pushed off the wall and stepped out of the makeshift barracks. Seeing a light on in the office that he shared with Sheridan, he made his way towards the structure. As he got closer, he could hear Sheridan talking, but he couldn't quite make out what he was saying. He was purposely keeping his voice low, and Apollo immediately became suspicious. He crept along the outer wall and approached the door of the office, his ears straining to listen.

"So he didn't actually give you an answer?" Bigby asked.

"Not in so many words, mate, but I'd bet Aunt Molly's knickers he's in." Sheridan sounded extremely sure of himself. "A man like Apollo doesn't have many options once you've removed him from the squads. What's he going to do, serve hamburgers and chips at a local fast food drive in?" The two laughed and Apollo felt his hackles rise.

"Well, let's say that he takes you up on your offer. What will we do with him?"

Apollo shifted slightly and could see Sheridan sitting in his favorite swivel chair. "I told him he'd be a full partner."

"Hey now,I'm not keen on splitting the profit three ways." Bigby sounded angry and Apollo didn't blame him.

"Who said he'd be an even partner?" Sheridan laughed. "No, my friend,Apollo is a fine warrior, but he isn't exactly someone you want to stick into a suit and have represent your company, now is he?"

"The same could be said for me, mate."

"That's why *you're* a silent partner." Sheridan swiveled his chair and tossed something to Bigby. "This is where I've got our goods stored. Tomorrow I want you to go by and secure the location."

"What will you be doing?"

"I'll be here doing what I do best,keeping the men in line and keeping Mr. Williams distracted. And, hopefully, setting up our next operation."

Bigby sighed and hopped off the chair, his feet making a thud when he hit the floor. "Fine,I'll secure the gear. You just make sure the next gig we get is less threatening and pays better."

"Don't you worry, mate," Sheridan assured. "Any life threatening activities we'll leave for our friend Mr. Williams."

Apollo slipped away from the office and worked his way back to the barracks. As he got back into his cot, he caught the door opening with his peripheral vision and watched as Bigby worked his way through the other beds and fall into his own cot.

Apollo lay awake and stared at the ceiling. Besides having been manipulated, now he was being played. *I think it's time Sheridan had a fatal accident.*

*****

Little John paced the lounge, practically wearing a hole in the flooring. Spalding approached him and placed a hand on his shoulder. "What's the deal?"

John looked down at the man and the tension on his face nearly made Spalding take a step back. "They've been in there for too long."

"Who and what? Slow down and take it from the beginning."

John took a deep, cleansing breath then did his best to tell Spalding the entire story of how he had been ordered to take Brooke to the interrogation room and then a fellow he had never met before came in and took over. Once Spalding heard the name, he broke into a slow and deliberate smile. He held up a hand to stop the larger man and tried to calm him. "Look, John…Jack's good people. If he's in there with her, then you can take a deep breath and relax. I've known the man forever and he's…well…"

"Well, what?" John looked like he was about to blow a gasket.

"I'd trust him with my life." Spalding shrugged. "He's a four-oh, squared away kind of guy. He doesn't have any kind of axe to grind."

"But what if he hates vampires or what if he…"

"He works for a vampire." Spalding interrupted. John paused and stared at him wide-eyed. "Yeah, I know. Pretty tough one to swallow, but yeah. He left here, got married, moved off and took a job working for a vampire. One of those *Beastia* guys I told you about. So, if anybody knows vamps, it's Jack."

John gave Spalding a disbelieving look and shook his head. "I still don't like it."

Darren smiled and pulled the larger man over to the couch. "Sit down, relax. Take a load off and try to trust me. If anybody can reach her, it's Jack."

John slumped into the couch and stared at the door. "I still don't like it."

"I'm sure she won't either." Spalding grinned at him.

*****

Damien slowly picked himself up from the floor. His head spun as he tried to get his bearings and his arms felt weak as he propped himself up and slowly looked around. The candles lay in melted puddles near where he had placed them and the windows of the warehouse had been blown out. Something violent had taken place and he missed the show.

Slowly, he rolled to his side and looked about. The tub of blood was laid over, its contents congealing on the cold concrete floor, the edges drying into a reddish brown mess. He leaned against a concrete support column and rubbed at his neck while his body tried to heal, his eyes taking in all of the damage to the building.

"You survived."

He spun and looked for the source of the voice and wished he hadn't been so quick. His head spun and his breathing was labored as he searched her out. "Barely, it feels like." He stepped from the column and into the brighter fluorescent overhead lighting. "What happened?"

Lilith stepped from the shadows and his eyes drank her in as she moved like liquid silk across the floor. Her movements reminded him of a large cat stalking prey. "The spell is complete."

"Spell?" He gave her a quizzical look then his damaged mind remembered. "Oh, yeah. Your legion…"

"They have arrived." Her smile disarmed him and he felt a newfound fear form in the pit of his stomach.

"W-where…are they?" He heard his voice crack as he spoke and knew he sounded weak. He tried clearing his throat. A feeble attempt at covering up his lack of strength.

"They are procuring bodies as we speak." She stopped just out of reach and eyed him. "They will be here soon."

"Bodies?"

Lilith laughed a deep and hearty laugh, her voice reminding him more and more of a dangerous predator. "They are demons, child. They need vessels to do my bidding here in this plane."

"Ah." Damien nodded as though he truly understood. He glanced about the warehouse again and shook his head. "Will they be, uh, staying here?"

"They will stay where they like. They will answer to my call as needed." She turned and began to walk away.

"And how exactly will that work?" He held his ribs as he fell into step behind her.

"They are warriors. They serve me. When they are needed, they shall come." She turned and gave him a cold, narrow gaze. "It has been ordained."

"I understand, my Mistress." He bowed slightly, his ribs protesting. "But, who exactly are they? What purpose will they serve?"

She paused and turned back to him, her eyes glimmering with mischief. "They are my demon legion. The most vile souls to have ever walked this Earth were condemned to eternity in Hell. And Samael gifted them to me. To serve me. To return me to my rightful place as ruler of this planet."

"Your legion was once…men?" He swallowed hard.

"They were once truly a legion of warriors. A Roman legion. The Fifth Macedonia. The things they did in Potaissa…" She smiled as her voice trailed off, her memories taking her back.

Damien shivered at the possibilities. "And once they find vessels?"

She waved him off and continued on her way. "They will wait for me to call them to service."

He fell into step behind her and quickly caught up. "How soon, Mistress? How soon before you make your move?"

She stepped into the offices and turned to shut the doors on him. "When I am ready. There is much I need to discover first."

Damien stood outside the office and stared at his reflection in the dusty glass of the door. She scared him. Well and truly frightened him to his core.

Perhaps he should have listened to her protestations when she was still Rachel?

12

Evan knocked lightly on the door to Major Tufo's room and pushed the door open. "How are we feel—?" He paused and stared open mouthed at the man who stood in front of his bed, hastily replacing his bandages.

Mark glanced up and his face flushed. "Uh, better?" Mrs. Tufo sat nearby, relief painted across her features.

Evan stepped inside and quickly shut the door behind. He nearly pushed Mark to the bed and pulled his stethoscope. "This isn't right."

"I know, right? It must be the wolf virus making me—"

"Shh!" Evan chided as he slid the stethoscope from one part of his chest to another. He slid the device to Mark's back and listened intently then withdrew and hung the scope from his neck. The look of worry on his face twisted Mark's guts. "This is too much...too soon."

"Wait, you mean this *isn't* from the wolf virus?" Mark had been sitting upright, almost at attention until now. He seemed to almost wither with the news. "If not the wolf virus, then what?"

Evan shook his head, his face a mask of bewilderment. "I honestly have no idea." He stared into Mark's eyes, then his mouth, paying particular attention to his upper teeth. He finally withdrew and tapped a finger along the edge of his jaw.

"Don't candy coat it, Doc. What gives?"

Tracy scooted forward and reached for Mark' hand. "You think its vampirism, don't you?"

Evan gave her a startled look. "What?" Her comment seemed to snap him out of a deep thought. "Oh…uh, well. At first I thought maybe, but his heart is very strong. His temperature feels normal. His fever has definitely broken. But yes, I was checking his teeth to see if a pocket was forming for…" He turned away, trying to think of a way to explain the thoughts forming in his mind.

"Spill it, Doc. Don't you dare leave me hanging," Mark's voice cracked as he spoke.

Evan seemed to rock back and forth as he considered the different possibilities. "I simply cannot explain this. It's almost as though you had been infected by the vampire virus, but you were attacked by a wolf. The only thing I can think of is since the full moon is so close…maybe…"

"I need the pills, Doc. The bane that we give the squads. I refuse to shift. Do you hear me?" Mark was on his feet, his gauze pads coming loose and falling from his chest, exposing the bright pink scars.

Evan waved him off. "We were pumping bane extract into you through your IV. I'll have the pills brought to you though. No harm in doubling up." It was still evident that something troubled him, his mind racing through different possibilities.

"So…what else are you thinking?" Tracy got up from her chair and sat next to Mark on the bed. "I can tell that there's something else going on in that head of yours."

Evan shot her a wan smile and shook his head. "It's nothing. Actually, it's impossibility. I was just…" he trailed off.

"What?" they both asked.

Evan cleared his throat and tried to look them both in the eye. "I was just wondering…if it were even possible…if I had accidentally infected you during your surgery. Before the wolf virus took hold. That *would* go a long way in explaining how you were healing so quickly. Especially considering that we had you on a whole blood IV." He shook his head again, his mouth forming a tight smile. "But, it's totally impossible to be infected by both. The two viruses cannot manifest in the same individual. And besides that, you're not dead. You still have a heartbeat. And…" he trailed off again, his mind racing along another possibility.

"Doc? Don't do that. You scare me when you do that." Mark tightened his grip on Tracy's hand to the point she had to pry his fingers loose.

"Well…it occurs to me that you were fighting a pretty high fever."

"And…?"

"And, I suppose if your body were trying to fight off two different viral vectors at the same time, it might be possible that…no. It's still not possible." Evan chuckled at himself. "Like I said, you still have a heartbeat."

Mark turned a worried eye to Tracy. "I don't want to be a vampire. I might be able to handle being a wolf. Especially if the bane keeps me from shifting, but not a vampire."

Evan gave him a rather droll stare. "You're not a vampire."

"Then what?!" Mark was nearing hysterics.

"I dunno. Maybe some kind of hybrid." Evan stood up and pushed the chair away. "But as long as you have a heartbeat…"

"What the hell do you mean, *some kind of hybrid*? Doc?!"

Evan sighed and shrugged at the same time. "What do you want me to tell you? I can't explain why you're healing so fast. We have you on bane so you won't shift. You have a heartbeat and a normal temperature, so you aren't a vampire. It sounds to me like you're on the fast track to recovery."

"What if it was something other than a wolf? Maybe a shape-shifter that just happened to take the form of a wolf?" Tracy asked.

Evan leaned down and squeezed her shoulder gently. "Then he'd have absolutely nothing to worry about. Shape-shifters can't transmit their ability. You're either born into it or you're not."

She gave Mark a worried look. "So, worst case scenario, he's infected with both?"

Evan let out a long breath. "If he is, he would be the first person *ever* in the history of…well, ever, to have contracted both."

"What would that mean, though, Doc? What would I become?" Mark's eyes were lined with worry.

Evan shrugged again. "Your guess is as good as mine. A wolfpire? A werevamp? I have no idea. Something that can only go out at night, bites people for their blood and then humps their leg?" His attempt at humor fell flat. "Major, if I knew, I'd honestly tell you."

"Isn't there a test you can run or something?" Tracy asked as she got to her feet.

Evan thought about her question and saw the fear in Mark's eyes. "I suppose I could come up with something. I don't have the proper equipment here to delineate the different viruses, but give me a little bit and I'll come up with some non-fatal tests."

"Non-fatal?" Mark swallowed hard.

Evan chuckled. "You wouldn't want me spearing you with the Holy relics we made for the Sicarii if you were carrying the vampire virus, would you? I need to be careful since both are reactive with silver."

"Does this mean I can't go out in the sun?"

"Let's get you healed up completely and figure out what we're facing first." Evan patted his shoulder reassuringly. "Until then, just try not to eat your sweet missus." He shot Mark a wink and then saw Tracy quickly withdraw her hand from Mark's. "Um, that was a joke, ma'am. He wouldn't…" He exhaled hard and then turned for the door. "I'll be back as quick as I have something definitive."

*****

"So who is Loren?" Brooke picked at her nails as though the question were an afterthought. "Your wife?"

Jack snorted as he sorted through the pages in her file, putting things back into order. "Hardly. She's...complicated."

Brooke looked up over the edge of her hand and hiked a brow. "Complicated? Sounds interesting."

"She's not, I assure you." Jack picked up the completed file and pressed it to his chest. "Now. What to do with you?"

"Do? What do you mean, 'what to do with'?" Brooke leaned back in her chair and studied the man in black military garb. "I'm not a tool to be *done* with."

"You are now." Jack hooked his jaw to the side and headed toward the door. "Follow me."

"For what?" Brooke pushed the chair out and fell into step behind him.

"I guess I need to bring you up to speed on things since you're one of the crew now." He turned down the hallway and she balked on him.

"Whoa there, cowboy. Back up the truck. I'm not part of anything." She lifted her hands in surrender and shook her head at him, slowly backing away.

Jack turned and gave her a bored stare. "Yes, you are. I don't like it, you don't like it, but that's just the way it is. So stop the protesting and get your fanny with the program."

"My...fanny?"

"You look twelve, so I'm not going to tell you to stop dragging your ass." He shot her a smirk and watched as her eyes narrowed.

"I'll have you know I'm old enough to be your mother." Her voice hissed as she spoke.

"I doubt that." Jack turned again and headed down the hallway. "Either way, you're part of the squad now. Time to introduce you. You already met Kalen. He's our resident warrior Elf and apparently the only one that Loren likes to talk to these days."

"Again, who the hell is Loren?" She trotted to catch up with him.

Jack inhaled deeply and blew the breath out hard. Loren had really gotten under his skin lately by giving him partial answers or teasers. Then bypassing him directly and going straight to Kalen? Yet she claims that he was supposed to be leading this ragtag team of young warriors. And why the youngest instead of the most experienced?

"Are you going to answer me or what?" Brooke called from behind him.

Jack stopped mid-step and turned. "Loren is like the village elder from the tribe that Kalen comes from. She looks to be your age, but she's much older and very wise. She said that there was some big, scary, dark force about to threaten mankind and that I was supposed to lead this group of young warriors in helping to deal with it."

"What does that have to do with me?" She planted her hands firmly on her hips and glared at him.

"You," Jack poked her firmly in the shoulder, "are one of our key players. Or...something like that." He shrugged and threw his hands in the air. "Who the hell knows? She isn't telling me anything anymore. She apparently only talks to Kalen."

"Wait...I didn't agree to anything." Brooke protested as Jack turned and headed back down the hallway.

"Doesn't matter, sweetheart. You're in." He shot a smirk over his shoulder, "And you didn't even have to go through initiation."

"Hey! Hey, wait a minute. I'm serious here." Brooke caught up with him and grabbed him by the shoulder, spinning him around. Jack grabbed her arm and spun her, effectively sweeping her foot and planting her to the ground and putting her in an arm bar at the same time. "Get off me, you big oaf!"

"I'm told you're a pretty effective fighter, but you should have seen that coming a mile away." He leaned down and all but whispered. "Do you want to learn how to be the most effective killing machine to ever walk the planet or not?"

She ground her teeth as she glared at him through the edges of her vision. "Is that what you're offering me?"

"I'm offering you the chance to be part of a team. A team of warriors like you've never seen before." He leaned closer and lowered his voice. "A team that can hone your skills to the point that nothing could ever stand in your way."

She felt him relax his grip on her and she pulled her arm free. She turned and found him still standing over her, his hand extended, offering her a hand up from the floor. "How long?"

"Until I say you're done."

She narrowed her eyes again and studied him. "And if I refuse?"

Jack shook his head slightly, his hand still offered. "You can't. I'm sorry, but Loren says you're part of the team."

"I think I want to meet this Elf," Brooke grunted as she took his hand.

Jack helped her to her feet and wiped imaginary dust from her back. "No, you don't." He turned and faced the young vampiress. "So, what's it going to be? Are you with us or not?"

Brooke glanced away, her mind considering the possibilities. "You'll teach me other ways to fight? Besides the sword?"

"I'll teach you everything I know. Weapons, hand to hand. Hell, I'll even teach you some Lycan moves."

Brooke found herself smiling at the possibilities. "When do we start?"

* * * * *

"We have to find you a safe place to shift." Laura paced in Jennifer's small room, her nerves getting the better of her.

"But they're wolves, too. Surely they'd understand—"

"No! You don't understand. They've been infected with the virus, but they take bane to prevent the shift. They don't *know* what they are. And we're under orders to keep it that way. The only team that knows anything is our own team."

Jennifer chewed absently at her thumbnail, a nervous habit she picked up from Laura. "What if we slipped out and then…"

"They have the entrances guarded and they're under orders to keep us protected," Laura interrupted. "We'd have to make a break for it and even then…they might go looking for us and if they discovered you while you were shifted…"

Jennifer's face screwed up. "Not good."

A banging at the door jerked both of their heads and Jennifer hesitantly opened it. Mick stood outside the door and gave her a sad look. "I know I'm the last person you want to see right now."

"You're right." She started to the push the door shut when Mick pushed it open and walked in.

"I've got a plan, and it might work."

"I don't want to hear it." Jennifer turned her back on him and walked the short distance back to her bed,flopping on top of it.

Mick looked to Laura who also turned away from him. "I could fly you to the States before the full moon. Your Fated one? Surely he has a place to shift? A safe place?"

Laura turned and gave him a wide eyed stare. "He does, but how could you get us there in time?"

Mick sighed heavily and slumped his shoulders. "I made some calls. I have a friend. He's delivering a 550 Gulfstream to a buyer in the States. He said that I could deliver it. It's plenty fast enough to get us there in time. I can…" he trailed off, his face displaying emotions that Laura couldn't read.

"You can what?"

"I can drop you off and then deliver the plane. Or…not. You know. Wait and see if things don't work out. Then I can take you away from there so you don't get hurt."

"How quickly can you get the plane?" Laura stared at her watch, trying to extrapolate the time differences.

"It's sitting at the airport, waiting. We'd just need a ride there."

"What about your other plane?" Jennifer asked, afraid of the answer.

Mick sighed heavily and refused to look her in the eye. "It's your dad's plane. I don't really care what happens to it." His voice was so quiet that Laura could barely hear him.

Jennifer, on the other hand, heard every word. She stiffened and her jaw ticked. "So the whole 'get away' was a set up?"

"Just to get you some place safe, Jen,I promise." Mick leaned against the wall and his face looked ready to break into tears at any moment.

"Get the plane. Tell your friend we'll take their offer. I'll go get us the ride to the airport." Laura headed for the door then froze. "Wait…your friend. This isn't her dad again, is it?"

Mick's face registered shock at first, then he shook his head. "No,this is a real person. A real dealer. I can give you his number if you like."

Laura eyed him again, then glanced to Jennifer who gave her a slight nod. "Just make the arrangements while I get us a ride. Pack your gear. We're out of here."

*****

Evan returned to his lab and found a small group milling about in the shadows. At first he paid little attention to the group. His mind was still on Major Tufo's condition and his healing so rapidly. He had sent for a blood sample to run some preliminary tests and was startled when the group entered his lab. He spun on his chair and eyed them warily.

"May I help you?"

A tall fellow stepped out of the shadows and Evan felt his eyes grow wide. A gargoyle stood in his very lab! "Chief Jack sent us to you."

"Oh my…" Evan stood slowly and approached the group carefully. "What an extraordinary group you are." His eyes travelled from the gargoyle to the elf to the gnome back to the gargoyle. "Please, excuse me, I've never had live subjects in my lab before."

The trio turned to each other then back to the vampire. "Subjects?" Azrael asked.

"Apologies. I…" Evan paused and laughed to himself. "Please, excuse my rudeness. I am Doctor Evan Peters, and I've been studying your kind…all of your kinds, for many years. But I've never actually had living, breathing specimens in my lab before." Evan stepped back and took them all in. "This is incredible."

Azrael stepped forward and crossed his large arms over his chest, his gaze narrowing. "Chief Jack sent us to you. To be checked out."

"Oh! Of course. How silly of me." Evan pushed some items off of his examination table and patted it. "I didn't realize you were working with Mr. Thompson. Please, up here." While Azrael tentatively took a seat, Evan broke out a new notebook and began jotting things down. He ran through a barrage of tests and declared each of them healthy.

"If you don't mind my asking, Azrael, what triggers your stone sleep?" Evan asked, writing furiously in his notebook.

"The sun."

Evan peered up from his writing and tapped the pencil against his chin. "Do you know what aspect of the sun causes the transition?" Azrael shook his head. "Would you mind if I ran a couple of tests?"

Azrael looked to Kalen who simply shrugged. "I guess it wouldn't hurt. Will it?"

"I don't believe it will. But before we begin, I have more questions." Azrael nodded and Evan began. "When you are wounded, does the stone sleep heal you?"

"Yes."

"Excellent. And if the wound is otherwise a grave one?"

"It is still healed by the sleep."

Evan wrote quickly. "What about damages done during the stone sleep?" Azrael gave him a quizzical look. "If somebody were to…I dunno, take a hammer and break off a finger while you were stone?"

"Then it would be removed when we awoke. Healed, but gone."

"Amazing. Truly amazing." Evan pushed his notebook aside and pulled out a small device. "This emits a concentrated UV ray. To a vampire, it acts like a laser and…well, it would sear flesh. Lots of fire and smoke and, well, it just plain stinks. Hurts like the dickens, too."

"And you intend to set me afire?" Azrael did not look pleased.

"No, not at all. If I'm right, then the spot that I hit with it should turn to stone." He looked at Azrael questioningly. "It should turn back afterward, shouldn't it?"

Azrael shrugged. "I suppose."

Evan lowered the device. "You've never been exposed to a single ray of sunlight before? Maybe hiding in the shadows or…"

"No." Azrael shook his head. "Only once have I remained indoors during the day and avoided the stone sleep."

"Okay. Well then, let's be careful, shall we? Maybe we start with a fingernail or toenail?"

Azrael held out his hand and extended a claw-like nail from his finger. Evan turned on the device and allowed the ray to brush the nail quickly. Almost immediately, a fine crusting of stone formed on the outer portion of the nail. Evan looked up at Azrael who was eyeing him closely. "Does that hurt?"

"No." Azrael flexed his hand and the crusting of stone flaked away. "Try again."

Evan held the device a little longer and they watched as more of the finger slowly turned to stone. He pulled the device away and they watched as the finger slowly turned back to flesh. "Amazing." He picked at the flakes of stone and peeled them away as though they were flakes of dandruff.

Evan wheeled his chair over to a drawer and pulled out a tube of something, then slipped it into a spray bottle. "I want to try another little experiment."

"Will it hurt?"

Kalen stepped forward and clapped the large gargoyle on the shoulder, "I thought you were tougher than that, old friend."

"I just want to prepare myself so I don't react and possibly hurt someone," Azrael's voice deadpanned, but his eyes indicated it might not be the first time he had done such a thing.

"This won't hurt a bit." Evan pressurized the sprayer and sprayed a fine mist across his hand and lower arm. "I developed this years ago in hopes that I could go out in the daylight. It didn't work for me. It's basically an industrial strength UV blocker."

"It didn't work?" Azrael gave him a questioning stare.

"Not for me. Apparently there are just too many aspects to being a vampire...simply applying a UV blocker won't allow walking in daylight." He sprayed a light and even coating,watching as it soaked in like fine water on concrete. "You have the most remarkable skin."

"What's going on, Doc?" Jack stepped into the lab, a young, dark haired woman in tow.

"Testing a theory." Evan grabbed the UV emitter and flipped it on again. "Here goes nothing." He pointed it at Azrael's hand and felt the corners of his mouth curl when nothing happened. He ran the UV emitter up and down his forearm and only when he reached the elbow did the fine crusting of stone start to appear once again. "Eureka!" Evan flipped off the emitter and tossed it aside. "I finally found a use for my UV blocker."

"Well…that's good, isn't it?" Jack shrugged.

"Most definitely. Up until now I thought I had invented a sunscreen for watching atomic testing but…who's your friend?" Evan had just noticed the young woman standing slightly behind Phoenix.

"Meet Brooke Sullivan."

"Raven," The young woman corrected. "Just…Raven."

"Well, just Raven. I am Doctor Evan Peters. Please, step in here and we'll have a look at…" Evan paused then turned to Jack. "She's a vampire."

"Yeah, Doc,she's a vampire." Jack smirked as he leaned against the doorway.

Evan swallowed hard and then gave the young woman a quaint smile. He motioned to Jack and the two stepped down and outside of his lab, "A word, please?" Evan pulled Jack out of hearing range of the others. "Why is she here?"

"She's going to be part of my new team. The…teen squad or diaper brigade or some such shit."

"No,Jack, no. She's a *vampire*. You have an elf on your squad. The two should never work together. Vampires are drawn to elves. Their blood makes vampires…high. Or drunk. Or…both. It's bad juju."

Jack shook his head and held his hands up. "Not my decision, Doc. The Wyldwood made this choice for me. Besides, she's a *Beastia*. I mean, not part of a family like you or anything, but she only feeds on animals."

Evan's eyes narrowed on Jack. "Promise me you will watch her, Jack."

Jack noted his concern and nodded. "I promise, Doc. I'll watch her like a hawk."

Doctor Peters turned back and stared at the young woman through the glass surround of his lab. "She's a vampire, so she shouldn't need a checkup. Anything that was wrong with her would be healed."

"Indulge me, Doc."

*****

Sheridan stepped outside the office and pulled the door shut. He was just turning when he caught the scent of something. Something familiar. Something…large. He slowly lowered himself and wafted the air closer to his face. He inhaled deeply and the scent hit him hard. Apollo.

Sheridan's eyes narrowed as he looked around the warehouse. He inhaled deeply and followed the scent to the edge of the office. It lingered just outside one of the frosted windows and he felt his guts twist on him. Apollo had been spying on him. But when?

He thought back to his phone call to Mr. Simmons. He hadn't given anything away then. He thought back through his other actions through the evening. *Dammit. The conversation with Big.*

Sheridan ground his teeth and gazed out through the warehouse. If the man was lying in wait for him, he couldn't sense him. He took a tentative step away from the office and none of the hair on the back of his neck rose. Somehow, he doubted the large man was waiting in the rafters with a sniper rifle.

Sheridan exhaled slowly and felt the tension leave his shoulders. If Apollo intended to confront him, he didn't plan to do it tonight. That gave him until morning to find a way to either coerce him back to his side or figure out a way to get rid of him.

*****

Little John paced the lounge, his hands instinctively clenching and unclenching. Spalding had tried every trick he could think of to get him to relax, but the man couldn't take it any longer. "I have to know what's going on."

"You just have to give them time." Spalding spun and held a finger up. "Hey, how about we go to the gym and you can burn off some of this nervous energy on the weights?"

Sullivan paused and stared at the smaller man. "This isn't just nervous energy. This is me…worrying about my sister."

Spalding smirked at him. "The same sister you swore to put a bullet in the next time you saw her?" He regretted the words as soon as they escaped his mouth. "I'm sorry. That didn't come out the way I meant."

"That was a cheap shot."

"I didn't mean it the way it sounded,I promise." Spalding deflated and shrugged. "Okay,how about we work our way down the interrogation room, and I'll see what I can find out."

That offer caught John's attention. "You would do that?"

"Of course." Spalding waved him on. "Let's go see what we can see."

The two worked their way down a flight of stairs and slowly approached the interrogation room. "You hang back, and I'll see what I can see." Spalding eased up on the room and stole a quick peek through the door glass. He eased back up and stared inside the room. Turning to Little John he asked, "You sure this is the room they had her in?"

John quickly closed the gap. "Of course I'm sure." He stared through the glass and uttered a curse under his breath. "Where could they have taken her?"

"No idea, but we can find out." Spalding turned and headed back down the hallway. He hit the stairwell and took the stairs two at a time. He entered the overlook heading to Colonel Mitchell's office. "I'll ask the boss, but you need to stay back. Otherwise, he might not be so forthcoming in…"

"In what?" Mitchell asked.

Spalding spun and blanched. "Colonel! How you doing, sir?"

"Spill it, Spalding. What are you up to?"

"We, uh…were wondering where Sully's sister might have ended up?"

Mitchell glanced past Spalding to Little John. The man appeared to be a nervous wreck. "She's with Phoenix." Mitchell turned and entered his office.

"And where would that be, sir?" Spalding inquired.

"How the hell should I know? He just said that the Wyldwood said that little vamp was supposed to be on his new team and…" Mitchell threw his hands up in surrender. "Jesus, last I heard somebody had put *me* in charge of this Mickey Mouse outfit, but no…" He shut the door behind him, effectively ending the conversation.

Spalding turned to Little John. "Well, there you have it. Apparently Jack has her. Somewhere." Spalding rubbed at his chin in thought. "I wonder why the Wyldwood would say that Brooke is supposed to work for Jack?"

"Would you please explain to me what in the hell is going on?" Little John's worry was painted so deeply that Spalding thought the man would pop.

"Yeah, I'll try, but it won't be easy." He motioned the man to follow him. "It's sort of a long story, so try to keep up."

"Give me the *Reader's Digest* version."

"I intend to, but even that can get complicated." Spalding went to the rail and leaned on it, looking out over the training area. "It all started when…"

13

Mark sat in silence while his wife went to grab a quick bite from the cafeteria. She promised to bring him something more substantial than the broth and gelatin he had been served. Mark would stand and peel the gauze back and stare in the mirror. Each time it seemed that the pink scars had healed that much more and he would shudder, cover the wounds again and sit back down.

Out of pure boredom, he picked up the broth and sniffed it. He could nearly *smell* the salt in the clear liquid, and it made his mouth water. He lifted the bowl to his mouth and took a sip. He didn't realize how hungry he truly was until he pulled the bowl back and saw that it was empty. The gelatin lasted about two seconds. He sucked down the juice and made quick action of the milk as well. He sat on the small bed and could feel his stomach rumble for something more substantive. Something with *meat*. Something rare. Something bloody.

He shook his head and tried to clear it of the thoughts he was having, but images of large steaks sizzling on a charcoal grill, juices dripping and popping on the coals danced in his mind. If he closed his eyes, he could almost smell the roasted flesh. His stomach protested again and almost cramped with want. He grabbed the plastic cup the juice came in and filled it from the ice water pitcher, downing the liquid to try to fill the emptiness inside. He knew it wouldn't work but he had to try.

Sitting back on the bed a smell rose to meet his nose, and it wasn't pleasant. He sniffed the air again then stood, inhaling deeply. *What the hell is that funk?*

He stepped from the bed and sniffed at the air. Whatever it was it seemed elusive. As he approached the bed again, the smell intensified. He bent low and sniffed the sheets, withdrawing in disgust. "Oh, my God." He grabbed the sheets and pulled them from the small bed, wadding them into a ball and tossing them toward the door. The mixture of sweat, betadine and fear had saturated the sheets. The odor was enough to turn his stomach.

The door opened and Tracy stood in shock at the state of the room. "What the hell, Tufo?"

"They stunk."

"Well, no duh. You soaked them with sweat and…oh, my God." She placed the tray she was carrying on the side table and quickly closed the small gap between them. She reached up and pulled the gauze from his chest. "Your wounds."

He quickly grabbed at the gauze and pulled it back into place. "I know." He turned from her and grabbed the tray from the table.

"Mark? This isn't right."

"You think I don't know that? What can I do about it? Keep opening up the wounds so they take longer to heal?" He lifted the plastic lid covering the plate and his mouth watered at the Salisbury steak smothered in brown gravy. "I wish you had brought about seven of these. I'm famished."

"What? Good heavens there's no way you could eat…" She paused in mid-sentence as he cut the steak in half and shoved one piece in his mouth, brown gravy running from the corners of his mouth. "You're going to make me sick if you keep that up."

"I told you, I'm starving." His words sounded muffled as he spoke through the mouthful of food. He scooped up a triple fingerful of mashed potatoes and shoved them into his mouth.

"Oh, for the love of…use a spoon!"

He turned and gave her a sheepish stare. "Thorry."

"I can get you more. You don't have to eat it all in two bites." She moved past him and opened the door. "I can't guarantee you seven, but I'll get you as many as they'll let me leave with."

He gave her a smile, potatoes and gravy dripping from the sides of his mouth. "Thank you."

"Just, please, use the utensils I brought you. And try not to eat the dishes until I get back."

He plopped down on the vinyl covered mattress and gave her a wan smile. "I'll try."

She paused and gave him one last look before heading back to the cafeteria. Had he gotten…larger?

*****

"There's supposed to be one more coming our way, but for now, we might as well get everybody situated and once all the dust is settled, we'll get started with your training." Jack addressed the group of young warriors surrounding him, his eyes assessing each of them. He had to admit, when he first went into battle with the original three, he had no idea that they were so young. He had his doubts about the gnome, but that was quickly quelled once the fighting started. But now that he knew that they were barely more than kids? "I know that for most of you, you've already been trained in one form of combat or another. I intend to assess your abilities and round out your training."

Azrael raised a hand slightly. "Who else are we expecting?"

Jack shrugged. "Your guess is as good as mine. I suppose when the Wyldwood gets around to letting us know…" he cast an accusing glance at Kalen. "I'll be the second to know."

Kalen averted his eyes. He knew that Chief Jack held it against him that the Wyldwood chose to speak to him over his leader, but he couldn't help it. It was simply easier for her to contact and speak with Kalen. The same stone in Kalen's wristband that allowed him to open the gateway to the Anywhere also gave him a direct link to the Wyldwood. She could contact him at will, and nobody else would know. She could, in effect, spy on their every action if she chose. Kalen sighed as he considered the responsibilities of being the Gatekeeper.

"How soon before we can start our training?" Brooke's face may have appeared passive, but her voice sounded more than anxious.

"We have a few things to take care of first." Jack tapped his watch. "First things first, the full moon is right around the corner and unfortunately, I'll be out of commission during that time."

Gnat stepped forward and leaned on his hammer. "What are we supposed to do during the times that you aren't available?"

Jack shook his head. "I honestly don't know. I really should name a Second. Somebody who is responsible for the group, a leader amongst the team, but right now I just don't know who to assign that to."

Azrael looked amongst the group present and reached out, pushing Kalen forward. "Him." Kalen looked back at Azrael in shock, his eyes darting between the large gargoyle and Jack.

Jack raised a brow, his eyes narrowing. "Why would you say that?"

"The Wyldwood. You claim she speaks to him, and it is because of her that we have all been called together, yes?"

"Well…" Jack trailed off; unsure that was enough to make Kalen the leader amongst the group.

"Chief Jack, I understand you do not want to trust me to assist you with leading our group." Kalen lowered his eyes to the floor.

Jack cleared his throat, buying time to choose his words. "It's not that I don't trust you, Kalen. It's just…you're usually so quiet and withdrawn. Most leaders are more…I dunno. Out there."

Brooke snorted and shook her head. "What a bunch. One who can lead, another who should and doesn't think he can."

"I can lead." Kalen corrected. "I just don't want Chief Jack to feel compelled to do anything he isn't comfortable with."

"Whatever." She turned and hopped onto a table, her long leather coat feathering out around her. "I say let the gargoyle do it.

He's big enough to keep everybody in line. Sugar cookie doesn't have what it takes anyway."

Kalen ground his teeth and Azrael gave her a sideways stare. "Sugar cookie?"

"She thinks I smell like cookies. It is because she is a vampire and I am Elf. That is all." Kalen refused to make eye contact with either as he spoke. He stepped forward and squared his shoulders. "Chief Jack, if you will have me as your Second, I will take the mantle and wear it proudly. I will not fail you."

Jack cast a sideways glance at Brooke then turned back to Kalen. If the kid thought he could control a vampire hunter, he was either made of tougher stuff than Jack gave him credit for, or he had a lot to learn. "Okay, kid, it's all yours. At least until I find somebody better or you prove you're not worthy."

Kalen paled with the caveat and Brooke hid a wicked smile.

*****

Laura climbed aboard the G550 and walked to the rear of the plane. The seats were overstuffed leather recliners and the plane had two full bathrooms, a wet bar, three televisions, game systems, DVD players, a small kitchenette…*I could live on this thing.*

"Grab a seat and get strapped in. These types of planes can really pull you back." Jennifer tossed her bag into an overhead storage bin and fell into a chair, pulling the lapbelts across and buckling them.

"In a rush? Doesn't he have like a long list of pre-flight stuff to go through?"

"He said something about the plane being checked out before we got here. Another pilot was supposed to have taken it, and he pulled in his favor. Anyway, he knows I'm running against a clock, so I'm betting he'll be cutting corners."

Laura heard the engines whine to life and she sat in a seat opposite Jennifer. She no sooner strapped in when she felt the brakes release and the plane begin to taxi. "Holy cow, you weren't kidding."

"These things usually take two to fly, so maybe Mick is co-piloting? Or vice versa? I don't know, don't care, and don't want to know."

Laura grimaced at her tone and looked away, trying to think of what to say. "You know, he could be telling the truth. That he did what he did because he cares about you."

"If he cared, he wouldn't have lied. He would have simply told me from the beginning and...I don't know. Maybe I would have played along just to fool my father."

"Jen, you heard what your father did to him when you came up missing. He thought Mick was involved, and he tortured him."

"All the more reason not to do what my father wanted." She turned and glared at Laura. "I can't believe that you're defending him."

"I'm not defending him. I'm just trying to see things from his point of view." Laura shrugged. "Haven't you ever done something that you regretted?"

"No." Jennifer looked away and Laura knew she was lying.

"Really?" She leaned over in her seat and stared at the smaller woman. "Even when you shredded your Fated Mate?"

"He had that coming."

"Who's to say he didn't. But you didn't feel the slightest bit of regret once you realized who he was? Or once you realized that he just wanted to try to talk to you? To try to help you calm down?"

"Don't go there, Laura." Jennifer turned and gave her a stony stare. "You have no idea what it's like to lose ten years of your life. To be...frozen and used as a lab rat."

"And yet, here you are. Rushing back to see him." Laura raised a brow at her.

"No, I'm going back to see if there's anything to this Fated Mate thing." Her voice softened and she turned away again. "I'd be lying if I said I was perfectly okay with it all. Every time I close my eyes and see his face, my breath catches in my throat and I…" she gulped air and her hands shook. "I'm scared to death. I see that same face. So angry. So full of hate. And he's shooting me, Laura. He shot me in the face."

"So why are you going back?" Laura reached a hand out to hold Jennifer's, but she pulled away.

"Because I *have* to. If he's truly my Fated Mate…then I *have* to,I have no choice." Jennifer's voice broke, and Laura thought she would burst into tears at any moment.

"I guess you're right,I don't understand. If somebody caused me that much distress just thinking about them, there's no way I could go back and…" she shook her head. "I just couldn't go back."

Jennifer sighed heavily and turned her face to the window. "Because you're not wolf. You'll never understand."

"Look, Jen, Matt's my boss. He's my friend. I'd do just about anything for him. But let's be honest here, you were doing just fine on your own before you knew he was who he was. You don't have to do this. Justfollow your heart. Do what will make you happy."

Jennifer finally turned and Laura saw her tear streaked face. "You still don't get it, do you? The Fates arranged this. This isn't an arranged marriage worked out in some back room by two wealthy families. This is the *Fates*. You don't mess with the Fates. If they say you're supposed to be together, then you're supposed to be together. Whether you want it or not. There's a reason for it. A purpose bigger than ourselves. It may not manifest now, or even a generation from now. It may not manifest for fifty generations, but if our coupling brings about something important in the future, then I HAVE to see it through."

"Horse shit." Laura sat back and crossed her arms over her chest. "Seriously. If the Fates are all that important, they'll find another way to make something happen. The future of mankind…er, well, *wolf*kind, won't be dependent on whether or not you mate with Matt."

Jennifer sighed and shook her head. "See? You can't understand."

"Because I'm not wolf. I get it." Laura sat back and closed her eyes for the long flight.

*****

Sleep refused to come. Apollo shifted on his narrow cot and stared towards where Bigby lay on his own cot, snoring lightly. *I ought to slit his throat in his sleep.* He turned back and stared at the ceiling, knowing that any direct actions taken toward either Bigby or Sheridan would give him away.

He closed his eyes, and his mind played out numerous scenarios where a well-placed C4 charge could remove both of them and leave him to his own devices.

Apollo groaned and tested the frame of his cot as he rolled to the other side. He glanced back through the group of sleeping men and decided his fate. He stood beside his cot and cast a glance along the line of sleeping warriors, ensuring his movements didn't rouse any. He crept along the empty aisle and slipped out the door, back into the main warehouse.

Apollo knew that Sheridan was no fool. He saw the light was off in the office, but the man slept in the room right next to it. He crept alongside the edge of the warehouse and approached Sheridan's quarters. He could hear the man snoring loudly behind the closed door and once he was satisfied it wasn't fake, he slipped back into the office and to the phone.

If their 'army' of mercenary wolves were going to be out of commission the following night due to shifting, what better time for the Monster Squad to come in and clean house? Apollo snickered to himself as he lifted the phone and dialed the number for the hotline.

When the duty officer answered, he gave his now defunct code and requested Colonel Mitchell. The duty officer nervously put him on hold and tracked the CO down.

Apollo didn't expect the venom that came across the phone when Mitchell answered, but he should have. "You got a lot of nerve calling here."

"Shh." Apollo lowered his voice to a whisper, "They're asleep. I'm sure you're tracking this number, so I'll stay on the line long enough for you to get a fix. They have silver-lined shipping crates for these assholes to shift in tomorrow."

"Like I'm supposed to care?" Mitchell could barely contain his anger as he spoke into the phone.

"You don't get it, sir. While they're shifted and locked up, send the boys in to clean house. It'll be like shooting fish in a barrel." Apollo leaned forward and glanced out the open window, straining his ears to listen for Sheridan's snoring. "You can clean the whole mess out in one move, sir. Nobody gets hurt."

"And how the hell am I supposed to trust you, Apollo?"

Apollo hung his head and sighed into the phone. "I don't know, Colonel. I guess you ain't. But…let's just say that I seen the error of my ways, and I came back to try to find a way to make things right. Or…as right as I can make them."

"Good men died because of you," Mitchell's voice growled low and menacing across the phone line.

"I know, sir. And believe me, if there was some way I could trade places with them, I would. But all I can do is tell you what they got planned. It's some guy named Simmons behind all this. I still don't know exactly *who* he is, just that he has more money than brains, and he has a huge hard-on for the squads."

"I know who he is. And I know why." Mitchell's own guilt found a way to worm into the situation and his voice softened. A little. "Where are you going to be when they shift?"

"I don't know yet. Probably some type of guard duty. I figured maybe I could ash them, but I ain't got no silver grenades.

Or…well, something that could take out a bunch of them in one fail swoop." Apollo glanced out the window again then lowered his voice even more. "Besides, I figured the boys would rather have the honor of doing this."

"We have your location."

"Good. Just have them wait until after the shift. These guys will be locked up in their crates and it will be easy pickings."

"It had better be. If any more men are lost because of you—"

"Colonel," Apollo interrupted, "I didn't have to call."

Mitchell stiffened slightly and considered his words. "True enough."

"If I can, I'll try to reach the squads again before they arrive. Just in case anything comes up."

"Roger that."

Apollo gripped the phone tighter and felt his chest grow heavier. "Colonel…"

"What?"

"I know there's no forgiveness for what I did." Apollo took a deep breath and blew it out slowly. "But is there any kind of reparations I can make?"

Mitchell squeezed his eyes shut and pinched at the bridge of his nose. His wolf was demanding blood for the betrayal. "I just don't know, Apollo."

Apollo nodded in the darkness. "Understood, sir."

*****

"Just have them in place before we arrive." Paul Foster hung up the satellite phone and practically fell back into his seat. "The good news is that we have a small contingency of assassins that can be in place before we arrive in Geneva."

Rufus raised a brow at the news. "And the bad news?"

Paul sighed heavily. "It's only a *small* contingency. If the Monster Squad comes looking for us there, then I can't guarantee they'll be enough to handle them."

"Relax, *mon ami*. Either we shall be successful, or we shall not." Rufus closed his eyes and eased back in the seat, apparently not a care in the world.

"Please forgive my lack of faith, brother." Foster sat forward and lowered his voice. "But I'm not ready to simply hang it all up and say, 'well, I guess it wasn't meant to be' if a group of commandos show up and shoot a silver bullet up my ass."

Rufus snorted a laugh and opened his eyes. "That was not my meaning at all." Rufus sat forward and patted his brother's arm. "I meant only that *if* we were to meet up with a squad of hunters, it will not be Monsieur Thompson's. They have teams scattered all over the world, and they are not allowed to operate in another's territory. These hunters do not know us. They do not know our assassins, our techniques. They would not be expecting what will hit them." He gave Paul a reassuring smile before sitting back and closing his eyes again. "I think your preparations are more than adequate."

Foster leaned back in his chair and stared at his brother, attempting to sleep. "I wish I had your confidence."

"You will see. All will be well." Rufus tilted his head and seemed to deflate further in the seat.

How anybody could sleep at a time like this... Paul pulled the small table over and locked it into place. Pulling the list of names from his case, he went through and tried to assign positions for the different vampires in their entourage based on strengths and abilities and different scenarios he played out in his mind. He rearranged the different vampires numerous times and finally found a lineup he was pleased with. He copied it and passed it on to the enforcers with them.

He wanted there to be no slip-ups once they touched ground.

*****

"Jesus, that's the *Reader's Digest* version?" Little John stared at Spalding, his eyes wide. "You could write a friggin book and it would be shorter."

Spalding shrugged. "It is what it is." He patted Spalding on the shoulder, "But at least now you know what's what and who's who and why's why."

"Not really. Just that my sister is being enlisted into working with an ex-squad member who is taking orders from some crazy hippie elf." He rolled his eyes.

Darren chuckled. "Well, I guess *that* is the *Reader's Digest* version."

The two heard the doors to the training area open and turned to watch as Jack and his new recruits walked in below them. "Hey, there's Brooke."

"And she isn't broken," Spalding ribbed him.

"I need to talk to her." John turned and headed for the stairwell.

"Whoa, buddy, cool your jets a minute." Spalding grabbed him by the back of his tactical vest and pulled him to a stop. "It looks to me like she's in the middle of something down there, and I don't know about you, but this may not be the best time to be interrupting."

"Butshe's my sister." John turned sad eyes to him, and Darren felt his pain.

"I know. Believe me, I can only imagine what you must be feeling right now, but it would be best if you waited until Jack's done with her." Darren nodded with his chin toward the group as Jack walked them through the CQB rooms.

"How about…how about if we both go down there and maybe volunteer our services? I mean, surely he's going to have to bring them up to speed on stuff around here, isn't he? We could help with that, couldn't we? I mean, during our down time anyway."

"Listen to yourself, John. You sound like—"

"Like what?" the larger man interrupted.

"Like desperation." Darren stared the man in the eye. "Look, I understand you want to be a part of your sister's life. Catch up and discover all the little things that have happened over the years. But until she's ready to open up to you, you can hang around her all you want and she isn't going to take part in any of that."

Spalding watched as the large man physically deflated. "I guess you're right."

"I'm not saying this to be mean, buddy. You know that."

Little John nodded. "Yeah,I get that." He cast a longing glance over the edge of the railing once more and watched as the group worked their way out of the CQB rooms and across into the indoor range, out of view. "I guess I just hoped that…" he trailed off.

Spalding patted his shoulder reassuringly. "I know. I know you did."

*****

Damien glanced up at the door banging shut. He knew that his Mistress was still in her room and their building was supposed to be abandoned. He dropped the boxes he carried and ran for the door, skidding to a stop when he rounded a corner and came face to face with a rather intimidating male.

"What the hell are you?" the man asked, his brow rising in consternation.

"I should ask the same of you." Damien crossed his arms defensively.

Without the strength of the elder vampires, he knew he was on the weaker side of this face off. If it came to blows, he wouldn't survive. He wasn't sure who or what, he faced here, but the power emanating from this being was magnificent.

"Lilith must really be scraping the bottom of the barrel if she has you serving her." The male pushed past Damien and walked toward the middle of the warehouse.

"Now see here, you can't simply come marching in here like you…ack!" His words were cut off by a swiftly moving hand that gripped his throat. The air being cut off was only a minor concern compared to the crunching sound he heard in his ears as the being squeezed.

"Your voice annoys me." He tilted his head and studied Damien as his eyes bulged from their sockets.

"Put him down." Lilith's voice was smooth and passive from behind the pair. The male visitor immediately dropped the vampire to the ground and turned to face her, lowering himself to one knee.

"My Mistress."

"Gaius. Your *triarii* awaits?"

She watched as his eyes rose and met her own. "Yes, Mistress. They have all found suitable vessels. They are ready to assemble on your word."

She reached out and touched him at the shoulder, beckoning him to rise. She ran her hands up and down his strong arms and across his broad chest. "Oh, this is a *very* fine specimen indeed." Her voice purred and her eyes devoured him as she circled him slowly. Damien lay prostrate on the ground, holding his shattered throat and whimpering as his queen all but dry humped this newcomer. "How are your people doing for weapons?"

"We have some vessels that are military. Some who are lawkeepers. Weapons will not be problematic." He stood at attention as she continued to circle him, her hands probing and squeezing.

"Excellent." She gave him a knowing gaze and pulled him toward her private abode. "We shall not be disturbed. We have…*plans* to discuss." She laughed as he she pulled Gaius into her room and shut the door behind them.

Damien lay on the floor and watched in horror as the love of his life just dragged a stranger to her bed. He had never felt so impotent in his entire life.

He rolled to his knees and massaged his damaged throat while it tried to heal. He silently cursed her name as tears rolled down his face. He stole another glance toward her abode and heard her scream out in ecstasy, repeatedly screaming 'yes' behind the closed door. For just a moment, Damien felt as if the dried up husk of a heart in his chest had physically shattered.

All of the time he had spent with her as Rachel…the plans they had made. The trips they taken. Her coming to him when he was little more than a shattered ghoul. Her revealing her plans to him and using him as her tool to implement those plans…all for nothing. All so she could jump the first overly muscled male to kick his way into their hiding spot.

It was *him* that gathered all of her parts. It was him that collected the virgin blood. It was him that cast the spell and sacrificed all of the strength he had gathered. It was him who collected all of her knickknacks and did her bidding so she could call forth her legion. It was ALL him. She would have nothing…nay; she would *be* nothing if it weren't for him. And what does she do?

Damien rocked himself up and to his feet. He tested his throat and was finally able to swallow again. He cleared his throat and a bloody chunk of something dislodged deep in the back, catching in his mouth. He quickly swallowed it again and made his way on shaky legs toward the door. He could see the sun beginning to rise and knew that whoever it was in there with her was most definitely *not* a vampire. The first rays were breaking the horizon and he kicked the door shut from the back side.

Damien wondered, not for the first time, if he were to simply walk out into the sunlight and turn to ash, would she miss him? Would she even realize it was because of her treatment of him? Would she care?

He slumped to the floor and held his head in his hands. He knew the answer. Even if she realized it was her fault, she wouldn't care. She didn't care. She'd never care again.

He lifted his eyes and stared toward her room, her rising screams and gasping breaths tearing at whatever it was inside that made him feel. He knew it wasn't a soul. He knew it wasn't a heart. But it was something.

And she was destroying it with each thrust.

14

Tracy watched Mark from an angle, nearly averting her eyes as he inhaled the food she brought. He finally leaned back against the wall and belched, rubbing his stomach. "Man, that hit the spot."

"It hit something." She looked at the splatters that hit the wall, the floor, and she swore there were some bits clinging to the ceiling. "I swear, Tufo, you need a shower now. You have bits of…gore, clinging to your whiskers."

Mark rubbed the back of his hand absently across his face and felt something greasy smear his arm. "I'll live," he answered absently.

He looked down at the gauze barely clinging to his chest and lifted it again. The bright pink scars were barely visible now. He peeled the rest of the bandages away and turned so that she could see.

"Oh my…" Her breath caught in her throat as she stared at him. Other than faint pink lines across his midsection, he looked nearly normal. "Cover that up. You're giving me goosebumps."

Mark shook his head as he pulled at the tape holding the stained bandages away and wadded them. "Screw that." He tossed the waste into the trash and stood in front of the sink. He stared at the light pink lines then turned his attention to his eyes. "I need to know what the hell is going on with me."

"What are you planning now?"

"First things first, I'm gonna grab a shower, wash this dried blood and gravy off me, then I'm gonna hit up Doc and see if he has any ideas."

"Mark, it's only been a few hours since—"

He turned on her suddenly and she withdrew, her hands coming up defensively. He cocked his head to the side and stared at her. "You know I'd never hurt you." He closed the gap between them slowly and took her hand in his. "Tell you what, I'm obviously not going to relapse. Head back to the house. Try to get some rest. If I get any answers from Doc, I'll call you."

She shook her head vehemently. "No, I'm staying with you."

"You can't, Honey. I'm going back to work, and I need answers. Trust me. When we get to the bottom of this, you'll be the next to know." He kissed her knuckles and she fought the urge to cringe. She couldn't explain why she felt that urge, but she did. She stared up at him and nodded slowly. He cupped her face and gave her a smile. "That's my girl. I'll call you as soon as I know anything." Kissing her softly on the forehead, he turned and headed for the door.

She sat and watched as he turned in the hallway and marched off smartly, looking every bit like a new man. She stood slowly on shaky legs and leaned against the sink. Lifting her face she caught her own reflection. Worrying and fretting over him had left her ragged and exhausted. Her face looked as if she had aged ten years overnight.

She inhaled deeply and blew it out hard. "You need sleep." Her reflection didn't respond. And it was a good thing it didn't. If it had, she would have signed herself into the Looney Bin.

*****

"So he just called out of the blue?" Jack sat back slowly, letting the news process.

"It took everything I had not to send a strike team after them as soon as we had a location lock on the call." Mitchell poured another cup of coffee and leaned back in his chair, facing Jack. "I thought I'd better get you in here and bounce this off of you since you were the last one to talk to him."

"I don't know what else I can add, Colonel. I thought I had him talked down at the island. I didn't even realize he had slipped off until the dust settled." Jack sipped his own coffee as Mitchell stared into his cup.

"He asked if there was anything he could do to get back in our good graces."

Jack's eyes widened at that. "What did you tell him?"

"No, what else could I tell him, Phoenix? The guy turned on his own teammates. He turned on all of us. And for what? Because Sheridan of all people told him his girlfriend was playing kissy face with somebody else?" Mitchell shook his head. "I would have bet the farm he was made of stronger stuff than that."

"So would I, sir." Jack set his cup on the corner of the desk and stared at him. "So what will you do with him?"

Mitchell shook his head. "I honestly have no idea." He ran a hand through his hair and stared at the ceiling. "By all rights, he should be killed in action when we raid that warehouse." Jack raised a brow at that but held his tongue. "We lost some damned good men here, and I know you lost good people due to him." Mitchell stood and paced his office, the tension building. "What would I do with him if we simply took him into custody? Lock him up in the silver cells? For how long? Forever? Ban him? Put him in a military prison?" He threw his hands up in disgust.

"I can only imagine what you're going through, Colonel. Something like this is unprecedented."

"You're damned right it is. We operate outside of so many rules...but the rules *have* to apply or what are we doing this for?" Mitchell paused and lowered his head. "Jack, I'm at a loss here."

"Are you asking me to lead a team in there to take him out, sir?" Jack prayed the colonel would say no.

"Negative." He worked his way back to his seat and stared at it as though it were a foreign object. He slowly lowered himself into it and rubbed the back of his neck. "He wants us to direct an attack on the full moon while their men are shifted. They have silver lined cargo containers or some such for them to lock themselves into. He'll be the only one still in human form." Mitchell looked up to meet Jack's gaze. "You and I will be locked up down below. We're going to have to trust the squads to take care of this."

"So, either Jones or Gregory will be taking lead on this op…" Jack trailed off, his mind racing through different scenarios. "Mark will be out of the game for a while."

Mitchell picked up his coffee again and sipped at it. "We'll be spread thin for this full moon, but we've been there before."

"I could call in reinforcements if you don't want the squads to dirty their hands with this one." Jack actually looked forward to having a reason to contact the Wyldwood and grill her personally, even if it was under the guise of asking for reinforcements for a night.

"Naw, we have this covered." Mitchell fought the urge to stand up and pace again. "I just wish that everything didn't have to go to Hell in a hand basket all at once, ya know?"

"Try to look at the silver lining, Colonel. The attacks pointed out the weak spots in the armor. You're having those fixed. Now we know who directed the attacks, even if we don't know who was behind it."

Mitchell looked up at him and set his coffee cup down. "We know now. Laura came through on that one."

"Clue me in, sir."

"Remember that little blonde gal that wolfed out and tore me a new one? Alpha One?"

"Your Fated Mate. She's the one behind this?" Jack was floored at the prospect.

"Negative. Her *father*. Apparently he's some rich son of a bitch…literally. He wants revenge for what was done to his little girl."

Jack let out a low whistle. Thinking about his own child soon to grace the world and putting himself in the father's place, he couldn't truly blame him.

*****

Laura opened her eyes and turned slightly to watch Jennifer. She sat stiffly in her chair, her eyes pinned forward toward the cockpit door, her cheeks wet with wiped tears. Laura couldn't be sure the full extent of her relationship with Mick, but she knew what being torn looked like and Jennifer was definitely torn. Laura gazed out the side window and tried to place herself in her friend's position. A lifelong friend and possible lover betrayed her to a father whose evil spans multiple continents. A Fated Mate that once shot her in the face then held her as a lab rat for a decade. Forced to choose what is expected of her and not what her heart wants. Laura cast a furtive glance toward the smaller woman and saw her wipe at her face again.

"It's not too late you know. We could have Mick divert the flight and…"

"You know we can't."

Laura turned back to the window and leaned her head against the plastic. "Because I'm not wolf, I know." She shook her head in confusion. "You know, I used to be jealous of the strength and agility that our men had because of the wolf. I even caught myself daydreaming more than once what it might be like. To be like you, I mean. A natural born wolf." She turned once more and saw Jennifer studying her. "But I'll be honest, this whole idea that a force outside of myself dictating who I'm supposed to marry? That doesn't sit well with me."

Jennifer smiled and cast her gaze off into the distance. "Not all wolves meet their Fated Mates. Many...actually, *most*, never do. They'll meet somebody, fall in love and get married. Some will have kids and live a perfectly normal life together. Most stay married until death." She turned and faced Laura, her face suddenly solemn. "But those who have the chance...the opportunity to be with their Fated one? That is something that simply can't be ignored."

"So you've said."

"No, Laura, you don't comprehend. Being *mated* isn't the same as married. Your souls are bound together. You feel what each other feels on such a level that words cannot describe. Your lives are physically bound together. If one wolf dies, the other dies as well. It isn't just a mating or coupling...not a pairing. It's...truly becoming one with your mate. Your lives become so intertwined that you become a part of your mate."

Laura raised a brow. *She's really drank the Kool-Aid if she buys all that.* "And you want to bind to somebody like that? I mean, if they die, you die? Really?"

Jennifer smiled. "It's an honor to find your Fated one. If he truly is mine, I can't imagine saying no." She sighed as she turned back toward the front. "And when I became a woman, I gave up childish things."

Oh yeah. She didn't just drink the Kool-Aid, she guzzled from the pitcher. "What if Mick is who you were supposed to be with?"

Jennifer's head spun around and she stared at her. "What do you mean?"

"I mean, what if all of this is just a test? You created Matt, didn't you? He isn't even a natural born wolf, right? You said yourself that this shouldn't be happening. So, what if you were supposed to be with Mick and the fates are testing your resolve?"

Jennifer shook her head. "A wolf cannot be with a cat. It isn't natural."

"Yeah, lots of things aren't natural. That doesn't stop it from happening." Laura sighed and slumped into her seat. "I'm just playing Devil's Advocate here. What do I care if you go against your heart."

"Who are you to know my heart?"

Laura didn't even turn to look at her. "Any idiot can see that you and Mick love each other. If you're both too proud to admit it, that isn't my fault."

*****

Sheridan shuffled through his papers and stuffed a small handful into a leather portfolio. "Big, do you have the inventories for the southside storage containers?"

Bigby reached across his small workspace and pulled a short stack of paper. "Right here." Handing them to Sheridan he watched as the man sifted through them then added them to the portfolio with the others. "How're we doing on our supplies?"

"With the next shipment, we should be able to arm a nice sized force." Sheridan dropped the leather folio to the ground and kicked it under the counter. "When are the reinforcements supposed to arrive from Mr. Simmons?"

"The day after the full moon." Bigby leaned back in his chair and interlaced his hands behind his neck. "Do the boys know that we'll have company?"

"A small handful of Mr. Simmons' more trusted wolves do." Sheridan booted up his computer and clicked on the internet, wanting to check their last shipment and estimated arrival times. "Once they're here, we'll leave the proper breadcrumbs so that the squads will come to us, and we can take care of them once and for all."

"So that's the plan? Make them come to us?"

Sheridan turned and gave him a smirk. "Partly. I'm sure they'll want payback, so I'm hoping they'll send most of their forces. The reinforcements will be here to handle them while we finish what we started at their stupid little hangar."

"You don't think they'll be expecting that?"

"They won't be expecting what I'm bringing this time." Sheridan chuckled to himself. "I'm taking Mr. Williams' advice this time and drop a bit of gas on them. Let their own ventilation system deliver the killing blow."

"I like the sound of that. Let the gas take them out and then we go in and mop up the bastards." Bigby got to his feet and stretched.

"We won't have to do much mopping up, old boy. Hit them with mustard gas and regardless of whether they're wolf, vampire or human, their flesh will blister, their lungs will fill with their own fluids…it will be quite painful. The supernatural beings might recover with time, but we'll have put silver slugs into their brain pan by then."

Bigby shook his head at the idea. "You truly are a nasty one."

"I know. One of my more redeeming qualities, if you ask me." Both men laughed at the offhand comment as Apollo walked into the office.

"Did I miss a joke?"

"Not at all my dear boy. We were just discussing our upcoming tactics." Sheridan pushed Apollo's favorite stool toward him with his foot. "Have a seat."

"You decided what we're going to use to lure the squads out here?" Apollo tried to appear nonchalant.

"We have a few ideas." Bigby leaned against the counter. "But we haven't decided for sure yet."

Apollo leaned against the workbench and nodded. "You could just call them and let them trace the call." He glanced to Sheridan and shrugged. "That would definitely get their attention."

"A little obvious, don't you think?"

Apollo smiled. "They got their asses handed to them. You really think they'd care? They'd *have* to respond." He glanced to Bigby. "Wouldn't you?"

Bigby considered the situation and nodded. "Actually, yeah. I think I would. Even if I suspected a trap, I'd still go." He glanced to Sheridan.

Sheridan looked between the two men and nodded. "Very well then. When the time comes, we may well do that."

"It's safer than sending some of our able bodied boys out there to lead them in." Apollo shrugged.

"True enough." Sheridan clicked off the computer and turned to Apollo. "So have you given my offer any more thought since we last discussed it?"

Apollo detected something in his voice that he couldn't quite identify. He almost felt like he was about to walk into a trap. He leaned back in his chair and crossed his meaty arms over his chest. "Actually, I have." He glanced at Bigby then back to Sheridan. "In fact, I made up my mind last night and came out here to find you but you was laughing it up with Big here, so I did an about face and went back to bed."

Sheridan raised a brow and glanced at Bigby who visibly stiffened. "Really? Why didn't you join us?"

Apollo cocked his head to the side and gave Sheridan a knowing look. "What I had to say was between you and me." He hooked a thumb toward Bigby. "I didn't want to interrupt you two and tell him to beat feet."

Sheridan nodded then turned to Bigby. "Excuse us for a moment, would you old boy?"

Bigby huffed and pushed off the counter. "Yeah, yeah. You two have your little tea party. I'll go do some real work."

After he was far enough away Apollo turned back to Sheridan. "I'll do it."

"Just like that?"

"You said it. You ain't in physical shape to run missions like what needs done and Bigby? If brains were dynamite, the boy couldn't blow his own nose."

Sheridan smiled then extended his hand. "Welcome aboard. Partner."

*****

"This is the satellite imagery for the area. According to Apollo they have silver lined cargo containers, so I'm assuming that's what these are here." Mitchell pointed to the long rows of shipping containers set in rows along the abandoned truck parking area between the two warehouses. He looked up at Jericho Jones and shook his head. "I honestly don't know how much faith to put into what Apollo says after what he's pulled."

"No worries, Colonel. I'll have a drone in the air and as long as we don't have two ops going at the same time, I'll pull a second team to act as security." He pointed to the high points. "If I put men here, here, here and here, we'll have a bird's eye view of the entire compound. Nothing will be able to move in there without our knowing it."

"Make sure your primary and secondary teams have IR beacons. I don't want anybody getting pinged by friendly fire because they saw a shadowy fast mover."

"Copy that." Jericho stood tall and stretched his back. "What of Apollo himself? Will he be in a container, or…"

"He thinks he'll probably be standing security." Mitchell turned away and shook his head. "To be honest Captain, I don't know what to do with him."

"Shall we consider him a hostile, sir?"

Mitchell sighed and practically fell into his chair, his eyes focusing on a photo of Second Squad when Apollo first made Team Leader. "I'm not prepared to give that order, Captain." His eyes crept up and read the young man's face. Jericho would make an excellent poker player. He gave away nothing.

"Very well, sir." He bent and scooped up the satellite photos. "If you change your mind, let me know."

"Jericho."

He turned and faced the Colonel, his face still stoic. "Sir?"

"When you address the squads and go over the mission?" Mitchell felt like he was listening to somebody else say the words that came out of his mouth next. "Leave Apollo's fate in their hands. He was their peer. He was their Team Leader. He turned against them as much as he did me." He turned in his chair and gave Jericho his back. "I don't want to know their decision."

"Yes, sir."

*****

Foster clicked off the satellite phone and reclined in his seat. "Transportation has been taken care of. There was an issue with the number of vehicles. Apparently they thought we were a small party. They didn't take into account our enforcers."

"Had Monsieur Thompson came with us, it would have been a small party." Thorn cracked open an eye and fought a smile. He knew how much Paul hated Jack, and he still found humor in his brother's bristling at the mention of his name.

"We don't need the likes of him." Foster spat. "Anyone who swears allegiance to you and then turns the first time you don't inform him of one of your little pet projects doesn't deserve to be your Second."

Thorn nodded slightly, his eye closing. "Monsieur Thompson never swore allegiance to me. Only to his beloved."

"All the more reason to kick his hairy ass to the curb." Foster crossed his arms over his chest and fumed. "He should know that the master of the castle has affairs that he couldn't possibly understand."

"Perhaps." Thorn sat up and turned to his brother. "But if we are to be honest, we both know that he is simply a man of honor. He couldn't work for someone who both stole from his former employers but also attempted to build a Doomsday weapon."

"Pish-posh. He is weak minded. Anybody who can't understand your *need* for such a weapon…"

"*Non.* We both know that is not the case. Jack is many things, but he is not weak minded. He is perhaps one of the best tactical minds I have met." Thorn sat back and allowed his words to soak in. "Just one of the many reasons I enjoyed having him around."

Foster turned slowly to face his brother. "You miss him?"

"At times. Like I miss Viktor." Thorn sighed and shook his head. "Sometimes an unorthodox point of view is refreshing."

"He was a heathen. Unorthodox? He was uncouth!"

Thorn laughed and nodded. "*Oui.* That he was. Very much so. But he was very good at what he did."

"Keeping you safe."

"Among other things." Thorn turned to his brother again. "Do you know how many times the Council made attempts on me while Jack was in my employ?" Foster shook his head. "Seven. In the few short months that I knew him, he thwarted their efforts seven times. The first was a dear friend of his. A man he had known for decades. A man that should have been unreachable, yet, the Council found a way to get to him. And Jack stopped him. Because he believed in me. He believed in what I stood for." Rufus Thorn paused and stared out the window, realizing perhaps for the first time just how deeply he had let down the man he called 'friend'. "I assured him that I, too, was a man of honor." His voice dropped to a whisper. "I assured him that I would sooner die than harm another human. And yet…"

"You needed to regain your strength, brother." Foster sat up and leaned toward him. "You were dying. Your work is important and it…"

"*Non*. If I could go back and do it over again, I would rather have died than take a human life." He slowly shook his head. "But beside that, I lied to him. I had a weapon built that had the potential to destroy all 'others'."

"A minimal risk. You said so yourself."

Thorn shook his head. "Perhaps it was divine intervention that the device didn't work." He turned his troubled face back to Foster. "Tell me brother, do you still believe in God?"

"I believe that there is one. But not for the likes of us."

Rufus turned back to the window and the night sky. "I pray that you're wrong." He stared out into the inky blackness. "And I pray that both He and Jack will one day forgive me my trespass."

*****

"What do you mean, 'our discretion'?" Gus Tracy asked his face puzzled.

Jericho closed the file folder he held and pressed it to his chest. "That's exactly what I said. Rather, what I was told. Apollo didn't just turn against the Colonel or the Squads in general; he turned against each and every one of you." He shook his head as he looked at each of the operators. "I don't envy your decision either way. Bring him back to face eternity behind bars and in silver shackles or drop him. Not an easy choice."

Donovan shook his head. "That's not justice. That's murder. He's not a monster."

Wallace turned and gave him a cockeyed look. "I think Carbone might disagree with you on that."

"Along with all of the techs and security forces that bit it that night." Lamb's mouth was a tight line as he leaned against the back wall of the briefing room.

"Are we really considering this?" Spalding stepped forward and turned to face the crowd. "Apollo was one of us. He was a team player. He trained with us, bled with us…"

"He turned against us." Wallace crossed his arms over his chest. "Look, I know you worked with him a lot longer than most of us, but the fact is, he's a wolf, he turned against the squads and he got good men killed. Not just here, but at the island where Phoenix and Mueller live."

"And if it weren't for him, we wouldn't have the Intel that we have now." Spalding stepped back and spread his arms wide. "Tell me that none of you have ever made a mistake in your life? In your entire life you've never screwed up?"

"I never opened fire on my buddies." Wallace refused to back down. "I never led a team of assassins to where my brothers lived and trained and let them loose on them. That's FUBAR man, and you know it."

"The guy was messed up in the head." Spalding tried to plead with the men. "He was torn up over Maria and this jack-off Sheridan got to him. Twisted him all up and…messed with his head."

"Tell me something, Spank." Jacobs stepped forward, his eyes red. "Could anybody mess with your head enough to make you go rogue on us?"

Spanky opened his mouth to reply but held his tongue. He lowered his eyes and shook his head. "No."

Jacobs laid a gentle hand on his shoulder and squeezed. "Look, I'm not saying we need to mow Apollo down. I'm not. I'm not saying we need to bring him back in chains either." He turned and looked at the rest of the group. "But maybe…just maybe, there is another choice here. I say banishment is the best option here. Just, cut him loose. Have nothing more to do with him. Forget he was ever one of us and leave him to his own devices. If he resurfaces later and he's a threat to humanity, then we do what we do best. But if he doesn't? If he fades into the darkness and disappears…maybe finds a pack or something and just stays away, then we let him."

Spalding looked up at Jacobs then scanned the room seeing the other operators' heads bobbing in agreement. "I like that idea, Ing." Spalding looked from man to man. "It's all or nothing. Either we're all in this together or we're not. It has to be unanimous."

"Banishment." Lamb nodded then looked to the man next to him. Each repeated the vote until it was unanimous throughout the room.

Jacobs smiled and squeezed Spalding's shoulder tighter. "Then banishment it is. You fought hardest for him, Spanky. I think you should explain it to him."

Spalding lowered his eyes, grateful that a solution was found that allowed his friend to live. "Gladly."

*****

Gaius stepped out of Lilith's room covered in sweat, bloody scratches and bite marks. He made no effort to cover his nakedness as he strode toward Damien. "You!" He pointed to Damien cowering in the shadows. "Water and wine. Now."

He turned back toward the room as Damien came to his feet, his anger rising as he did. "I'm not a slave."

Gaius stopped in midstep and turned to face the trembling vampire. "Did you dare speak back to me?"

"You heard me. If you want something to drink, get it yourself." Damien caught his breath and stuck his chest out.

Gaius tilted his head as he considered the little vampire. He suddenly tilted his head back and laughed. A deep, dark, throaty laugh that made Damien's anger rise even further. When he stopped laughing, he wiped at his eyes then crossed his arms over his chest. "You *will* do as I say, little ghoul, or meet the true death."

"The true death would be preferable to being a slave to a demon."

Gaius smiled as he walked slowly toward him. Damien did his best to keep his eyes on the man's face, but he instinctively lowered his eyes to what dangled below his waist, his curiosity getting the better of him. "Like what you see, little ghoul?"

Damien's eyes shot back up to the demon's face, and he nearly took a step back. Red, glowing eyes stared back at him, a grey, smoldering smoke wisping from the sides of his face. "Y-you don't scare me."

"Yes I do." Gaius raised a hand toward Damien and outstretched his fingers. Damien felt something compel his body to go rigid. "Kneel before me, little ghoul." As Gaius lowered his hand, Damien felt his legs grow weak and his body slowly lower to the ground.

"N-no…I won't." His voice cracked as he cried through gritted teeth, every fiber of his being fighting against the unseen pull of the demon before him.

"Ah, but you already have." Gaius stepped directly in front of Damien and swung his hips back and forth, smacking Damien in the face with his wet, sticky, flaccid penis. "I told you to get water and wine. And you *will* do it. Or you'll find out just how much stamina this body has left in it." Gaius laughed again as his manhood began to swell with each slap against the vampire's face.

Damien fought to not reply lest he get a mouthful of something that he'd rather not. The demon continued to torture and humiliate him, slapping him unmercifully with his member.

"Gaius, don't tease him. He is a flesh eater, you know." Lilith's voice called from behind the pair.

"He's enjoying it, my queen. See how he leans into it. He wants so badly to open his mouth and accept it, don't you little ghoul?"

Damien realized that the demon was making 'little ghoul' sound like 'little girl' as he spoke. He mustered all of his hatred and stared up at the demon, a smile crossing his features. Thank the goddess for reminding him what he truly was. He *was* a flesh eater. And he'd eaten the flesh of men before. Perhaps not this particular piece of flesh…but male flesh was still flesh.

Damien opened his mouth to snap off a certain dangling portion of flesh when he found his jaws locked open and a foreign invader jammed deep into his throat, Gaius' laughter echoed through the warehouse as he grabbed Damien by the hair and did unspeakable things to him.

"Gaius. Don't waste that beautiful thing on the likes of him. I still have needs. Do you have any idea how many centuries I've gone without? We have a lot of lost time to make up for." Damien choked as Gaius made one last deep ramming motion then withdrew from his mouth, releasing his grasp and allowing him to collapse to the floor. He could hear his goddess purring as Gaius turned and marched back to her.

"Don't forget the water and the wine." The door slammed shut and Damien curled into a ball again.

From scourge of the vampire world to demon fluffer. Could my life get any worse?

15

Mark stepped from the showers and wrapped the towel around his middle. He stepped to the next room and unzipped his shave kit. He flipped on the hot water and wet his razor then set it aside as he picked up the shave gel. Squirting a small gob in his palm he worked it into a lather, then spread it on his face and rinsed his hands. Picking up his razor he glanced into the mirror and paused. His eyes dropped to the top of his chest and the barely visible scar that hardly showed up in his reflection. He stepped back and stood taller, taking in his full abdomen. Nearly all of the scars were faded to nothing. He let out a low whistle and shook his head. "Why doesn't this scare the ever loving dogshit out of me?"

"Yo, asshole. I thought you were near death?"

Mark spun and saw Dom leaning against the far wall, smiling at him. "The rumors of my death have been wildly exaggerated."

"Apparently." Dom stepped closer and glanced at his chest. "You got infected, huh." It was obviously a statement.

Mark shrugged. "It's looking like it." He turned and wet his razor again, dragging it across his face, being careful to follow the lines of his goatee. "The real question is, 'with what'?"

Dom watched him go through the motions a moment then shrugged. "Does it matter what it was if it's keeping you alive?"

Mark paused in mid stroke and stared at Dom's reflection. "I would think it matters." He went back to shaving, trying to concentrate on not cutting his own throat. "I don't want to transform into something we don't understand and hurt my family."

Dom nodded as he considered the possibilities. "I thought we were pretty positive that it was a bunch of wolves that attacked the hangar."

Mark shrugged as he rinsed his razor and brought it back to his face. "Yeah, it sure looked like a wolf that tore my guts out." He shuddered involuntarily as the memories resurfaced. "But what if it was somehow Doc that infected me instead? He said that the wolf never bit me. It was all claw marks. No teeth were involved."

Dom watched him curiously a moment then stepped forward and jerked Mark's arm. "Hey! What the...son of a bitch. You made me cut myself. Now I'm bleeding."

Dom smiled. "You'll live." He raised a brow. "So it must be wolf. If it were vampire, your heart wouldn't be beating."

"*You* need a beating." Mark muttered as he rinsed away the shave cream and dabbed at the cut. It was nearly healed before he could pull out his septic stick. "Son of a...well." He slumped his shoulders and dropped the septic stick back into his shave kit.

"Like I said. If you were infected with vampirism, you'd be dead. No heartbeat, no bleeding."

Mark glared into the mirror. "Thanks for the lesson." He watched Dom through the corner of his eye as he finished shaving.

"Hey, you won't age as fast. And you'll get stronger."

Mark glanced into the mirror and squared his shoulders. "I didn't think it would be this quick." He flexed his arms in the mirror and shot Dom a smirk.

Dom's brows creased. "It usually isn't." He stepped closer and stared at Mark. "You look...bigger."

Mark pulled out his towel and glanced down. He shot Dom a smile. "Thanks for noticing."

"That's not what I..." Dom threw his hands up in surrender. "I'll take your word on that one."

Mark rinsed his face with steaming hot water and tossed his stuff back into the shave kit. "All I know is I'm freaking starving. Like, *all* the time."

Dom nodded knowingly. "It will subside. Probably after the full moon." He looked up suddenly. "You are on the bane, right?"

"Doc put me on it right away, just in case. Looks like it was a damn good thing he did." Mark tucked his shave kit under his arm and made his way to the locker room. "Now that I'm healed up, I can't wait to get back to work. I need the distraction."

Dom followed him. "You sure the Colonel will be okay with it? I mean, you were near dead just a few hours ago."

Mark shrugged as he opened his locker and pulled out his spare uniform. "I don't care what he says. I *need* the distraction. I'll go stir crazy if he makes me sit out any longer."

"What does the missus think of you just jumping back into the fray?"

Mark paused and stared at her picture in his locker. He gave a slight shrug and shook his head. "I sent her home. She doesn't need to worry if I'm going to pull through and…honestly? Her sitting by my side was making me a nervous wreck."

"You didn't answer my question."

Mark sighed and sat down hard on the bench. "Dom, I didn't ask her for her input, okay? I just told her to go home and rest. I'm healed up, bouncing off the walls with energy and…" He turned and stared at the big man. "I needed to get back to work so I have *something* to do."

"I think I understand." Dom sat next to him and patted his shoulder. "Really. I think I understand where you're coming from. But remember, she's supposed to be your number one priority. Not this job. Not the next mission. And certainly not Mitchell."

Mark turned and stared at him as if he were daft. "Duh."

Dom chuckled. "So don't keep her out of the loop. Even the little stuff. Include her. Unless she tells you to knock it off, let her know. Because it's her job to worry and believe me, she will."

"So how long have you been married to her?" Mark smirked at him.

Dom stood and held his hands up in surrender. "I had a mom, dude. I remember."

"Thank you, Doctor Phil." Mark pulled on his boots and laced them tight. "But if you'll excuse me, I'm going to finish dressing then sneak off to the chow hall and eat a cow or two."

"If you ask nicely, they'll even knock off the horns for you." Dom patted his shoulder as he passed by him in the narrow passage. "Just remember to keep her in the loop and maybe she'll let you live."

"And don't hump her leg, no matter how good she looks in that dress. Got it."

*****

"So that's the thing?" Jack stared at the small stone on Kalen's wrist and shook his head. "And you can talk to her any time you want?"

"Not any time I want, but any time she wants to reach me, she can." Kalen shrugged. "I'm not supposed to tell anybody who isn't Elf about the stone, but you are my leader. You must be able to trust me Chief Jack."

Jack sat back in his chair and gave Kalen a long, hard stare. "Are you breaking some kind of code or rule or something by letting me in on this?"

Kalen shrugged again. "In a way, yes."

"So, you broke the rules?" Jack raised a brow at him.

Kalen nodded. "In order that you might better understand how the Wyldwood speaks with me so often. It isn't that she refuses to speak with you, it's just much easier for her to speak with me."

"When she does, will anybody close to you be able to see her? Hear what she's saying?"

Kalen shook his head. "The stone is designed so that only the bearer can communicate with it."

"So." Jack rocked forward and got to his feet. "I guess that makes you my radioman."

Kalen gave him a confused look. "I'm sorry Chief Jack. I do not…"

"You'll be in charge of communications." Jack poured a cup of coffee and returned to his desk. "At least, with the Wyldwood. And do me a favor, the next time you talk to her, find out who our missing player is and when we can expect him. Or her."

"Yes, sir." Kalen swallowed hard. "There is one thing I need to speak with you about."

"Let me guess. The Wyldwood told you something."

Kalen nodded and seemed to squirm in his chair. "Yes, she did mention another, but not a warrior."

"Great. Somebody we need to hunt down?" Jack sipped the coffee and grimaced.

"No sir." Kalen hesitated slightly. "Have you ever dealt with griffins?"

Jack raised both brows on that one. "Griffins?" He shook his head as he thought back through his numerous missions. "Not that I can recall. Actually, to be honest, I thought they were fables."

"We're supposed to find a griffin named Allister. He will be your aid. A Second, if you will." Kalen's eyes searched Jack's face but the man remained stoic.

"A Second?" Jack sipped his coffee again. "I thought you were going to be my Second."

"As did I." Kalen looked away. "The Wyldwood claims that Allister brings much ancient knowledge that will help us."

"Ancient knowledge?"

Kalen nodded avoiding Jack's gaze still. "Griffins are very studious and much of history is handed down from generation to generation orally. They have fantastic memories, and Allister is a very old griffin. He knows much."

"Great. A smart bird." Jack sipped his coffee again and considered having to work with a griffin. "I guess we can put down a lot of newspapers."

Kalen gave him a surprised stare. "No! Chief Jack, griffins are not simply birds. They are majestic creatures."

Jack leaned forward and stared at him. "When you talk to them, do you, or do you not, speak to a bird head?"

"Well, yes. Technically their faces appear like an eagle, but they are more…"

"Like I said. A smart bird. May as well be a parrot." Jack leaned back and finished his coffee setting the cup down hard. "Is there anything else she may have slipped in during the conversation?"

Kalen opened his mouth to argue but held his tongue. He shook his head. "No, sir."

"Very well." Jack waved him out with his hand. "Until this talking bird shows up, you're still my Second. Just keep on eye on Brooke. Something tells me she's going to test you."

Kalen nodded and stood to leave. "Technically, we need to go in search of Allister."

Jack raised a brow at him. "If parrot boy is supposed to work with us, our paths will cross." He gave Kalen a wink. "But if Loren gives you an address, maybe we can stop by and pay him a visit."

Kalen smiled then turned to leave. Jack called out to him as he reached for the door, "I meant what I said about Brooke. When me and the Colonel are locked up, don't be surprised if she tests you."

Kalen opened the door and turned to face him. "I'd be disappointed if she didn't."

*****

Mick walked back through the passenger compartment and noticed Jennifer turning away from him. He paused only a moment at the brush off and instead turned to Laura. "We'll be landing shortly. If you'll make arrangements…" His voice sounded almost mechanical.

"Where are we landing at?" Laura glanced out the window but didn't recognize anything.

"An airport called Wiley Post, I think. From there, the plane will continue on to Dallas and the new owner." Mick looked to Jennifer again who seemed to find the clouds on her side of the plane mesmerizing.

"Will you be going on with the plane or disembarking with us?" Laura asked Mick, but her eyes were glued to Jennifer.

Mick looked from Laura to Jennifer, then back. He shrugged. "I suppose that's up to her. If she thinks she can stand for me to be around, then I'd like to go with the two of you."

"It's a free country." Jennifer crossed her arms over her chest and continued to stare out the window. "I can't stop you."

"That's not the same as an invitation." Mick's eyes pleaded with the side of her head.

Laura caught his attention. "That may be the best you'll get Mick. It's your decision."

Mick exhaled hard as he stared at Jennifer. "I have a plane to fly." He spun on his heel and headed forward again.

Laura waited until the cockpit door had shut before she turned to Jennifer. "You were a little rough on him, don't you think?"

"I don't love him."

"That's not what I said…"

"You did earlier." Jennifer turned slowly and glared at her. "You said that Mick and I were in love and too stubborn to act on it."

"What I said should have no bearing on how you treat him." Laura shifted in her seat to better see Jennifer. "Did you really have to be so mean?"

"He was a traitor." Jennifer's voice was barely a whisper. "I trusted him and he was working for my father."

"To keep you safe." Laura argued. "If your father truly was behind the attacks on the squad, then it just might have saved your life."

Jennifer huffed as she turned away again. "No excuse to betray our friendship."

"Your…friendship?" Laura snorted. "If it was *just* a friendship, I don't think you'd be so bent out of shape."

Jennifer turned on her and glared. "What did you just say?"

"I said, 'methinks she doth protest too much'."

Jennifer's eyes widened with shock before she turned her back on her again.

*****

Mitchell sat in his office and reviewed Apollo's service record. *How could I have missed it?* He continued to blame himself for one of his men turning against the squads and felt that somehow, he should have seen a warning sign. There had to have been something. A sign, a trigger, a *something* that could have given him a heads up of what was about to happen.

Mitchell shut the file and slipped it into his basket. He stood and walked to the window overlooking the training area. It sat empty at the moment and in his mind's eye, he could still see Apollo leading his squad through the close quarter's drills. Was he risking his other men by not scrutinizing the other members?

A knock at his door snapped him from his thoughts. "Come."

Mark opened the door and walked in, shutting the door behind him. "Reporting for duty, Colonel."

Mitchell nearly stumbled when he saw the man standing in his office, apparently no worse for wear. "What the…how the hell are you even standing?"

Mark exhaled hard and began unbuttoning his BDU blouse. He pulled his undershirt up and showed the minor scarring. "I have no explanation and neither does Doc. All I know is, I'm healed, I'm antsy as hell, hungry enough to eat half the chow hall and ready to get back to work before I go nuts."

Mitchell sat hard in his chair and stared at his oldest friend, a warning claxon going off in his mind. "Mark, this isn't good."

"You're telling me?" Mark tucked his shirt back in and buttoned his blouse. "What can I do? Doc is running some tests to see if he can figure out what the hell is going on with me. All I can tell you is my mind isn't muddled. I don't have weird thoughts or suicidal behavior. As far as I can tell, I'm fit for duty."

Mitchell slowly shook his head. "This…this isn't right."

Mark approached his desk and stood at parade rest. "Colonel, I don't know what I can tell you to put your mind at ease. All I can do is assure you that it's still me. I may be infected, but Doc has me on the bane. I'm healed and if you don't let me get back to work, I'm going to…"

"What?" Mitchell raised a questioning brow.

Mark shook his head. "I'm going to lose my damned mind." He met Mitchell's gaze and pleaded with his eyes. "Please, sir. Just let me do my job. It's all I have to keep my sanity."

Mitchell rocked back and forth in his chair as he considered his XO's request. "This is so unorthodox. By all rights, you should be in a sick bed for at least three weeks. Maybe longer."

"I realize that, sir, but…"

"But here you stand with barely a stinking scratch on you." Matt stood and approached him, his eyes studying every inch of the man. "I have no idea how that's even possible."

Mark sighed heavily and turned to face him. "Permission to speak freely, sir?"

"What's with all the formality, Mark? Take a seat and speak your mind."

Mark pulled the chair out and sat in it, his mind racing as he considered the ramifications of what he was about to do. He looked to his boss and searched his face for some readable sign. "This is just between us, okay?"

Mitchell shook his head. "I'm sorry, buddy. I can't do that. After all this crap with Apollo…I can't risk that. Not any longer." He spun in his chair and poured another cup of coffee. "But I will keep this conversation off the record. It may well sway my decision, but it doesn't have to be a part of anything formal."

Mark hung his head and clenched his teeth. "Is that the best you can do? For me?"

Mitchell sipped at his coffee and nodded. "I'm afraid so, buddy. I can't afford to screw up any worse than I already have. You know how we operate here. If we mess up, we try to learn from it so it never happens again."

"So that means we can't trust each other?"

"No, not at all. It just means that I have to take everything into consideration when…Mark, look at you. You should still be a pile of hamburger and lying in bed healing. I can't promise you something without knowing what it is."

Mark nodded and leaned back. "Fine." He closed his eyes and tried to think of a way to tell Matt the scenarios playing out in his fear-filled mind. "As I said, Doc is running tests, but…I think there may be a chance that I got infected with something other than the wolf virus."

Mitchell leaned forward and stared at him. "Define *other*."

Mark took a deep breath and blew it out slowly. "I haven't said anything to anybody else. Only Doc and Tracy know that this is even a remote possibility."

"Spill it, XO." Mitchell was starting to become agitated.

"I'm worried that maybe somehow I got infected by Doc during surgery. Maybe somehow both viruses are running through my body."

Mitchell sat back and gave him a wide eyed stare. "You're serious?"

"Deadly."

"What makes you think this?"

"Look at how fast I healed. Only vampires can do that, right?"

"But organisms can't harbor both viruses at the same time. It's just not possible." Mitchell almost laughed, except there was nothing funny to the situation.

"You think I don't know this?" Mark stood and began pacing, hoping to burn off some of the nervous energy he felt. "But nothing else makes sense. It can't be *just* the wolf virus. I wouldn't have healed as fast. It can't be *just* the vampire virus. I wouldn't have a heartbeat."

"But you do. Right?"

"Yeah. And trust me, Dom made sure that I can still bleed." Mitchell gave him a curious stare and Mark waved him off. "Nothing…suffice to say, I still have a heartbeat. I'm not craving blood. Although a nice, big, rare steak sounds pretty good right about now."

"That's probably the wolf virus."

"Oh, I'm sure the hunger is all wolf virus, but it doesn't explain the rapid healing." Mark stopped pacing and turned to face him. "Doc is trying to isolate the virus, but he doesn't have the equipment. All he can do is try to 'test me' to see what I react to. Since both are allergic to silver…"

"Yeah. I see the problem." Mitchell scratched at his chin as he thought. "Have you tried sunlight?"

"It's still dark out, but I intend to."

"We do have UV generators." Mitchell stood and went to the other side of his office. Pulling the blinds back he pointed to Evan's lab. "Right down there."

Mark sighed as he stared at Dr. Peters working in his lab. "I guess I could at least test that part first."

"Beats stepping outside and bursting into flames."

Mark gave him a stupid look. "You think?"

"Contrary to popular belief, I kind of like you the way you are. I'd rather you not become a human french fry." Mitchell clapped his back. "You're reinstated, but on limited duty for the time being. I want you to work with Doc and figure out what the hell is going on with you."

"And if we can't figure it out?"

"We'll cross that bridge when we get to it."

*****

Foster's head turned on a swivel as they worked their way to the waiting cars. Although the plane was parked safely inside a sealed hangar, he didn't discount the possibility that a squad of assassins were lurking in the shadows ready to drop each and every one of them. He ushered Rufus quickly to the waiting limo and slammed the door behind them. "I think it may be safe."

Thorn raised a brow at him. "Truly?" The sarcasm was missed as Foster continued to bounce from window to window, watching the enforcers load up in the escort vehicles.

"Yeah, I'm pretty sure we're good."

"What a relief." Thorn leaned back in the thick leather seat and nodded to the driver. The limo pulled out and the garage door opened allowing them out. "Once we get to the hotel, we'll only have a few hours before our meeting with the Council. Are your people prepared?"

"They're ready and standing by. Each one is prepared to give their life for you, brother."

Rufus nodded, unsure whether to believe Paul and his paranoid driven fantasies. "I'm not sure that will be necessary."

Foster turned and gave him a hard stare. "This is the Council we're talking about here. They've tried seven times in the last six months to kill you. You don't think it will be necessary?"

"They've given us safe passage for this meeting. Or did you forget?"

"And you trust them?" Foster wasn't sure he heard his brother correctly.

"Of course not. But they'll want to know the nature of our request before they try anything." Thorn smiled and patted Paul's knee. "That is when we shall win them over."

"You hope."

"*Non.* I know."

"How can you be so certain, brother?"

Thorn turned and gave Foster a hard stare. "Because our lives depend upon it."

*****

"A griffin?" Azrael shook his head as the words sunk in. "I've never met one."

"Tastes like chicken." Brooke shot him an evil smile. "A bit more chewy though."

Gnat snorted and leaned on his hammer. "I doubt you've ever laid eyes on a griffin. They're not fond of vampires."

Brooke gave him a narrow stare. "Nobody likes gnomes. You're just here as a mascot."

"Ease down." Kalen raised a hand to gather their attention again. "Chief Jack says that for now, we have to…"

"Who died and made you boss?"

Kalen turned to Brooke and tried not to react. "You were here when Chief Jack made me his Second."

"I thought the griffin was his Second?" She leaned against the table and shot Kalen a smirk.

"He will be once we find him. Until then, I am Second." He turned back to the group. "As I was saying…"

"We have to *find* this griffin?"

"Brooke, please." Kalen did his best to hide his displeasure.

"Raven," her voice was like ice as she spoke,"my name is Raven."

"Very well. Raven, please." Kalen implored with his eyes. "We have things to do while Chief Jack prepares for the full moon."

Brooke huffed before hopping onto the table and turning away from the others. Kalen watched her for just a moment before returning his attention back to the others. "As I was saying, there is still another that will be joining us, but we still don't know who or when. Allister will be able to provide us much insight into whatever we are to face in the future. He is a most wise and powerful griffin."

"You do realize," Gnat spoke up, eyeing Brooke as she ignored them, "griffins are predators. They've been known to eat everything from gnomes to elves. Even humans."

Kalen nodded. "Wild, feral, lesser griffins, yes. This is true." He lowered his gaze to Gnat. "But saying that all griffins are this way would be like saying that all gnomes are rock farmers."

"Blasphemy!" Gnat snapped to attention and had his hammer in his grip in a flash. "There are as many types of gnomes as there are elves!"

"Precisely." Kalen held a hand up to calm the small warrior. "Just as there are many types of griffins."

Azrael pushed past Gnat. "The 'other' that will be joining us. We don't know who or when, but did the Wyldwood say what to expect?"

Kalen shook his head. "Only to expect another."

"So it could be another gargoyle?" Azrael appeared hopeful.

"Or a gnome?" Gnat smiled from between Azrael's legs.

Kalen shrugged. "Or a vampire. Or an elf. I honestly do not know."

"If it's another vampire, can I leave?" Brooke finally turned to face him.

Kalen paused, his mouth open but words not coming. Eventually he shook his head and lowered his eyes. "Raven, I have no control over who is to be part of our hunting party."

"Hunting party? Is that what you call this mish-mash of unfortunate players?" Brooke laughed as she stared at the others. "We have a rock gardener with a hammer, a rock beast by day and winged demon by night, a blonde Indian and a friggin' vampire. Does that sound like a 'hunting party' to you?"

Kalen's eyes narrowed as he stared at her. "You are so very wrong." His voice was low and menacing. He took a step toward her, his jaw set. "You have a gargoyle *warrior*, a *warrior* gnome, a *warrior* elf and YOU." He squared off with her, his gaze set. "While I can't speak for your abilities, I can tell you from experience that these warriors are all battle tested and work well together as a team. We didn't choose for you to join our hunting party, but the Wyldwood proclaimed it. Therefore, we must accept it."

Brooke stiffened and slid off the table, squaring her own shoulders. "I didn't ask to become a part of this circus either ya know."

"Regardless, you will show them respect or find yourself on the wrong end of a warrior's wrath."

Brooke shot him an evil smile. "Any time you're ready cotton top."

Kalen moved to advance when a mighty hand stayed him. "Forgive me." Azrael bowed his head to Kalen as he held him back. "You are the Second and your word shall be heeded. I felt it necessary to prevent the two of you from doing something you'd both regret."

"Let 'em go at it." Gnat shot Brooke a dirty grin. "She needs to be knocked down a peg or two."

"No." Azrael shook his head. "Our leader needs to lead and *all* of us need to heed his words." He cast a lingering glance to Brooke. "That includes you, vampire."

"What the hell is going on here?" Jack stepped into the room and glared at each of them.

"I didn't do nothing,I was just standing here." Gnat stepped back and propped his hammer over his shoulder.

"There are no issues, Chief Jack." Azrael let go of Kalen's shoulder and bowed slightly to Jack. "Just a slight disagreement. It is settled now."

"Is it?" Jack looked to Kalen and Brooke.

Brooke threw her hands in the air. "Hey, I can't help it if Sugar Cookie can't take a joke."

Kalen turned to Jack and bent to one knee. "I have failed you as your Second, Chief Jack. I humbly request that you select another."

Jack chewed at the inside of his lip as he watched Kalen lower his eyes to the floor. "Sorry, kid,you're the one." He tapped him on the shoulder. "On your feet."

Kalen glanced up, shock and surprise plain to see across his features. "I don't…"

"Squaring off is one thing. If I'd had to bring a bodybag in here, then I'd relieve you."

"The body bag would have been for him." Brooke stared at her nails as she pretended to clean them.

"Possibly." Jack stepped between the two. "But I can tell you both this right here, right now. If you don't bury the hatchet and figure out how to work together, you're going to have to figure out how to live with a size-twelve boot in your ass."

Brooke shot him a rebellious stare and Jack shook his head. "Don't test me." He watched as she lowered her eyes and nodded. "We're a team now. You have to learn to work together, fight together and trust that each has the other's back. The future may well depend on it."

*****

Damien stood outside the office that Lilith called her bedroom. He shook with righteous anger and prayed that somebody would give him the power to destroy Gaius. The humiliation dished upon him was more than he could bear. He stared at the platter with the pitcher of water and bottle of wine and ground his teeth together. He was *not* a slave. He was a vampire!

Damien shook with righteous rage as he listened to the two of them go at it beyond the door. The screams of ecstasy and the grunting, huffing and puffing was enough to make him want to burn the building down around their ears. If he thought for a moment that it would work…

He set the platter down and fought the urge to kick it over, sending the drinks across the concrete floor. His rage only grew as he considered the turn of events. He had gone from being promised to rule at her side to being nothing more than a…what did she call him? A pet?

He stomped away and growled under his breath. *If I had a soul, I'd sell it for the chance to put that bastard in his place!* He swung at empty air and wished that Gaius' head had been there.

Damien slumped to the ground and pressed his hands over his ears, his eyes clamped shut in a vain attempt to block their activities from his ears.

For the briefest of moments, Damien felt a tingling, a pull like nothing he'd felt before. He opened his eyes and saw a strange green glow coming from within the warehouse. He dropped his hands and immediately a buzzing invaded his mind. It wasn't so much in his ears as it was in his head.

He stood and looked around the empty warehouse, the source of the noise and light…apparently everywhere. There was no single thing causing it that he could see. For just the briefest of moments, Damien felt fear. Fear of the unknown, fear of what was to come, fear of a power unlike any he had ever sensed before. But just as quickly, the fear passed and he opened himself to the possibilities. *Is this the answer to my prayer?*

He stepped away from the wall and walked closer to the office that Lilith called her bedroom. He looked about and noticed…the light…was shining on him, focusing its brilliance on him! He looked up and saw nothing that could be a source.

YOU SHALL BE MY VESSEL. The voice boomed in his skull, echoing in his mind unlike anything he had ever experienced. Damien nearly fell to his knees as the voice hit him like a hammer. He pulled his hands from his head and looked up. "Who are you?"

Damien knew he had no soul. He had forfeited it the moment he became vampire, but he still had a consciousness. He could feel his grip on reality begin to slip…his memories fading, his sense of *self* disappearing. Whatever was happening, Damien knew, he was losing himself.

He wasn't sure exactly what was happening, but he knew without a doubt, once the transformation was complete, he would be gone forever. He could feel himself slipping. More and more of himself was being stripped from his body. He stood and shook with fear as what little was left tore in futility to remain. Damien turned his eyes skyward and screamed as the last remnants of what made him who he was got ripped from the shell of his body.

As he fell to the ground, the being that once was Damien Franklin caught itself then stood erect. He turned toward where Lilith now lay with the Roman and a sneer crossed his face. Somebody was going to pay for touching his woman.

16

Mark stared as Evan dropped silver nitrate solution onto the sample of blood he had given. Evan stared into the microscope then sat back and gave him a wide eyed stare. "What's wrong, Doc? Did it smoke and sizzle?"

Evan slowly shook his head. "Not exactly." He turned back to the slide and made an adjustment to the ocular. "This isn't supposed to be happening."

"Don't leave me hanging here." Mark stood and hovered over the vampire's shoulder. Evan reached for another amber bottle of solution and dripped a few drops onto the sample. After a moment he pushed away from the microscope and rubbed at his eyes.

"What's happening, Doc? What's it telling you?" Mark's agitation was causing his voice to rise in volume.

Evan shook his head. "I honestly can't tell you. I've never seen anything like this."

"What do you mean? Is it reacting like a sample of werewolf blood should?" He plopped into a chair next to him, his eyes imploring.

"Actually? No." Evan shrugged. "Nor is it reacting as a vampire's blood should."

"So…it's what? Acting normal? That can't be right." Mark scratched at his chin in thought.

"Oh, it's definitely not acting normal." Evan wheeled over to a set of lockers and donned heavy rubber gloves. He withdrew a wooden arrow shaft and pushed his chair back to the microscope.

"What are you doing?"

"Testing another idea." Evan poked the end of the wooden arrow shaft into the sample of blood and watched as the blood separated and moved away from the arrow shaft. "This can't be happening."

"Jeezus, Doc. Would you at least tell me what's happening?" Mark was on his feet and trying to look over the man's shoulder.

Evan sat back and placed the arrow shaft on the table. He pulled his safety goggles off and turned to face him. "Your blood is acting most strangely. When I drop silver nitrate onto the slide sample, it…spits it out, for a lack of a better description."

Mark gave him a deadpan look. "Come again?"

"Your blood refuses to allow the silver nitrate to interact with it." Evan turned and pointed to the arrow. "That is one of the arrow bolts that we turned from the Cross of Christ fragment. It is treated with a sealant that has the blood of Christ in it. When I poked it into the sample of your blood…it literally parted."

"Like the Red Sea?"

Evan shrugged. "I suppose." He shook his head. "I have no idea what's going on with you."

Mark sighed and slumped back into his chair. Suddenly he looked up. "Is whatever this is…is it affecting my mind? I mean, do you think it compromises me?"

Evan shook his head. "I have no idea what it is. How could I possibly know how it might be affecting you?"

Mark slumped again. "I may never get to go back to work."

"We'll keep at it." Evan turned around and grabbed another syringe. "I just need to draw another blood sample."

"Is there no way to simply test for *which* is running through my veins?"

"I don't have the equipment to test for…" Evan froze and stared at him, a silly smile crossing his face. "I may not be able to differentiate the different viruses, but there are other tests."

"Like?"

Evan grabbed his UV light emitter. "Roll up your sleeve and let me see your forearm."

Mark rolled up his BDU sleeve and stuck his arm out on the table. "Is this going to hurt?"

Evan shrugged. "I don't know yet. My guess is that if it does, it will only burn for a little while." He pulled on his UV goggles and plugged in the light. "At the rate you're healing, it won't be long before you're back to normal."

Mark groaned as Evan flipped on the light and ran it up and down the soft underside of his arm. He looked up at the Doc who had a puzzled look on his face. "I really thought there would be a reaction."

"So, you think there's vampire virus inside me." It was more a statement than a question.

Evan turned off the light and pulled off his goggles, his eyes scanning the skin of Mark's arm. "I'm beginning to lean more and more toward both viruses living inside you, but I can't explain how."

"Fucking great." Mark chewed his bottom lip as he considered the possibilities. "But you're pretty sure I'll heal, right? I mean, if something happens that…well, I mean, I'm not dead so…"

"What are you getting at, Major?"

Mark reached across the table and grabbed the arrow in his hand. Evan's eyes went wide as Mark gripped it tightly in his hand. Both men watched, waiting for smoke to rise or his flesh to light afire. When nothing happened, Mark slammed the wooden shaft into his left hand and ground his teeth to keep from screaming.

"Good heavens, man!" Evan pulled the heavy rubber gloves back on and reached for the arrow. As he grasped it and began to remove it, the first small wisps of smoke began to rise from Mark's flesh. "Oh, my…"

"I guess that answers our question, doesn't it?"

Evan pulled the arrow out and both men watched as the wound slowly began healing. "Besides hurting like a bitch that burned."

Mark gave Evan a knowing look. "I think it's safe to say that somehow you infected me while you were saving my life."

Evan swallowed hard and nodded. "I believe you may be correct." He turned away from the man and slowly came to his feet. "I was working so fast…it's more than possible I nicked myself with either a suture needle or scalpel or…" He turned back and Mark saw the tears forming in his eyes. "I am so sorry, Major."

Mark inhaled deeply and let it out slowly. "It was an accident, Doc." He flexed his hand, the light pink scar barely visible as he squeezed and flexed. "Apparently the timing was perfect for both viruses to be able to live inside one organism."

"I suppose so. Technically though, this isn't supposed to be possible."

"I realize that." Mark sat up and stared at the man. "The real question is what do we do now?"

*****

"Are you sure the hotel is secure, brother?" Foster continued to pace the room, occasionally glancing out the corner of the window to stare at the shadows outside.

"For the final time, if the Council wanted to kill us before granting us an audience, they would have done so already." Rufus stretched out on the bed and closed his eyes.

"Forgive me, brother, for not trusting the very organization that has tried to kill you for the last two hundred years." Foster fell into the chair opposite and glared at him.

Thorn opened one eye. "And not once have I reminded you of exactly *why* they want my head. Have I?"

Foster's glare turned to a stare of shock as the realization hit him. He knew it was his fault. He always had known. Being forgiven and made his brother's Second had allowed him a reprieve from the guilt and for the briefest of moments allowed him to forget. "Forgive me, brother." His voice fell to a whisper, "I have no excuse for…"

"Do not apologize, Paul." Rufus sat up and ran a hand through his hair. "You did what you had to at the time. I came to realize that a long time ago. If you hadn't, they would have had your head." He turned a weary eye to his brother. "My only regret…my only misgiving in the whole matter is that our father had to pay for your actions."

Foster turned away and stared at a blank wall, his emotions threatening to betray him. "You may not believe me brother, but a day doesn't go by that I don't regret my actions."

"I know." Rufus stood and slowly approached Foster, his hand resting on his shoulder. "That is why I was able to forgive you."

"Better than I deserved."

"Perhaps,perhaps not. A hard lesson was learned." Rufus squeezed his shoulder then turned for the cases of clothes stacked in the room. "We can discuss the follies of our youth another time. It is nearly time. Come. Let us dress for our meeting with the Council and pray that we both survive the night."

*****

Laura flashed her ID card at the main gate and was quickly waved through. "With hours to spare," she commented to Jennifer. "I'm sorry you won't really have time to get to know Matt before the shift." She glanced at her watch then out the window of the car as she maneuvered her way through the base.

"I'd be lying if I didn't say that I was nervous." Jennifer bit at her thumbnail as she stared at the buildings that she only vaguely remembered passing as she escaped the last time she had been here. "My heart is beating like a drum."

Laura slowed the car and gave her a weak smile. "I can only imagine. Do you want me to stop so you can maybe walk around and get some air?" Jennifer shook her head quickly. "I don't mind, and we have the time."

"No, really,I'll be okay. I think."

"Are you more nervous about meeting Matt or because you were a prisoner the last time you were here?"

"Both, I think." Jennifer stared out the windows, her eyes darting about.

"Just keep reminding yourself that you're not a prisoner this time. You're free to leave whenever you want." Laura patted her arm. "Well, after the shift is done, I mean."

Mick leaned up from the back seat. "What am I supposed to do while she's shifted?"

Laura shrugged. "Whatever you want. I'm sure that they'll want to debrief you."

"Debrief me? What the hell could I know that they'd want to debrief me?"

"Uh, for one thing, Jennifer's father?You were more or less working for him." Laura's eyes met his in the rear view mirror. "They'll want all the intel you can give on the man. Where his houses are, the manpower at his disposal, everything and anything you might know."

"If that ain't a fine poke in the ass." Mick flopped back in the seat and shook his head. "So, she'll be free to move about, but I'll be a prisoner until they get what they want. Ain't that a dandy?"

"Well, maybe you shouldn't have betrayed me," Jennifer shot at him.

"I didn't betray you love. I was trying to keep you safe!" Mick huffed in exasperation. "I swear. Women are so *thick* sometimes."

Laura glanced in the rear mirror. "Telling a lady that she's thick isn't going to win you any points."

"If she refuses to see reason, then she's by-gawd thick." Mick crossed his arms and stared out the window.

"You should have just taken the plane to Dallas, Mick. You shouldn't even be here." Jennifer's voice threatened to crack.

"There it is." Laura pointed to the hangar and felt the tension level rise as Jennifer fought to catch her breath. Laura pulled to the side of the road and reached for her as Jennifer continued to stare, her eyes wide. "Easy, sugar. It's just a building."

Jennifer slowly began to nod. "Y-you're right. Just a building."

"You shouldn't make her do this," Mick argued from behind them.

"This is her choice. I'm more than happy to turn the car around and…"

"No!" Jennifer turned and shook her head at Laura. "Keep going."

"Okay. But remember…just keep telling yourself. You're not a prisoner this time." Jennifer nodded as Laura put the car back into gear and pulled into the parking lot.

*****

Apollo checked his weapon then slung it over his shoulder. He strode into the office and went to his locker. Pulling his tactical vest and gear from the locker, he began preparing for his night as security patrol.

"You are one hell of a scary looking individual in that get up, mate." Apollo turned to see Sheridan following him into the office.

"All part of the job. If you can scare 'em away all the better."

"Do you expect any trouble tonight?" Sheridan seemed distracted as he dug through his mounds of paperwork.

"Not really. In all the time we've been here, none of the other roving patrols ever had an issue. I figure it will be a long night of drinking coffee and walking the perimeter." He turned to Sheridan. "You don't reckon there will be much howling, do you? That might draw attention if it's very loud."

Sheridan shook his head. "All of the other facilities around here are empty, mate. Long since abandoned." He paused to look at the list of personnel and nodded. "We've got the cargo units dead center of this place. Even if they do make a ruckus, we're far enough from any place populated that I doubt it will be heard. Those containers will muffle more noise than you might think."

"Good. I'd hate to think I'd have to kill somebody just because they got curious." He finished with his gear and pulled his rifle back around to the ready position. "When you plan to shove their hairy asses into 'em?"

Sheridan glanced at his watch. "Sundown is in two hours. We'll be in the containers with a thirty minute safety window."

Apollo nodded. "Do I need to come in behind each one and secure it or can they do it theyselves?"

Sheridan reached to the table top and pulled a small box with a large red button on it. "Once everyone is inside, push this. It's a radio transmitter and locks the cargo containers with an electronic lock. That way you can unlock them in the morning without running yourself ragged."

Apollo smiled as he hefted the small box then shoved it into a pocket on his vest. "Perfect." He stood straight and squared his shoulders. "If I don't see you later, have a good night in the box."

"I'll be fine, mate. You be safe out there on the wall. Well, so to speak." Sheridan shot him a wink and a cheesy grin.

Apollo clapped his shoulder as he walked by. "Time to make the doughnuts."

*****

Jack walked Brooke and Kalen to the CQB station. "This is where we teach entry and room clearance. Close quarters battle training." He pushed open the lightweight plywood door and ushered the pair inside. "Normally we do this with firearms, and eventually I'll run your team through with whatever firearms I can find that best suits you."

"I don't do guns." The defiance in Brooke's voice was palpable.

"Maybe not, but you will learn." Jack's tone left little doubt that it *would* happen. "I'm about to be out of commission until dawn. I expect you two to run this drill together until you can do it with your eyes closed."

"Us two?" Kalen's confusion wasn't missed.

"That's right." Jack pointed at them both. "Using the weapons that you are already most familiar with. Your bow and your sword. I've already set this up with the training officer and he's got numerous targets that he can set up that can accommodate your weapons."

"Wait. Why just us two?" Brooke was beginning to feel nervous and it tinged her voice as she looked around the CQB simulator.

Jack planted his hands on his hips and gave her a smirk. "Because I know that Kalen can work with Azrael and Gnat. I've seen it firsthand."

"So now I'm the problem child?" Brooke's tone turned defiant once more.

"You said it, not me." Jack turned back to Kalen. "I expect you two to continue this drill until you are proficient. Understood?"

"Yes, Chief Jack." Kalen bowed slightly.

"Now, hold on just a minute." Brooke stepped between the two and pointed a finger at Jack. "What's the point of just putting the two of us in this thing? How long do we have to run through this like mice in a maze?"

"Until you can work like a team. Until you can get it right." Jack smirked at her. "Until you can pass."

"What does it take to pass?" Her eyes narrowed, not sure she wanted to know the answer.

"No civilian casualties and all bad guys are down." Jack patted her shoulder. "You both need to know that the other has their back."

He could hear her growling under her breath as he walked away.

*****

Mitchell finished his paperwork and signed off on the one operation that he knew for a fact would be going down that night. He stared at the paperwork authorizing two of his squads to go into Oklahoma City and take down Walter Simmons' attack dogs. He felt a sick feeling in his gut that he couldn't shake and wished that he knew how to get in touch with Max. If ever there was a time when he wanted to skip the shift, it was this night.

Mitchell slipped the paperwork into his out box and stretched his neck to try to work some tension out. He glanced at his watch and knew that it was nearly time to prepare for the shift. A light knocking at his door pulled his attention back to the here and now.

"Come." He looked to the door and had to remember to breathe as Laura stepped inside his office.

"Colonel,I've brought somebody who's actually anxious to meet you."

Mitchell was on his feet so quickly that he nearly toppled his chair. "Laura...I didn't...I mean. I..." He glanced around his office, unsure what he should do next when a small framed brunette stepped inside the door. Her eyes were glued to the floor and she slowly raised her face to meet his. Mitchell could feel his wolf fighting to rise to the surface. She was here and it could sense it.

"Colonel Matt Mitchell, this is Jennifer Simmons." Laura escorted the woman into Mitchell's office and Matt stood frozen in place. His mouth opened to speak, but nothing came out. Laura stared at the two and finally stepped forward. "It's customary to say, 'hello'."

Mitchell gave her a droll stare then turned back to Jennifer. "I apologize. I'm just…at a loss. I had imagined this day for so long and now that you're finally here, my mind escapes me."

Jennifer nodded sheepishly. "I understand." Her voice was soft and shaky.

Mitchell motioned for her to come in and take a seat at the couch. "Please, forgive my awkwardness. I'm still not sure exactly what to say."

"I'm going to leave you two alone for a little bit. I have to get Mick downstairs and checked in so we can start debriefing him."

Mitchell turned and gave her a curious stare. "Mick?"

"A friend who may have some intel on Jennifer's father."

Mitchell nodded then turned back to Jennifer as the door shut. He noted the slight jump she made when the door clicked. He stepped back and held his hands up. "We can leave the door open if you'd prefer." He watched as her eyes darted about his office and finally met his gaze. She shook her head slowly. "I don't know how to tell you how sorry I am about…well, everything."

She sat up straighter and squared her shoulders. "I'm not sure why I'm so nervous." She looked about his office from her seat on the couch. "As I recall, the last time we met, it didn't end well for you." She gave him a half smile.

Mitchell snorted. "No, it did not." He pulled a chair around and sat facing her. "I suppose I should thank you for letting me live."

"I didn't think I had." She caught his expression and shrugged. "As long as we're being honest…"

Mitchell nodded, a smile forming. "Would you like something to drink? I've tried to limit myself to coffee, but I can get you something harder if you like."

She shook her head. "I'm fine, really."

Matt rubbed his hands nervously as he studied her. "You, uh…you changed your hair."

She nodded and touched her hand to the side of her head. "Yes. I thought maybe it would be harder for you to find me."

"You thought correctly. I still see you as a blonde." Matt sighed heavily and shook his head. "I'm sorry. I'm at such a loss here. I'm told that you and I are…"

"Fated Mates," she finished for him. "Yes, that's what I'm told as well."

"I have no idea what that truly means other than what I've been told. But I know that the moment you stepped in here, my wolf has tried like hell to rise to the surface."

She swallowed hard and nodded. "Mine too. It's taking quite a bit of effort to hold her at bay."

"I'm sure that Laura told you that we have a place to shift for the moon?"

Jennifer nodded. "Silver-plated cells?"

"Yes, I'm sorry that they're not the most comfortable of places, but for the longest time, it was just me." He shrugged. "Well, me and a vampire that…it doesn't matter."

Jennifer inhaled deeply and stared at the ceiling. For a brief moment, Mitchell feared she was going to scream that she couldn't handle this and run from his office. She blew the breath out slowly and faced him. "Would it help you any if I told you that I'm probably twice as nervous as you are?"

Matt shrugged. "Somehow I doubt that. My wolf has been driving me nuts since we started searching for you."

"Well, try to put yourself in my shoes. I've just returned to a place that, for all intents and purposes, was a prison for me for nearly ten years. I'm facing a man that…my strongest memories are of him shooting me in the face and of my wolf tearing him to pieces. Now I've come back only to find out that my father has declared war on him and his people, and I'm supposedly his Fated Mate."

Matt sat back and considered what she told him. He rolled the words around in his head and while a part of him wanted to tell her that he was sorry and promise that it would all be okay, he found himself hearing words come from his mouth that he didn't expect to say. "Consider *my* point of view. Until you came into my life, I didn't even know that monsters existed. You attacked me and my family while we were camping and you killed my wife and daughter right in front of me and then transformed me into...this. Yes, I hunted you down, but not until I was ordered to by the military. It was their decision to keep you on ice and for the longest time, I thought you were dead. Once I realized you weren't, I tried my best to get you freed, but..." Matt looked away. "Then imagine how I felt when they told me that the very same person who killed my wife Jo Ann and my daughter Molly was *my* Fated Mate?"

He turned and looked at her and saw the tears running down her face. His heart broke when he saw the pain etched in her features and his wolf howled deep inside him, demanding that he do something to make her feel better. Mitchell leaned forward, reaching for her hand and she jerked away from him. "I shouldn't have come here." She jumped up and headed for the door.

Mitchell shot to his feet and stepped between her and the door, effectively blocking her. "Don't go!" He held his hands out hoping she would calm down and give him a moment to recant his words. "I didn't mean for it to sound like..."

She growled low in her throat and he saw her eyes turn amber once more. Matt groaned as he stepped back. "Not again..."

*****

Lilith's door flew open and bounced against the wall as the body of Damien Franklin stepped inside, fury reflected in his eyes. "Get off my woman."

263

Gaius rolled away from Lilith and glared at the vampire. "How dare you interrupt me, little ghoul." He pushed off of Lilith and stepped toward the intruder. "I guess he liked what I did to him earlier. Come back for more, did you?" Gaius grasped his manhood and shook it at him.

The vampire stared at him in surprise. "Unless you want that ripped from your corpse and shoved down your throat, begone and be smart enough never to darken my doorstep again."

Lilith sat up in her bed and stared at the vampire. "My love!" She slipped from the mattress and moved closer to him. "You've returned to me!"

"Your love? I thought this little ghoul was your pet?" Gaius laughed as he strode purposefully toward him. "Once I put him in his place, he won't be—" Gaius found himself being thrown across the room, his body impacting the wall of the office with such force that the metal studs bowed outward. As his body crumpled to the floor, the being that was once Damien Franklin stepped closer and with a wave of his hand, pulled the demon from the ground, suspending him in midair.

"You are Gaius, yes?" He squeezed his hand tighter and watched as the demon's eyes began to bulge in their sockets. "I think it's time you found a new form to inhabit."

"W-who…are…you?"

Lilith slid in next to the being and ran a hand over the much broader chest. "Your lord and master, demon. You should be bowing to his greatness."

Gaius watched as the intruder's hand opened and he fell to the ground, gasping for air, his head feeling as though the skull had been crushed by a mighty, unseen force. He rolled to his back and stared as the vampire stepped forward and bent its head to the side, studying him. "On your knees, Roman."

Gaius fought to roll over and get to his feet. He refused to bow to this vampire, even if he did seem to have the upper hand this time. As he pulled one leg under him in an attempt to stand, he felt the bones in that leg twist and snap, sending him to his knees on the hard concrete floor.

"I told you, Roman, on your knees." The ghoul's voice took a tone that he recognized but couldn't place. He knew he should know it, but from another time and place. He raised his eyes to study the vampire, hoping to get a glimpse of why.

"You aren't allowed to lay eyes on me, Roman." The hand flexed again, and Gaius felt his eyes bulge then burst like grapes being crushed between unseen fingers. He inhaled deeply to scream only to have his throat squeezed off, squelching the cry.

Gaius fell to his hands and tried to force air into his lungs as the unseen hand squeezed tighter. "As I said, Gaius, I believe it's time you find a new form to inhabit. This one has touched my woman and I can't have that."

Lilith laughed and practically squealed with joy. "You should recognize your betters, Roman." She rubbed against the intruder and stroked his arm, rubbing her face against his chest. "My Samael has returned to me."

17

"What do you mean, 'what do we do now'?" Evan gaped at Major Tufo. "I have no idea how to proceed from here."

Mark stood and paced the small lab space. "Tell me something, Doc. If I had been infected with just the wolf virus, would there have been any restrictions on my going back to my duties once I was healed?"

Evan shook his head. "No, of course not. Once your body was healed we would simply—"

"And if I had been infected with just the vampire virus?" Mark interrupted. "Would there be any restrictions then?"

Evan sat down slowly, his mind racing. "I honestly don't know Major. We've not had any vampires in our employ before. Besides myself, of course."

"But do you see any reason to keep me from my duties?"

Evan exhaled hard and ran through a number of possible scenarios. Eventually he turned back to the XO and shook his head. "Technically, no. You are healed. You seem to be of proper mind. You don't appear to be a threat."

"Then would you please sign off on my going back to work before I go stir crazy? I have all this pent up energy and if I don't do something with it, I will go bat shit crazy."

Evan sat back down and pulled the major's medical record to him. "I can put you back on temporary duty. I need you to check in with me daily." He scribbled something into the record and closed it. "If anything changes, and I mean *anything* at all, I want you to come to me immediately. This is the first time I've ever encountered a successful human/wolf/vampire hybrid. By all rights, I should have you on my table."

Mark shot him a questioning look. "Dissection?"

"Of course not. Just to study. To find out how this happened. How it's even possible." Evan paused and turned back to the major. "Is there any chance that there's Elf or Fairy blood in your family history?"

Mark snorted as he accepted his medical record. "I think I had a cousin who was a little limp wristed, but I don't think I'd call him a fairy. He played professional football and would kick your ass."

"That's not what I…" Evan fought a smile. "Ha-ha-ha. A pun at the vampire's expense. I was serious."

"And I seriously have no idea. I would have to say no." Mark seemed more than anxious to vacate the lab and was just waiting for Evan to dismiss him.

"That's something we'll have to investigate further at a later date. Until then, go about your normal routine, but I meant it. Every morning I expect you to be here for blood draws and physicals."

"Aye-aye, Captain Blye. First thing in the morning." Mark turned to leave then stopped at the door. "Hey, Doc? Thanks."

"Just come to me before you do anything rash. Like decide to eat one of the enlisted personnel."

*****

Thorn exited the vehicle and looked up at the tall building that the Council now used as their chambers. Although he couldn't see them, he knew that at least a dozen of the best assassins that Foster could locate here in the EU were present, hidden in the shadows, their weapons of choice at the ready.

Rufus waited until their entire party exited the vehicle then turned and made his way up the steps. As he approached the oversized double doors, two vampires appeared from the shadows, blocking their path. Thorn reached into his trench coat and withdrew his ID. "Rufus Thorn to see the Council. They're expecting me."

One of the vampires examined his ID while the other whispered into his sleeve. He nodded at the voice speaking through his earpiece then turned and opened the door for Thorn and his party. "They're waiting for you upstairs. There's an elevator to your left."

"Thank you." Rufus placed his ID back in his coat as the small group made their way through the lobby and to the elevators. "Remember, we are guests here. Nobody is to speak unless they are addressed specifically and nobody is to make any aggressive moves. Are we understood?"

The enforcers nodded and Paul slipped in beside his brother. "There's something I should probably tell you before we get up there, brother."

Rufus waved him off. "It will have to wait. I need to concentrate." Foster turned and stared at Rufus, his eyes closed, appearing as though he were sleeping standing up. When Rufus opened his eyes, he turned to the enforcers. "They have their own enforcers stationed at the ends of the chambers. I need you to make your way to them and stay hidden. If you hear things getting out of hand, you know what to do. The rest of you will enter with Paul and me." The enforcers all nodded and split apart into separate groups when the doors opened.

As the small party made their way to the grand chambers, two vampires waited to open the double doors leading to the ornate oval room. A large table with chairs took up the center of the room and the Council members were all seated, presumably going over the business at hand. One of the vampires who opened the door escorted them inside and announced them. "Monsieur Thorn and party." He bowed slightly and backed away and through the double doors again, pulling them closed behind him.

Rufus and his group stood still while waiting to be acknowledged. Foster was about to clear his throat to draw attention to them when one of the Council members suddenly pushed back his chair and stood. He stared at Thorn and the malice in his eyes was unmistakable. "Advance and be recognized."

Thorn bowed slightly and stepped forward. "I am Monsieur Rufus Thorn. This is my adopted brother, Paul Foster, both of the United States of—"

"We know who you are." Rufus turned to the vampire still seated who interrupted him. "You are either very brave or very foolish to have asked for this audience, Monsieur."

Rufus fought not to raise his voice as he spoke. "We have come to address the Council to seek a reprieve and pardon."

The stunned silence was not missed as members of the Council glanced to each other then finally back to Thorn. The vampire who stood and addressed them spoke, "You know that the Council does not give pardons for deadly crimes against our own. You waste our time and your own." He turned and took his seat again, in essence declaring the meeting over.

"Perhaps not, but it is our belief that special circumstances call for special considerations." Rufus advanced slowly and removed his overcoat, handing it to one of his enforcers. "You know as well as I do that I did not commit the act for which I have been accused. And my brother is here to retract his previous statements of fact to the Council."

"Once a judgment has been handed down, it cannot be changed. There are no reprieves, no pardons." A dark haired vampire stood and glared at Rufus. "You have avoided meeting our judgment numerous times in these past months, but your luck will soon run out, Monsieur. Of that, I can assure you."

"*Oui*, I am most positive that if you were so inclined, you could meet out justice now and feel wholly justified in breaking your promise of safe passage." He turned and waved Foster forward. "But I bring news and a proposition that I hope will change your collective minds."

"Our verdict is stone. It cannot be changed."

Rufus nodded knowingly and turned to wink at Foster who quivered like a leaf in a swift wind. He turned back to the Council and bowed slightly. "Then forgive my intrusion. I thought perhaps this esteemed body would be interested in stopping Damien Franklin and his attempt to resurrect Lilith. I stand mistaken." He turned for the doors, "By your leave."

"Wait!" The voice echoed throughout the chamber and Rufus smiled knowingly at Foster who still stared wide eyed at his brother.

Rufus turned slowly to face the Council once more. "*Oui?*"

"What do you know of our concerns? How do you know of Franklin and his efforts?"

Rufus gave the Council members a slight smile and stepped forward once more. "I am aware of your efforts,and your inability to stop young Damien. I believe you have found your people… *eaten, oui?*"

A much older vampire stood and walked slowly toward Rufus. He studied the vampire standing before him and tucked his hands behind his back as he spoke. "What is your proposal, Monsieur Thorn?"

"My proposal is simple. A reprieve in any further attempts on my life. My compatriots and I will find Franklin, put a stop to him, and his efforts in resurrecting Lilith. Once we bring you proof that his efforts are thwarted and he has been permanently stopped, you grant the pardon." Rufus crossed his arms over his chest, his gaze unwavering.

The older vampire studied the younger man and chuckled lightly. "And if you fail?"

"Then it will cost me my life. For I will not stop until I have succeeded or am dead. You will have your verdict seen through,and your issues with Franklin may or may not have been taken care of for you."

The older vampire narrowed his gaze on Rufus. "Our intelligence tells us that there is a good chance that Lilith has already been restored."

"Then she will be stopped along with Franklin." Rufus turned back to Foster and motioned him forward. "My brother is his creator. It is my belief that although Franklin has become a ghoul, he can still be reached by his maker."

"And if he can't?"

"Then he shall be brought to the blade. His head will be returned to you regardless."

"And Lilith?"

"Her remains shall be scattered to the four corners once more, her heart and head brought to this esteemed body to be held."

The older vampire turned to the seated Council members. A silent passing of agreement was made by imperceptible nods. When he turned back to Thorn, the older vampire's face was stern. "You have your reprieve, Thorn. But heed my words. If you fail to perform…if you fail to hold up your end of the agreement, we will hold nothing back in bringing *your* head back. Am I understood?"

"Completely."

*****

Lieutenant Gregory sat at the stainless steel table going over the notes he had made while questioning Mick. "And you're sure that he only employs wolves?"

"To my knowledge, yes." Mick sighed and stared at his watch. "How many more times are we going to go over the same stuff?"

Gregory ignored him as he made more notes and read through his previous questions. "But you claim you're not a wolf, correct?"

"Correct. I'm a werecat."

"Yet, Mr. Simmons employed you to take care of his daughter?"

"He didn't really employ me. He just threatened to have me killed if I didn't." Mick crossed his arms and glared at the human.

"And that was simply to keep her away from here while they attacked?"

"I don't know. I guess so." Mick stood and pulled a cigarette from his shirt pocket.

"There's no smoking in here." Gregory turned back to his notes.

Mick crumpled the cigarette and fell back into the chair. "How much longer will this take?"

"Until we have covered everything. Do you know when Mr. Simmons plans to attack again?"

"No." Mick glared at the man, his hands tightening into fists.

"He didn't say anything that might give you an idea his timeline?"

"Look, mate, I wasn't exactly on his best friend list, okay? He told me that if Jennifer took off again and came to me, that I should do everything in my power to keep her away from this place. That's it. There is no more. He didn't show me any plans. He didn't tell me anything else. He didn't pull out a map and point to anything. He didn't name any names. He didn't…" Mick threw his hands into the air. "How much longer, mate?"

Gregory closed his notes and stared at the man. "Why? You taking medication?"

"No. Actually I'd like a chance to talk to Jennifer before she has to shift for the moon." Mick's frustration level was at an all-time high.

Gregory shook his head. "I highly doubt that's going to happen."

"To hell with this." Mick sat up so quickly that his chair flew backward, hitting the wall behind him. As soon as he was on his feet, the door to the interrogation room flew open and guards flooded the room, shackles in hand. "What the hell?"

"If you refuse to cooperate, then we do this the hard way." Gregory stood and nodded to the guards. "Take him to the secure room."

Mick struggled and fought as the guards shackled him and dragged him down the hallway and into a room very much like the room they were in. The difference being that the chairs and table were bolted down and there were steel loops in the floor and tabletop to run the shackle chains through. "This is bullshit!" Mick struggled as they held him down and chained him in place.

"Had you cooperated, this wouldn't be necessary." Gregory sat down opposite him and opened his notes once more.

"I came here of my own accord, asshole!" Mick fought against the chains and slammed his fists on the table.

Gregory stared at him stonily and closed his notes. "You conspired with a megalomaniac who sent an army of supernatural creatures to our base of operations and attacked us unannounced. Good men died in that attack. If you truly wanted no part in Mr. Simmons' actions, all it would have taken was a simple phone call and we could have at least been alerted."

Mick's glare softened and he slumped in his seat. "I didn't know. I swear I didn't. He didn't say who he was going after. I had no idea who you chaps were; where you were located…all I knew was somebody in the States had kidnapped his daughter and held her for nearly ten years." Mick raised his face and stared at the man opposite him. "Tell me something. You got kids? What would you do if somebody had stolen your little girl and ran all sorts of ungodly experiments on her for ten years? Would you just sit back and do nothing? Would you let bygones be bygones?"

Gregory shifted uncomfortably in his chair. "I don't…I'm not the one in question here."

"Yeah, that's what I thought." Mick smirked at the man. "Once that shoe is on your own foot, it doesn't fit so well, does it, mate?"

Gregory opened his notebook and clicked his pen. "Back to the questions. When you were with Mr. Simmons…"

*****

"Jennifer, you need to get a grip." Matt backed to the door and reached behind himself to lock it. He watched as he eyes continued to glow amber. "I'm not going to hurt you and I'm not trying to…"

"Get out of my way. Coming here was a mistake." Her voice growled as she spoke and he could almost watch as her teeth elongated.

Matt squared his shoulders and shook his head. "No."

Jennifer backed up a step. "What? I'm not joking."

"And neither am I. I can't let you leave. Not like this." He crossed his arms and stared down at her. "My wolf would never forgive me. And to be honest…neither would I."

She shook her head as she continued backing up. "I can't be here."

"I need you to calm down," he lowered his voice,speaking to her as soothingly as he could. He extended a hand to her. "I'm sorry, Jen. I don't know why I said what I did. Maybe it was nerves. Maybe it was…fear. I don't know. But I know that if you leave now…"

Her eyes slowly ebbed and faded back to normal. "My wolf senses your emotions." She watched as Matt slowly slid down the door and sat on the floor, his face buried.

"I have no idea what I'm doing." His voice threatened to break.

Jennifer felt herself soften and she took a tentative step forward. She reached out for him then slowly withdrew her hand. "I don't know what to say."

Mitchell lifted his face and she saw his eyes, reddened and wet with unshed tears. "Neither do I." He sniffed back the pain and wiped at his nose. "This is so damned confusing to me. I'm torn, and I don't know what to do about it."

She squatted down next to him and rested a hand on his arm. "Talk to me."

Matt shrugged and tried to look away. "And say what? That I used to stare at your image when you were frozen and feel…something. That I hated myself for having feelings for you?" He gave a short self-loathing laugh. "For the longest time, I truly did hate you." He saw the pain return to her face, and he placed his own hand on hers. "I think it's more accurate to say, I hated what your wolf did. And I kept trying to blame you, but…I knew. You didn't do it. Your wolf did."

"I'm still responsible." Her voice was barely a whisper as she slid onto the floor beside him.

"You can't be held responsible for what your wolf does." Matt sighed and lowered his face again. "Just like I couldn't help what I allowed to happen over the years as you were locked away."

"You're saying you have feelings for me?"

"I'm saying I don't know what I feel. All I know is I'd have dreams of you. And I really did try to get you released, but…" He shook his head in frustration. "They just wouldn't hear of it."

Jennifer scooted closer and wrapped her arm around his. "This feels right somehow."

"I know. And that scares the bejeezus out of me." He turned and stared at her. He could see her emotions painted across her face just as he knew his must be. She was just as scared, just as confused and just as worried as he was. "Part of me worries about betraying what I had with Jo Ann. Another part of me completely freaks out at the idea of not having you in my life."

She nodded. "I'm in the same boat. I have all these haunting memories of when you shot me. When you hunted me down. When I escaped here. It's like a big part of me just wants to turn and run away, but an even bigger part of me is scared to death of going against the Fates."

"Aren't we a fine pair?" he snorted and rubbed her arm. "Maybe two basket cases make one complete person?"

She chuckled and squeezed his arm. "Or it makes an even bigger basket case."

"Oh, we're screwed then." He turned to stare at her and saw the vulnerability in her eyes. Everything he feared suddenly slipped away as he stared into her big, beautiful eyes. Matt felt himself being drawn closer, her chin lifting as he closed to kiss her.

A buzzing sounded from his desk, snapping him out of the trance he was in. He pulled back quickly and stood from the floor. He held out a hand to lift her up then reached for his phone. "Go for Mitchell."

"Colonel, it's Jack. It's about time, sir."

Mitchell glanced at the clock and cursed silently. "Thanks for the heads up, Chief. We'll be down there in a moment." Mitchell turned to Jennifer. "It's time. The sun is almost down."

Jennifer wiped at her face and stepped aside for Mitchell to open the door for her. "I guess this is it, isn't it?"

Matt gave her a puzzled look. "What do you mean?"

"Our wolves are about to meet for the first time. They may not let us change our minds." She looked to him hopefully.

He gave her a reassuring smile. "I don't care what the wolves think. I'm not letting you go again."

*****

Apollo watched as each man strode outside to the shipping containers. They had the foresight to leave their clothes behind lest they be ruined either during the shift or by their wolf after the shift. Sheridan directed each man to his container then headed for the unit on the end. He turned to Apollo and gave a mock salute before rounding the corner and disappearing from view.

Apollo gave each man a few minutes to secure their door themselves then announced over the bullhorn that he would be sealing the electronic locks in 30 seconds. He counted down the time then pushed the button. He heard the series of bolts being thrown simultaneously and smiled to himself.

Like shooting fish in a barrel.

He made his way back inside and tossed the electronic lock mechanism onto the counter then picked up the phone. He dialed the number for the duty officer and reported that the area was secure. Once they hung up, he'd head toward the gates and open them for the squads.

Apollo hung up then worked his way outside. He paused as he listened to the men begin their shift, grunts and howls coming from the containers followed by angry outbursts as the wolves discovered the silver mesh lining each container. For the briefest of moments, he almost felt sorry for the poor bastards. "Better to go out like this than having you pull another sneak attack."

He worked his way to the front gates and quickly unlocked the padlocks holding the ends of chain together. Pulling the chain out from between the two chain link gates, he slid one side open, then the other. Apollo worked his way back to the warehouse and dropped the tailgate on a pickup parked within. Hopping onto the back of the truck, he waited for the squads to show up and make quick work of the wolves locked away.

*****

"Failure. Back to the beginning," a voice echoed over the intercom.

Kalen was nearly ready to collapse. He collected his arrows and walked back to the entrance of the CQB simulator. "If you'd just come in behind me and look pretty, we could get this over with once and for all." Brooke stuffed her throwing stars back into her belt and sheathed her sword.

"Simply follow you? Did you forget we are supposed to work together?"

"Yeah, yeah. Teamwork building. I get it." She leaned against the pillar outside the door of the CQB sim room. "But face it, Sugar Cookie, that just ain'tgonna happen."

"Because you refuse to be a team player." Kalen hung his bow over his shoulder and stood at the ready.

"Because I'm *not* a team player." Brooke pushed off the pillar and come to stand beside him. "I've been on my own for far too long. I don't play well with others."

"Learn," Kalen growled. "I do not wish to be out here all night. I'd like to get a little rest before dawn."

Brooke snorted. "This is my daytime, Keebler. I can drag this out for days."

Kalen turned on her, his pain and exasperation painted clearly on his features. "Why? Why do you insist on being this way? Is it truly so hard to rely on another?"

Brooke turned away from him. "I don't do well with partners."

"You need to accept assistance from others. Learn that your team is there to help you. We all have strengths and we all have weaknesses. Those who excel in one area can assist the others who do not. It truly is a simple concept to grasp."

Brooke shook her head almost imperceptibly. "I don't need help."

The claxon sounded and a yellow strobe light went off indicating the beginning of another round. With each round through the training simulator, different bad guys and good guy targets were popped up in different locations. No two drills were exactly alike and Kalen truly felt that if Raven didn't get her act together, they would see every possible combination more than once.

"You want left or right?" Kalen stacked on the right side of the door.

"Just go in. I'll take what you don't." She shot him a hateful glare.

Kalen counted down…three…two…one…and kicked open the door, immediately turning to the right, his bow drawn and ready to fire. Raven disappeared to the left and began sweeping the room left to right. Kalen ascertained the targets and just as he put his arrow into the 'bad guy' target, Brooke's throwing star sliced into the target just below his arrow. He shot her a warning glare then advanced to the next area. Brooke entered without stacking up outside the room and began throwing stars at all of the targets, regardless of their identifier. Immediately, the claxon sounded indicating their failure once more.

The voice echoed through the simulator, "Failure. Back to the beginning."

Kalen slumped his shoulders and began collecting his arrows. "I told you, Sugar Cookie. Just fall in behind me and we'll be—"

"No!" Kalen turned and threw a finger into her face. "We will work this drill as the instructor stated. We will work as a team or we will continue to run it until Chief Jack returns and *makes* you become a team player."

Brooke gave him a crooked smile. She opened her mouth as if to say something then pulled his finger into her mouth and sucked the end of it. "Mmm. You even *taste* like a sugar cookie."

Kalen pulled his hand back and stared at her wide eyed. "Why would you do such a thing?"

"To diffuse your anger, Keebler." She shot him a wink. "Fine. You want to play like a real team and get this over with? Then let's do it. One time like we really mean it."

Kalen narrowed his gaze at her and set his jaw. "Are you being truthful?"

"Yup,I mean it." Brooke stepped out of the CQB simulator. "But as soon as we kick this drill's ass, you have to learn how to have a little fun."

Kalen stiffened. "I know how to have fun."

She shook her head. "No, Sugar Cookie,I mean real fun." She winked at him then squared off for the next round.

"I don't think I like the sound of that."

"Is it a deal or isn't it?"

Kalen considered her bargain then nodded. "Agreed. It is a deal. But nothing against the rules."

Brooke laughed as the claxon sounded. "You didn't say *whose* rules."

*****

The teams loaded their gear and extra ammunition into the black trucks parked in the parking lot. Neither truck had been fitted with the ceramic armor plating or the 30MM canon. As of now, this was simply a transport vehicle.

Spalding called for a coms check and each member checked in. He nodded to Lamb who started the truck and pulled the Raptor out of the gravel lot and out onto the paved roads of Tinker Air Force Base.

"First Squad, you are essentially under Spalding's command for this operation," Jericho Jones announced over the communications channel. "Drone will be airborne in one-zero mics."

"Copy that, OPCOM. ETA to target site two zero mics." Spalding looked to the GPS unit on the dash and turned to Lamb. "We're going through our own backyard here so keep the speed down and try to look inconspicuous."

Lamb pulled through the main gates and accelerated up the onramp to I-40. "This thing has a lot more go to it than the Hummers."

"I imagine so, but we aren't in a huge hurry. Unless Apollo is completely selling us out, they're all contained and waiting on us. They can just keep waiting. I'm in no hurry and don't want to have to explain to any local law why we're out in town with automatic weapons."

"Understood." Lamb let off the accelerator and set the cruise control. He turned to Spalding and elbowed him. "You don't really think Apollo would set us up like that, do you?"

Spalding shook his head. "No, but I also wouldn't have thought he'd turn on us either." He glanced up and noted the men in the back seat listening to their conversation. Raising his voice, he added, "All the same, expect anything."

"Copy that." Ing pressed the button on his throat mic. "First squad Bravo Three, break away, take the lead. Once you are within a half click, shut her down and set up the perimeter."

"Copy that," Popo's voice came back over their ear pieces and the squad watched the black truck accelerate and pass them. Within moments, it exited from the interstate and headed for the industrial park. Lamb followed, but far enough behind that First Squad would have time to advance and set a perimeter watch.

Second Squad watched as the Raptor's brake lights turned the area red then they winked out. Lamb pulled the matching truck in behind the first and shut off the engine. The members of Second Squad sat silently in the cab of the truck for a moment before Donnie opened the back door and stepped out. "Time to make the doughnuts."

18

Mark appeared in the hallway causing Mitchell and company to pull up short. "Doc cleared me, boss. I'm heading to OPCOM to observe Jones on this op."

Mitchell shot him a questioning stare. "Doc cleared you? Already?"

Mark shrugged. "We figured out what caused the rapid healing and he's convinced that I'm not a threat. He wants me to check in every morning for a workup." Mark grimaced at the thought of all the needles he'd have to endure in the near future. "I guess I'm not done being a lab rat."

"What was the verdict?"

"Worst case scenario. Both viruses working in tandem. I know I know…it's not supposed to be possible, but I'm a walking, talking conundrum."

"You're carrying both the wolf virus *and* the vampire virus?" Mitchell shook his head. "You do realize what this means, don't you? We're going to have to rethink our inoculation protocols. Apparently the men aren't immune from…"

Mark interrupted, "I believe they still are, sir. The only reason I got infected with both was a timing thing. I was pretty much down for the count and got infected by both at the same time."

"Still that shouldn't be possible."

Mark hesitated then added softly, "Doc asked if I might have Elf or Fairy blood in my heritage."

Mitchell shot him a confused look. "Would that make a difference?"

"Possibly," Jennifer added, stepping into the conversation. "If there was Fae blood especially."

Mitchell glanced at his watch. "We don't have time to get into this too deep right now, XO. Go. Do your thing, but listen to Doc. Check in with him every morning."

"Roger that, Colonel." Mark watched as the two entered the elevators and Mitchell punched in the code for the basement. "God speed, sir."

"I'll see you in the morning, Mark. Try to take it easy until then."

Mark watched the doors close then headed for the stairwell. He took the stairs two and three at a time until he reached the floor the OPCOM was housed. He exited and headed down the hallway with purpose. Seeing the center rigged for red light, he quickly opened the door and slipped in.

Jericho Jones glanced up from the command chair and registered surprise. "Major? Should you be out of bed, sir?"

"Cleared for duty." Mark slipped in behind him and stared at the screens. "Don't get up, Captain. I'm just here to observe and assist if needed."

"Yes, sir." Jones turned his eyes back to the screens and relayed the position of the incoming drone. "Team Leader, Predator is in a holding pattern above your location."

"Roger that, OPCOM. Preparing to make contact."

*****

Rufus waited outside the Council chambers for his enforcers to come to him. "I would call this meeting a success, *oui*?"

"I still don't trust them, brother." Paul paced slowly in the hallway. "What's to stop them from letting you do their dirty work and then going ahead as planned?"

Thorn sighed softly and placed a reassuring hand on Foster's shoulder. "It is called honor, dear brother. These are ancient vampires. Even with being the head of the *Beastia*, and having your people aligned with me, my power pales in comparison to theirs."

Paul's face twisted as he stared back at the closed doors. "What kept them from answering the call of the Sicarii?"

"They are their own *familia*." Rufus shrugged. "By charter, the heads of each of the largest familias come together and form their own *familia* to rule over the rest. Unless the Sicarii was aware of that, he wouldn't have known to bring them under his rule."

"They were never conscripted?"

"*Non*." Rufus glanced back toward the closed doors. "They were very lucky that their charter called for such or they all would have been."

"Lucky bastards." Foster turned at the approaching enforcers. "Any troubles?"

"Negative. They never knew we were there."

Rufus clapped his hands together. "Excellent." He motioned toward the stairs. "Let us be off. We have a lot of work yet to do."

"Do you know yet how we'll track down Damien?" Foster fell into step beside Thorn.

"I have an idea that may work."

*****

Laura collapsed in her chair and leaned back to stare at the ceiling. She allowed herself a chance to breath and a smile crossed her features. She was finally home. Nobody was trying to kill her and she could finally start making plans to pack her belongings and actually leave. She giggled lightly to herself and spun her chair back and forth while the realization set in that she was nearly free.

A knock at the door snapped her from her exhausted daydreaming and she leaned her head to the side. "Enter."

Evan stepped inside carrying a rose and quietly shut her door. "I heard you were back."

She gave him a sleepy stare and continued smiling. "Finally." She debated sitting up, but it felt so good to just lean back and relax. "I'm so tired."

Evan dropped the rose on her desk and scooped her from her chair. He carried her to the couch and gently lay her down on the overstuffed leather. "Let me see if I can help you relax a little bit." He sat behind her and rubbed gently at her shoulders. She let out a low moan and leaned into him.

"You have wonderful hands."

"So I've been told." He gently kissed her earlobe and worked his way to her neck. "If memory serves, it was you who told me that."

"Mm-hmm. I was right." She leaned her head to one side and he gently bit her neck, drawing blood. "Ooh…skip the foreplay, big boy."

Evan chuckled low in his throat as he sipped from her. "You know me, go straight for the jugular."

Her hand reached up and behind her to grip the back of his neck, pulling him tighter toward her. "Harder," she whispered.

Evan opened his mouth wider and bit hard, eliciting a shudder from her as she sucked in her breath. Her hand reached for his hair and she balled her hand into a fist. "Oh, my God…"

Evan sucked harder and Laura's eyes rolled back as her toes curled. He pulled his mouth from her neck and whispered, "I missed you."

"Don't stop." She pulled his head closer to her neck and ground his face into the bloody bite. Evan tasted her again, but held himself back. "Harder…"

"No. Remember, we have to restrain ourselves." He pulled back and turned her so that he could stare into her eyes. "We can't risk it."

She took a deep breath and nodded, her desires not quite sated. "If you say so."

He pulled her into a tight embrace and held her. "You know me. Always the cautious one."

She lay on the couch wrapped in his arms for quite some time. Evan watched her breathing to see if she had fallen asleep and was prepared to slip out when she shifted and laid her head in his lap. "I still plan to leave."

He felt himself stiffen slightly at her words. He ran a hand through her long mahogany hair and stared at her profile. "When?"

She closed her eyes, unable to look at him. "As soon as the Colonel cuts me loose."

Evan knew better than to show his disappointment. It would do no good. Once her mind was made up, there was no changing it. "Will you come back?"

"Of course. I'll have to. I have to see you, don't I?" He watched as the corners of her mouth curled upward. "I can only go so long without a dose of you."

"I really wish you'd stay. Just…tell Mitchell that you want fewer duties. Maybe you could work in supply or something?" He continued to stroke her hair. "You could always be my assistant."

She chuckled and squeezed his leg. "I need to get away, Evan. I've been in this game for way too long."

"But if you're going to be coming back anyway, why not just stay?"

She shook her head slowly. "I can come back and visit you without having any strings attached. If I stay, I'll just end up having to do something else that will strip another piece of my humanity."

Evan stiffened again, but continued to stroke her hair. "Strip your…how do you mean?"

She turned on the couch so that she was looking straight up at him. "Over the years, I've had to do things that I never thought I'd do. I think it all came to a head with Senator Franklin." She lifted her hand and brushed her fingers against the side of his face. "He killed himself because of what I did."

Evan shook his head. "He *chose* to end his own life. He was a mean bastard and if it weren't for him trying to take down everything we've been doing, it wouldn't have happened."

She closed her eyes again and replayed events through her mind. "I suppose we'll just have to agree to disagree on that one." She opened her eyes again and the sadness painted across her face would have broken his heart if it were still beating. "Franklin was just the tip of the iceberg though. Losing First Squad, then losing Dom. The whole 'end of the world' thing. Mueller's wife and kid. It just starts adding up after a while. And, Evan, I'm just tired of it all. I'm tired of…" She stared into his eyes and stroked his jaw again. "Honey, I'm just tired."

Evan moaned as he leaned down and kissed her, the taste of her own blood adding a salty, coppery tinge. "I really don't want you to go."

"I promise it won't be forever."

"I hope not. Forever is a very long time." Evan wiped at his eyes absently. "I'm a vampire. I should know."

*****

Matt opened the door the cell and escorted Jennifer inside. He gently pushed the cell door shut and the clang echoed off the painted concrete walls. "I'll be right next door." He watched her as she looked around the cell and began stripping her clothes off, tossing them outside the bars.

Jack sat in the adjacent cell in a black spandex bodysuit. He averted his eyes not from shyness or respect. The time he'd spent with the wolves on the island had long ago taught him that nudity was nothing to concern himself with. Rather, he was concentrating on the pull of the moon. Hoping to time his shift just moments before the moon called.

Mitchell stepped into the cell next to Jennifer's and pulled the door shut. He turned to her as he began to undress. "The doors are on a timer. They'll open at dawn."

Jennifer tossed the last of her clothes outside the cell and gave him a smile. Mitchell tried not to stare at her as she stood in the center of her cell, nude. She truly was beautiful and it took him a moment to remember what he was supposed to be doing. As he tossed his socks and shoes outside the cell door he could feel his wolf clawing to surface, eager to meet its mate.

Mitchell removed the last of his clothing and tossed it outside the door and turned to stare at her once more. He saw that her eyes had already shifted to amber, glowing in the low light. Suddenly she took on a golden brilliance and he saw a grey timber wolf standing where Jennifer once stood. The wolf never took its eyes off him as he felt the shift begin to pull at him. He glanced over the wolf's shoulder and saw Jack stand to his full height then shift to his Halfling form, the Spandex suit expanding to fit.

Mitchell cocked his head to the side, curious about the bodysuit when the shift hit him and he began his own shift. His vision changed from color to black and white and Mitchell's memory faded as the wolf rose to the surface and howled.

*****

"All clear. Operators, stand by."

The overhead speaker sounded more tinny than usual as Kalen and Brooke retrieved their weapons and stepped outside the simulator.

"Nailed it." Brooke held the door for Kalen as he exited.

"You did very well, Raven. I actually felt like you could be counted on during that drill."

Brooke gave him a droll stare then let the door fall back to hit him as she walked away. "That was the point, Keebler."

Kalen opened his mouth to say something, but thought it better to hold his tongue until after the training officer informed them of their performance.

"You passed. A report is being generated and will be sent to Phoenix. Cadets, dismissed." The young officer turned and walked away without any further discussion.

Kalen watched Brooke spin on her heel and head for the exit. "Why did you get upset? I was trying to compliment your performance and you—"

Brooke spun and shoved a finger into his chest, cutting him off. "You still don't get it, do you Sugar Cookie?"

Kalen shook his head, unsure what he was supposed to get. "I suppose I do not."

"I didn't do this for you. I did this for...for..." She huffed suddenly and turned to leave again.

"What? What did you do it for?" He fell into step behind her. "Please explain to me what it is I'm missing."

She threw her hands into the air, her back still to him as she marched away. Kalen watched her leave, completely unaware of what he did wrong. "Please tell me."

"Figure it out on your own, Elf." She slammed the door as she left, leaving Kalen alone. He stared after her, but for the life of him, he couldn't understand what he may have said that upset her so.

Kalen worked his way back to their quarters and knocked lightly on the door of Azrael. It still surprised him each time he saw the gargoyle up close. He stared upward into the Azrael's face. "I could use your guidance, friend."

Azrael opened the door further, allowing Kalen to enter. Once inside, he noted just how small the room was with Azrael inside it. The gargoyle motioned to the small chair. "Please. It is much too small for me to use."

Kalen sat and stared at nothing. Azrael waited patiently for the Elf to open up. Finally Kalen turned to him. "What am I doing wrong with Brooke?"

"You mean Raven?"

"Yes, Raven. It seems that everything I do upsets her. Even when I try to compliment her, she gets extremely upset."

Azrael sat down gently on the edge of the bed. "Tell me what occurred."

"We had to go through a drill that teaches teamwork. She continually caused us to fail. I said something to her about it. I told her that failing it on purpose served no purpose. She finally came around and when she applied herself, we passed the first time."

"Good." Azrael nodded. "So she *can* be a team player."

"Yes, and I even told her as much. I told her that towards the end of the drill that I actually held the belief she could be counted on. It upset her." Kalen gave him a confused stare. "I do not understand."

"Perhaps you should have stated your belief in a different manner?" Azrael scratched at his chin. "Is it possible that she took offense to your remark? Perhaps she felt that you should have been able to count on her the entire time?"

Kalen shrugged. "I do not know. But I do know that she is now upset with me and without explanation."

Azrael shook his head. "I'm afraid I cannot explain this one to you. This could be a 'female' thing or it could be a 'vampire' thing. Either way, it is beyond my grasp on human interaction."

"But, Azrael, she is not human. She is vampire."

Azrael patted the young elf on the shoulder. "Ah, but therein lies the conundrum. She once was human then became vampire. I fear that human complexities still exist, even if they are turned to the undead."

Kalen sighed heavily. "I am not well versed in either dealings with humans or dealings with vampires."

"What of dealings with females?"

Kalen gave him a surprised look. "Even less."

*****

Lilith purred as Samael threw the inert body of Gaius out of the office that she used as a bedroom. He stood and glared at her, fury burning in her eyes. "You allowed the Roman to touch you?"

She sucked on her lower lip and gave him a pouty stare. "You weren't here." She swayed her hips as she approached him then doubled her fist and punched him hard across the jaw. "In fact, you haven't *been* here in well over two millennia!" Samael stared at her in shock as she puffed out her chest. "What did you expect me to do? Wear a chastity belt and cry each night for your return?" She waved him away flippantly as she spun and pranced back to her bed.

"Do not turn your back on me, woman!" Samael advanced, growing in stature with each step.

Lilith sensed his reaching for her and jumped to her bed just as his hands closed on empty air. She bounced on the bed and spun to face him, a mischievous smile crossing her face. "Oh, so now you care?" She kicked at him as he crawled across the bed, reaching for her.

"Do not mock me, woman." He grabbed her ankles and pulled her to him. "I have waited too long to be with you again."

She giggled and laughed as he pulled her into a rough embrace. "Don't act like you're truly jealous, Samael. I know better." She kissed him; gently at first,and then with reckless abandon. He dropped her to the bed and pinned her with his arm, his tongue exploring her mouth. She pushed him away and sucked in air, trying desperately to catch her breath. "Oh, my God, I missed you."

"Wait until I've taken my full form," his voice growled, low and menacing.

"You can do that? I thought you could only inhabit others?" She pushed him back and stared into his crystal blue eyes.

"Even now, I am altering this body. This...dead flesh." Samael stared down at the body of the vampire he had taken. "Why did you keep a ghoul?"

She smiled and stroked his chin. "A pet, my love. A means to an end, that is all."

He grabbed her roughly and pulled her to him. "A toy? For your pleasures?" He bit at her neck, and his rough whiskers excited her.

"He collected the pieces of my body and performed the ritual to breathe life back into my physical form." She giggled and kicked as he nipped and nibbled his way down to her breast.

"Why keep him around afterward?" Samael suddenly looked up. "And how did he survive the ritual? A life for a life. Vampires and ghouls have no life to offer."

She laughed and threw her head back. "He stocked up on power. A regular vessel that one." She wrapped her arms around his ever widening back and pulled herself closer to him, pressing herself to his flesh. Her probing hands felt the nubbins on his back that would soon burst forth and form wings. "Oh my...you are altering this body quickly."

Samael grasped her hair and pulled her head back, staring at her. "It's been too long since I've had a physical form. I want this one perfected as quickly as possible." He bit her neck, and she screamed with delight as his teeth scraped along the tender flesh.

"Oh yes. You will be perfect, that's for sure." She pulled him closer and bit his earlobe. "Now quit teasing me and do what you came here to do."

Samael jerked her hair back and pulled her writing body flat to the bed. "Your soul is mine. I now claim your body."

"Don't just claim it. Take it, dammit!"

She wrapped her legs around his waist and thrust herself upward to meet him. "Take me...take me now!"

*****

"Bravo team, this is Team Leader, sound off," Spalding whispered into his throat mic.

"Bravo Two, southeast corner secure." Wallace scanned his coverage area with the SCAR 17. "Zero Tangos."

"Bravo Three, northeast corner secure. Zero Tangos," Popo reported.

"Bravo Four, northwest corner secure. Limited visibility. Zero Tangos." Gus Tracy shifted his position as he reported, trying to get better coverage.

"Copy that, Bravo team. Approaching now." Spalding used hand signals to send Delta team forward and fan outward.

"Team Leader, be advised, you have a single guard heading your location. Five Zero meters," Bravo Two reported in a whispered voice.

"Copy that Bravo Two. That should be Apollo. Hold fire unless you see hostile movement." Spalding stepped from the shadows and walked down the middle of the roadway to the open gates.

"Spanky, that you?"

Spalding released the breath he'd been holding and keyed his throat mic. "Affirmative. Contact made. Confirm Tango as Apollo." Spalding stepped out of the shadows and into the glow of the sodium light. "Apollo, it's good to see you again, brother."

Apollo shot him a toothy grin and reached out to take the man's hand. "Damned good to see you, too." He pulled the operator in and clapped him on the back. "How many are you?"

"Delta and what's left of Bravo." Spalding kept his voice low, but was sure the other team members heard the conversation.

Apollo's stature slumped and he lowered his eyes. "I can't tell you how sorry I am that..." he turned away and shook his head. "Who's left from my team?"

Spalding cleared his throat and answered softly. "You lost Bone. If it's any consolation, he went down fighting."

Spalding could have sworn he saw the big man's lower lip quivering as he nodded. "He was a good man. Hell of a warrior."

"Listen, Apollo, I have to tell you something." Spalding wasn't sure exactly how to broach the subject and had played this conversation out in his mind numerous times. It never went well. Since there wasn't really a good way to broach the subject, he felt the best thing to do was to simply spit it out.

"Yeah? What's that?"

"Before we left, Mitchell pretty much gave us two options."

"You mean me, don'tcha?" Apollo rubbed at the back of his neck then wrapped his arms around his chest. "Hit me with it, baby. Whatever it is, I have it coming."

"Well, see…he pretty much said our choices were to bring you back in chains or a bodybag."

Apollo exhaled hard as the words struck him like a physical blow. He shook his head and stared down at Spalding. "I don't want to go to no prison, Spanky. I can't do it. I know I deserve it, but—"

Spalding held up his hands to stop him. "We came up with a third option." He pointed into the shadows. "Actually, Ing came up with it and the rest of the guys all signed on. All of them."

Apollo inhaled deeply. "I don't guess that third choice was anything like ten HailMarys and come back to work, was it?"

Spalding shook his head. "No, brother, it wasn't. I'm sorry." He placed a reassuring hand on the big guy's shoulder. "We're calling it banishment. Basically, after tonight, you disappear. You just fade into the night and forget that the squads exist. Try to find a pack or something, or…hell, anything. Just steer clear of mercenary work, don't let yourself become a threat to humans and we both forget the other exists."

Apollo nodded, his eyes staring into the shadows. "But if I ever pop back up on the radar…"

"Then we do what we do best." Spalding watched as the big man's eyes turned to him. "Neither of us wants that, Apollo."

"No. You got that right." He turned and blew out a hard breath. "Thank you, Spanky."

"Don't thank me, brother. It was unanimous. Both squads voted on this and…it wasn't just me."

Apollo pulled his friend into a tight bear hug. "In case something happens tonight, thank you, brother."

Spalding tried not to groan or break as Apollo squeezed him. "Any time, buddy."

Apollo let him drop to the ground and wiped at his face. "We got work to do." He waved Spalding and the other operators on. "Follow me."

Leading the team through a myriad of abandoned metal buildings, they soon came out to a clearing where multiple rows of shipping containers formed lines through the facility. "They're in there. Silver lined coffins."

"Accesses?"

"Rooftop. Ventilation and access ports." Apollo pointed to a ladder and Lamb and Jacobs immediately hit the metal rungs and were standing atop the first container.

Lamb dropped a silver nitrate grenade down the ventilation shaft, and the pair waited for it to go off. The following roars and howls let them know that the grenade did its job. Ing opened the access port and the pair opened fire on the weakened wolves.

Other members of Delta passed Jacobs and Lamb and jumped to the next container. Lamb whistled to get their attention. "Save the grenades. There's silver over the access port. Just pop the top and let 'em have it."

"Roger that." Donnie gave him a thumbs-up and Little John cracked open the access port and eased it open. Confirming that the silver mesh covered the area, he threw open the lid and the pair opened fire. As they were cleaning up, Lamb and Jacobs passed them and jumped to the next one.

Spalding elbowed Apollo. "Care to join them?"

Apollo nodded. "Why the hell not. These sons of bitches deserve every shot." The pair went to the next row and climbed atop the containers. Spalding keyed his throat mic again. "This is going a little too easy. Keep your eyes open."

Three clicks echoed back in his earpiece as acknowledgment. Spalding watched as Apollo tossed open the first of the access ports and the pair opened fire. Satisfied that the wolves were dead, they jumped to the next container.

"Movement," Gus Tracy reported. "Can't get a clear bead."

"Bravo Four, Bravo Two, location, over?"

Tracy shifted again on the rooftop and tried to spot whatever it was he saw moving. "Bravo Two, east of the blue metal outbuilding. Over."

"Scanning." Bravo Two shifted his line of sight and scanned the area, coming up empty. "I've got nothing. Bravo Three?"

"Negative. Field of view is empty from here."

Spalding paused in his clean-up efforts and keyed his throat mic. "Bravo Four, are you sure you saw something?"

"Bet my life on it, Spanky." Tracy continued to scan the area, his finger hovering just above the trigger of the SCAR heavy.

"What's wrong?" Apollo asked as he closed the access port.

"One of the perimeter overwatches noted movement." Spalding turned and stared in the direction of the reported incident. "Nobody can verify."

Apollo shook his head. "Everybody but me should be in these crates."

Spalding continued to stare toward the sighting. "Should be are the key words there, brother. What are the odds somebody didn't go in?"

Apollo shrugged. "They'd be a wolf. Sort of hard to miss."

Spalding keyed his throat mic, "All units, be advised, we may have a rogue wolf in the area. Overwatches, cover your six. Delta team, on your toes."

A series of clicks confirmed the order and Spalding motioned for Apollo to jump over to the next container. As Spalding sprung through the air, something grasped his ankle and dragged him down and between the containers. His screams were followed by gunshots.

19

"Sir, the satellite is online and we're bringing it to bear."

Jericho spun the command chair around. "When you have the location zeroed in, put it on the big screen."

Mark looked up from his station. "Drone is in a holding pattern. Random heat signatures scattered on-scene."

"Delineate and tag those heat signatures, Major. I need to know who's who." Jericho spun his chair back to the front and tapped at his command console. "Anything out there that's not supposed to be needs to be reported to Delta Team Leader."

"Bravo Two through Four delineated and tagged. Delta Actual, is talking with an unknown." Mark zeroed in the camera from the drone and switched from thermal to microwave to infrared. "Looks like Apollo has made contact."

"Cut into their local coms," Jericho ordered. The communications tech relayed the communications through the overhead speakers. After listening for a moment, Jericho nodded. "That's Williams. Tag his signature and…who is that fast runner?"

Mark looked up at the big screen to see where the runner was. The heat signature cut and weaved from building to building then slipped between the cargo containers. "Checking. Signature is too hot and too large to be one of ours. Recommend warning the squad."

"Agreed." Jericho was keying the coms, preparing to inform the teams that an interloper was in the area when another heat signature disappeared from the top of the containers and a scream mingled with gunfire came across the coms. "Sitrep!" Jericho was punching in the command for a magnification of the satellite's imagers as the coms erupted with the shouts and yells of the squad as they converged on the area between the two containers.

"That sounded like Spalding." Major Tufo was on his feet and staring at the large screen above the far wall of the OPCOM. He watched as the screen resolution changed and the picture zoomed in on the area immediately surrounding the cargo containers. A very large heat signature disappeared from the top of the tall metal containers, and he couldn't tell from the video what was happening on the ground.

Jericho had turned the volume down from the local communications and stared at the screen as well. "That's too tight an area to bring the drone in without risking our people."

Mark nudged the Captain. "Any of the overwatches have eyes on what's happening?"

Jericho immediately switched to the helmet cams of the three different Bravo members. "Negative." He cursed under his breath. "We're blind."

*****

"So what's this big idea you have?" Foster reclined in the rich leather interior of the car and waited for his brother to expand on his thoughts.

"You remember Viktor, *oui*?"

"Of course. The first wolf that you tamed." Foster gave him a wry smile. "Who could forget the giant hairball?"

Rufus ignored the barb and continued. "He has repaired the relationship he once shared with his mother. I intend to take advantage of that."

Foster narrowed his gaze and shook his head in confusion. "I'm not following you."

Thorn watched the town zip by through the tinted windows of the limo, his mind wandering to a different time and place when he could walk in the sunlight and enjoy all that the old world once offered. He turned slowly to Foster, his eyes still distant. "Viktor's mother's sister. She is a witch." He allowed a moment for the words to sink in. "She can see things. Unseen things."

Foster snorted, "You believe in witches?"

Thorn gave him a deadpan stare. "Says the vampire…"

"Touché."

"She can tell us where Damien and his collection of body parts have hidden. Once we find out, we simply take a task force and collect him."

"And if he resists?" Foster felt the corners of his mouth curling upwards, his anticipation growing along with his desire to destroy the wayward child.

"Then we convince him that it is in his best interest to discontinue his activities." Rufus turned and faced Foster. "If he still resists, we simply remove his head from his body and bring the ashes back to the Council."

Foster leaned forward and lowered his voice, his eyes casting furtive glances toward the enforcers in the front of the vehicle. "And if the Council is correct and he has already resurrected the demon whore? What then, brother? You know that she'll be more than we can handle. Remember what the ancient books said. She can control the dead."

Rufus sat back and contemplated such a scenario. "I believe that if we encounter that bridge on our journey, then it will be time to call in Jack once more."

"Jack? Thompson? The wolf that wants your head on a platter? Just how do you think you could convince him to aid us?"

Thorn smiled and leaned his head back, his eyes closing. "By convincing the Monster Squad that Lilith is a threat to humans. They'll have no choice but to deal with her." He turned his head slightly and cracked an eye open. "At which point we will step in and retrieve the pieces and ensure they are scattered."

Foster laughed and leaned back in the seat, emulating his brother. "I like the way you think."

*****

Kalen exited Azrael's room and turned to go to his own room. He ran into Brooke and took a step back. "Excuse me,I didn't mean—"

"Move it, Keebler." She shoved past him and continued on her way.

Kalen lowered his eyes as she stormed away then stepped back into the hallway and squared his shoulders. "Stop!"

Brooke paused and turned to eye him cautiously. "I know you didn't just use that tone with me."

"I am your Second. You will comply." Kalen stared her down as she slowly faced him.

"Oh, no you didn't." She planted her feet and glared at him. "No man speaks to me like he owns me."

"I don't own you, but I am in charge while Chief Jack is indisposed. You will comply."

The corner of her mouth curved upward and Kalen wasn't sure if it was a snarl or a smile. "Go ahead then, Sugar Cookie. Tell me to do something, so I can tell you where to shove it."

Kalen shook his head. "There is nothing for you to do, but you need to listen to me." He stepped forward and began closing the gap between them.

Brooke brought her hands up and planted them on her hips. "I don't need to listen to anybody. I shouldn't even be here."

"And yet, here you are. You have been included as a member of our team and whether you like it or not, we need you."

Her eyes registered the surprise at his words. She didn't expect to hear him say that they 'needed' her. Her mind spun as she tried to think of a snappy comeback. "Well…I don't need you."

"I understand that." Kalen stopped just in front of her. He lowered his voice and tried to soften his words. "You've always been alone and done things on your own,I get that. I understand that you don't like being a force of one. But there is safety in numbers. We all have the same goal here and the Wyldwood claims that we need you. She wouldn't have said so if it weren't true."

"That may be, but still, I don't need you." She narrowed her gaze at him and tightened the line of her mouth. "I've done just fine on my own."

"I concede that point." Kalen lowered his voice further and leaned in, essentially whispering to her. "What if the Wyldwood included you because she somehow knew that we couldn't complete our mission without you? Perhaps she somehow knew that you were the key?" He shrugged. "I'm not saying that is the case, but it may well be. If it is, then *we* need *you*."

"We?" She turned her head slightly and whispered into his ear. "Or *you*?"

Kalen stepped back as if he had been struck. "W-what? I don't..." He averted his eyes and shook his head. "The entire team needs you. And we need you to be a team player."

She raised a brow at him. "Truly? A lone assassin like myself truly becoming a 'team player'? Do you really think that's possible?"

Kalen squared his shoulders again and nodded. "I believe that anything is possible if you set your mind to it. Especially for you, Brooke. I've seen you fight. I watched you in the simulator. You have real skill." He turned and waved down the hall toward the other rooms where the other warriors rested. "They have skills as well. Imagine if you allowed yourself to actually become a part of what we are and not only added your skill set to our cause, but allowed yourself to trust the rest of us? Our assets on the battlefield would make this small force..."

"What?" she mocked him. "A laughing stock?"

"No." He searched her face. "A force to be reckoned with."

Brooke leaned against the wall of the hallway and studied the elf standing before her. "I'll give you this, Keebler, you have a way with words."

"What is this 'Keebler' you keep calling me?"

Brooke laughed and turned back down the hall. "I'll tell you tomorrow. For now, Sugar Cookie, get some sleep." She turned back and faced him. "I'll give you and your little monster hunters a chance. But there needs to be something in it for me."

"Besides doing the right thing? Besides learning from others with a different skill set? Besides having the opportunity to hunt down killers again, but with backup?"

"Yeah, yeah. You still owe me a night of fun, Sugar Cookie. I fully intend to keep you to that deal."

Kalen watched as she turned and walked the short distance to her room then disappear behind the door. He felt a familiar pang but couldn't quite identify it. He knew that she drove him mad with her attitude. She made him crazy when she rebelled against the authority. She irritated him with her flippancy. But she also held his respect as a warrior. She had this insane ability to get under his skin...and make him like it. He sighed heavily as he turned and opened the door to his own room.

Stepping inside, he realized that she was in the room adjacent to his. He lay down on the bed and tried not to think of the woman in the black leather jumpsuit. He tried not to think of the way she wielded her swords. He inadvertently placed a hand against the cinder block wall between them and wished that he could *feel* her presence through it.

He closed his eyes and tried not to imagine the female warrior that kept invading his thoughts.

*****

Jack sat in the far corner of his cell watching the interaction between Mitchell and his Fated Mate. The female timber wolf paced in agitation, wanting desperately to get through the bars and Mitchell's Halfling form had long ago determined that the silver bars meant pain. It didn't stop him from trying to reach through the bars to touch the timber wolf. Smoke rose from the areas that brushed the silver plated bars and the Halfling howled as the searing pain forced it to withdraw.

Jack's mind drifted to Nadia and the baby. He knew that time was drawing closer to the arrival of their new addition, and he ached to be with her. Yet something told him that he was needed here. Besides tracking down the thieving bastard, Thorn, he felt like this was his second home.

Jack leaned back against the rear concrete wall of the cell and stared at the bars surrounding him. His mind drifted back to a better time when he was still on the island. Although he was Rufus' Second, he knew nothing of the weapon that the vampire had constructed. He shook his great head as he considered how he'd been duped. If it hadn't been for Thorn destroying his trust, he would probably be in Geneva right this moment with a handful of squad members, preparing to...

Jack sat up, his eyes wide. He stared at the cell door and wished he had a way out and a way to communicate. How could he have been so stupid? Of course Thorn would still go to Geneva! He *had* to. He had an audience with the Council. If Thorn were alive, he would be in Geneva. Come Hell or high water, he would find a way.

Jack beat his head against the concrete wall in frustration. He could feel it in his bones where the lying vampire was, and there was nothing he could do about it. Jack glanced at the clock on the wall and began calculating. Was it ahead or behind in Geneva? If Rufus met with the council, would he try to return to the states immediately afterward? If he did, what plane would he use?

Jack's nerves started getting the better of him. He stood and began to pace in his cell, the nervousness of the other two inmates only adding to his frustration. He found himself unable to think in the Halfling form and Jack fought to maintain control. He had to remember his revelation so that he could begin his search the next morning. It was far easier to track someone when the trail is still warm.

*****

"Spanky!" Apollo took a giant leap and dove between the two containers. He tackled the large, hairy beast, wrapping his arm around its neck as his momentum carried them to the concrete below.

The pair rolled and Apollo found himself tucked under the huge mass of the monster. Teeth snapped near his nose and spittle flew as the monster attempted to chew his face off. Apollo worked his knee up and under the creature, holding it just out of biting range.

Spalding rolled to the side and sucked in a lungful of air, the creature having squeezed most of it from his body in a failed attempt to crush him. He turned his head to see Apollo wrestling with the monster and Spalding reached for his weapon. His carbine had been knocked loose so he pulled his pistol from the thigh holster. Rolling to his side Spalding used the concrete ground to steady his aim.

"I gotchu now, motherfucker!" Apollo grabbed a handful of werewolf throat and squeezed for all he was worth.

The creature batted his arm away and grabbed him by his tactical vest, sliding him out from under its massive form. Spalding lost his shot as Apollo was dangled in front of him. With a speed that neither man suspected, the creature pushed Apollo out and away, sending him smashing into the closed end of the container next to them, rattling the metal sides.

Spalding pointed the pistol and let loose three rounds into empty air...the creature had vanished. "Where the hell did it go?" He crawled to his knees and stared around the corner of the container. "Bravo Two, do you have eyes on that thing?"

"Negative, Spank. It appeared then vanished." Wallace scanned the area and ground his teeth in frustration. "It's fast."

Spalding duck-walked to Apollo and helped him to sit up. He keyed his throat mic, "OPCOM, do you have visual on a fast runner?"

"Sporadic sightings. Heat signatures appearing and disappearing too fast to zero in."

Spalding pulled Apollo to his feet. "You bit?"

"Naw, man. That mug just got slobber all over me. Worse than a Mississippi leg hound." Apollo wiped at the thick mucousy liquid covering his face and neck.

"I thought they were all locked up." Spalding squared off on the big man.

"I swear to God, Spank. I thought they were." Apollo stepped out from the containers and glanced down both lengths. "You and me can hunt this mutt. Let your squad finish cleaning house."

Spalding nodded and looked up to the top of the containers where Delta Squad still waited. "Carry on with the mission. Clear out *all* of these containers. We're going hunting."

"Roger that." Donnie slapped John across the shoulder. "You're with me."

Spalding turned back to Apollo. "Where do we start?"

"The warehouses. The big one is where we staged everything. The smaller one is where we kept the vehicles." He broke off at a trot with Spalding hot on his heels.

"OPCOM, Bravo units, keep your eyes open. If you see a fast mover, drop it!" Spalding huffed into his mic. "Don't wait for it to stop. And for the love of Pete, keep it off Delta Squad. They have their hands full."

"Copy that, Team Leader." Jericho cursed as he watched the cameras from the drone tilt and the altimeter numbers drop. They put the drone into a low circular orbit over the operation. "Keep that satellite hot. Watch the fences,I don't want that thing escaping."

Lamb and Jacobs had just flipped open a new access port and took aim when they heard a metallic clang. Lamb looked to Jacobs. "What was that?"

Jacobs shrugged. "Beats me, brother. I thought you did it."

They turned and directed fire inside the container, dropping the wolves within when their earpieces came alive. "Delta Squad! Those containers are opening!"

All four members of Delta Squadron had a simultaneous 'oh shit' moment then turned and made their way to the ends of the containers they stood on. "Contain these things!" Donnie yelled as he opened fire.

Jacobs jumped to the next container and Lamb ran past him to take the container beyond. Both men squared up with the slowly opening doors and prepared to shoot anything that came out.

"Bravo Two, Bravo Three, I have no line of sight," Tracy reported as he continued to shift his position in order to help cover the area. "Relocating."

"Negative, Bravo Four!" Spalding yelled into his mic. "I need you to cover your package. You are our only eyes on the west side."

Gus Tracy groaned as he settled back in. *Why the hell am I here if I can't help?* "Roger that, Team Leader." He placed his eye back to the reticle of his scope and covered his package area. *Please, if there's a god; let that hairy bastard cross into my zone.*

"Apollo reports there's an electronic lock on those boxes. The controller is in the warehouse. The rogue must have punched the button." Spalding's voice sounded jumpy as he ran between the buildings and into the warehouse. "Be advised, our rogue wolf is most likely Sheridan."

All of the operators felt a cold chill at the sound of the name. Each of them prayed for the opportunity to put the traitorous dog down before the night was over.

*****

"Tell me, my love, what are your plans for this Legion of yours?" Lilith ran a nail lazily along Samael's back, tracing the outline of where his wings would soon burst forth.

"I have no plans for them." He stretched and flexed his growing body. "They are yours to command. I promised them to you, remember?"

She paused and pressed her nail deeper into his flesh watching him twitch as she drew blood. "The same Legion you promised me before the humans killed me the first time?"

He grabbed her hand and pulled her bloody digit from his skin. Tossing her hand aside roughly he gazed at her sternly. "Yes,the very same. They weren't ready to be commanded yet."

"I see." She licked the blood from her finger and smiled at him seductively. "Did you have to harden them for me?"

Samael snorted and rolled to his side to face her. "They had to be taught."

"Taught? They're Roman centurions, no?"

"And like all elite soldiers, they have to be broken and then built back up. Otherwise they have it in their heads that they don't have to take orders from a woman." He reached out and cupped her breast. "Even one as delicious as you."

"You had to mold them to my service." She rolled to her back and stared at the ceiling. "And to what purpose do I use these demons?"

Samael shrugged. "World domination, of course. Isn't that what you've always wanted? To rule the world of men?"

She gave him a sideways look. "I'm supposed to take over this world with a thousand demons? Have you seen the weaponry that man has now? They have firearms that can shoot a hundred projectiles in a matter of moments."

Samael chuckled as he stood and walked to the sink to relieve himself. "And you think the weapons of mortal men can harm my demons?"

"They have bombs that can level entire cities. I think they can destroy the bodies of your demons."

"Then they simply move on to another body." He strutted back to the bed and knelt at the edge. "For as long as there are men walking the earth, my demons have a body to inhabit."

"*Your* demons?" She raised a brow at him.

"Your demons. I simply created them." He fell to the bed and watched as she bounced next to him. "But I created them nearly perfect. They're evil of heart, wicked of mind, capable of inflicting pain in ways that most have only imagined, and they are the most proficient of killers."

Lilith considered his words and nodded. "And they're all at my command."

"Yes, they are." He pulled her to him roughly and rolled her over. "Yours to command, to kill, to do with as you please." He grabbed a double handful of her buttocks. "But if you allow another of them to touch you…I'll kill you both myself."

She smiled over her shoulder at him and gave him a sultry look. "Jealous, are we?"

"I don't share." He pulled her up to her knees and impaled her. "I told you. You belong to me."

Lilith gripped the edge of the mattress and bit her lip. "Yes, m'lord. I am yours."

"Only mine. None other."

"Only yours. I am yours, completely."

She watched his reflection in the glass of the office as he took her roughly and she fought back the urge to scream. He was no longer Damien. He appeared as he did all those centuries ago when he first appeared to her. When he first claimed her. When he first took her. She felt a pressure building from deep within and she inhaled sharply. Finally. A man worthy of her.

*****

Mick sat within the empty interrogation room and stared at the two way mirror on the other side of the room. He note the dark circles under his eyes and shook his head. *How the hell did I end up in chains?*

Mick stared at his hands and controlled his shift, allowing a nail to grow and protrude from his finger. It wasn't much and hopefully it was a small enough change that nobody would notice is they were watching. He glanced to the mirror and pretended to scratch at his wrist. He turned away and coughed lightly, trying to cover his mouth with his shackled hands.

Moving by feel, Mick worked his claw to the handcuffs holding his wrists and slipped the tip of his claw inside. He wiggled the hardened nail back and forth, praying that he could pick the lock. In moments, he felt the cuff give slightly, a light clicking sound catching his sensitive ears. He used his wrist against the cuff and felt it fall open. He held the cuff against his arm and worked his other nail into the other cuff. Working left handed wasn't the easiest thing, but he managed to unlock that side as well.

Mick sat in his chair and continued to stare at the mirror. *No time like the present.* He let the cuffs slip from his arms then stood to make a break for the door. The shackles around his ankles tripped him, and he fell against the metal table with a loud bang. Mick jerked his eyes to the mirror then fell to the floor, working his claws into the shackles at his feet. After getting both loose, he rolled under the table and stood by the door.

Pressing his ear to the door, he listened intently for rushing footsteps; he heard nothing. He reached out tentatively and grasped the knob, turning it slightly. The door opened, and he stuck his head into the hallway. Nobody in sight, he slipped from the room and into the hall. He pulled the door shut behind him and made his way to the elevator at the end of the hall.

Mick stood at the elevator door and debated testing his luck. He glanced down the other hallway and noted a set of doors leading to a stairwell. *Probably safer.* He pushed open the door to the stairs and began working his way upward, listening intently for anybody entering the stairwell with him. As he reached the second floor he heard voices below him and the echoing sound of a door shut. Mick took the stairs two at a time and came to the first floor landing. *In for a penny…*

He cracked open the door and stared into the barrel of a gun. Both hands went up in surrender and he stepped back. Gregory stepped into the stairwell with him and gave him a bored look. "Took you long enough."

Mick was unsure the proper response. He debated trying to lie his way out but knew better. He slumped his shoulders and averted his eyes. "I didn't know if anybody was watching."

"We're always watching. Cameras. Ever hear of them?" Gregory holstered his weapon and motioned for Mick to follow him. "You're not under arrest, but Ms. Simmons is currently shifted downstairs in a silver lined cell. You have a few hours before they're through."

"They?" Mick fell into step behind Gregory. "Oh, you mean…her Fated…"

"We have three wolves shifted below decks." Gregory went down a flight of stairs and opened the door, holding it for Mick. "We have a room ready for you, or if you prefer, you can rent a hotel room off base."

Mick glanced at his watch then shook his head. "Just a place to get a little rest, I'll be fine."

Gregory walked him to the end of the hall and opened the door to a small room. "It's not much, but it has the basics. Bed, table, chair, lamp. Latrine is at the end of the hall and clearly marked.

There are showers there as well. Your bag is under your bunk." He turned to Mick and gave him a look that Mick couldn't discern. "Any questions?"

"None that I can think of." Mick stepped into the room then turned back to Gregory. "What was with all the theatrics back there?"

Gregory paused. He gave Mick a serious stare that made the man wish he'd not asked. "I wasn't joking when I said that we lost a lot of good people in those attacks. There are those who want the heads of anybody and everybody who might be even remotely involved."

"So it wasn't theatrics."

"It was a test of sorts. If you had tried anything aggressive, you would have been shot."

Mick gave him a crooked grin. "What if I'd taken your weapon? You couldn't have shot me then."

"My weapon? It wasn't loaded." Gregory pulled the pistol and cleared the chamber, showing that the magazine and chamber were both empty. "Just in case you *had* gotten my weapon. But there were two security guards a few feet away that you couldn't see with fully loaded M-16s ready to open fire."

Mick swallowed hard. "Gotcha, mate. Good thing I have a nice, wide yellow streak, eh?"

Gregory raised a brow at him. "Somehow, I doubt that." He turned to leave, "Have a good night, sir."

"Yeah. You, too." Mick pushed the door shut and fell onto the narrow bed. "Holy shit. What have I gotten myself into?"

20

Mark studied the monitor at his station then turned back to the big screen. "Captain, can we get a wider spread on the satellite image?"

Jericho typed in the commands and the pair waited while the imager refocused, bringing the industrial area back under scrutiny. The image focused and Mark tapped the man on the shoulder, "Switch from IR to thermal."

Jericho gave him a confused look but typed in the command. Moments later, the image glowed with hotspots. "The drone has too narrow a spot beam for this." Mark sat at his station and began tapping his keyboard. "Let's see if this works."

He overlaid the tags applied earlier from the drone and watched as each member of the two squads came up with red triangles above their heat signature. "And then there's this." He typed another command and a green triangle appeared over the heat signatures that weren't already tagged. "That's our bogeys."

Jericho shot Tufo a toothy grin. "Major, I don't know how you did that, but—"

"Pure freakin' genius, Cap." Mark tapped the side of his head. "Big kidneys."

Jericho keyed his coms. "Team Leader, OPCOM, we have your bogeys on thermal. If you boys will step aside, we can exercise the Predator."

Mark and Jericho both watched as Spalding and Apollo ran through the warehouse in pursuit of a fast mover who seemed to simply run through the wall. Both Spalding and Apollo slowed and nearly stopped at the wall, then took up the trail again. "Copy, OPCOM. All units prepare for drone strike."

Jericho watched as the squad members stepped out of the fray and took up defensive positions along the side of the main warehouse. Jericho turned to the technician directing the drone pilots. "Make it rain."

"Bringing the rain, sir."

Mark watched as white lines of heat crossed the image on the big screen and fast moving heat signatures seemed to splatter with each pass. After the second pass, the fast moving targets broke away and began to scatter throughout the open yard of the industrial area.

"Engaging targets," Bravo Two announced.

"Targets engaged," Bravo Three seemed to echo.

Spalding's voice came across the channel again. "Bravo Four,eyes open for Sheridan. He exited the warehouse through a second-story window. Possibly headed your direction."

"Scanning." Tracy eyed the area with his scope and waited for any kind of movement. He caught a glance of heat between two buildings and zoomed in with his scope. He continued to watch the narrow area and saw the faint glow of heat once more. Placing the crosshairs on the largest part of the red, he squeezed the trigger.

The heat signature disappeared once more between the buildings and Gus cursed to himself. He was almost certain that at best, it was a glancing blow. "Team Leader, Bravo Four. I think he slipped past. I didn't have a clear shot, but I think I winged him."

"If it slows the son of a bitch down, that's better than we had, Four." Spalding turned to Apollo. "Feel like chancing a walk in the rain?"

Apollo listened to the sound of the drone firing on the targets outside and shot the smaller man a stupid grin. "I don't hear no thunder. I'm thinking it's safe to go out." He slammed a fresh magazine into his rifle and motioned for Spalding to go first. "After you, oh-ballsy-one."

"Always the gentleman, aren't ya?" Spalding slipped out the open door and hugged the outer wall of the warehouse. They worked their way westward and searched for any sign of Sheridan.

Apollo tapped his shoulder and pointed, using hand signals to keep quiet. Spalding turned and caught movement near a small outbuilding. Spalding motioned for Apollo to go left and that he'd go right. Unless the target could fly, one of them was bound to lay eyes on him.

Apollo took off at a trot, keeping his head low. Spalding branched off and rounded the other corner of the building. Both men breeched the rear of the building at the same time and stood staring at an empty space.

"Where the hell did he go?" Apollo stared back over the open ground leading back to the main gate and the litter of bodies left by the drone. "Surely he wouldn't have tried to go out there?"

Spalding scanned the area and shrugged. "I've got nothing."

"I know I seen something."

A dark figure launched itself from the roof of the outbuilding and tackled Apollo, taking him to the ground once more. Spalding turned and saw the two massive figures rolling on the ground and brought his weapon to bear. He laid his finger on the trigger but couldn't bring himself to pull it. The odds of hitting Apollo were just too high, and he'd worked too hard to get the man a reprieve.

Spalding slung his rifle over his back and leapt into the air, hoping to tackle the wolf and roll it off of Apollo. Instead, he was clotheslined in midair and sent spiraling away.

Apollo punched, clawed, kicked and would have bitten if he were close enough. The beast rolling atop him seemed unfazed by the cascade of blows striking it about the head and neck. On the rare occasions that Apollo was rolled to the top, he'd try to push away from the beast. Any effort to put distance between them was futile. The wolf had too long of a reach and claws that could grip his clothing and flesh to prevent him from escaping.

Apollo pulled his pistol and tried to bring it to bear on the monster's head, but the weapon was slapped away and sent skittering across the concrete. Blow after blow, punch after punch, Apollo tried to weaken the beast, to inflict as much damage as he could before the hairy bastard ripped his heart out. Each strike seemed to only sap his strength and leave the monster unshaken.

Apollo was able to grasp the handle of his knife and rather than use the blade, he used the handle as reinforcement for his punches. He felt either his knuckles break or the monster's teeth shatter as he punched it across the jaw, the blade dragging a ragged cut along the length of the snout. The monster howled in pain, fueling Apollo's resolve. He beat at the monster's face and chest, each punch slicing small bits of flesh from the beast's hide.

Feeling drained and winded, Apollo felt his hand pinned to the ground as the monster loomed over him. Bits of bloody flesh and broken teeth showering his face as the creature snarled at him.

Apollo closed his eyes, unable to watch as the monster ripped his throat out. He inhaled deeply and yelled for all he was worth. If he was going out at this bastard's hand, he wouldn't go silently.

A gunshot echoed between the metal buildings, and Apollo felt the weight of the monster collapse onto him. He fought and struggled for air as he worked his huge arms up and under the hairy creature. He pushed as Spalding pulled the massive carcass from his prone body.

"Sorry it took me so long. I lost my pistol when I tackled Scooby." Spalding held out a hand, offering Apollo help to his feet.

Apollo lay on the ground sucking in air, struggling to regain his breath. "Took you long enough."

"Get up, you sissy." Spalding pulled the big man to his feet and was nearly pulled to the ground. "This is yours." He handed the pistol to Apollo.

"I guess I owe you my life. Again."

"I don't think so, brother. You dove off that cargo box and saved my bacon." Spalding clapped his shoulder. "I think we're even."

The ripping sound of the drone firing on another set of targets snapped both men back to the present. Spalding threw himself against the side of the small outbuilding. Apollo grabbed him by the tactical vest and hauled him back toward the main warehouse. "I don't think this will protect us."

Spalding hunkered in the shadows of the main warehouse and glanced out over the industrial park. "Team Leader, OPCOM, sitrep?"

"Mopping up now. Bravo units are tagging the stragglers."

Spalding sighed and slumped to the ground. "Remind me to bag Sheridan's head as a gift for Jack."

"Brother, I'll help you cut the damned thing off."

*****

Thorn lay down on the expansive bed in the penthouse suite and stretched out. He sighed as he allowed himself to slowly begin to shut down in preparation for dawn. The heavy curtains blocked all sunlight and he was more than ready to sleep.

"Shouldn't you call Viktor?" Foster asked from the doorway leading to the next room.

Thorn shook his head. "It's the full moon. He won't be able to answer this night."

"Isn't it daylight there yet?" Foster tried to calculate the time difference in his head.

"*Non.* It is early night there, just as it is dawn here." He leaned up on his elbows and nodded to Foster. "Go, sleep the day away. Soon I will set the wheels in motion."

Foster leaned against the doorjamb and eyed Rufus. "You remember when I told you that there was something I needed to tell you? Before we went to meet the Council?"

Rufus lay back on the bed and closed his eyes. "*Oui*."

Foster swallowed hard and studied his brother. "When I came out to your place…when you summoned me?" He cleared his throat and prepared for the worst. "The Council wanted me to give them the location of your island." Foster waited for Rufus to explode. He fully expected a tirade, perhaps even a physical attack. He continued to stand in the doorway and study his brother's prone body. Rufus almost appeared dead. Perhaps he had already fallen asleep?

Foster rubbed his hands together nervously and stepped into Thorn's room. "Did you hear me, brother?"

"*Oui*, I heard you."

"They had me take a tracking device with me." Foster watched nervously, waiting for Rufus to become enraged. He swallowed again and stepped even closer. "I was supposed to activate it once I got there. Except…I couldn't. I tossed it into the ocean."

"*Oui*. I know."

Foster stood silently, his mouth open in shock. He continued to stare at his brother's body lying so peacefully on the bed and he couldn't think of a reply. He heard his mouth speaking without realizing what he was saying. "What do you mean, 'you know'? How could you have known?"

Rufus sighed and sat up, eyeing his brother. "Do you not remember that I have spies within the Council? I knew you would have the tracking device before you did." Rufus gently shook his head as he stared at Paul. "They threatened you with the true death if you did not reveal my location. I know this. Yet, you still did not tell them. I wonder why that is?"

Paul swallowed hard and averted his eyes. "Because, you are my brother."

Rufus chuckled lightly and lay back down. "We both know that at the time, you did not think of me as 'brother'. So I had to ask myself, why wouldn't Paul Foster do as commanded by the Vampire Council? What was in it for him?"

Paul shrugged. "There was nothing in it for me. Except the promise of the true death." Foster walked further into the room and sat at the edge of the bed. "But somewhere along the way, I came to realize…you may have control of my people. You may have tripled your strength because of my acquisitions. You may have been the brunt of my anger for…how many centuries?"

"Too many."

"Yes. Too many." Paul shifted uncomfortably on the bed and looked to Rufus. "But somewhere along the way, I figured out that…you *are* my brother. Our father loved you as though you were a natural born son. And you're truly everything he wanted in a son." Paul sighed and ran a hand over his face. "I was faulting you for my own shortcomings."

"And this realization caused a change of heart?"

Foster shrugged, unable to put into words exactly what he felt. "I knew that I had to choose a side. And if there were a side that involved you? I'd be a fool to go against you."

"You chose wisely."

"Well, things certainly worked in my favor once I did." Foster stood and went to the bar. He poured a cognac and leaned against the counter. "Once I threw in completely with you, things stopped going against me. I started seeing things differently as well."

Thorn sat up in the bed and watched Foster intently. "Such as?"

"Such as…being a *Beastia* wasn't all that horrible." He sipped his cognac. "And when that bastard Thompson turned against you, you made me your Second. I realized then that you *wanted* to believe in me. I guess it caused me to step up."

Rufus glanced at the clock then turned to Paul. "While I find pleasure in the fact that you have come to accept certain truths, the hour is late and I must rest. We have a big day tomorrow."

"True." Foster tilted the glass and drained the cognac. "I'll leave you be."

"Good morning, brother."

"Good morning."

*****

"When do you plan to leave?"

Laura looked into Evan's eyes and cupped his face. "As soon as Matt knows I'm ready." She stroked his cheek with her thumb and knew that her eyes reflected the same sadness that his did. "I've needed to get away for so long and getting Jenny back here was my ticket."

Evan closed his eyes and turned from her. "It was hard enough saying goodbye the first time, I don't know if I can stand saying it again."

"I told you I'd be back." Laura tossed her bag onto the small pile and turned back to him. "Look, most of my stuff is either in storage or shipped home already. I can leave some of my stuff here for when I come back. That way you know I have to return. There's no way I'd leave my favorite sweater with you and not come back for it, right?" She painted a cheesy grin on her face, but the desired reaction failed to manifest. She stepped closer to him and pulled him into an embrace. "I promise you, it's not forever."

Evan wrapped his arms around her and squeezed gently. "It will feel like it." His whispered breath tickled the side of her neck. "It seemed like forever while you were gone searching for the woman."

"It may have felt like it, but it truly wasn't. I wasn't gone but a few days." She kissed him gently on the cheek and he leaned in closer.

"A moment away from you feels like an eternity."

"Then come with me." She leaned back and stared deeply into his eyes. "We can travel by night. We can hole up during the day and you can sleep."

Evan shook his head and sat down hard. "I promised Mitchell. And my work…"

"Your work can wait." She sat next to him and pulled his hand into her own. "Come with me, meet my father. Meet my brothers."

Evan snorted and cocked a curious brow at her. "They'd fight each other over who got to stake me first."

"No they wouldn't." She smiled at him and laid her head on his shoulder. "I told my dad about you. I'll be honest, he wasn't thrilled at first, but he slowly came around."

"What convinced him?"

"Everything, I think. The fact that you're helping us. That you don't...*didn't* drink human blood."

"I still wouldn't if there was a choice," Evan corrected.

"I know. And as far as dad knows, you're still *Beastia*."

Evan ran a thumb across the back of her hand absently. "And your brothers? You don't think they'd pump me full of hot silver the moment they met me?"

She laughed and shook her head. "They enjoy breathing too much. They know that if they did anything to hurt you, I'd kill them."

"Ah, sisterly love." Evan returned her smile and moved his caresses to her hair. "I really wish I could. But Mitchell thinks there's something big brewing and wants me working on new weaponry. I really need to make that a priority."

Laura sighed heavily and leaned away from him. "Evan, the world will always have some kind of major threat rattling its saber and threatening to destroy everything. You need to decide to live a little for yourself." She lifted his chin with her thumb and stared into his eyes once more. "For me."

Evan nodded and leaned into her once more. He wrapped his arms around her and enjoyed the warmth she radiated. "Maybe after a little bit, I can come out and visit you?"

She lowered her eyes and nodded, knowing that he'd never leave the safety and security of the hangar. "Sure. That sounds really swell."

*****

A banging at the door stirred the two lovers once more. Lilith stood and wrapped a robe around her before going out to the main doors. She looked back at Samael who stood nude in the doorway of her bedroom. "I have no idea."

"Turn them away, I need to rest this body."

Lilith stared at the Fallen One and smiled. In the short time that he had been back, he had nearly converted the dead flesh of Damien Franklin into an exact duplicate of his old body. She marveled at his chiseled chest and abs, the strength of his arms, the corded muscle of his legs. She had no idea how he did what he did, but she didn't care. Her angel had returned to her.

She turned toward the offending noise and strode with purpose. Reaching for the knob of the metal door, she pulled it open and was nearly run over by a burly, bearded man, a knit cap atop his head. He reminded her of the pictures she had seen of a lumberjack, only...not in this area. "Where the hell is he?"

"You need to leave. You are not welcome here." Lilith raised a hand to grab the large man when he swatted her arm away.

"Don't toy with me, woman. Where's that damned vampire? He has a whipping coming."

Lilith stared at the burly man and recognition crossed her features. "Gaius?"

"Of course, it's me. Now where the hell is that little ghoul?" He stomped deeper into the warehouse and glared toward her bedroom. "He's in there, isn't he?"

"Gaius, that is no longer Damien," Lilith purred, tugging at his arm to pull him back toward the door. "It is Samael returned."

"That isn't possible." Gaius turned and glared at the door to her bedroom. "I want the ghoul."

"No you don't," she chuckled as she continued to tug at his arm. "You truly need to leave and prepare the others."

Gaius turned on her and grabbed both of her wrists, pulling her hands to her side. "I said I want the ghoul."

"Then you shall have him!" Samael stood behind Gaius, his voice booming.

Gaius' eyes shot wide, his muddled mind recognizing the voice behind him. He turned slowly and stared at what used to be Damien. Dropping to one knee, he lowered his eyes to the floor. "Forgive me, m'lord. I didn't realize it was you."

"After the lady told you? You're either deaf or stupid." Samael lowered his voice and approached Gaius slowly. "I can't believe that a commander of your status to be stupid."

"N-no, master." Gaius prostrated himself to the floor and averted his eyes. "Please, forgive my insolence."

Samael rose to his full height and stared down at the burly demon. "Rise, my servant." He watched as Gaius slowly stood, his eyes still staring at the concrete floor. "You have chosen another body."

"A strong body, m'lord. Not as well connected as the previous host, but it will work to complete our task."

Samael smirked and slowly circled the large man. "Tell me, Gaius. Do you know what our task is?"

"To serve the lady. To aid her in taking over the world of man."

Samael nodded his approval. "He can be taught." Lilith fought back a smile as her lover poked the bear of a man. "How soon until your Legion is ready?"

"A matter of days, m'lord."

Samael turned to Lilith and raised a brow. "Can you wait that long, my love?"

She strode purposefully to him and ran a hand across his chest. "I'm sure we can come up with ways to pass the time." She bit at his ear and watched as his eyes closed in pleasure. "I've waited this long, my love. What's a few more days?"

Samael turned to Gaius. "Prepare your men. Have them report here when ready."

"Yes, m'lord." Gaius rose and turned for the door.

"Two days, Commander. No later."

"As you willm'lord."

*****

Kalen slept fitfully, disturbing images running through his mind. He saw Horith and his gaping, shredded wounds, begging for death. He saw the Wyldwood and the disappointment she felt for his inability to lead. He watched Chief Jack turn his back on him for letting him down on the battlefield. Azrael turning against him because…something…something bad happened to Gideon. And it was *his* fault.

Kalen awoke with a start, his breath coming in rapid gulps, his eyes darting around. He had to take a moment to control his breathing, to force his heart to slow down. *It was just a dream. Just a dream…*

"I was getting worried about you," Brooke's soft voice broke the silence of the darkness.

Kalen jerked to the side and stared in the direction of her voice. "Why are you here?"

She stood and walked the short distance to his narrow bed. "I heard you talking in your sleep." She kept her voice low, whispering in the darkness. She lay down next to him on the narrow cot; the coolness of her skin wrapped in the black leather surprised him. "Actually, it sounded like you were yelling. I came to check on you." Her hand slid up and brushed a lock of his long white hair from his face.

"I am fine now. It was just a dream." His heart began to hammer in his chest once more but not from the fear he experienced in his dream.

"It sounded more like a nightmare to me…" She leaned closer and brushed her lips across his chin, chills covering his body as she settled in nearly on top of him.

"P-perhaps it was. I really don't remember now," he lied. "But I am obviously in no harm. You may return to your own room now."

She smiled at him in the darkness and he could see her fangs extended, the shine of her lips pulling his eyes from hers. "Now, where's the fun in that? Remember, you're supposed to have some fun now. Break a few rules…" She leaned closer and kissed him gently on the bottom lip, sucking it ever so gently into her mouth.

Kalen's excitement confused him. The coldness of her skin combined with the heat he felt from her actions totally confused him…but he liked it. No. If he were totally honest, he *loved* it. He tried to kiss her back and she pulled away, not allowing him the pleasure. Every time he leaned forward to kiss her, she pulled away. When he lay back, she moved forward and sucked his lip into her mouth, running her cool tongue across his flesh. A moan escaped his mouth as she probed his mouth with her tongue. She pulled his tongue into her mouth and sucked it gently. He felt the point of her fangs, and it excited him even further.

When Brooke pulled away, Kalen inhaled deeply and forced his eyes open. "Why are you doing this?"

She smiled wickedly at him and ran her hands along his muscular chest. "Because I can." She moved in again and kissed him deeply, refusing to allow him to kiss her back. She moved her lips to his jaw, his neck and to his collarbone.

"You're killing me here." Kalen's breath hitched as he spoke.

Brooke ran her hands down his chest and across his abdomen, feeling him flinch as she touched sensitive and ticklish spots. "Wait until I *bite* you there," she whispered. Kalen's eyes shot wide at the prospect. She continued to kiss her way down his body, nipping and nibbling at his soft flesh until she reached his abdomen. Her hands had worked their way further down and Kalen stiffened.

"Brooke…perhaps you should…"

"Shhh." She nipped at his waist and he flinched, eliciting a soft giggle from her. She leaned up and hovered over his face, a glimmer of mischief in her eye. With one hand she unzipped her top. He could just make out the curve of her breasts although the leather still covered them. "I could just eat you up, Sugar Cookie." She suddenly struck like a snake, biting him viciously on the neck and drawing a mouthful of blood.

Kalen inhaled deeply to scream; fear, agony and ecstasy filling his body at the same time. He pushed against her and suddenly found himself sitting up in bed. Alone. His breath came in ragged pants as he stared into the darkness. He could feel the cold sweat covering his body and his hand reached to his neck. Nothing. Not so much as a scratch.

Kalen sat on the edge of the bed and considered what just happened. *Was it all just a dream?* He stood and walked to his door. Still locked. He went to the sink and splashed cold water in his face then cupped his hands and drank greedily. Climbing back into bed, he lay in the darkness and considered the ramifications. *What does it mean? Am I attracted to her? Of course I am. She is beautiful. She is an excellent warrior. She is…lovely.*

Kalen punched his pillow in frustration. How could he work with her knowing that she meant more to him?

*****

Spalding and Apollo strode out into the aftermath and reviewed the carnage. "Damn, I'm glad I'm not part of the cleanup crew." Apollo kicked a body over, watching as it slowly transformed back to something like a human-wolf hybrid. "Ugly sons of bitches, ain't they?"

"They aren't so pretty in either form. They're even less pretty in between." Spalding keyed OPCOM and requested the cleanup crews converge on the location. He looked up at his haggard squad. "Everybody okay?"

A string of affirmatives and thumbs up settled his nerves somewhat. "Donnie, you and Sullivan double-check the crates. Make sure everything inside is no longer breathing. Jacobs, Lamb, take the main gate and escort the cleanup crews in." Spalding made a motion with his hand to attract the attention of Second Squad. Keying his throat mic, he announced, "We're mopping up down here. Keep your eyes and ears open and do not secure your stations until the cleanup crews are finished."

"Roger that," Bravo Four was the first to respond. The other two chimed in as well.

Spalding turned and began walking toward the main warehouse. "Brother, how about you point me to Sheridan's personal stuff and then you need to disappear before the cleanup crews arrive."

Apollo stood tall and nodded. He inhaled deeply, the scent of spent gunpowder still lingering in the air. He glanced about the site then back to Spalding. "I'm really going to miss it, ya know."

"I know. Once an operator, always an operator." Spalding turned and walked slowly with him toward the main building. "But they meant it, buddy. No popping up on radar. No mercenary stuff. Just…disappear."

Apollo shrugged. "I ain't the merc type, man. You know that." He paused and stared off into the darkness. "The hardest part is not saying goodbye."

"It's probably for the best, brother. There's a lot of people at the base that won't be happy…we haven't told them what we decided yet."

Apollo fought the urge to get misty. He sniffed back the tears and nodded at Spalding. "I understand. I don't like it, but I understand. I just wish there was some way to turn back the clock, ya know?"

"I know. Believe me, buddy,I know." The two stood in silence for a moment longer then Apollo turned and motioned toward the main doors of the hangar. "Come on,Sheridan's crap is in the office in here. Probably got contact info for that Simmons cat."

"That's what I wanted to hear." Spalding fell into step with him and the two began working their way across the expanse.

A muffled shot echoed in the darkness, the flash hidden by the suppressor attached to the barrel. Apollo jerked suddenly and froze in midstep, his eyes dropping to his chest.

Spalding stopped and turned to him. "What's wrong, buddy?" He didn't notice the fresh blood splatter on Apollo's tactical vest. He was covered in blood, flesh and spittle from the wolf attack earlier.

Apollo turned and stared at him blankly, his mouth opening to say something, but the words never came. A second shot hit him in the temple, dropping him where he stood.

Spalding leapt to the side, catching the big man before he hit the pavement. "Medic!" His scream was instinctive, from years in the field, as no medic had ever gone out with the squads before.

Spalding cradled Apollo as he quivered and shook, his nerves firing, causing his body to jerk. Keying his throat mic, Spalding screamed into the coms, "Stand down! Stand down! Hold fire!" He lay Apollo down gently on the ground, "Stay with me, buddy! Stay with me!" He glanced around with desperate eyes, "I need a medic over here! Man down!"

Jacobs and Lamb rushed to his side, pulling their emergency packs as they slid in beside Spalding. "What happened?"

"Gunshot!" Spalding stepped back as Lamb and Jacobs did their best to stench the flow of blood. Lamb gently turned Apollo's head only to realize that the other side of his skull was missing. He turned shocked eyes to Spalding and shook his head. "There's no way, Spank."

Jacobs pressed his fingers to the big man's neck and felt for a pulse. "I got nothing."

Spalding slowly came to his feet and stared off toward the points where his Bravo members supposedly sat overwatch. Hatred flashed in his eyes and he ground his teeth as he tried to calculate which man had murdered his friend.

CUSTOMERS ALSO PURCHASED:

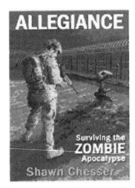

SHAWN CHESSER
SURVIVING THE
ZOMBIE APOCALYPSE
SERIES

T.W. BROWN
THE DEAD
SERIES

JOHN O'BRIEN
NEW WORLD
SERIES

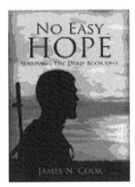

JAMES N. COOK
SURVIVING THE DEAD
SERIES

MARK TUFO
ZOMBIE FALLOUT
SERIES

**ARMAND
ROSAMILLIA**
DYING DAYS
SERIES

ABOUT THE AUTHOR

Heath Stallcup was born in Salinas, California and relocated to Tupelo, Oklahoma in his tween years. He joined the US Navy and was stationed in Charleston, SC and Bangor, WA shortly after junior college. After his second tour he attended East Central University where he obtained BS degrees in Biology and Chemistry. Heath then served ten years with the State of Oklahoma as a Compliance and Enforcement Officer while moonlighting nights and weekends with his local Sheriff's Office. He still lives in the small township of Tupelo, Oklahoma with his wife and three of his seven children. He steals time to write between household duties, going to ballgames, being a grandfather to five and being the pet of numerous animals that have taken over his home. Visit him at heathstallcup.com or Facebook.com

43920194R00206

Made in the USA
San Bernardino, CA
03 January 2017